P9-DOD-849

WHAT WE BECOME

WHAT WE BECOME

—◊—

A Novel

ARTURO PÉREZ-REVERTE

Translated by Nick Caistor and Lorenza García

ATRIA BOOKS

NEW YORK   LONDON   TORONTO   SYDNEY   NEW DELHI

ATRIA BOOKS

An Imprint of Simon & Schuster, Inc.
1230 Avenue of the Americas
New York, NY 10020

First Atria Books hardcover edition June 2016

ATRIA B O O K S and colophon are trademarks of Simon & Schuster, Inc.

For information about special discounts for bulk purchases, please contact Simon & Schuster Special Sales at 1-866-506-1949 or business@simonandschuster.com.

The Simon & Schuster Speakers Bureau can bring authors to your live event. For more information or to book an event, contact the Simon & Schuster Speakers Bureau at 1-866-248-3049 or visit our website at www.simonspeakers.com.

Interior design by Kyoko Watanabe

Manufactured in the United States of America

10 9 8 7 6 5 4 3 2 1

Library of Congress Cataloging-in-Publication Data
Names: Pérez-Reverte, Arturo, author. | Caistor, Nick, translator. | Garcia,
    Lorenza, translator.
Title: What we become / Arturo Pérez-Reverte ; translated by Nick Caistor
    and Lorenza Garcia.
Other titles: Tango de la guardia vieja. English
Description: First edition. | New York : Atria Books, 2016. | "Originally
    published in Spain in 2012 by Santillana Ediciones Generales, S. L. as El
    tango de la Guardia Vieja"—Verso title page.
Subjects: LCSH: Male dancers—Fiction. | BISAC: FICTION / Romance /
    Historical. | FICTION / Historical. | FICTION / Suspense.
Classification: LCC PQ6666.E765 T3613 2016 | DDC 863/.64—dc23
LC record available at http://lccn.loc.gov/2015037715

ISBN 978-1-4767-5198-6
ISBN 978-1-4767-5200-6 (ebook)

WHAT WE BECOME

I N NOVEMBER 1928, Armando de Troeye traveled to Buenos Aires to compose a tango. He could permit himself that luxury. At forty-three, the man who wrote "Nocturnes" and "Pasodoble for Don Quixote" was at the height of his fame, and all the Spanish illustrated magazines published a photograph of him, arm in arm with his beautiful wife aboard the *Cap Polonio*, an ocean liner of the Hamburg Südamerikanische company. The most glamorous picture appeared in the society pages of *Blanco y Negro*: in it the de Troeyes are on the first-class deck, he with a trench coat draped over his shoulders, one hand in his jacket pocket, the other holding a cigarette, as he smiles at the people on the quayside waving him off; and she, Mecha Inzunza de Troeye, wearing a fur coat and a stylish hat that sets off her eyes, which the caption writer described enthusiastically as "splendidly deep and sparkling."

That night, with the lights still twinkling on the distant coast, Armando de Troeye dressed for dinner. He was late in doing so, delayed by a slight but nagging headache. In the meantime, he insisted his wife go on ahead to the ship's ballroom and keep herself amused listening to the music. A meticulous fellow, de Troeye took his time filling the gold cigarette case he kept in the breast pocket of his tuxedo, and distributing among the other pockets some of the things he would need that evening: a gold fob watch, a cigarette lighter, two carefully folded white handkerchiefs, a pillbox for antacids, a crocodile-skin wallet containing calling cards, and a few low-denomination notes for tips. Afterward, he switched off the electric light, closed the door of the luxury cabin behind him, and attempted to sway with the gentle roll of the huge vessel as he walked across the thick carpet that muffled the distant thrum of engines propelling the ship through the Atlantic night.

Before crossing the threshold into the ballroom, as the head-waiter approached holding the dinner reservations list, de Troeye studied his own starched bib and cuffs and his shiny black shoes in the ornate foyer mirror. Evening dress always accentuated his elegant, slender appearance (he was of medium build, his face well-proportioned rather than attractive, enhanced by intelligent eyes, a trim mustache, and a mop of curly black hair with some prematurely gray streaks). For an instant, the composer's trained ear picked up the rhythm of the music the orchestra was playing: a slow, melancholy waltz. De Troeye smiled benevolently. The performance was merely passable. He slipped his left hand into his trouser pocket, and, responding to the headwaiter's greeting, followed him to the table he had reserved for the entire crossing in the most select part of the room. A few gazes followed him. An attractive woman with emerald earrings blinked in astonishment. People knew who he was. The orchestra was striking up another slow waltz as de Troeye sat down at the table, where a champagne cocktail stood untouched next to the fake, electric candle flame in a tulip glass shade. Among the couples swaying in time to the music on the dance floor, his young wife smiled at him. Mercedes Inzunza, who had arrived twenty minutes earlier, was dancing in the arms of a slim, handsome young fellow in evening dress: the ballroom dancer, whose job it was to entertain the unaccompanied ladies in first class or those whose companions did not dance. After returning her smile, de Troeye crossed his legs, and with a somewhat affected air plucked a cigarette from his gold case and lit it.

I

The Ballroom Dancer

THERE WAS A time when he and all his rivals had a shadow existence. And he was the best of them. He always kept flawless rhythm on a dance floor, and off it his hands were steady and agile, his lips poised with the appropriate remark, the perfect, witty one-liner. This made men like him and women admire him. In those days, in addition to the ballroom dances (tangos, fox-trots, Bostons) that helped him earn a living, he had mastered the art of verbal pyrotechnics and sketching melancholy landscapes with his silences. During many a long and fruitful year he had rarely missed his mark: it was rare for a wealthy woman of any age to resist his charms at one of the tea dances at a Palace, Ritz, or Excelsior Hotel; on a terrace on the Riviera; or in the first-class ballroom of a transatlantic liner. He had been the type of man one might come across in the morning in a café, wearing a tuxedo and inviting to breakfast the domestic staff from the house where he had attended a dance or a dinner the previous night. He possessed that talent, or that shrewdness. Moreover, at least once in his life, he was capable of betting everything he had on the table at a casino and traveling home by tramcar, cleaned out, whistling "The Man Who Broke the Bank at Monte Carlo," apparently unconcerned. Such was the elegance with which he could light a cigarette, knot a tie, or sport a pair of perfectly ironed shirt cuffs, that the police never dared arrest him, unless they actually caught him red-handed.

"Max."

"Yes, sir?"

"You may put my suitcase in the trunk."

The sun over the Bay of Naples makes his eyes smart as it bounces off the Mark X Jaguar's chrome plating, the way it did off the automobiles of long ago, driven by him and others. But all that has changed, and his old shadow is nowhere to be seen either. Max Costa glances beneath his feet, tries shifting slightly, to no avail. He can't remember exactly when it happened, but that hardly matters. His shadow has gone, left behind like so many other things.

He grimaces resignedly, or perhaps it is simply the sun in his eyes, as he tries to think of something real and immediate (the tire pressure for a half or fully loaded car, the ease of the synchronized gearbox, the oil gauge) to fend off that bittersweet pang that always comes when nostalgia or loneliness gets the better of him. Taking a deep, leisurely breath, he finishes polishing the silver statuette of a leaping cat above the front grille with a chamois cloth, then slips on the jacket of his gray uniform that was lying folded on the front seat. Once he has carefully buttoned it up and straightened his tie, he slowly mounts the steps, flanked by headless marble statues and stone urns, leading up to the front door.

"Don't forget the small bag."

"I won't, sir."

Dr. Hugentobler doesn't like the way that in Italy his employees address him as "doctor." This country, he frequently says, is swarming with *dottori, cavalieri,* and *commendatori.* I am a Swiss doctor. A professional. I don't want people mistaking me for a cardinal's nephew, a Milanese industrialist, or some such thing.

As for Max Costa, everyone at the villa on the outskirts of Sorrento simply calls him Max. This is paradoxical, because most of his life he used various names and titles, noble or otherwise according to the needs of the moment. But for a while now, ever since his shadow fluttered its handkerchief in a last farewell (like a woman who vanishes forever amid a cloud of steam, framed in the window of a sleeping car, and one is never sure if she is leaving at that moment or if she started to leave long before), he has been using his own name. A shadow in return for the name which, until his forced retirement (recent, and in some ways natural), has appeared in thick case files in police departments all over Europe and America. In any event, he thinks as he picks up the small leather bag and the Samsonite suitcase and places them in the trunk of the car, never, not even in his darkest moments, did he imagine he would end his days replying "Yes, sir?" when addressed by his first name.

"Let's be off, Max. Did you bring the newspapers?"

"They are on the backseat, sir."

The clunk of two doors. Max Costa has donned his chauffeur's cap, taken it off, and put it back on again in order to install his passenger. Once behind the wheel, he leaves it on the seat beside him, and in a reflex of vanity glances in the rearview mirror before smoothing down his gray, still abundant hair. Nothing like the detail of the cap, he thinks, to highlight the irony of his situation: the absurd beach where the tide has washed him up after his final shipwreck. And yet, when he is in his room at the villa shaving before the mirror and registers the lines on his face like someone tallying the scars of love and war, each with a name of its own (women, roulette wheels, uncertain mornings, evenings of glory or catastrophe), he always ends up winking at himself in absolution, as though recognizing in that tall, no longer so slim, old man with dark, weary eyes, the image of a former accomplice for whom any explanation is unnecessary. After all, his reflection seems to be saying in a tone that is familiar, gently mocking, and possibly a little spiteful, that, at age sixty-four and considering the dreadful hand life has dealt him of late, he can still count himself lucky. In similar circumstances, others (Enrico Fossataro, old Sandor Esterházy) were forced to choose between public charity or last moments spent writhing uncomfortably at the end of a necktie, in the bathroom of a miserable boardinghouse.

"Anything of importance happening in the world?" Hugentobler inquires.

A rustle of newspapers in the backseat of the car: pages leafed through absentmindedly. This was a remark rather than a question. In the rearview mirror, Max sees his boss's eyes directed downward, spectacles perched on the end of his nose.

"The Russians haven't dropped the A-bomb, have they?"

Hugentobler is joking, naturally. Swiss humor. When he is in a good mood, he often tries to joke with the servants, probably because he is a bachelor, without a family to laugh at his funny stories. Max gives a professional smile. Discreet and keeping the proper distance.

"Nothing much, sir: Cassius Clay has won another title, the astronauts on Gemini XI have returned safe and sound. . . . The war in Indochina is heating up as well."

"You mean in Vietnam."

"That's it. Vietnam . . . And in the local news: the Campanella Chess Contest is about to begin. Keller versus Sokolov."

"Good heavens," says Hugentobler, dismissive and sarcastic. "How sorry I am to miss that. . . . There really is no accounting for taste, eh Max?"

"How right you are, sir."

"Imagine spending your whole life poring over a chessboard. That is how those chess players end up. Crazy, like Bobby Fischer."

"Indeed."

"Take the low road. We have plenty of time."

The crunch of gravel beneath the tires ceases as they pass through the iron gate and then the Jaguar begins to roll gently along the asphalted road through groves of olive, gum, and fig trees. Max downshifts effortlessly as he comes to a sharp bend, at the end of which he glimpses the calm sea, glittering like polished glass, silhouetting the pine trees and houses clustered on the mountain, with Vesuvius on the far side of the bay. For a moment he forgets his passenger and concentrates on the pleasure of driving, the movement between two places whose location in time and space is of no consequence to him. The air wafting through the open window smells of honey and resin—the lingering aromas of summer, which in that part of the world always refuses to die, engaging in a sweet, ingenuous battle with the calendar.

"It's a beautiful day, Max."

Max Costa blinks, collecting his thoughts, and once more glances up at the rearview mirror. Dr. Hugentobler is no longer reading the newspapers and has a Havana cigar in his mouth.

"Indeed, sir."

"I'm afraid the weather will have changed by the time I return."

"Let's hope not. You'll only be gone three weeks."

Hugentobler lets out a grunt, accompanied by a puff of smoke. He is a placid-looking man with a pink complexion, who owns a private clinic near Lake Garda. He amassed a fortune in the postwar years dispensing psychiatric treatment to wealthy Jews traumatized by the Nazi atrocities: the sort who would wake up in the middle of the night believing they were still in the barracks at Auschwitz, with Dobermans snarling outside and SS men shepherding them to the shower rooms. Hugentobler and his Italian associate, Dr. Bacchelli, helped them wrestle with their phantoms, and to round out their treatment recommended a trip to Israel organized by the clinic, after which they were presented with an exorbitant bill that allowed Hugentobler to maintain a house in Milan, an apartment in Zurich, and the villa at Sorrento with five cars in the garage. For the past three years, it has been Max's job to keep them serviced and to drive them, besides overseeing the general maintenance of the villa, whose other employees are a married couple from Salerno, the gardener and the maid, Mr. and Mrs. Lanza.

"Don't go straight to the port. Drive through the center of town."

"Very well, sir."

He glances at the accurate but inexpensive watch on his left wrist (a gold-plated Festina), and joins the traffic on Corso Italia, which is light at that hour. There is plenty of time for them to reach the motor launch that will ferry Dr. Hugentobler across the bay, sparing him the tortuous road to Naples' airport.

"Max."

"Yes, sir?"

"Stop at Rufolos and get me a box of Montecristo No. 2s."

Max Costa's working relationship with his boss began like love at first sight: the moment the psychiatrist laid eyes on Max, he disregarded his exemplary references (entirely fictitious, in fact). He was a pragmatist, convinced his professional instinct and experience would never mislead him about the human condition. Hugentobler decided that this fellow who dressed with an air of faded elegance and bore a calm, frank expression, exhibiting polite discretion in both word and gesture, was the living embodiment of honor and decency. Thus he would lend just the right note of dignity to the doctor's magnificent car collection (the Jaguar, a Rolls-Royce Silver Cloud II, and three vintage cars, including a Bugatti 50T coupé). Naturally, Hugentobler does not have the slightest notion that his chauffeur once enjoyed cruising around in cars, owned by himself or others, every bit as luxurious as those he is now paid to drive. Had he known, Hugentobler would have been forced to revise a few of his opinions about the human condition, and to hire a driver with a less elegant appearance but a more conventional résumé. But that would have been a mistake. Anyone familiar with the darker side of life understands that a man who has lost his shadow is like a woman with a dark past who marries: no one is more loyal, because she knows how much is at stake. However, it will not be Max Costa who at this stage of the game enlightens Dr. Hugentobler about fleeting shadows, tarts with hearts of gold, or the forced honesty of ex-ballroom dancers who turn into gentleman thieves. Even if they didn't always behave like gentlemen.

—∞—

When the motor launch pulls away from the Marina Piccola jetty, Max Costa remains leaning for a moment against the breakwater surrounding the harbor, watching the vessel's wake cleave the blue surface of the bay. Afterward, he removes his jacket and tie, and, draping them over one arm, returns to the car, which is parked near the Guardia di Finanza building, at the foot of the cliff top where Sorrento is perched. He tips the youngster keeping an eye on the Jaguar fifty lire, starts the car, and drives slowly along the road that curves sharply as it climbs toward the town. As he enters Piazza Tasso, he rolls to a halt before three pedestrians, two women and a man, who are leaving the Hotel Vittoria, and watches idly as they cross a few inches in front of the car. They look like wealthy tourists, the type who vacation out of season so that they can enjoy the sun, the sea, and the mild weather, which lasts well into autumn, without the inconvenience of the summer crowds. The man, probably in his late twenties, is wearing sunglasses and a jacket with suede elbow patches. The younger of the two women is a pretty brunette in a miniskirt, her hair in a long braid down her back. The older woman has on a beige woolen cardigan, a dark skirt, and a crinkled tweed man's hat, beneath which her cropped, silver-gray hair is showing. She is quite elegant, Max observes, with a sophistication that comes not from her clothes but rather from the way she wears them. A cut above the average woman to be seen in the villas and smart hotels in Sorrento, Amalfi, and Capri, even at this time of year.

Something about the second woman compels Max to follow her with his eyes as she crosses Piazza Tasso. Possibly her slow, relaxed bearing, with her right hand placed casually in the pocket of her cardigan, moving with the ease of those who have spent their lives sashaying across the carpets of a world that was theirs. Or perhaps what catches Max's attention is the way she tilts her head toward her companions to laugh at their conversation, or to utter words whose sound is muffled by the car's silent windows. In any case, for a split second, as fleetingly as someone recalling the confused fragment of a forgotten dream, Max is confronted with the ghost of a memory. With an image from the distant past, a gesture, a voice, a laugh. He is so taken aback that only the blast of a car horn behind makes him shift into first gear and crawl forward, still watching the trio, who have arrived at the other side of the sunlit square and are seating themselves at one of the tables on the terrace of Bar Fauno.

He is about to turn into Corso Italia when the memory crystalizes with full force: a face, a voice. A scene, or a number of them. Suddenly Max's surprise gives way to astonishment, and he slams on the brakes, inviting another blast from the car behind, followed by angry gesticulations from the driver as the Jaguar turns sharply to the right, braking once more before pulling up alongside the curb.

He removes the key from the ignition and sits there motionless, staring at his hands still resting on the wheel. Finally, he gets out of the car, puts on his jacket, and crosses the square beneath the palm trees, heading toward the terrace outside the bar. He is nervous. Afraid, perhaps, of confirming his suspicions. The trio is still there, talking animatedly. Max tries to stay out of view, pausing beside the shrubs in the landscaped area. The table is ten yards away, and the woman in the tweed hat is in profile, talking to the others, unaware of Max's intense scrutiny. No doubt she was once extraordinarily attractive, he confirms, as her face still shows traces of a faded beauty. She might be the woman he thinks she is, he concludes tentatively, and yet he can't be sure. There are too many other women's faces in the way, both before and long since. Watching from behind the bushes for any details that correspond to his memory, Max reaches no satisfactory conclusion. Finally, aware that he will eventually draw attention to himself standing there, he circles the terrace and goes to sit down at a table at the far end. He asks the waiter to bring him a Negroni, and for the next twenty minutes he observes the woman in profile, studying each of her movements and gestures to compare them with those he remembers. When the trio leaves the table and crosses the square again toward the corner of Via San Cesareo, he has finally identified her. Or so he believes. He rises and follows them, at a distance. His old heart hasn't beaten this fast for centuries.

—⁓—

The woman danced well, Max Costa realized. Easily and with a certain boldness. She followed him confidently when he tested her ability with a more complicated, inventive sidestep that a less nimble woman would have stumbled over. He guessed that she was about twenty-five. Tall and slender, with long arms, slim wrists, and legs that seemed to go on forever beneath her dark taffeta dress with violet overtones, cut low at the back. Thanks to the high heels she was wearing, which set off her gown, her serene face with its well-defined features was on a level with his. She wore her ash-blond hair crimped according to the prevailing fashion that season, and cut in a short bob that exposed her neck. As she danced, she kept her eyes fixed on a point above the shoulder of her partner's tailcoat, where her left hand adorned with a wedding ring was resting. Their eyes had not met since he'd approached with a polite bow, offering to lead her in one of the slow waltzes they called a

Boston. Hers were the color of liquid honey, almost translucent, enhanced by a perfect application of mascara (no more than was necessary, the same as with her lipstick) beneath the fine arc of her plucked eyebrows. She was nothing like the other women Max had accompanied that evening in the ballroom: middle-aged ladies reeking of musky perfumes such as lily and patchouli, or awkward young girls dressed in light-colored dresses with skirts below the knee, who bit their lips as they struggled to keep in step, blushed when he placed a hand on their waist or clapped to a hupa-hupa. And so, for the first time that evening, the ballroom dancer on the *Cap Polonio* began to enjoy his job.

Their eyes didn't meet again until the Boston (called "What I'll Do") was over and the orchestra launched into a rendering of the tango "A media luz." They had stood there facing each other for a moment in the middle of the half-empty dance floor. At the first bars, realizing she wasn't intending to return to her table (where a man in a tuxedo, doubtless her husband, had just sat down), he opened his arms wide, and the woman instantly responded, impassive as before. She placed her left hand on his shoulder, extended her right arm slowly, and they began moving across the dance floor (*gliding* was the word, Max thought), her eyes once more gazing past the ballroom dancer without looking at him, even as she shadowed his movements with surprising precision, his slow, sure rhythm, while, for his part, he endeavored to maintain the proper distance, their bodies touching just enough to perform the figures.

"Was that all right?" he asked after a difficult figure eight, which the woman had followed effortlessly.

At this she finally afforded him a fleeting glance. Possibly even the semblance of a smile, which faded instantly.

"Perfect."

In recent years, the tango, originally Argentinian but brought into vogue in Paris by the Apache dances, had been all the rage on both sides of the Atlantic. And so the floor was soon filled with couples twirling more or less gracefully, linking steps, embraces, and releases, which, depending on the dancers' ability, could be anywhere from passable to grotesque. Max's partner, however, responded with ease to the most complex moves, adapting to the traditional, obvious steps as well as to the occasional embellishments which, increasingly sure of his companion, he would improvise, always in that slow, restrained style, introducing breaks and delicate side steps, which she followed effortlessly, without missing a beat. It was obvious she too was enjoying moving to the music, from the smile she graced Max with each time they performed a difficult turn, and from her bright gaze that would occasionally stop staring into space and alight for a few seconds, contentedly, on the ballroom dancer.

As they twirled around the dance floor, Max studied the husband with the steady eye of a professional hunter. He was accustomed to observing the husbands, fathers, brothers, sons, and lovers of the women with whom he danced. Men, in short, who accompanied them with pride, arrogance, boredom, resignation, or other similarly masculine emotions. There was much useful information to be gleaned from tiepins, fobs, cigarette cases, and rings; from the thickness of wallets opened as waiters approached; from the quality and cut of a jacket, the pleat of a trouser leg, or the shine on a pair of shoes. Even from the way a tie was knotted. All these details allowed Max Costa to elaborate plans and goals to the rhythm of the music, or, expressed in more mundane terms, to progress from ballroom dancing to more lucrative prospects. Time and experience had finally persuaded him of the truth of the comment Count Boris Dolgoruki-Bragation (second lieutenant in the First Regiment of the Spanish Foreign Legion) had made to him seven years earlier in Melilla, a minute and a half after regurgitating an entire bottle of cheap brandy in the backyard of Fatima's bordello:

"A woman is never just a woman, dear Max. She is first and foremost the men she once had, those she has, and those she might have. Without them, she remains a mystery . . . and whoever discovers that information possesses the combination to the safe. The access to her secrets."

When the music had finished and he accompanied his partner back to her table, Max took a last, closer look at the husband: elegant, self-assured, in his forties. Not a handsome man, yet pleasant-looking with his dapper mustache, curly hair flecked with gray, and lively intelligent eyes that missed nothing, including what was taking place on the dance floor. Max had searched for his name on the reservations list before approaching the woman, when she was still unaccompanied, and the headwaiter had confirmed that he was the Spanish composer Armando de Troeye, traveling with his wife. They had a deluxe first-class stateroom and a table reserved in the main dining room next to that of the ship's captain.

"It has been a pleasure, Madam. You dance magnificently."

"Thank you."

He bobbed his head in almost military fashion, a gesture that always pleased the ladies, as did the graceful way he took their fingers and drew them to his lips, but she responded to his gesture with a quick, cold nod before sitting on the chair her husband had pulled out for her. Max turned around, smoothing his sleek, black hair back from his temples, first with his right hand then his left, and moved away, skirting around the people on the dance floor. He walked with a polite smile on his lips, his gaze directed at the room, all five foot ten of him in his impeccable tailcoat (on which he had sunk the last of his savings before boarding the liner with a one-way contract to Buenos Aires), aware of the female interest coming from the tables where a few passengers were already standing up to make their way to the dining room. Half the room hates me right now, he concluded with a mixture of boredom and amusement. The other half are women.

The trio pauses in front of a store selling souvenirs, postcards, and books. Although in Sorrento some of the shops and restaurants and even a few of the luxury boutiques on the Corso Italia close at the end of the summer, the old quarter around Via San Cesareo remains a tourist haunt all year round. The street is narrow, and Max keeps a prudent distance, hovering outside a salumeria where a chalkboard propped on an easel in the doorway offers discreet protection. The girl with the braid enters the store while the woman in the hat stays outside talking to the young man, who has taken off his sunglasses and is smiling. He is dark-haired, good-looking. She must be fond of him, because on one occasion she strokes his face. Then he says something and the woman laughs out loud, the distinct sound reaching the ears of the man spying on them: a clear, forthright laugh that makes her seem much more youthful and awakens precise memories from the past that set Max aquiver. It is her, he concludes.

Twenty-nine years have passed since he last saw her. A light rain was falling then on a coastal landscape, in autumn: a dog was scampering across the wet pebbles on the beach, beneath the balustrade on Avenue des Anglais, in Nice. Beyond the white façade of the Hôtel Negresco, the city melted into the gray, misty landscape. All the years that have gone since then could confuse the memory. And yet, the ex-ballroom dancer, current employee, and chauffeur to Dr. Hugentobler is no longer in any doubt. It is the same woman—the identical way of laughing, of tilting her head to one side, her composed gestures. The casual elegance with which she keeps one hand in the pocket of her cardigan. He would like to move nearer, to see her face close up, but he does not dare. While he wrestles with his indecision, the girl with the long braid emerges from the store, and the three of them walk back the way they came, past the salumeria where Max has quickly taken refuge. From inside, he sees the woman in the hat go by, studies her face in outline, and is absolutely certain. Eyes like liquid honey, he notes with a shiver. And so, carefully, at a safe distance, he follows them once more across Piazza Tasso to the hotel.

—◊—

He saw her again the next day, on the boat deck. It was pure chance, as neither he nor she had any business being there. Like the other employees on the *Cap Polonio* who were not part of the ship's crew, Max Costa was supposed to steer clear of the first-class area and promenade decks. In order to avoid the passengers in teak and wicker deck chairs taking the sun as it shone on the starboard side (those playing skittles and quoits, or skeet shooting, occupied the port side), he decided to climb a ladder to another deck, where eight of the sixteen lifeboats stood lined up on their chocks alongside the liner's three gigantic red-and-white smokestacks. It was a peaceful place, a neutral area few passengers used, for the lifeboats were an eyesore and blocked the view. The only concession to anyone wanting to go there were a few wooden benches. On one of these, as he passed between a hatchway painted white and one of the huge ventilation outlets that sucked fresh air into the bowels of the ship, Max recognized his dance partner from the previous evening.

It was a bright, clear day, pleasantly warm for that time of year. Max had left his cabin without a hat, gloves, or cane (he was dressed in a gray suit with a vest, a soft-collared shirt, and a knitted tie) and so as he walked past the woman he simply bowed politely. She wore a smart flannel suit: a three-quarter-length jacket and a pleated skirt. She was reading a book resting in her lap, and as he walked in front of her, momentarily blocking the sun, she looked up at him, her oval face framed beneath the narrow brim of her felt hat. Perhaps it was the glimmer of recognition Max thought he detected in her eyes that made him pause for a moment, with the discretion appropriate to the situation and to their respective positions on the ship.

"Good morning," he said.

The woman, who was lowering her gaze again toward her book, responded with another silent stare and a brief nod.

"I am . . . ," he blurted, feeling suddenly awkward, on shaky ground, and already sorry he had spoken to her.

"Yes," she replied calmly. "The gentleman from last night."

She said gentleman instead of dancer, and he was secretly grateful for it.

"I don't know whether I told you," he added, "that you dance magnificently."

"You did."

She was already returning to her book. A novel, he noticed, glancing at the cover, which she was holding half-open on her lap: *The Four Horsemen of the Apocalypse* by Vicente Blasco Ibáñez.

"Good-bye. Enjoy your reading."

"Thank you."

He moved on, unaware of whether her eyes remained glued to her book or if she was watching him leave. He did his best to walk nonchalantly, one hand in his trouser pocket. When he reached the last lifeboat, he paused beside it, took out a silver cigarette case (engraved with initials that weren't his), and lit a cigarette. He took advantage of the gesture to cast a surreptitious glance toward the prow, to the bench where the woman was still reading, head down. Not interested.

—⚬⚬⚬—

Grand Albergo Vittoria. Buttoning up his jacket, Max Costa passes beneath the gold sign on the arched, wrought-iron gateway, nods at the security guard, and walks down the driveway bordered by ancient pines and every kind of tree and plant. The gardens are spacious, stretching from Piazza Tasso to the edge of the cliff, which looks out over Marina Piccola and the sea, and where the hotel's three main buildings are perched. In the middle one, at the bottom of a small flight of steps, Max finds himself in the lobby, in front of the glass doors leading to the conservatory and the terrace, which (unusually for that time of year) is full of people enjoying an aperitif. To the left, behind the reception desk, is an old acquaintance: Tiziano Spadaro. Their association dates back to a time when the man who is currently chauffeur to Dr. Hugentobler was a guest in such places as the Hotel Vittoria. Many a generous tip, changing hands discreetly according to a set of unwritten codes, laid the basis for a friendship, which over time had become sincere, or complicit.

"Well, if it isn't Max. You're a sight for sore eyes. It's been a long time."

"Almost four months."

"Good to see you."

"And you. How is life?"

Spadaro shrugs (he has thinning hair, and his protruding belly strains under his black vest), reeling off the usual list of complaints about his job out of season: fewer tips, weekenders accompanied by aspiring young actresses or models, groups of loud Americans doing the Naples-Ischia-Capri-Sorrento-Amalfi tour, a night spent in each place, breakfast included, who are forever ordering bottled water because they don't trust what comes out of the tap. Fortunately (Spadaro gestures toward the door to the bustling conservatory) the Campanella Cup has come to the rescue: the Keller-Sokolov duel has filled the hotel with chess players, journalists, and fans.

"I want some information. Off the record."

Spadaro doesn't remark "just like in the old days," and yet his expression, surprised at first and then mocking, taken somewhat off guard, lights up with the familiar look of collusion. Close to retirement, with fifty years of experience behind him after starting as a bellhop in the Hotel Excelsior in Naples, Spadaro has seen everything. And that includes Max Costa in his prime. Or not yet past it.

"I thought you'd given all that up."

"I have. This is different."

"I see."

The old receptionist appears relieved. Then Max asks him about an elegant older lady, accompanied by a girl and a good-looking young man, who entered the hotel ten minutes ago. Perhaps they are guests.

"They are, of course . . . the young man is none other than Keller himself."

Max blinks absentmindedly. The girl and the young man are what least interest him.

"Who?"

"Jorge Keller, the Chilean grand master. Contender for the title of world chess champion."

Max remembers at last, and Spadaro fills in the details. The Luciano Campanella Cup, held this year in Sorrento, is sponsored by the Turin multimillionaire, one of the biggest shareholders in Olivetti and Fiat. A great chess enthusiast, Campanella organizes an annual contest in landmark sites all over Italy, always in the most luxurious hotels, where he invites the most famous grand masters, whom he pays handsomely. The encounter takes place over four weeks, some months before the official contest for the world championship, and has come to be considered the unofficial world championship between the two best chess players of the moment: the titleholder and the most prominent challenger. In addition to the prize money (fifty thousand dollars for the winner and ten thousand for the runner-up), the prestige of the Campanella Cup resides in the fact that, so far, the victor of the contest has either gone on to win the world title or has retained it. Sokolov is the current champion; and Keller, who has beaten all the other candidates, is the challenger.

"That young man is Keller?" Max says, astonished.

"Yes. A pleasant lad, relatively normal, which is unusual in his profession. . . . The Russian is less friendly. Always surrounded by bodyguards and cautious as a fox."

"What about her?"

Spadaro makes a dismissive gesture, the one he reserves for low-status guests. Those without much history.

"She's the fiancée. And part of his team (the receptionist leafs through the hotel register to refresh his memory). Irina. Irina Jasenovic. The name is Yugoslav, but her passport is Canadian."

"I meant the older woman. The one with the short gray hair."

"Ah, she's the mother."

"Of the girl?"

"No. Of Keller."

—m—

He bumped into her again two days later, in the ship's ballroom. Dinner was to be a black-tie affair: the captain was honoring some distinguished guest, and a number of male passengers had exchanged their customary black tuxedo for a tight-fitting tailcoat, starched bib front, and white bow tie. The diners had gathered in the ballroom, drinking cocktails and listening to the music before going on to dinner. After the meal a few of the youngest or more fun-loving would return there and stay on until the small hours. The orchestra started with the usual slow waltzes and smooth melodies, and Max Costa danced half a dozen sets, almost all of them with young girls and married women traveling *en famille*. Max reserved a slow fox-trot for an Englishwoman, past her prime but not bad-looking, who was there with a girlfriend. He had seen them whisper and nudge each other whenever he swept past their table. The Englishwoman was blonde, plump, with a rather abrupt manner. Although perhaps a little vulgar (he thought he detected too much My Sin on her) and festooned with jewelry, she was not a bad dancer. She had pretty blue eyes, too, and enough money to make her attractive: the clutch bag on the table was of gold mesh, he confirmed at a glance as he stood before her to invite her onto the dance floor; and the jewels looked real, in particular the sapphire bracelet and matching earrings, the stones of which, once removed from their settings, would fetch five hundred pounds sterling. He had discovered from the reservations list that her name was Miss Honeybee. Widowed or divorced, the headwaiter, a man called Schmöcker (nearly all the officers, seamen, and permanent members of staff on the ship were German) had hazarded, with the assurance of someone having fifty Atlantic crossings under his belt. And so, after a careful study of the woman's responses to his manners and proximity, and without making a single inappropriate gesture—maintaining proper distance and a professional aloofness throughout, and ending as he returned her to her table with a splendid, manly smile (met with a perfunctory "so nice" from the Englishwoman)—Max placed Miss Honeybee on his list of possibles. Five thousand sea miles and a three-week crossing could provide rich pickings.

That evening, the de Troeyes arrived together. Max was taking a breather next to the bank of palms alongside the stage, drinking a glass of water and smoking a cigarette. From there he saw the couple enter, preceded by the obsequious Schmöcker, with her walking slightly ahead. The husband had a white carnation in his black satin lapel, one hand in his pocket and the other holding a lighted cigarette. Armando de Troeye appeared indifferent to the interest he aroused in his fellow passengers. As for his wife, she looked as if she had just stepped out of the society pages of an illustrated magazine: she was wearing a long string of pearls with matching earrings. Slender, calm, walking confidently in high-heeled shoes to the gentle roll of the ship, her body etched long, straight lines onto her flowing jade gown (with an expert eye Max calculated it as costing at least five thousand francs on Rue de la Paix in Paris), which exposed her arms, shoulders, and back down to her waist, and was fastened around her neck by a fine strap, charmingly visible beneath her bobbed hair. Entranced, Max came to a twofold conclusion. She was one of those women who at first glance appeared elegant, but when you looked again were beautiful. She also belonged to the select class of women born to wear gowns like that as if they were a second skin.

He did not dance with her immediately. The orchestra played a Camel Walk then a shimmy (the absurdly titled "Tutankamon" was still in fashion), and Max was obliged to satisfy the wishes of two energetic young girls, watched over from a distance by their parents (two amiable-looking Brazilian couples), who were intent upon practicing the dance steps, not without skill: right shoulder followed by the left forward then back, until they decided they were exhausted, and had almost exhausted him. Afterward, when the first beats of a black bottom started (the title of the song was "Love and Popcorn"), Max's services were solicited by an American woman, still in her prime, somewhat ungraceful but more than adequately clothed and bejeweled, who turned out to be an amusing dance partner, and, when he accompanied her back to her table, discreetly slipped a folded five-dollar bill into his hand. Several times during this last dance Max came close to the de Troeyes' table, and yet each time he directed his gaze there, the woman seemed to be looking elsewhere. The table was now unoccupied and a waiter was clearing away two empty glasses. Busy attending to his partner of the moment, Max had not seen them get up and leave for the dining room.

He took advantage of the dinner break, which was at seven, to enjoy a bowl of consommé. He never ate anything solid when he had to dance—another habit acquired during his time in the Legion, although the dance then was of a different nature, and a light meal was a healthy precaution in case of a bullet in the belly. After the soup he put on his coat and went out on the starboard promenade deck, to smoke another cigarette and to clear his head as he watched the crescent moon shimmering on the ocean. At a quarter past eight he returned to the ballroom, installing himself at one of the empty tables, close to the orchestra, where he chatted with the musicians until the first passengers began to float in from the dining room: the men on their way to the casino, the library, or the smoking room, and the ladies, younger people, and more game couples occupying the tables around the dance floor. The orchestra began tuning up, Schmöcker rallied his waiters, and there was the sound of laughter and champagne corks popping. Max stood, and, after making sure his bow tie was still straight and checking that his shirt collar and cuffs were in place, he smoothed down his tailcoat and scanned the tables in search of anyone requiring his services. Then he saw her enter, this time on her husband's arm.

They sat at the same table. The orchestra struck up a bolero and the first couples took to the floor. Miss Honeybee and her friend had not returned from the dining room, and Max had no way of knowing if they would that evening. In fact, he felt relieved. With that vague pretext in mind, he threaded his way through the people swaying to the fluid rhythms of the music. The de Troeyes were sitting in silence, watching the dancers. When Max paused in front of their table, a waiter had just placed on it a couple of champagne glasses and an ice bucket out of which peeped a bottle of Clicquot. He bowed to the husband, who was leaning back slightly in his chair, legs crossed, one elbow on the table, and another of his perpetual cigarettes in his left hand, where, next to his wedding band, Max noticed a thick, gold signet ring with a blue lozenge. Then he looked at the woman, who was studying him with interest. She wore no bracelets or rings, apart from her wedding band, only the splendid string of pearls and matching earrings. Max did not open his mouth to offer his services, but simply gave another, more fleeting bow than the last, clicked his heels together in almost military fashion, and stood stock-still until she, with a slow smile and apparently appreciative, shook her head. Max was about to withdraw, when the husband slid his elbow off the table, carefully straightened the crease in his trousers, and peered at his wife through a cloud of cigarette smoke.

"I'm tired," he said in a lighthearted manner. "I think I ate too much at dinner. I'd like to watch you dance."

The woman did not stand up immediately. She looked for an instant at her husband, who took another draw on his cigarette, squinting in silent approval.

"Enjoy yourself," he added after a moment. "This young man is a magnificent dancer."

Scarcely had she risen from her chair when Max opened his arms, discreetly. Holding her right hand aloft, he placed his free hand on her waist. The unexpected touch of her warm skin took him by surprise. He had noticed the cut of her evening gown exposing her back, but it hadn't occurred to him, despite his experience of embracing ladies, that when dancing with her he would place his hand on her naked flesh. His unease lasted only an instant, concealed beneath his professional mask of composure, and yet his partner sensed it, or he thought she did. For a split second she looked straight at him, before her gaze wandered again across the dance floor. Max leaned gently to one side to begin the dance, and she responded with perfect ease. They began to circle amid the other couples. On two occasions he glanced at the necklace she was wearing.

"Are you ready to do a crossover here?" Max whispered after a moment, anticipating a favorable passage in the music.

Her silent gaze lasted a couple of seconds.

"Of course."

He removed his hand from her back, halting abruptly on the dance floor, and spun her full circle, first this way then that, sketching an arabesque around his still form. They came together again in perfect harmony, his hand resting once more on the supple curve of her waist, as if they had rehearsed the step half a dozen times. There was a smile on her lips and Max nodded, satisfied. A few couples had moved aside slightly to stare at them with admiration or envy, and she alerted him with a gentle squeeze of his hand.

"Let's not draw attention to ourselves."

Max apologized, for which he was rewarded with another indulgent smile. He enjoyed dancing with her. She was the perfect height for him, and he enjoyed feeling the curve of her slender waist beneath his right hand, the way she rested her fingers on his other hand, how easily she pivoted in time to the music, always with poise and finesse, maintaining the figure. With a hint of defiance, perhaps, and yet without any fuss, as when she had agreed to his spinning her around, doing so with all the elegance in the world. As they continued dancing, her eyes remained distant, nearly all the time staring into space, allowing Max to study her perfect features, the contour of her mouth colored with a subtle lipstick, her discreetly powdered nose, the neat arc of her eyebrows on her smooth forehead, above long eyelashes. She had a soft smell, a perfume he couldn't quite identify, for it seemed to blend with her youthful skin: possibly Arpège. Max looked at her husband, who was watching them from the table, apparently paying little attention, as he raised his champagne glass to his lips, and then glanced again at the necklace, whose pearls of exceptional quality glowed faintly in the light of the electric chandeliers. Thanks to his own experience and a few unorthodox acquaintances, the twenty-six-year-old Max knew enough about pearls to distinguish between the button, round, teardrop, and baroque varieties, including their official or unofficial value. These were round pearls of the highest quality: almost certainly Indian or Persian. And worth at least five thousand pounds sterling: more than half a million French francs. That could pay for several weeks with a beautiful woman in the best hotel in Paris or on the Riviera. But, carefully administered, it could also keep him in relative idleness for a year or more.

"You really dance very well, Madam," he repeated.

Almost reluctantly, her eyes focused on him once more.

"In spite of my age?" she said.

It did not seem like a question. She had clearly been watching him before dinner, when he was dancing with the young Brazilian girls. Max looked suitably shocked.

"Old? For heaven's sake. How can you say such a thing?"

She continued studying him quizzically. Or perhaps with amusement.

"What's your name?"

"Max."

"Very well, Max. Go ahead, guess my age."

"I wouldn't dream of it."

"Please."

He had quickly collected himself, for he never lost his composure in front of a woman. She had a broad, dazzling smile, which he contemplated with feigned concentration.

"Fifteen."

She gave a loud, vivacious laugh. A healthy laugh.

"Correct," she nodded, playing along good-naturedly. "However did you guess?"

"I have a talent for that sort of thing."

She nodded, her expression half-mocking, half-pleased, or perhaps she was admiring the way he continued to lead her around the floor, amid the other couples, without their conversation distracting him from the music and the dance steps.

"And not just that," she said, rather mysteriously.

Max searched her eyes for any added nuance in her comment, but once again they were staring blankly over his right shoulder. At that moment, the bolero came to an end. They separated, still facing each other as the orchestra prepared to launch into the next number. Max glanced again at the splendid pearls. For a moment he thought she had caught him in the act.

"That's sufficient," she said suddenly. "Thank you."

The periodicals archive is on the upper floor of an old building, at the top of a marble staircase surmounted by a vaulted ceiling decorated with flaking paintings. The hardwood floor creaks when Max Costa, carrying three bound volumes of the magazine *Scacco Matto*, goes to sit down in a well-lit part of the room, beside a window overlooking half a dozen palm trees and the white-and-gray façade of the Basilica di San Antonino. On the desk he places a spectacle case, a notepad, a ballpoint pen, and several newspapers purchased at a kiosk on Vía de Maio.

An hour and a half later, Max stops taking notes, removes his reading glasses, rubs his tired eyes, and looks out at the square, where the evening sun is casting long shadows from the palm trees. By now, Dr. Hugentobler's chauffeur has read almost everything published about Jorge Keller, the player who over the next four weeks will be challenging the world chess champion, Mikhail Sokolov, in Sorrento. There are several photographs of Keller in magazines, invariably sitting in front of a chessboard, and in some of them he looks very young: a mere boy tackling opponents much older than himself. The most recent one is from that day's edition of a local paper: Keller is posing in the hotel lobby at the Vittoria in the same jacket he was wearing when Max saw him strolling through Sorrento that morning with the two women.

—⁂—

"Born in London in 1938, the son of a Chilean diplomat, Keller astounded the chess world when he maneuvered the American Reshevsky into a tight spot during a simultaneous exhibition in the Plaza de Armas in Santiago: he was fourteen years old at the time, and in the ten years that followed, he went on to become one of the most talented players of all time . . ."

Despite Jorge Keller's meteoric rise to fame, Max is less interested in his professional biography than in other aspects of his family history, and he has finally unearthed some information about that. Both *Scacco Matto* and the newspapers covering the Campanella Cup agree on the influence which, after her divorce from her Chilean husband, the young chess player's mother has had on her son's career.

—∞—

"The Kellers separated when their son was seven years old. Wealthy in her own right following the death of her first husband during the Spanish civil war, Mercedes Keller found herself ideally situated to offer her son the finest education. When she discovered his talent for chess, she sought out the best teachers, took the boy to every tournament both inside and outside Chile, and persuaded the Chilean-Armenian grand master, Emil Karapetian, to oversee his instruction. The young Keller did not disappoint her. He had no difficulty beating his peers, and under the supervision of his mother and Karapetian, both of whom still accompany him today, he progressed rapidly . . ."

—∞—

After leaving the archive Max returns to the car and drives down to the Marina Grande, parking near the church. Then he makes his way to the Trattoria Stéfano, which is still closed to the public at that time of day. He has gone out in his shirtsleeves, cuffs turned up twice to expose his forearms, jacket slung over his shoulder, pleasurably inhaling the easterly breeze with a tang of salt and the shores of a calm sea. On the terrace of the small restaurant, beneath a bamboo canopy, a waiter is laying tablecloths and cutlery on four tables situated close to the water's edge and the fishermen's boats, beached amid piled-up nets and coils of fishing line.

Without looking up from the chessboard, Lambertucci, the restaurant owner, grunts in response to Max's greeting. With the familiarity of a regular customer, Max strolls behind the little bar where the cash register is, sets his jacket on the counter, pours himself some wine, and approaches the table where Lambertucci is busy concentrating on one of the two chess games, which at the same time every day for the past twenty years he has been accustomed to playing with Captain Tedesco. Antonio Lambertucci, a lanky fellow in his midfifties, is wearing a none-too-clean T-shirt that reveals an army tattoo, a souvenir from when he was a soldier in Abyssinia before being sent to a prisoner-of-war camp in South Africa and later marrying the daughter of Stéfano, the previous owner of the trattoria. Lambertucci's opponent, a black patch over the left eye he lost in Benghazi, gives him a somewhat scowling look. Being called Captain is not a joke: on the contrary, like Lambertucci a native of Sorrento, Tedesco won his promotion during the war, although the difference in rank between the two men lost significance over the three years of captivity both men endured, with nothing to do but play chess. Besides the basic moves, Max knows little about this game (he has learned more that day in the archive than during his entire lifetime), but these two seem like genuine chess lovers. They are regulars at the local chess club and know all about international tournaments, who the grand masters are, and lots more besides.

"So, how good is this Jorge Keller?"

Lambertucci gives another grunt, as he studies an apparently dangerous move his opponent has just made. Finally he makes his move, there is a rapid exchange of pieces, and then Tedesco nonchalantly says "checkmate." Ten seconds later, the captain is putting away the pieces in their box while Lambertucci picks his nose.

"Keller?" he finally remarks. "Very promising. The next world champion, if he defeats the Russian. . . . He's brilliant and not as eccentric as that other young man, Fischer."

"Is it true he's been playing since he was a child?"

"So I hear. As far as I know, he became a phenomenon after winning four tournaments between the ages of fifteen and eighteen. Lambertucci glances at Tedesco for confirmation and proceeds to enumerate on his fingers: "Mar de Plata, the international tournaments at Portorož and Chile, and the challengers' tournament in Yugoslavia, tremendous . . ."

"He beat all the big names," Tedesco adds, equitably.

"Meaning?" says Max.

Tedesco smiles like someone who knows what he's talking about.

"Meaning Petrosian, Tal, Sokolov . . . The best players in the world. His consecration came when he beat Tal and Sokolov in a twenty-game tournament."

"No mean feat," adds Lambertucci, who has fetched the carafe and is topping up Max's glass.

"All the greats were there," Tedesco concludes, narrowing his one good eye. "And Keller trounced them all without turning a hair: he won twelve games and drew seven."

"So why is he so good?"

Lambertucci looks quizzically at Max.

"Have you got the whole day?"

"Yes. My boss has gone away for a few days."

"In that case stay to dinner . . . eggplant parmigiana washed down with a nice little Taurasi."

"Much obliged, but I have a few things to do at the villa."

"This is the first time I've seen you show any interest in chess."

"Well . . . you know how it is." Max smiles wistfully. "The Campanella Cup and all that. Fifty thousand dollars is a lot of money."

Tedesco narrows his one good eye again, pensively.

"You can say that again. Who'll get their hands on it?"

"Why is Keller so good?" Max insists.

"He has a natural talent and is well taught," replies Lambertucci. Then he shrugs and looks at Tedesco, leaving it to him to fill in the details.

"He's a tenacious young fellow," Tedesco says, mulling it over for a while. "When he was starting out, many of the grand masters played a conservative, defensive game, but Keller changed all that.

He defeated them with his spectacular assaults, astonishing sacrifices of his pieces, daring gambits . . ."

"And now?"

"That's still his style: bold, brilliant, heart-stopping endgames. . . . He plays like someone immune to fear, with terrifying casualness. Occasionally he makes seemingly sloppy, incorrect moves, yet his opponents are confounded by his complex strategies. . . . His ambition is to be world champion, and the contest here in Sorrento is considered a preliminary competition, a warm-up for the championship being held in Dublin five months from now."

"Will you be attending the games here?"

"We can't afford it. The Vittoria is reserved for moneyed folk and journalists. . . . We'll have to follow the games on the radio and television, with our own chessboard."

"And is it all as important as they say?"

"It is the most anticipated meeting since the Reshevsky-Fischer head to head in sixty-one," Tedesco explains. "Sokolov is a hardened veteran, coolheaded and rather dull: his best games usually end in a draw. They call him the Russian Wall, just imagine. . . . The fact is there is plenty at stake. The prize money, of course. But politics as well."

Lambertucci gives a shrill laugh.

"They say Sokolov has rented an entire apartment house next to the Vittoria, and is surrounded by advisers and KGB agents."

"What do you know about the mother?"

"Whose mother?"

"Keller's. She's mentioned in all the magazine and newspaper articles."

Tedesco remains pensive for a moment.

"Well, only what I've heard: that she is his manager. That when she saw her son's talent she got the best teachers for him. Chess is an expensive sport until you make a name for yourself. All that traveling, hotels, inscription fees . . . You need to have money, or to obtain money. It seems she had some. I believe she is in charge of everything: his team of trainers, his physical fitness. She even keeps his accounts. . . . People say he is her creation, but I think they exaggerate. Regardless of any help they get, players of genius like Keller create themselves."

—⁓—

Their next encounter on the *Cap Polonio* took place on the sixth day at sea, before dinner. Max Costa had been dancing for half an hour with female passengers of various ages, including the American woman who tipped him five dollars, and Miss Honeybee, when the headwaiter Schmöcker led Mrs. de Troeye to her usual table. She was alone, as she had been on the first evening. When Max passed close by (at that moment he was dancing with one of the young Brazilian girls to "La Canción del Ukelele"), he saw a waiter bringing her a champagne cocktail while she lit a cigarette in a short ivory holder. She wasn't wearing the pearl necklace this time, but one made of amber. Her black satin dress was cut away at the back, and her hair, smoothed down like a boy's, sleek with brilliantine, a thin line of kohl slanting her eyes. Max glanced at her several times, unable to catch her eye. He exchanged a few words with the musicians as he went by, and when they obligingly struck up a tango that was all the rage ("Adiós Muchachos"), Max took his leave of the young Brazilian girl and walked up to her table during the opening bars. Bowing his head briefly, he smiled and stood there motionless as a few other couples got to their feet. Mecha Inzunza de Troeye looked up at him, and for an instant he feared she would turn him down. But a moment later he saw her deposit her cigarette in the ashtray and stand up. It took her an eternity to do so, and the action of placing her left hand on his right shoulder seemed unbearably languorous. Then the tango, already in full swing, swept them both up, and Max knew instantly that the music was on his side.

He realized yet again that she danced outstandingly. The tango did not demand spontaneity, but rather implicit intentions carried out swiftly, in sullen, almost resentful silence. And that was the way they moved, embracing and separating, performing calculated *quebrados*, and following a shared instinct that allowed them to glide effortlessly around the floor, amid couples tangoing with the obvious clumsiness of novices. As a professional, Max knew it was impossible to perform the tango without a skilled partner capable of following a dance whose flow would suddenly stop, the man slowing the rhythm, reenacting a struggle, in which, entwined around him, the woman would continually attempt to flee, only to yield each time, proud and defiant in her submission. Mecha Inzunza de Troeye proved to be that sort of partner.

They danced two tangos in a row (the second was called "Champagne Tango"), during which neither of them uttered a word, surrendering completely to the music and the pleasure of the dance, to the occasional brush of her satin against his flannel and to the heat Max could feel coming from his companion's youthful body, the outline of her face and combed-back hair descending to her exposed neck and shoulders. And when in the pause between the two dances they stood facing each other (slightly breathless from their exertions, waiting for the music to start again, without her showing any sign of returning to her table), and he noticed tiny pearls of sweat on her upper lip, he pulled out one of his two handkerchiefs, not the one protruding from the top pocket of his tailcoat, but another, clean and ironed, from his inside pocket, and offered it to her spontaneously. She accepted the piece of folded white linen, scarcely dabbing her mouth with it before returning it to him, a little damp and smudged with lipstick. She did not even go over to the table for her bag, as Max had anticipated, to powder her nose. Max also wiped the sweat from his upper lip and brow (it did not escape her notice that he touched his lips first), then put away the handkerchief. The second tango started and they danced as before in perfect harmony, only this time her gaze did not stray across the ballroom. After faultlessly executing a particularly complicated turn or step, they would pause for an instant and look straight at each other, before breaking the stillness on the next beat, and turning once more around the dance floor. Once, when he halted abruptly, in midmovement, cool and aloof, she clung to him, suddenly, swaying to one side then the other with a mature graceful elegance, as though fleeing his embrace without really wanting to. For the first time since he had become a professional ballroom dancer, Max felt the urge to brush the nape of her slender, youthful neck with his lips. It was then that he realized, with a casual glance, that his dance partner's husband was sitting at the table, legs crossed, a cigarette between his fingers, watching them closely, despite his apparent indifference. And when Max looked back at her, he discovered golden reflections that seemed to explode into silences of eternal, ageless women. Keys to all the mysteries men could not fathom.

—∿—

The ship's smoking room connected the first-class promenade decks on the port and starboard sides with the poop deck. Max Costa made his way there during the dinner break, knowing it would be almost empty at that hour. The waiter served him a double espresso in a cup bearing the Hamburg Südamerikanische crest. After loosening his white tie and starched collar, he smoked a cigarette next to the window, through which, amid the reflections of light within, the night outside was visible, the moon shining on the poop deck. As the dining room gradually emptied and passengers started to appear and fill the tables, Max got up to leave. In the doorway he stood aside to let a group of men holding cigars pass, among whom he recognized Armando de Troeye. The composer was unaccompanied by his wife, and as Max strolled along the starboard promenade deck, he searched for her among the groups of ladies and gentlemen wrapped in overcoats, mackintoshes, and cloaks, taking the air or contemplating the ocean. It was a warm evening, but the sea was beginning to get choppy for the first time since they had set sail from Lisbon, and although the *Cap Polonio* was equipped with state-of-the art stabilizers, the roll of the ship brought expressions of concern. The ballroom was quiet that evening, and many of the tables remained empty, including that of the de Troeyes. The first cases of seasickness were occurring, and the musical entertainment was cut short. Max barely had a couple of waltzes, and could finish early.

As he was about to descend to his cabin in second class, they bumped into each other next to the elevator, their reflections caught in the huge mirrors on the main staircase. She was wearing a gray fox fur cape and carrying a lamé purse. She was alone, on her way out to one of the promenade decks, and, with a swift glance, Max marveled at how steadily she walked in high heels despite the roll, for even the floor of a vessel that size took on a disconcerting three-dimensionality when the ocean was rough. Turning back, Max held the exterior door open for her until she was outside. She responded with a curt "thank-you" as she crossed the threshold. Max bobbed his head, closed the door, and walked back along the passageway, eight or ten steps. The last of these he took slowly, thoughtfully, before coming to a standstill. What the hell, he thought. Nothing ventured nothing gained, he concluded. Providing he trod carefully.

He soon found her, walking along the upper deck, and stopped casually in front of her, beneath the muted glow of lights covered in sea salt. Doubtless she had come up for some air to avoid feeling seasick. Most of the passengers did the exact opposite, shutting themselves away in their cabins for days on end, prey to their own churning stomachs. For a moment, Max was worried she would walk past, pretending not to see him. But instead she stood still, gazing at him in silence.

"I enjoyed our dance," she blurted out.

Max managed to stifle his astonishment almost instantaneously. "So did I."

The woman went on gazing at him, perhaps quizzically.

"How long have you danced professionally?"

"For five years. But not all the time. The job is . . ."

"Amusing?" she interrupted.

They continued strolling along the deck, adapting their steps to the vessel's slow sway. Occasionally they passed the dark figures or familiar faces of other passengers. The only parts of Max visible in the less illuminated areas were the white blotches of his shirtfront, waistcoat, and tie; the meticulous inch and a half of each starched shirt cuff; and the handkerchief in the top pocket of his tailcoat.

"That wasn't the word I was looking for." He smiled softly. "On the contrary. I was going to say part-time. It has its advantages."

"Which are?"

"Well . . . As you can see, it allows me to travel."

By the light of a porthole he could observe that she was the one smiling now, approvingly.

"You do it well, for something that's only part-time."

Max shrugged.

"For the first few years it was more steady."

"Where was that?"

Max decided to omit part of his employment history, to keep certain names to himself. Including the red-light district in Barcelona and le Vieux Port in Marseille. And the name of a Hungarian dancer, Boske, who used to sing "La petite tonkinoise" while shaving her legs, and had a penchant for young men who woke up in the middle of the night drenched in sweat, troubled by nightmares that led them to believe they were still in Morocco.

"Luxury hotels in Paris in the winter," he said, summing up. "And in the high season, in Biarritz and the Côte d'Azur . . . I also worked in the cabarets of Montmartre for a while."

"Ah." She seemed interested. "We may have bumped into each other."

"No. I would remember you."

"What did you want to tell me?" she asked.

For an instant he couldn't think what she was referring to. Then he realized. After bumping into her below, he had caught up with her on the promenade deck, appearing before her without any explanation.

"That have I never danced such a perfect tango with anyone."

She was silent for three or four seconds, possibly contented. She had come to a halt (there was a lightbulb close by, screwed into the bulkhead) and was gazing at him through the briny blackness.

"Indeed? . . . Well. You are very kind, Mr. . . . Max, isn't that your name?"

"Yes."

"Good. Believe me, I appreciate being flattered."

"It isn't flattery. You know that."

She laughed. A frank, healthy laugh. The same one as a few evenings before when he had jokingly calculated her age as fifteen.

"My husband is a composer. I am surrounded by music and dance. But you are an excellent partner. It's easy to follow your lead."

"I wasn't leading you. You were yourself. I know the difference."

She nodded, thoughtfully.

"Yes. I suppose you do."

Max placed his hand on the wet gunwale. Between rolls, he could feel the throb of engines deep inside the ship vibrating through the deck beneath his feet.

"Do you smoke?"

"Not now, thank you."

"May I?"

"Be my guest."

He fished the silver case out of his inside jacket pocket, took out a cigarette, and raised it to his lips. She watched him.

"Egyptian?" she asked.

"No, Turkish. Abdul Pashas . . . With a hint of opium and honey."

"Then I'll have one."

He leaned forward holding the book of matches, and cupped the flame with his hand as he lit the cigarette she had inserted into a small ivory cigarette holder. Then he lit his. The wind quickly carried the smoke away, smothering the taste. She seemed to be shivering with cold beneath her fur cape. Max gestured toward the door of the nearby palm court, a conservatory-like room with a large light on the ceiling, furnished with wicker chairs, low tables, and potted plants.

"Dancing professionally," she commented as they went in. "That seems like a strange occupation, for a man."

"I don't see the difference. . . . We make a living from it just as easily, as you can see. Dancing isn't always about intimacy or amusement."

"And is what they say true? That a woman expresses her true nature when she dances?"

"Sometimes. But no more than a man."

The room was empty. She sat on one of the chairs, casually allowing her cape to slip open. Examining her reflection in the lid of a vanity case she had pulled from her bag, she applied a touch of pale red Tangee lipstick. Her sleek hair gave her face an alluringly angular, androgynous appearance, while the black satin dress, Max thought, clung to her body in a fascinating way. Aware that he was looking at her, she crossed one leg over the other, rocking it slightly back and forth, and propping one elbow on the arm of the chair, raised the hand in which she was holding the cigarette (her nails were long and manicured, painted the same color as her lips). Every now and then, she flicked the ash onto the floor, Max noticed, as if all the ashtrays in the world were nothing to her.

"I mean strange seen from close up," she said after a while.

"You're the first ballroom dancer I've exchanged more than two words with: thank you and good-bye."

Max had brought over an ashtray and was standing, his right hand in his trouser pocket. Smoking.

"I enjoyed dancing with you," he said.

"Likewise. I would do it again, if the orchestra was still playing and there were people in the ballroom."

"There's nothing to stop you doing so now."

"Pardon me?"

She studied his smile as if analyzing an impertinence. But the professional dancer held her gaze, unflustered. You look like a good fellow, both the Hungarian woman and Boris Dolgoruki had told him, agreeing about that although they had never met. When you smile like that, Max, no one could ever doubt that you are a damn good fellow. Try to use that to your advantage.

"I'm sure you can imagine the music."

Once again, she flicked her ash on to the floor.

"You are very forward."

"Could you do that?"

It was her turn to smile this time, with a hint of defiance.

"Of course I could." She blew out a puff of smoke. "I'm married to a composer, remember. My head is full of music."

"How about 'Mala Junta'? Do you know it?"

"Perfect."

Max stubbed out his cigarette, then smoothed down his vest. She remained motionless for a moment: she was no longer smiling, and was watching him thoughtfully from her chair, as if to make sure he wasn't joking. Finally, she left the cigarette holder smeared with lipstick in the ashtray, stood up very slowly, her eyes fixed unwaveringly on him, and placed her left hand on his shoulder and her right hand in his, as it hovered, outstretched. She remained like that for a moment, erect, tranquil, unsmiling, until Max, after gently squeezing her fingers twice to indicate the first bar, leaned slightly to one side, moved his right foot forward, and the couple started to dance in silence, closely embraced, looking straight at each other, amid the wicker chairs and potted plants in the palm court.

—⁓—

A twist ("Rita Pavone") is playing on the white plastic portable Marconi. In the garden at the Villa Oriana there are palm trees and umbrella pines, and between them, leaning out the open window of his bedroom, Max can see across the Bay of Naples: the cobalt-blue background with the wide, dark cone of Vesuvius and the coastline stretching toward Punto Scutolo, with Sorrento on the cliff top and the two marinas with their stone jetties. Dr. Hugentobler's chauffeur has been reflecting for some time, without taking his eyes off the view. Since eating breakfast in the quiet kitchen he has been standing by the window, mulling over the possibilities and probabilities of an idea that kept him tossing and turning all night, unable to make up his mind, and which, contrary to his hopes, the light of day hasn't thrust from his thoughts.

At last, Max appears to collect himself and paces for a moment around the modest room on the villa's ground floor. Then he looks out the window again, toward Sorrento, before going into the bathroom to splash cold water on his face. After drying himself he looks at his face in the mirror with the care of someone trying to see how age has caught up with him since the last time he looked. He stands like that for a while, as if searching for someone in the distant past—wistfully studying his silver-gray hair, already thinning, his skin ravaged by time and life, the furrows on his brow and at the corners of his mouth, the white bristles on his chin, the drooping lids that deaden the gleam in his eyes. Then he feels his waist (the notches closest to his belt buckle are marked from where he has gradually loosened it) and shakes his head disapprovingly. He is dragging around a surfeit of years and pounds. And possibly of life as well.

He walks out into the corridor, past the door leading to the garage, and continues until he reaches the drawing room. Everything in there is clean and neat, with white dust sheets draped over the furniture. The Lanzas are spending their days off in Salerno. For Max this means absolute peace and quiet, with nothing to do besides keep an eye on the house, forward any urgent mail, and ensure that Dr. Hugentobler's Jaguar, Rolls-Royce, and three vintage cars are all in working order.

Still pensive, he goes over to the cocktail cabinet in the drawing room, opens the door to where the drinks are kept, and helps himself to a small measure of Rémy Martin in a cut-glass tumbler. He proceeds to sip it, knitting his brow. Generally speaking, Max doesn't drink much. Almost his entire life, even during the harsh, early years, he has drunk in moderation (perhaps the word should be prudently, or carefully), and, whether imbibed by himself or by others, he was able to turn alcohol into a useful ally rather than an unpredictable enemy; into a professional tool of his ambiguous trade, or trades, which, depending on the situation, could be as effective as a smile, a blow, or a kiss. In any case, at this point in his life, heading toward the inevitable scrap heap, an occasional glass of wine or vermouth, a perfectly shaken Negroni cocktail, still quickens heart and mind.

Finishing his drink, Max wanders around the empty house. He is still thinking over what kept him awake the previous night. On the radio, which he has left on, a woman's voice rings out from the other end of the corridor. She is singing "Resta Cu'Mme" as if the words were truly making her suffer. Max becomes distracted for a moment, listening to the song. When it has finished he returns to his bedroom, opens the drawer where he keeps his checkbook, and verifies his bank balance. His meager savings. Just enough, he thinks, to cover the necessities. The basics. Amused by the idea, he opens his wardrobe and surveys the contents, imagining probable situations, before making his way to the master bedroom. Max is unaware of it, but he walks with a relaxed spring in his step. With the same agile, self-assured gait he possessed years before, when the world was still a dangerous, thrilling adventure: a constant challenge to his wit and ingenuity. He has finally made a decision, which simplifies things, joining past and present in a surprising circle that seems to make everything fall into place. In Dr. Hugentobler's bedroom a golden glow is seeping in through the curtains. As Max draws them back, light floods the room, revealing the view over the bay, the trees, the neighboring villas clustered on the hillside. He turns toward the closet, takes down a Gucci suitcase from the top shelf, and opens it on the bed. Hands on hips, he contemplates his boss's well-stocked wardrobe. Dr. Hugentobler and he have more or less the same neck and chest measurements, and so he selects half a dozen silk shirts and a couple of jackets. The shoes and trousers aren't his size, because Max is taller than Hugentobler (he sighs: he will have to pay a visit to the expensive men's shops along the Corso Italia), but a brand-new leather belt is, and he puts it in the suitcase together with half a dozen pairs of soberly colored socks. After a final glance, he adds a couple of silk neckerchiefs, three attractive ties, a pair of gold cuff links, a Dupont lighter (although he gave up smoking years ago), and an Omega Seamaster De Ville wristwatch, also gold. Back in his own room, suitcase in hand, he hears the radio again: now Domenico Modugno is singing "Vecchio frac" ("The Old Tuxedo"). Incredible, he reflects. As if this were a good omen, the coincidence makes the former ballroom dancer smile.

Tangos to Cry for and Tangos to Die for

"HAVE YOU GONE mad?"

Tiziano Spadaro, receptionist at the Hotel Vittoria, leans across the desk to take a look at the suitcase Max has placed on the floor. Then he eyes Max from the bottom up: brown, Moroccan leather shoes; gray flannel trousers; silk shirt and cravat; navy-blue blazer.

"On the contrary," the newly arrived guest replies evenly. "I just felt like a change of scenery for a few days."

Spadaro strokes his bald head thoughtfully. His suspicious eyes meet those of Max, scouring them for hidden intentions. Dangerous connotations.

"Have you forgotten what a room costs here?"

"Of course not. Two hundred thousand lire a week . . . So what?"

"I told you: we have no vacancies."

Max's smile is friendly and self-assured. Almost benevolent. In it there is a trace of old loyalties and unshakable belief.

"Tiziano . . . I have been staying in hotels for forty years. There is always a vacancy."

Spadaro lowers his gaze grudgingly toward the polished mahogany counter. Max has put a sealed envelope containing ten ten-thousand-lira notes in the space between his hands. The hotel receptionist at the Vittoria contemplates it the way a baccarat player might hesitate before turning the cards he has been dealt. Finally, he moves his left hand slowly toward the envelope, brushing it with his thumb.

"Call me a bit later. I'll see what I can do."

Max likes the gesture: fingering the envelope without opening it. Old codes.

"No," he says gently. "Sort it out now."

They remain silent while a group of guests walks past. The receptionist glances around the lobby: there is no one on the stairs leading up to the rooms, or at the glass door to the conservatory, where they can hear the murmur of conversation; and the concierge is busy at his post, placing keys in pigeonholes.

"I thought you had retired," says Spadaro, lowering his voice.

"I have. I told you so the other day. I just want a break, like in the old days. Champagne on ice and some nice views."

Spadaro looks at him suspiciously again, after a second glance at the suitcase and his elegant clothes. Through the window, the receptionist glimpses the Rolls-Royce parked at the top of the steps leading down to the hotel entrance.

"Things must be going very well for you now in Sorrento. . . ."

"Splendidly, as you can see."

"Just like that?"

"Precisely. Just like that."

"And your boss, the one at Villa Oriana?"

"I'll tell you about him some other time."

Spadaro rubs his bald head again, weighing the situation. His years in the job have given him a bloodhound's sense of smell. This is not the first time Max has placed an envelope on the counter in front of him. The last was ten years ago, when Spadaro still worked at the Hotel Vesuvio in Naples. A priceless moretto brooch from Nardi's that belonged to an aging screen actress called Silvia Massari—a regular guest there—went missing from her room, which (courtesy of Spadaro) adjoined Max's. The disappearance took place while she was having lunch with Max out on the hotel terrace with its spectacular vista, after the two of them had spent the previous night and most of that morning engaging in autumnal yet vigorous intimacies. During the regrettable incident, Max only left the terrace and his companion's tender gaze for a few moments to wash his hands. Consequently, it did not occur to Miss Massari to question the integrity of his conduct, his splendid smile, and other tokens of affection. In the end, the affair was resolved with the interrogation and dismissal of a chambermaid, although there was no evidence against her. The actress's insurance dealt with the matter, and as Max was settling his account and handing out tips with the air of a perfect gentleman, Tiziano Spadaro received an envelope similar to the one before him now, only thicker.

"I didn't know you were interested in chess."

"Really?" The old professional smile, broad and dazzling, the one he most favors from among his old repertoire. "Well, I was always something of an enthusiast. An intriguing atmosphere. A unique opportunity to see two great players . . . Better than football."

"What are you plotting, Max?"

Max holds Spadaro's inquisitive gaze, unflustered.

"Nothing that will jeopardize your approaching retirement. I promise. And I have never broken a promise to you."

A long, brooding pause. A deep wrinkle appears between Spadaro's eyebrows.

"That's true," he admits finally.

"I am glad you remember that."

Spadaro looks down at his waistcoat buttons and runs his hand over them pensively as though brushing off imaginary specks of dust.

"The police will see your registration card."

"So what? . . . I was always clean in Italy. Besides, this doesn't involve the police."

"Look. You're getting on a bit for some things . . . we all are. You shouldn't forget that."

Without responding, impassive, Max continues to look at the receptionist, who is contemplating the envelope, still lying unopened on the polished wood.

"How many days?"

"I don't know." Max shrugs. "A week will be sufficient, I think."

"You think?"

"It'll be enough."

The other man places a finger on the envelope. Finally he sighs and slowly opens the register.

"I can only guarantee you one week. After that we'll see."

"Very well."

With the palm of his hand, Spadaro rings the bell three times to call the bellboy.

"A small, single room, without a view. Breakfast not included."

Max reaches into his jacket pocket for his identity papers. When he lays them on the desk, the envelope has disappeared.

—⚏—

Seeing the husband enter the bar in second class on the *Cap Polonio* took Max by surprise. He was enjoying a glass of absinthe and water and some olives, sitting next to one of the big sliding windows overlooking the promenade deck on the port side. He liked this spot, because it allowed him to observe the entire room (wicker chairs replacing the plush, red-leather armchairs in first class) and also gaze at the ocean. The weather was still fine, sun all day long and clear skies at night. After the rough seas they had endured for the past forty-eight hours, the vessel had stopped rolling and the passengers were moving about the ship more easily, looking at one another instead of worrying about which way the deck was sloping. In any case, Max, who had crossed the Atlantic five times, couldn't recall a calmer trip.

A few of the passengers at the neighboring tables, almost exclusively men, were playing cards, backgammon, chess, or steeplechase. Max, who was only an occasional, practical player (not even during his army days in Morocco had he been as passionate about gambling as other men were), nonetheless derived pleasure from watching the professional cardsharps who plied their trade on ocean liners. The ruses, bluffing, variety of reactions, and codes of behavior all reflected the complexity of the human condition so faithfully that they provided an excellent open school for anyone who knew how to look, and Max invariably learned some useful lessons. As on every ocean liner, there were cardsharps on the *Cap Polonio* in first class, second class, and even in steerage. The crew was aware of this, of course, as were the ship detective, the headwaiters, and the stewards, who were acquainted with a few of the regulars and kept an eye on them, underlining their names on the passenger list. A while back, on the *Cap Arcona*, Max had met a gambler called Brereton, who was reputed to have finished a legendary game of bridge in the tilting first-class smoking room on the *Titanic* before it sank in the frozen waters of the North Atlantic, and to have won substantially just in time to dive into the water and swim to the last lifeboat.

Max Costa was astonished to see Armando de Troeye in the second-class bar on the *Cap Polonio* that morning because it was unusual for passengers to cross the boundaries defined by their social status. However, his astonishment grew when the famous composer—who was wearing a Norfolk jacket, a vest with a gold fob, plus fours, and a fedora—stood surveying the room from the doorway, and, on seeing Max, made a beeline for him, smiling affably as he sat down in the chair beside him.

"What are you drinking?" he asked, signaling to the waiter. "Absinthe? . . . Too strong for me. I think I'll have a vermouth."

By the time the waiter had brought over his cocktail, Armando had already praised Max's skill on the dance floor, and was engaging him in polite conversation on the subject of ocean liners, music, and ballroom dancing. As the composer of "Nocturnes" (and other successful works such as "Scaramouche" *and* the ballet "Pasodoble for Don Quixote," to which Diaghilev had brought international fame), de Troeye was someone Max saw as supremely self-confident, an artist who knew who he was and what he represented. And while de Troeye maintained an attitude of worldly superiority in this second-class bar (the celebrated composer opposite the humble employee from a lower rung on the musical ladder), he was clearly making an effort to be friendly. Despite his obvious reservations, his manner was far from the superciliousness of previous evenings, when Max had danced with his wife in the first-class ballroom.

"I assure you I was watching you carefully. And you are close to perfection."

"It is kind of you to say so. Although you exaggerate." Max gave a courteous half-smile. "These things depend on one's partner, too. . . . Your wife is a marvelous dancer, as you well know."

"Undoubtedly. I don't deny it. She is a remarkable woman. But the initiative came from you. You marked out the territory, so to speak. And that can't be improvised." De Troeye picked up the glass the waiter had placed on the table and held it to the light, as though mistrusting the quality of a vermouth in second class. "May I ask you a professional question?"

"Of course."

A tentative sip, then a satisfied expression beneath the trim mustache.

"Where did you learn to dance tango like that?"

"I was born in Buenos Aries."

"You surprise me." De Troeye took another sip. "You don't have an accent."

"I was a youngster when I left. My father was from Asturias and emigrated there in the nineties. . . . Things went badly for him, and he ended up returning to Spain, where he became ill and died. Before that, he had time to marry an Italian woman, have children, and take them all back with him."

De Troeye leaned over the arm of the wicker chair, attentive.

"How long did you actually live in Buenos Aires?"

"Until I was fourteen."

"That explains everything. The authentic feel of those tangos. . . . Why are you smiling?"

Max shrugged, unaffectedly.

"Because there is nothing authentic about them. Real tango is different."

The composer was genuinely surprised, or so it appeared. Perhaps it was nothing more than polite interest. The glass was hovering between the table and de Troeye's half-open mouth.

"Really . . . In what way?"

"It is faster, played by folk musicians from the poor neighborhoods. Lascivious rather than artful, to put it simply. Made up of *cortes* and *quebradas* danced by whores and lowlifes."

The other man burst out laughing. "And it still is in some circles," he added.

"Not really. Original tango changed a lot, above all when it became fashionable in Paris ten or fifteen years ago with the Apache dances of the underworld. . . . The upper classes started imitating them, and it came back to Argentina frenchified, transformed into a polished, almost respectable dance." Max gave another shrug, drained his glass, and looked straight at de Troeye, who was smiling affably. "I hope what I say makes sense."

"Indeed. And it's most interesting. . . . You are a pleasant surprise, Señor Costa."

Max did not recall telling de Troeye or his wife his surname. It was possible he had seen it on the staff list. Or looked for it there. He held that thought for a moment, without analyzing it too much, before continuing to indulge the composer's curiosity. He explained that, thanks to its Parisian stamp of approval, the Argentinian upper class, who had hitherto rejected tango as an immoral dance that belonged in the bordellos, instantly adopted it. Tango, no longer reserved for the hoi polloi from the slums, became the rage in dance halls. Prior to that, genuine tango, the tango danced in Buenos Aires by whores and ruffians from the poor neighborhoods, was frowned upon in polite society: it was something young well-to-do girls played in secret on their pianos at home, from sheet music brought to them by boyfriends and dissolute, carousing brothers.

"And yet," objected de Troeye, "you dance modern tango, so to speak."

Max smiled at the word *modern*.

"Of course. That is the kind everyone asks for. And the one I know. I never danced the old-style tango in Buenos Aires. I was too young. Although I saw it danced often enough. . . . Ironically, I learned the tango I dance in Paris."

"How did you end up there?"

"That's a long story. It would bore you."

De Troeye had beckoned the waiter, and was ordering another round, ignoring Max's protests. Ordering drinks without consulting anyone seemed to come naturally to him. Apparently he was the sort of fellow who behaved like a host even when he was a guest at someone else's table.

·"Bore me? On the contrary. You cannot imagine how fascinated

I am by what you're saying. . . . Are there still people in Buenos
Aires who play the old way? . . . Pure tango, as it were?"

Max thought about it for a moment and finally shook his head,
doubtfully.

"There is nothing pure. But there are still a few places. Not in
the fashionable dance halls, obviously."

De Troeye examined his own hands. Broad, strong hands. Not
tapered, the way Max imagined those of a famous composer would
be. Clipped, shiny nails, he noticed. He wore the gold signet ring
with the blue lozenge on the same finger as his wedding band.

"I am going to ask a favor of you, Mr. Costa. Something that
means a lot to me."

The fresh drinks had arrived. Max did not touch his. De Troeye
was grinning, sure of himself.

"I'd like to invite you to lunch," he went on, "so that we can
discuss this in more detail."

Max concealed his surprise beneath an awkward smile.

"I appreciate the gesture, but as an employee I am not allowed
in the first-class dining room . . ."

"You're right." The composer frowned, thoughtful, as though
wondering to what extent he could change the ship's regulations.
"That is an unfortunate inconvenience. We could eat together in
second class . . . but I have an even better idea. My wife and I have a
double stateroom that can easily accommodate a table for three. . . .
Would you do us the honor?"

Max hesitated, still taken aback.

"That is very kind of you, but I'm not sure that I should. . . ."

"Don't worry. I will arrange it with the steward." De Troeye took
a last sip before placing his glass firmly on the table, as if the matter
was decided. "So you accept, then?"

Any qualms Max still had were simply because he was cautious.
It was true that nothing was going the way he had imagined. Or
was it? he wondered after reflecting for a moment. He needed a

little more time and information to be able to weigh the pros and cons. Armando de Troeye's entrance was a new, unforeseen element in the game.

"Perhaps your wife—" he began to say.

"Mecha will be delighted," de Troeye declared, raising his eyebrows as he signaled to the waiter to bring the bill. "She says you are the best ballroom dancer she has ever met. It will be a pleasure for her as well."

Without glancing at the total, de Troeye signed with his room number, tipped the waiter with a banknote, and rose to his feet. Out of courtesy Max made to do likewise, but de Troeye detained him, placing a hand on his shoulder. A hand stronger than he would have imagined for a musician.

"In a manner of speaking, I want your advice." De Troeye had slipped his gold fob watch out of his pocket and was checking the time with a nonchalant air. "Until midday, then . . . Cabin 3A. We shall be expecting you."

Without waiting for a reply, Armando de Troeye left the bar, taking for granted that Max would keep the appointment. After he had gone, Max sat staring at the door through which he had just disappeared. He reflected on the surprising turn this gave, or might give, events he had been trying to set up for the days to come. On balance, the situation could offer richer pickings than he had initially imagined, he concluded. He placed a sugar cube in a teaspoon, balanced it on top of the glass of absinthe, and poured a small amount of water over it, watching the sugar dissolve into the greenish liquid. Grinning to himself, he raised the glass to his lips. This time, the sweet, pungent taste of the alcohol did not conjure memories of second lieutenant legionnaire Boris Dolgoruki-Bragation and the native shacks of Morocco. His thoughts were with the shiny pearl necklace glistening beneath the ballroom chandeliers in Mecha Inzunza de Troeye's cleavage. And with the line of her bare neck, rising from her shoulders. He felt an urge to whistle a tango, and would have done so had he not suddenly remembered where he was. When he rose to his feet, the taste of absinthe in his mouth was sweet like a promise of women and adventure.

—w—

Spadaro, the receptionist, has lied. The room is indeed small, furnished with a chest of drawers and an antique wardrobe with a full-length mirror, the bathroom is cramped, and the single bed is modest. But it is not true that the room has no view. Through its only window, Max can see the part of Sorrento that overlooks the Marina Grande, as well as the copse of trees in the park and the villas clustered on the rocky slopes of the Punta del Capo. And when he opens the shutters and leans out, the light dazzling his eyes, he can also see part of the bay, with the island of Ischia a blur in the distance.

Fresh out of the shower, naked beneath a bathrobe bearing the embroidered monogram of the hotel, Dr. Hugentobler's chauffeur observes himself in the wardrobe mirror. His critical eye, trained by the habits of his profession in the study of human beings (for his success or failure always depended on this), lingers on the motionless figure of an old man, contemplating his own wet, gray hair, his furrowed face and tired eyes. He is still in good shape, he concludes, providing one looks with a kind eye upon the ravages men his age usually show—the irreparable damage, diminishment, and decay. And so, in search of consolation, he prods the bathrobe: there's no doubt he is heavier, thicker set than he was some years earlier, but his waistline is still acceptable. He holds himself erect and his eyes remain lively and intelligent, proof of an elegance that the decadence, dark years, and ultimate loss of hope have never completely eradicated. As if to verify this, like an actor rehearsing a tricky part of his role, Max suddenly smiles at the old man in the mirror, who responds with a seemingly spontaneous gesture that lights up his face: friendly, persuasive, polished to perfection so as to inspire confidence. He stays that way a moment more, motionless, allowing his smile to slowly slip away. Then, taking a comb from the top of the chest of drawers, he smoothes his hair down in the old style, straight back, parting dead straight, on the left side close to the middle. Appraising the result with a critical eye, he concludes that his gestures are still elegant. At least they can be. They reveal an alleged good breeding (and in the old days that was a simple step away from alleged good birth), which years of practice have refined until anything that might betray their fraudulent origin has been eliminated. In short, the remains of a stimulating past, which in days gone by allowed him to venture with a hunter's ease into uncertain, often hostile territory. Not only to survive, but to prosper. Almost. Until quite recently.

Slipping out of his bathrobe, Max whistles "Torna a Sorrento" as he starts to dress with the meticulous care of the old days, when he devoted minute attention to the angle of a hat, the knot of a tie, the five different ways of folding a white handkerchief in the top pocket of a jacket. It would make him feel confident in his resourcefulness, like a warrior preparing for battle. That vague awareness of the past, the familiar whiff of expectation, of imminent combat, now soothes his rediscovered sense of pride, as he dons a pair of cotton underpants, gray socks (which take a bit of effort to put on, bending over on the edge of the bed), and the shirt from Dr. Hugentobler's wardrobe, slightly loose at the waist. In the last few years snug clothes have been in fashion, flared trousers, tight-fitting jackets and shirts, but Max, who cannot conform to such trends, prefers the classic cut of the Sir Bonser pale-blue silk shirt with button-down collar that looks like it was made for him. Before buttoning it up, his eyes linger on the small, star-shaped scar an inch in diameter on the left side just below the rib cage—courtesy of a bullet fired by a cop from the Rif in Taxuda, Morocco, on November 2, 1921, which narrowly missed his lung, and, following a spell in the hospital at Melilla, brought to an end the short-lived

military career of the legionnaire who five months earlier had enlisted in the 13th Company of the First Battalion of the Spanish
Foreign Legion as Max Costa, thus renouncing forever his original
name: Maximo Covas Lauro.

—◊◊—

Tango, Max explained to the composer and his wife, was a coming
together of several strands: Andalusian tango, Cuban habanera,
Argentine milonga, and black slave dances. When the Argentinian
gauchos first brought their guitars to the bars, stores, and brothels
on the outskirts of Buenos Aires, they brought with them the rural
milonga, based on songs, and eventually the tango, which began
as a milonga dance. The black elements were important, because
in those days couples danced farther apart than they do now, with
cross and back steps, simple or more elaborate turns.

"Black tango?" Armando de Troeye seemed genuinely surprised.
"I didn't realize there were black people in Buenos Aires."

"There used to be. Former slaves, of course. They were deci-
mated at the turn of the last century by a yellow fever epidemic."

The three of them were still seated at the table that had been
set up in the couple's double stateroom. It smelled of fine leather
trunks and eau de cologne. Through a large window they had
a view of the calm blue ocean. Max, who wore a gray suit, soft-
collared shirt, and paisley necktie, had knocked on the door at two
minutes past twelve, and, after a few initial moments during which
Armando de Troeye alone seemed to be at ease, the lunch (sweet
pepper soup, lobster salad, and a chilled Rhine wine) had passed in
an atmosphere of pleasant conversation. At first it was conducted
almost entirely by de Troeye, who, after recounting a few of his
own anecdotes, once again expressed interest in Max's childhood
in Buenos Aires, the return to Spain, and his time as a ballroom
dancer in luxury hotels and transatlantic liners. Habitually circum-
spect when talking about his own life, Max had skirted around

the issue with brief remarks and deliberate vagueness. Finally, over coffee and cognac, at de Troeye's request, he had resumed their discussion about tango.

"The white Argentines," Max explained, "who at first only watched the blacks, soon adopted their way of dancing, but slowed down steps they couldn't imitate and introduced movements from the waltz, the habanera, or the mazurka. . . . Remember at that time tango wasn't so much a kind of music as a way of dancing, or playing music."

From time to time, as Max spoke, his cuffs with their silver cuff links resting on the edge of the table, his eyes met those of Mecha Inzunza. The composer's wife had remained silent throughout most of the meal, listening to their conversation, and only occasionally commenting briefly or slipping in a question and awaiting the reply with polite interest.

"The tango danced by Italians and European immigrants," Max went on, "became slower, less disjointed, although the *compadritos* from the poor neighborhoods adopted some of the African mannerisms. . . . When a couple were dancing in a straight line, so to speak, the man would stop in midflow, to show off or to perform a *quebrada*, halting his movement and that of his partner"—Max glanced at Mecha, who was still listening attentively—"the famous *corte*, the respectable version of which you are so good at in the tangos we dance currently."

Mecha Inzunza honored the compliment with a smile. She was wearing a delightfully diaphanous, champagne-colored dress, and the light from the window set off her hair, bobbed at the nape of her neck, whose slender shape had filled Max's thoughts ever since the silent tango they had danced in the palm court of the ocean liner. The only jewels she had worn then were the pearls in a double string around her neck and her wedding band.

"What are *compadritos*?" she asked now.

"What were they, you mean."

"Do they no longer exist?"

"Things have changed a lot in the last ten to fifteen years . . . When I was a child, *compadritos* were young men of humble background, the sons or grandsons of the gauchos who rode in with the cattle and dismounted in the working-class suburbs of Buenos Aires."

"They sound dangerous," remarked de Troeye.

Max made a dismissive gesture. They were relatively harmless, he explained, unlike the compadres and compadrones, who were much rougher characters: some were real villains, others only appeared to be. Politicians would employ them as bodyguards, or during elections, and so on. But the authentic compadres, who often had Spanish surnames, were being replaced by the sons of immigrants who tried to emulate them: petty criminals who still adopted the old ways of the knife-fighting gauchos, but without possessing their code of honor or their courage.

"And is authentic tango a dance of *compadritos* and compadres?" asked Armando de Troeye.

"It used to be. Those early tangos were openly lewd, with couples bringing their bodies together, entwining their legs and thrusting with their hips, like I said before. Remember that the first female tango dancers were camp followers and women from the brothels."

Out of the corner of his eye, Max could see Mecha Inzunza's smile, scornful yet fascinated. He had seen that same smile before in other women of her class, when topics like this were mentioned.

"Hence its bad reputation, naturally," she said.

"Of course," Max went on, still addressing her husband out of politeness. "Imagine, one of the earliest tangos was called 'Give Me the Tin . . .'"

"The tin?"

Another sidelong glance. Max paused, searching for how best to put it.

"The token," he said at last, "which the madam gave each client, and which the whore in turn gave to her mack, who cashed them in."

"Mack, that sounds foreign," said Mecha Inzunza.

"It comes from *maquereau*," de Troeye explained. "The French word for *pimp*."

"I understood that perfectly, my dear."

Even when tango became popular and was danced at family gatherings, *cortes* were banned on grounds of indecency. When he was a child, tango was only danced at afternoon shindigs in the Spanish or Italian social clubs, in brothels, or in the *garçonnières* of well-to-do young men. And even now, when tango had taken the dance halls and theaters by storm, the ban on *cortes* and *quebradas* remained in place in some circles. The "leg thrust," as it was crudely termed. Once the tango became socially acceptable, it lost its character, Max concluded. It became slow, calculated, less lewd. This was the tame version that had traveled to Paris and become famous.

"It was transformed into that dull routine we see in dance halls, or into Valentino's ridiculous caricature of it on screen."

Max could feel her eyes on him. Avoiding them with as much calm as he could muster, he reached for his cigarette case and offered it to her. She took one of the Abdul Pashas, inserting it into her short ivory holder. De Troeye did likewise, and then lit his wife's with his gold lighter. Leaning slightly toward the flame, she raised her eyes, looking once more at Max through the first puff of smoke, which the light from the window turned a bluish shade.

"And in Buenos Aires?" asked Armando de Troeye.

Max smiled. He had lit his own cigarette after tapping one end of it gently on the closed lid of the case. The turn in the conversation enabled him to meet Mecha's eyes once more. He held her gaze for three seconds, maintaining his smile, then addressed her husband again.

"In the slums of the suburbs a few people still dance tango with the occasional *quebrada* and leg thrust. That is where the last of the Old School Tango survives. . . . What we dance is actually a watered-down version of that. A tasteful habanera."

"Is it the same with the lyrics?"

"Yes, but that's a more recent phenomenon. At first tango was only music, or couplets sung in the theaters. When I was a boy it was still rare to hear tango sung, and when it was, the lyrics were always obscene, stories with double meanings told by shameless ruffians. . . ."

Max paused, unsure if it was appropriate for him to carry on.

"And?"

It was Mecha who had posed the question, toying with one of the silver teaspoons. That decided him.

"Well . . . you only have to consider some of the titles from back then: 'Que polvo con tanto viento,' 'Seeds in the Wind; 'Siete Pulgadas,' 'Seven Inches'; 'Cara Sucia,' 'Dirty Face'—all of which have double meanings, or 'La c . . . ara de la l . . . una,' 'The F . . . ace of the M . . . oon,' written like that, with three dots in the title, which, forgive me for being crude, actually means 'La concha de la lora,' 'The Floozie's Muff.'"

"Floozie?"

"A word for 'prostitute' in Buenos Aires slang. The sort Gardel uses in his songs."

"And muff?"

Max looked at Armando de Troeye, without replying. The husband's amused expression gave way to a broad smile.

"Understood," he said.

"Understood," she repeated a moment later, without smiling.

Sentimental tango, Max went on, was a recent phenomenon. It was Gardel who popularized those melancholy lyrics, filling tango songs with cuckolded hoodlums and fallen women. His voice turned the ruffian's shamelessness to tears and regret. Poetic guff.

"We met him two years ago, when he was touring in Rome and Madrid," said de Troeye. "Charming fellow. A bit of a gossip, but pleasant enough." He looked at his wife. "With that fixed smile of his, remember? . . . As if he could never relax."

"I only saw him once, from a distance, eating chicken stew at El Tropezón," said Max. "He was surrounded by people, of course. I didn't dare approach him."

"He certainly has a good voice. So langorous, don't you think?"

Max took a puff of his cigarette. De Troeye poured himself another brandy and offered Max some, but he shook his head.

"Actually, he invented the style. Before, there were only bawdy rhymes in brothels. . . . He had no real predecessors."

"What about the music?" De Troeye had raised his brandy to his lips and was looking at Max over the rim of the glass. "What, in your opinion, are the differences between old and new tango?"

Max leaned back in his chair, tapping his cigarette gently so that the ash fell in to the ashtray.

"I am no musician. I simply dance to make a living. I can't tell a quaver from a crochet."

"Even so, I would like your opinion."

Max drew twice on his cigarette before replying.

"I can only talk about what I know. What I remember . . . The same happened to the music as to the dance and the words. The early musicians were self-taught, they played little-known tunes, from piano scores or from memory. On the hoof, as they say in Argentina . . . like jazz musicians when they improvise, inventing as they go along."

"And what were the orchestras like?"

Small, Max explained. Three or four musicians, the bandoneon providing the bass notes, simpler harmonies, faster paced. It was more about the way they played than the music itself. Gradually, those orchestras were replaced by more modern ensembles: piano instead of guitar solos, violin accompaniment, the drone of the squeezebox. That made it easier for inexpert dancers, the new fans. Professional orchestras adapted overnight to the new tango.

"And that is what we dance," he concluded, slowly putting out his cigarette. "That's what you hear in the ship's ballroom and the respectable establishments of Buenos Aires."

Mecha Inzunza stubbed out her cigarette in the same ashtray as Max, three seconds later.

"What happened to the other sort?" she asked, playing with the ivory cigarette holder. "The Old School Tango?"

Not without some difficulty, Max took his eyes off her hands: slender, elegant, refined. Her gold wedding band glinted on the ring finger of her left hand. He looked up to find Armando de Troeye staring at him, expressionless.

"It still exists," he replied. "On the fringes, though it's increasingly rare. Depending on where it's played, almost no one dances to it. It's more difficult. Cruder."

He paused for a moment. The smile now playing on her lips was spontaneous. Suggestive.

"A friend of mine once said there are tangos to cry for and tangos to die for. . . . The old-fashioned tangos belonged more to the second category."

Mecha Inzunza had propped her elbow on the table and was cupping her face in her hand. She appeared to be paying close attention.

"Some people call it the Old School Tango," Max explained. "To differentiate it from the new, modern tango."

"That's a good name," the husband said. "Where does it come from?"

His face was no longer expressionless. Yet again a friendly gesture, that of an attentive host. Max spread his hands as though to state the obvious.

"I don't know. The Old School was the title of an early tango. I couldn't say for sure."

"And is it still . . . obscene?" she asked.

Her tone was unemotional. Almost scientific. That of an ento-mologist investigating, for example, whether copulation between two beetles was obscene. Assuming, Max concluded, beetles copu-lated. Which, undoubtedly, they did.

"That depends where you go," he replied.

Armando de Troeye seemed delighted by the conversation.

"What you're telling us is fascinating," he said. "Far more than you could imagine. And it changes some of the ideas I had about tango. I want to see it for myself . . . in its authentic surroundings."

Max frowned, cagily.

"It certainly isn't played in any respectable venues. None that I know of."

"Are there authentic places in Buenos Aires?"

"One or two. But to call them unsuitable would be an under-statement." He looked at Mecha Inzunza. "They are dangerous places . . . inappropriate for a lady."

"Don't worry about that," she said with icy calm. "We've been to inappropriate places before."

—◊◊◊—

It is late afternoon. The setting sun over Punta del Capo casts a reddish glow over the villas on the green hillside. Max Costa, in the same navy-blue jacket and gray flannel trousers he was wearing when he arrived at the hotel (he has only changed his silk cravat for a red necktie with blue polka dots tied in a Windsor knot), comes down from his room and mingles with the other guests enjoying a predinner drink. Although the summer and its crowds have gone, the chess contest has kept the place busy: nearly all the tables in the bar and on the terrace are full. A poster resting on an easel announces the forthcoming game in the Sokolov-Keller duel. Max pauses to study the photographs of the two adversaries. Beneath pale bushy eyebrows of the same color as his hair, which reminds

Max of a hedgehog, the Soviet champion's watery blue eyes gaze suspiciously at the pieces on a chessboard. His round face and coarse features evoke the image of a peasant studying the board in the same way generations of his ancestors might have surveyed a field of ripening grain or clouds passing overhead presaging rain or drought. As for Jorge Keller, he looks almost distracted and dreamy as he gazes at the photographer. Max thinks he can detect a touch of naïveté, as though the young man were looking not at the camera but at someone or something slightly farther off that has nothing to do with chess, but rather with childish dreams or vague fantasies.

A warm breeze. The murmur of conversation and soft background music. The terrace at the Vittoria is spacious and splendid. Beyond the balustrade is a stunning view over the Bay of Naples, which is beginning to be bathed in a golden light that gradually spreads across the horizon. The headwaiter shepherds Max to a table beside a marble statue of a half-kneeling naked woman peering out to sea. Max orders a glass of cold white wine and glances around him. The atmosphere is one of elegance, as befits the time and place. There are smartly dressed foreign guests, mostly those Americans and Germans who visit Sorrento out of season. The rest are Campanella's guests, whose travel and hotel expenses he has paid. There are also chess lovers who can afford to pay their own expenses. At a neighboring table, Max recognizes a beautiful movie actress accompanied by a group of people that includes her husband, a producer at Cinecittà. Hovering nearby are two young men who look like local journalists. One has a Pentax camera slung around his neck, and each time he raises it, Max hides his face discreetly behind his hand or turns to look in the opposite direction. It is unconscious, a reflex, that of the hunter careful not to become the hunted. These old gestures, second nature to him now, he had developed instinctively as a professional to minimize risk. In those days, Max Costa was never more vulnerable than when exposing his face and identity to some detective capable of asking what an experienced con artist, or gentleman thief, as they were referred to euphemistically in another era, was doing in a given place.

When the journalists move away, Max surveys the scene. On his way down, he was thinking how extraordinarily lucky it would be to spot her at the first attempt, and yet there she is, sitting at a table quite close to his, with a group of other people that does not include young Keller or the girl who was with them. This time she isn't wearing her tweed hat, and he can see her short, silver-gray hair, which looks completely natural. As she speaks, she tilts her head toward her companions, showing polite interest (a gesture Max recalls with astonishing clarity), occasionally leaning back in her chair and nodding at their conversation with a smile. She is simply dressed, with the same casual elegance as the day before: a dark, flared skirt and a white silk blouse gathered at the waist by a wide belt. She has on a pair of suede loafers and the same wool cardigan draped over her shoulders. She wears no earrings or jewelry, apart from a slender wristwatch.

Max enjoys a sip of the chilled wine, which has made the glass go misty, and, as he leans forward to replace it on the table, the woman's eyes meet his. The encounter is momentary, barely lasting a second. She is saying something to her companions, and as she does so she glances about, her eyes momentarily meeting those of the man sitting three tables away. They do not settle on him, but keep moving as the conversation continues, and someone says something she listens to attentively, her gaze now fixed on her companions. Max, with a stab of regret and wounded vanity, smiles to himself and consoles himself with another sip of Falerno. It is true he has changed, but so has she, he decides. An awful lot, no doubt, since they last saw each other in Nice twenty-nine years ago in the autumn of 1937, not to mention in Buenos Aires, nine years before that. It has been a long time, too, since his conversation with Mecha Inzunza on the boat deck of the *Cap Polonio*, four days after she and her husband invited him to lunch with them in their stateroom to discuss tango.

—m—

He went searching for her deliberately that day, too, after lying awake all night in his second-class cabin, feeling the gentle sway of the ship and the distant throb of the vessel's engines deep inside the hull. There were questions that needed answering and plans to elaborate. Potential losses and probable gains. And yet, although he refused to admit it to himself, there was also an intrinsically personal reason for it that had nothing to do with material considerations. Something unusually devoid of calculation, made up of sensations, attractions, and uncertainties.

He found her on the boat deck, as before. The ship was traveling at speed, cleaving the thin mist, which the morning sun (a hazy, golden disk rising higher and higher in the sky) was slowly dispersing. She was sitting on a teak bench, beneath one of the three enormous red-and-white smokestacks. Dressed casually in a pleated skirt and striped sweater, she wore flat shoes and a straw cloche hat, whose short brim obscured half her face as she leaned over her book. This time Max did not pass her by with a mumbled greeting, but said good morning, halting in front of her and doffing his cap. He had the sun behind him, the sea was calm, and his shadow moved gently back and forth across the open book and her face when she raised her eyes to look at him.

"Well," she said. "The perfect dancer." She smiled, although her expression as she contemplated him seemed absolutely serious. "How are things, Max? . . . How many young women and old maids have stepped on your toes these past few days?"

"Too many," he groaned. "Don't remind me of it."

Mecha Inzunza and her husband had not been to the ballroom for four days. Max had not seen them since the lunch in their stateroom.

"I have been thinking about what your husband said . . . about places to go to in Buenos Aires to see real tango."

Her smile became more pronounced. Pretty mouth, he thought. Pretty everything.

"Do you mean old tango?"

"Old School. Yes, that's what I mean."

"Splendid." She closed her book and moved along the bench, with complete spontaneity, making a space for him to sit down. "Will you take us there?"

Although he had been expecting her to say "us," it still took Max aback. He remained standing in front of her, still holding his cap.

"Both of you?"

"Yes."

Max nodded. Then replaced his cap (pulling it down rather rakishly over his right eye) and sat on the part of the bench she had vacated. The spot was sheltered from the breeze by one of the huge white ventilation outlets placed at intervals on the deck. Max glanced at the title of the book in her lap. It was in English: *The Painted Veil*. He had not read anything by the author, Somerset Maugham, whose name was printed on the cover, although he thought he had heard of him. Books were not his thing.

"I have no objection," he replied. "Providing you are ready to run certain risks."

"Now you're scaring me."

She looked anything but scared. Max glanced beyond the life-boats, sensing her eyes on him. He wondered briefly whether he should feel irritated by some veiled sarcasm, and decided he should not. She could have meant it, although he found it difficult to imagine her being scared in that way. By certain risks.

"They are in poor neighborhoods," he explained. "Which you might describe as unsavory. And I'm still not sure whether . . ."

He fell silent as he turned to look at her. She seemed amused by his calculated, cautious pause.

"Whether I should venture into such places, is that what you mean?"

"In fact, it isn't so dangerous. It's more a question of not drawing attention to yourself."

"How?"

"With money. Jewelry. Expensive, or overly stylish clothes."

She threw back her head and gave a loud laugh. That relaxed, healthy laugh. Almost athletic, Max reflected absurdly. Fashioned on tennis courts, at beach resorts, and in Hispano-Suiza two-seaters.

"I see. . . . Must I disguise myself as a tart in order not to stand out?"

"It's no joke."

"I know." She looked at him, suddenly serious. "You would be surprised at how many little girls dream of dressing up as princesses, and how many grown women long to dress up as whores."

The word *whores* had not sounded vulgar coming from her lips, Max noticed with surprise. Only provocative. As one would expect from a woman capable of going to a disreputable neighborhood, either for pleasure or out of curiosity, to see tangos. Because there are ways of saying things, the professional dancer concluded. Of uttering certain words or gazing into a man's eyes, the way she was doing at that moment. Whatever she said, Mecha Inzunza couldn't be vulgar if she tried. Second Lieutenant Boris Dolgoruki-Bragation, when he was alive, put it quite well: when it happens, there is nothing you can do, and nothing you can do will make it happen.

"I'm surprised your husband is so interested in tango," he managed to say, collecting himself. "I thought he was . . ."

"A serious composer?"

Now it was Max's turn to laugh. He did so with the sophistication and calculated poise of a man about town.

"You could put it that way. One thinks of his music as being on a different level than that of popular dance."

"Let us call it a whim. My husband is an extraordinary man."

Inwardly, Max agreed with her. *Extraordinary* was undoubtedly the right word. As far as he knew, Armando de Troeye was among the half dozen most famous and best paid composers in the world. Of the living Spanish composers, only de Falla could compare.

"A great man," she added a moment later. "In thirteen years he has achieved what others can only dream of. . . . Do you know who Diaghilev and Stravinsky are?"

Max smiled, vaguely offended. I am a lowly ballroom dancer, his expression said. I have heard of them but that is all.

"Of course. The director of the Ballets Russes and his favorite composer."

She nodded and went on to say that her husband had met them in Madrid during the world war, at the house of a Chilean friend, Eugenia de Errazuriz. They were there to stage a performance of "The Firebird" and "Petrushka" at the Teatro Real. At the time, Armando de Troeye was a very talented composer, but relatively unknown. They got along, he showed them Toledo and El Escorial, and they became friends. The following year, he bumped into them again in Rome, and through them he met Picasso. When the war was over, and Diaghilev and Stravinsky took "Petrushka" to Madrid again, de Troeye accompanied them to Seville to see the Easter processions. They returned bosom pals. Three years later, in 1923, the Ballets Russes performed the premiere of "Pasodoble for Don Quixote" in Paris. It was an astonishing success.

"You probably know the rest," Mecha Inzunza concluded. "A tour in America, the triumph of "Nocturnes" in London, where the concert was attended by the King and Queen of Spain, the rivalry with de Falla, and the magnificent sensation caused by "Scaramouche" last year at the Salle Pleyel in Paris, with Serge Lifar dancing the lead and sets by Picasso."

"That is success," observed Max, dispassionately.

"What is success, for you?"

"Anything over five hundred thousand pesetas a year, guaranteed."

"Well . . . you are easily pleased."

He thought he detected a note of sarcasm in her voice, and looked at her curiously.

"When did you meet your husband?"

"At the house of Eugenia de Errazuriz, in fact. She is my god-mother."

"I imagine life with him must be interesting."

"Yes."

This time the monosyllabic reply had been abrupt. Neutral. She was staring past the lifeboats toward the sea, where the sun, climbing higher into the sky, was illuminating the gold and gray misty air.

"What has any of that to do with the tango?" asked Max.

He watched her tilt her head as if there were several possible answers and she was considering them one by one.

"Armando is a joker," she said finally. "He likes to play games. On many levels. Including in his work, naturally . . . Risky, innovative games. That is precisely what fascinated Diaghilev."

She remained silent for a moment, contemplating the cover of her book, which showed a debonair gentleman gazing out to sea from what looked like a Mediterranean cliff top, with umbrella pines and palm trees.

"He often says," she resumed at last, "that he doesn't care whether a piece is written for piano, violin, or the town crier's drum. . . . Music is music. And that's that."

Away from their sheltered spot, there was a gentle breeze stirred only by the ship's movement. The disk of the sun, increasingly resplendent, warmed the wooden bench. Mecha Inzunza rose to her feet and Max instantly followed suit.

"And always with that humor, so typical of my husband," she went on speaking openly, continuing where she had left off. "He once said in an interview that he would have liked to compose the way Haydn did, for the amusement of a monarch . . . A symphony?

Voilà, your Majesty. And if that doesn't please you, I shall turn it into a waltz and put words to it. . . . He likes to pretend his works are commissioned, although they aren't. It is his private joke. His affectation."

"It requires great intelligence to pass off your true feelings as artifice," said Max.

He had read or heard that somewhere. Lacking any real education himself, he was adept at taking other people's words and making them his own. At choosing the appropriate moment to use them. She looked at him, slightly taken aback.

"Goodness. Perhaps we underestimated you, Mr. Costa."

He grinned. By now they were strolling toward the rail on the poop deck, past the last of the three smokestacks.

"It's Max, remember."

"Of course . . . Max."

They reached the rail and leaned over to peer at the bustle below: caps, trilbies, white panamas, wide-brimmed sun hats, and cloche hats, all the rage, made of felt or straw with colored bands. Where the first-class promenade decks on port and starboard converged on the terrace of the smoking room, whose windows were flung open, the tables were crowded with passengers enjoying the calm sea and mild weather. It was the hour of the lunchtime aperitif, and a dozen waiters in scarlet jackets were swerving in and out of tables, holding aloft trays of drinks and snacks, while a uniformed headwaiter made sure everything ran as smoothly as expected.

"The waiters look friendly," she remarked. "Contented . . . Perhaps it's the sea air."

"Well, I can assure you they aren't. They live in fear of the chief steward and the ship's officers. Looking friendly is part of the job: they are paid to smile."

She looked at him with renewed curiosity. Differently.

"You seem to know a lot about it," she ventured.

"I do. But we were talking about your husband. About his music."

"Oh, yes . . . I was going to tell you that Armando likes delving into the apocryphal, inventing anachronisms. He enjoys working with a copy more than with the original. With nods to other composers, whether they be Schumann, Satie, Ravel . . . To dissimulate by pretending he's making a pastiche. Parodying above all the parodists."

"An ironic plagiarist?"

She studied him again in silence. Intensely. Sizing him up him both inside and out.

"Some call that modernism," he backtracked, afraid he had gone too far.

His had a well-rehearsed smile, that of an honest fellow—or a perfect dancer as she had called him earlier. After an instant, he saw her turn away, shaking her head.

"Don't be mistaken, Max. He is an extraordinary composer, who deserves his success. He pretends to explore what he has already discovered, or to disregard details he has already inserted with precision. He knows how to be vulgar, yet even his vulgarity is sophisticated. In the way elegant people sometimes dress deliberately nonchalantly. . . . Do you know the introduction to his 'Pasodoble for Don Quixote'?"

"I'm afraid not. My musical knowledge doesn't extend much beyond ballroom dancing."

"What a pity. You would understand better what I just said. The introduction to the 'Pasodoble' doesn't lead anywhere. It's a brilliant joke."

"Too complicated for me," he said candidly.

"Yes." The woman studied him carefully again. "I daresay it is."

Max was still leaning over the white rail. His left hand was six inches away from her right hand, which was clasping her book. He looked down at the passengers in first class. His long years of training allowed him to feel only a twinge of rancor. Nothing he couldn't live with.

"Will the tango your husband composes also be a joke?" he asked.

In a sense, she replied. But not only that. Tango had become vulgar. It was all the rage, as much in fancy ballrooms as in popular theaters, the movies, and local dance halls. Armando's idea was to play with that vulgarity, to give people back its original meaning, filtered through the irony they had just been talking about.

"Dissimulating in his usual way," she concluded. "With his enormous talent. A tango that will be a pastiche of pastiches."

"A chivalry novel to end all chivalry novels?"

For a moment she looked astonished.

"Have you read *Don Quixote*, Max?"

He quickly weighed his chances. Best not to take the risk, he decided. Out of senseless pride. It is easier to catch a clever impostor than an honest fool.

"No." The same irreproachable smile, spontaneously rehearsed. "But I have read things about it in newspapers and magazines."

"Perhaps *end* is the wrong word. But certainly one that goes beyond them. Something that can't be surpassed, because it has everything. A perfect tango."

They moved away from the rail. Over the water, gradually turning from gray to blue, the sun was dissolving the last traces of surface mist. The eight starboard lifeboats, painted white and resting on their chocks, were so dazzling that Max had to lower his cap a little more to shield his eyes. Mecha Inzunza took a pair of dark glasses out of the pocket of her sweater and put them on.

"What you told him about the origins of tango fascinated him," she said, after a few more steps. "He can't stop mulling it over. . . . He is expecting you to keep your word and take him there."

"What about you?"

She gave him a sidelong glance, turning her head twice, as

though not fully grasping the implications of his question. Inzunza bottled spring water, Max remembered. He had flicked through the illustrated magazines in the reading room in search of advertisements, and had questioned one of the stewards. At the turn of the century, her grandfather, a pharmacist, had made a fortune bottling water in Spain's Sierra Nevada. Later on, her father had built two hotels there, and a new health spa, recommended for people with liver and kidney ailments, which had become fashionable among the Andalusian upper classes in the summer season.

"What are you expecting, Mrs. de Troeye?" Max persisted.

By this stage of their conversation, he was hoping she might ask him to call her Mecha, or Mercedes. But she did not.

"I've been married to Armando for five years. And I admire him deeply."

"Is that why you want me to take you there? To take you both there?" He allowed himself a skeptical expression. "You aren't a composer."

She did not reply at once, but continued to stroll, her eyes hidden behind her dark glasses.

"What about you, Max? Will you travel back to Europe on the *Cap Polonio* or stay in Argentina?"

"I may stay for a while. I've been offered a three-month contract at the Plaza Hotel in Buenos Aires."

"As a dancer?"

"For now, yes."

A brief silence.

"That doesn't seem to hold much of a future. Unless . . ."

She fell silent again, yet Max had no difficulty completing the sentence: unless with your good looks, honest-John smile, and tangos you manage to seduce a millionairess perfumed with Roger & Gallet, who will take you on, all expenses paid, as a *chevalier servant*. Or, as the Italians put it more crudely, a gigolo.

"I don't intend to devote my entire life to that."

Now the dark glasses were turned toward him. He saw himself reflected in them.

"The other day you said something interesting. You spoke of tangos to cry for and tangos to die for."

Max made a dismissive gesture, as if to minimize its importance. His instinct told him to be honest this time, too.

"It was a friend who said that, not me."

"Another dancer?"

"No . . . He was a soldier."

"Was?"

"He isn't any longer. He died."

"I am sorry."

"There is no need to be." Max smiled wistfully to himself. "His name was Dolgoruki-Bragation."

"No ordinary soldier's name. More like that of an officer, wouldn't you say? . . . A Russian aristocrat."

"That is exactly what he was: Russian and an aristocrat. Or so he claimed."

"And was he really . . . an aristocrat?"

"Possibly."

Now, perhaps for the first time, Mecha Inzunza seemed unsettled. They had come to a halt beside the outer rail, at the foot of one of the lifeboats. The name of the boat was painted in black letters on its prow. She removed her hat (Max managed to read *Talbot* on the inside label) and shook her hair, loosening it in the breeze.

"Were you a soldier, too?"

"For a time. Not for long."

"In the world war?"

"In Africa."

She tilted her head slightly to one side, fascinated, as though seeing Max for the first time. For years, the war in North Africa had been grabbing the headlines in the Spanish press, filling the illustrated magazines with photographs of young officers—Captain

So-and-so of the Army, Lieutenant Such-and-such of the Spanish Foreign Legion, or of the Cavalry—who died heroically (they all died heroically in the society pages of *La Esfera* or *Blanco y Negro*) in Sidi Hazem, Ketama, Bab el Karim, and Igueriben.

"Do you mean in Morocco? . . . Melilla, Annual, and all those dreadful places?"

"Yes. All those places."

He was leaning back against the rail enjoying the cool breeze on his face, squinting in the bright sunlight reflecting off the sea and the white lifeboat. As he slipped his hand inside his blazer and retrieved the cigarette case engraved with a stranger's initials, he noticed Mecha Inzunza watching him intently. She continued to stare at him as he offered her a cigarette from the open case, and shook her head. Max took out an Abdul Pasha, snapped the case shut, and tapped one end of the cigarette on the lid before placing it between his lips.

"Where did you learn those manners?"

He had taken out a book of matches embossed with the Hamburg Südamerikanische crest, and was trying to light his cigarette in the lee of the lifeboat. This time, too, his reply was sincere.

"I don't know what you mean."

She had taken off her dark glasses. Her eyes seemed much paler, more translucent in that light.

"Don't be offended, Max, but something about you puzzles me. You have flawless manners, and you are blessed with good looks, of course. You are a wonderful dancer and more dapper than many gentlemen I know. And yet you don't seem . . ."

He smiled to disguise his awkwardness, and struck a match. Despite cupping his hands around the flame, the wind blew it out before he could light his cigarette.

"Educated?"

"That isn't what I meant. You don't display the clumsy exhibitionism of a social climber, or the crude affectation of those pretending to be what they are not. You don't even possess the natural arrogance of a handsome young man. You seem to please everyone, without even trying. And I am not only referring to the ladies. Do you understand what I'm talking about?"

"More or less."

"And yet the other day you told us about your childhood in Buenos Aires and your return to Spain. Life doesn't seem to have been very kind to you then. . . . Did things improve after that?"

Max struck another match, successfully this time, and looked at her through the first puff of smoke from his cigarette. All of a sudden, he no longer felt threatened by her. He remembered the red-light district in Barcelona, La Canebière in Marseille, the sweat and fear in the Legion. The bodies of three thousand men, baking in the sun, scattered along the road between Annual and Monte Arruit. And the Hungarian woman, Boske, in Paris, her sublime body, naked in the moonlight that poured in through the only window in the attic on Rue de Furstenberg, onto the crumpled sheets amid silvery shadows.

"Somewhat," he replied at last, looking at the sea. "Or rather, I improved somewhat."

The sun has hidden behind the Punta del Capo, and the Bay of Naples is growing slowly darker with a last shimmering glow upon the water. In the distance, beneath the dark folds of Vesuvius, the first lights are being turned on along the coast stretching from Castellammare to Pozzuoli. It is dinnertime, and the terrace at the Hotel Vittoria is gradually emptying. From his chair, Max Costa sees the woman rise and walk toward the glass door. Their eyes meet again momentarily, but her gaze, casual and distracted, passes over his face with indifference. This is the first time in Sorrento that Max sees her from close up, and he notices that although she still shows traces of her former beauty (especially her eyes and the delicate shape of her lips), time has left its mark on her: her cropped hair is almost like Max's; her skin is duller, less taut, and crisscrossed with countless tiny wrinkles around the mouth and eyes; and her hands, although still slender and graceful, are flecked with the unmistakable blemishes of age. Yet her gestures are the same as he remembers: calm and self-assured. Those of a woman who all her life has strolled through a world created especially for her to stroll through. Fifteen minutes earlier, Jorge Keller and the young woman with the braid joined the group around the table, and now they are accompanying her as she crosses the terrace, past Max, and disappears out of view. A thickset, bald fellow with a grizzled beard is with them. Scarcely have they gone by, when Max rises and follows them through the door, pausing for a moment next to the Liberty armchairs and the potted palms decorating the conservatory. From there he can see the glass door leading into the hotel lobby and the stairs to the restaurant. When Max gets there, they have already continued up the outside steps and are walking along the path through the hotel gardens toward Piazza Tasso. Max goes back to the lobby and approaches the concierge.

"Was that Keller, the chess champion?"

The man's feigned surprise is magnificent. He nods, discreetly. He is a tall, willowy youth, who wears two miniature gold crosskeys on each lapel of his black jacket.

"Indeed, sir."

If Max Costa has learned anything in the fifty years he has spent drifting in and out of such places, it is that employees are more useful than those in charge. Which is why he has always tried to form closer relationships with the actual problem solvers: concierges, porters, waiters, secretaries, taxi drivers, or receptionists. Those through whose hands the resources of a wealthy society pass. Such connections are not merely improvised, but take time, common sense, and something money can't buy, an ease of manner that can be understood to mean, today you scratch my back, tomorrow I scratch yours; or at least, I owe you one, my friend. In Max's case, a generous tip or a shameless bribe (his perfect manners invariably blurred the indistinct line between the two) were never more than precursors to the devastating smile he gave both victim and accomplice—willing or unwilling—before the final twist. In this painstaking way, all his life, he has accumulated a wide range of acquaintances bound to him by unique, discreet ties. And that also included men and women of dubious character, objectively undesirable, capable of unscrupulously stealing from him a gold watch but also of pawning it in order to lend him money if he was in need or to repay a debt with him.

"Keller will be dining out, I imagine."

The concierge nods once more, without fully committing himself, this time with a polite, mechanical expression: aware that the old, distinguished-looking gentleman on the other side of the counter, who has casually taken a fine leather wallet out of his inside jacket pocket, is paying for four nights at the Hotel Vittoria what he earns in a month.

"I'm mad about chess. . . . I'd love to know where Mr. Keller dines. I'm quite a fan, you know."

The five-thousand-lira note, discreetly folded into four, changes hands and disappears into the pocket of the jacket with the miniature gold keys on the lapels. The concierge's smile is more natural now.

"Ristorante 'o Parrucchiano, on the Corso Italia," he says after checking the reservations list. "A good place to eat cannelloni or fish."

"I'll go there one of these days. Thank you."

"My pleasure, sir."

There is plenty of time, thinks Max. And so he climbs the broad staircase adorned with vaguely Pompeian figures, until, running his fingers along the banister, he reaches the second floor. Before his shift ended, Tiziano Spadaro gave him the room numbers of Jorge

Keller and his entourage. The woman's is 429, and Max makes his way down the corridor toward it, along the carpet that muffles his footfall. The door is standard, with the classic lock that allows you to look through the keyhole, and it presents no problems. He tries his own key (it wouldn't be the first time luck triumphs over technical problems). Then, after glancing quickly left and right, he slips a simple picklock out of his pocket, as perfect in its own right as a Stradivarius: a metal rod, half the length of his palm, flat and narrow with a hook on one end, which half an hour before he tested on the lock of his own door. In less than half a minute, three quiet clicks indicate that he can enter freely. Max turns the handle and opens the door with the calm air of the professional who has spent the best part of his life opening other people's doors with an absolutely clear conscience. After a final precautionary glance down the corridor, he hangs up the *Non disturbare* sign and walks in, softly whistling to himself "The Man Who Broke the Bank at Monte Carlo."

3

Boys from the Old Days

THE ROOM HAS an attractive covered balcony with an arch overlooking the bay. The last light of day is seeping in through the windows. Cautiously, Max draws the curtains, goes into the bathroom, and returns with a towel, which he arranges on the floor to block the gap under the door. Then he puts on a pair of thin rubber gloves and turns on the lights. The room is simply decorated, with damask armchairs and prints of Neapolitan vistas on the walls. There is a vase of fresh flowers on the chest of drawers, and everything looks clean and neat. In the bathroom, a monogrammed canvas vanity case contains a bottle of Chanel perfume and Elizabeth Arden moisturizers and cleansers. Max looks without touching, then searches the room trying not to disturb anything. In the drawers and on top of the chest and bedside tables are a few personal belongings, a notebook, and a purse containing a few thousand lira in notes and small change. Putting on his spectacles, Max has a look at the books—two thrillers by Eric Ambler in English and one by an Italian author called Soldati: *Le lettere da Capri*. At the bottom is a biography of Jorge Keller, an envelope bearing the hotel crest marking the page. On the cover, beneath the title, *A Young Chessboard Life*, is a photograph of him, and inside several paragraphs are underlined in pencil. Max reads one at random: *"He remembers being so upset when he lost a game that he would cry inconsolably and refuse to eat for days. But then his mother would say to him: There is no victory without defeat."*

After replacing the book, Max opens the wardrobe. On the top shelf are two tattered Louis Vuitton suitcases, and below, clothes arranged on hangers, on shelves, and in drawers: a suede jacket, dresses and skirts in dark colors, silk or cotton blouses, knitted cardigans, fine French silk scarves, good-quality English and Italian shoes, comfortable, with a low heel or flat. Under the folded clothes, Max discovers a large, black leather box with a tiny lock. He gives a growl of satisfaction, like a hungry cat seeing a fish bone; his fingers tingle with the pulsation of ancient habits. Thirty seconds later, with the help of a paper clip bent into an L-shape, the box is open. Inside is a small bundle of Swiss francs, and a Chilean passport in the name of Mercedes Inzunza Torrens, born in Granada, Spain, 7 June 1905. Her current address is given as Chemin de Beau-Rivage, Lausanne, Switzerland. The photograph is recent, and Max studies it closely, recognizing her graying hair, cropped almost like a man's, her gaze fixed on the camera, the lines around her eyes and mouth, which he observed when she walked past him on the hotel terrace, and which are treated more ruthlessly by the harsh light of the photographer's flash. An elderly woman, he concludes. Sixty-one. Three years younger than him, excepting that time is more relentless in its devastation of women than of men. Even so, the beauty Max saw nearly forty years ago on board the *Cap Polonio* is still evident in the passport photograph: the serene expression in the eyes of a refined woman of society, the exquisite line of her mouth, the delicate shape of her face, the long, still graceful neck. There are species of beautiful animals that even manage to age relatively well, Max reflects sadly.

Replacing the passport and the money, taking care not to change anything, he checks the remaining contents of the box. A few pieces of jewelry: simple earrings, a slim, plain gold bangle, and a Vacheron Constantin ladies' watch with black leather strap. There is also another flat, square, brown leather box, worn with age. When Max opens it and recognizes the necklace inside (two hundred perfect pearls, with a simple gold clasp), he can't keep his hands from trembling, even as a smile of satisfaction flashes across his face; a look of unexpected triumph enlivens his expression, tense with the excitement of his discovery.

His fingers protected by the rubber gloves, he removes the necklace from its case and examines it under one of the lamps: it is perfect, pristine, exactly like when he last saw it. Even the clasp is the same. The exquisite pearls reflect the light with an almost hazy softness. Thirty-eight years before, when for a few hours the necklace was in his possession, a jeweler from Montevideo by the name of Troianescu, who valued it at less than its true worth, still gave him what was then the respectable sum of three thousand pounds.

Max studies the pearls, trying to estimate their current value. He has always been good at quick appraisals; his eye sharpened with time, practice, and opportunity. Natural pearls have depreciated with the overproduction of cultivated ones, but good-quality, antique pearls have kept their value, and these could easily fetch five thousand dollars. If he sold them to a reliable Italian fence (he knows one or two who still do business), he might get four-fifths of that sum: nearly two and a half million lire, equivalent to his salary of almost three years as a chauffeur at Villa Oriana. That is the value Max places on the necklace belonging to Mecha Inzunza, the woman he once knew. And the other one he no longer knows. The one in the passport photo, whose fresh, unfamiliar, perhaps forgotten scent he perceived as he entered the room and while he was searching through her clothes in the wardrobe. The woman who has changed, although not entirely, who walked past him less than an hour ago without recognizing him. Max's memories come flooding back, pell-mell, at the warm touch of the pearls: music, conversation, lights from a past era that seem to belong to a different century, the poor neighborhoods of Buenos Aires, rain tapping on a windowpane overlooking the Mediterranean, the taste of warm coffee on a woman's lips, silk, smooth flesh. Long-forgotten sensations that come rushing back like a gust of wind in autumn sweeping up dead leaves. Unexpectedly quickening his pulse, which he thought had calmed down forever.

Pensive, Max goes over to the bed and sits for a while, gazing at the necklace, fingering the pearls one by one as if they were the beads of a rosary. Finally he sighs, gets up, smooths out the bedspread, and places the necklace back in its box. He puts away his spectacles and takes a last look around before switching off the light. After removing the towel from the door, he folds it and returns it to the bathroom. Then he draws back the curtain in front of the terrace. It is already dark, and he can see the lights of Naples in the distance. Leaving the room, he replaces the *Non disturbare* sign and closes the door. Afterward, he takes off the rubber gloves and strides down the carpet, left hand in his trouser pocket, right hand straightening his tie knot with thumb and forefinger. He is sixty-four years old, and yet he feels young again. Interesting, even. And, above all, daring.

—⁓—

Bellboys carrying telegrams and messages, smartly dressed guests, and porters pushing luggage carts along the plush carpets emblazoned with the hotel's name. The bustle was typical of such an exclusive establishment. Max Costa had been waiting for an hour and a quarter in the smoking room next to the columned foyer of the Hotel Palace in Buenos Aires, at the foot of the monumental wrought-iron-and-bronze staircase. Beneath the high corniced ceiling decorated with paintings, the afternoon sun lit up the enormous stained-glass windows, enveloping him in a warm, colorful glow. He was sitting in a leather armchair, from which he could see the revolving door to the street, the entire main foyer, one of the elevators, and the reception desk. He had arrived at the hotel in the afternoon, five minutes before his arranged three o'clock meeting with the de Troeyes, but the clock on the mantelpiece in the smoking room said ten past four. After checking the time again, he recrossed his legs, careful not to stretch the knees of his gray trousers, which he had pressed himself that morning in his room at the boardinghouse, and put out his cigarette in a large tin ashtray nearby. He remained unflustered by the couple's lack of punctuality, aware that in most situations patience proved to be a highly practical virtue. Above all for a hunter.

He had been on land five days, the same length of time as the de Troeyes. After calling at Rio de Janeiro and Montevideo, the *Cap Polonio* had sailed up the muddy waters of Río de la Plata, and, after lengthy docking maneuvers, had moored alongside the cranes and huge redbrick warehouses, where a teeming throng awaited the passengers. Although it was autumn in Europe, in the Southern Cone spring was beginning, and seen from the soaring decks of the liner, everyone on the quayside seemed to be wearing linen suits and white straw hats. From the second-class deck, Max, who had to wait for all the passengers to disembark, saw Mecha Inzunza and her husband descend the main gangway, at the foot of which they were greeted by half a dozen people and a cluster of journalists, before continuing on in search of their luggage: a pile of suitcases and trunks guarded by three porters and an employee of the shipping company. The de Troeyes had said good-bye to Max two days earlier, following the farewell dinner, after which Mecha Inzunza had danced three tangos with him while her husband sat smoking at his table, watching them. Then they invited him for a drink in the first-class cocktail lounge, and although he was breaking the staff rules, Max accepted because it was his last day on board. They drank champagne cocktails and continued talking about Argentinian music until the early hours, agreeing to meet after they had docked, so that Max could keep his promise of taking them to a place where they could see tango played in the old way.

And here he was, in Buenos Aires, watching the hotel lobby with the same professional calm with which, trusting his intuition, he had been waiting for the last five days, lying on the bed in the room of a boardinghouse on Avenida Almirante Brown, as he chain-smoked and drank glasses of absinthe, which gave him a sore head in the morning. The time limit he had given himself before going in search of the couple, inventing some pretext, was about to run out, when the landlady knocked at his door. A gentleman was asking for him on the telephone. Armando de Troeye had a lunch date, but they were free the rest of the afternoon. They could have coffee together, and meet later for dinner, before setting off on the promised foray into enemy territory. De Troeye had said the words "enemy territory" in a lighthearted manner, as though he didn't take Max's warnings about the dangers of exploring the port city's dens of iniquity seriously.

"Naturally, Mecha will be going with us," he had said after a brief pause, in response to the question Max was unable to pose. "She is even more curious than I am," he had added after a further silence, as if his wife were within earshot (the Palace Hotel was equipped with every modern convenience, including a telephone in each room), and Max could imagine them exchanging knowing looks, and whispering while de Troeye placed his hand over the mouthpiece. That last night, when they were discussing the matter on the *Cap Polonio*, she had insisted on joining them.

"I wouldn't miss it for the world," she had asserted with complete equanimity.

On that occasion she was sitting on a bar stool in the first-class cocktail lounge, while the bartender mixed drinks. The gleaming pearls hung in three strands around Mecha Inzunza's neck, and a simple white Vionnet gown, cut away at the shoulders and back (the farewell dinner was a black-tie affair), accentuated her natural elegance to astonishing effect. That evening, when Max had danced those three tangos with her (he hadn't seen her do that with de Troeye during the entire crossing), he could appreciate once more the pleasurable sensation of her bare skin beneath the full-length satin gown, which, as it moved to the music, traced the curves of her body.

"We could get into some awkward situations," Max insisted.

"You and Armando will be there," she replied, unfazed. "To protect me."

"I'll take my Astra," her husband said, playfully, patting an empty pocket in his jacket.

He winked as he did so, and Max bridled at de Troeye's flippancy and his wife's self-assurance. He was beginning to wonder if it was worth the trouble, but a fresh glance at the necklace convinced him it was. Possible losses and probable gains, he told himself. All part of life's routine.

"I wouldn't advise carrying a weapon," he said simply, between sips of his drink. "There or anywhere. You might be tempted to use it."

"Isn't that the point of them?"

Armando de Troeye wore an almost conceited smile. He seemed to enjoy adopting that playful, gangsterish air, pretending to be an amused adventurer. Once again, Max felt the familiar stab of resentment. He imagined de Troeye, afterward, bragging about his escapade in the slums to his snobbish millionaire friends—to that Diaghilev of the Ballets Russes, for example. Or that fellow Picasso.

"To pull out a weapon is to invite others to use theirs."

"Well," exclaimed de Troeye. "You seem to know an awful lot about weapons for a dancer."

There was a sour, disdainful note beneath the apparently good-natured remark. Max was taken aback; perhaps the celebrated composer wasn't always as nice as he pretended to be. Or possibly he considered the three tangos Max had danced with his wife too many for one night.

"He certainly knows something about them," said Mecha.

De Troeye glanced at her, mildly surprised, as though wondering how much information his wife had about Max that he was unaware of.

"Of course," he said darkly, as if to put an end to the matter. Then he smiled in a perfectly natural way, and sank his nose into his glass, as though what was important in life remained outside it.

Max and Mecha Inzunza looked straight at each other for a moment. Earlier, they had taken to the dance floor as before, her gaze drifting somewhere above his right shoulder, their eyes scarcely meeting, or possibly avoiding each other. Since the silent tango in the palm court, there was something hovering between them that changed their way of communicating as they danced: a calm complicity, made up of silences, movements, and attitudes (they performed some of the *cortes* and side steps by mutual consent, with a hint of shared, almost subversive humor), and also of implicit glances, or apparently straightforward situations, such as when Max offered her an Abdul Pasha and lit it for her hesitantly, turning to speak to her husband as if he were in fact addressing her, or when he stood waiting, heels together, with an almost military air, while Mecha Inzunza rose from her chair, casually extending a hand toward his, placing the other on the black lapel of his tailcoat as the two of them started to move in perfect harmony, skillfully avoiding the clumsier or less attractive couples already swaying on the dance floor.

"It will be fun," Armando de Troeye said, draining his glass. It sounded like the conclusion to a long inner debate.

"Yes," she agreed.

Bewildered, Max didn't know what they meant. He wasn't even sure they were talking about the same thing.

—⁂—

The clock in the smoking room at the Hotel Palace in Buenos Aires said a quarter past four when Max saw them crossing the lobby: Armando de Troeye was sporting a boater and a cane; his wife wore an elegant georgette ruffled dress with a leather belt and a wide-brimmed sun hat. He picked up his own Knapp-Felt hat (perfectly acceptable if a little shabby) and went over greet them. De Troeye apologized for their lateness ("You know, the Jockey Club and that excessive Argentinian hospitality, everyone talking about frozen meat and English thoroughbreds"), and as Max had been waiting so long, Armando suggested they go for a walk to stretch their legs and have a coffee somewhere. Mecha Inzunza made her excuses, declaring she was tired, and arranged to meet them at dinnertime, then proceeded toward the elevators as she pulled off her gloves. Max and de Troeye left the hotel together, chatting as they strolled beneath the arcades along Leandro N. Alem, the landscaped avenue opposite the port bordered by ancient trees that spring had festooned with yellow and gold blossoms.

"Barracas, you say," de Troeye commented after listening with rapt attention. "Is that a street, or a neighborhood?"

"A neighborhood. I think that would be best . . . Or we could try La Boca."

"Which would you suggest?"

Max said he thought Barracas was better. They both had corner cafés and brothels, but La Boca was too close to the port, and therefore swarming with sailors, dockworkers, and passing immigrants. Dives full of foreign riffraff, for want of a better word. There they played and danced a frenchified tango in the Parisian style, interesting but less pure. Barracas, on the other hand, with its

Italian, Spanish, and Polish immigrants, was more authentic. Even the musicians were. Or seemed to be.

"I understand," de Troeye smiled, contented. "An immigrant's dagger is more tango than a sailor's switchblade."

Max burst out laughing.

"Something like that. Only don't be deceived. A knife can be equally dangerous in one place as in the other. . . . Besides, nowadays almost everyone prefers to carry a gun."

They turned left on the corner of Corrientes, near the Stock Exchange, leaving behind the arcades. Farther down the street, a stretch of asphalt road had been dug up as far as the old Post Office, in preparation for the new underground railway.

"What I would ask," Max added, "is that both you and your wife dress discreetly. As I said, no flashy clothes or jewelry. And no bulky wallets."

"Don't worry. We'll be discreet. I wouldn't want to get you into any trouble."

Max halted, letting his companion go ahead of him around a workmen's trench.

"If there's trouble, we'll all be in it together. . . . Is it absolutely necessary for your wife to accompany us?"

"You don't know Mecha. She would never forgive me for leaving her behind at the hotel. Our outing to the slums excites her like nothing else."

Max considered the implications of the verb "to excite" with a feeling of irritation. He detested the way the de Troeyes used certain words so glibly. Then he recalled the glint in Mecha Inzunza's eyes on board the *Cap Polonio* when she contemplated their trip to the poor neighborhoods of Buenos Aires. Perhaps, he concluded, some words were more appropriate than they seemed.

"Why have you agreed to escort us there, Max? . . . Why are you doing this for us?"

Taken off guard, Max glanced at de Troeye. The question had

sounded sincere, spontaneous. And yet the composer's face was blank. As if he were asking out of politeness, mere formality, his thoughts elsewhere.

"I'm not really sure."

They continued walking up the street beyond Reconquista and San Martín. Workmen were digging more trenches below the tramcar cables and electric street lamps, and numerous automobiles and carriages for hire circulated between them, slowing whenever they reached a narrow part of the street. The sidewalks were teeming with people.

"Needless to say, I'll reward you generously."

Max felt another stab of irritation. More acute this time.

"That's not why I'm doing it."

De Troeye was swinging his cane nonchalantly. He wore his cream-colored jacket unbuttoned, one thumb hooked onto the vest pocket from which a gold chain was dangling.

"I know it isn't. That's why I asked."

"I told you, I don't really know the reason," said Max, fingering the brim of his hat awkwardly. "On board ship, you two . . ."

He paused deliberately, gazing at the rectangular patch of sunlight at the intersection of Corrientes and Florida. In fact, he was merely extricating himself from a tight spot. He walked on a few paces in silence, thinking about her: the bare flesh of her back, or beneath her gown brushing softly against her hips. And the pearls around her splendid neck, beneath the electric lights in the ship's ballroom.

"She is beautiful, is she not?"

He knew without turning his head that Armand de Troeye was looking at him. He preferred not to speculate in what way.

"Who?"

"You know perfectly well who. My wife."

Another silence. Finally, Max turned toward his companion.

"And what about you, Señor de Troeye?"

Max suddenly realized he didn't like the fellow's smile. Certainly not then. The way his mustache curled. Perhaps he had never liked it.

"Please, call me Armando," said de Troeye. "We know each other now."

"Very well, Armando. . . . What do you hope to get out of the visit?"

They had turned left, into Calle Florida, which after three o'clock was reserved for pedestrians, with automobiles parked on the corners and lots of storefronts. The entire street looked like a twin gallery of window displays. De Troeye flapped his hand toward them as if the answer obviously lay there.

"You know what. To compose an unforgettable tango. To offer myself that pleasure and caprice."

He was gazing absentmindedly at men's shirts in the window of Gath & Chaves as he spoke. They began making their way through the throng of passersby, mostly well-dressed women who were milling on the sidewalks. A newspaper kiosk displayed the latest edition of *Caras y Caretas*, with Carlos Gardel's dazzling smile on the front cover.

"In fact, the whole thing started with a wager. I was at Ravel's house in San Juan de Luz, and he made me listen to a crazy piece of music he had written for a ballet by Ida Rubinstein: a repetitive bolero, without development, based solely on a gradual crescendo of orchestral instruments. . . . If you can write a bolero, I told him, I can compose a tango. We laughed for a while, and then wagered each other a dinner. . . . And so, here I am."

"I wasn't only referring to tango music when I asked what you were hoping for."

"You can't compose a tango with music alone, my friend. Human behavior is important, too. It paves the way."

"And how do I fit in?"

"In several ways. First of all, you are a useful means of entry into a milieu that interests me. Secondly, you are an excellent tango dancer. And thirdly, I like you. . . . You are different from most of the people born here, who are convinced that being Argentinian is a divine right."

As he walked past the window of a store selling Singer sewing machines, Max glimpsed his reflection alongside de Troeye's. Compared in this way, the famous composer was not noticeably superior. In fact, in terms of physique Max was the winner. Despite Armando de Troeye's elegance and manners, Max was slimmer and taller, by almost a head. He had good posture, too. And although his clothes were more modest, or older, they looked better on him.

"What about your wife? . . . What does she think of me?"

"You ought to know that better than me."

"Well, you're wrong. I haven't the faintest idea."

They had paused, at de Troeye's initiative, in front of the boxes outside one of the numerous bookshops in that part of the street. De Troeye hooked his cane over his arm, and without removing his gloves, touched a few of the volumes on display, although somewhat halfheartedly. Then he waved his hand dismissively.

"Mecha is an extraordinary woman," he said. "She possesses more than simple beauty or elegance. Or rather, a lot more . . . don't forget, I am a musician. However successful I may be, or however easy the life I lead might appear, my work comes between me and the world, and often Mecha is my eyes. My antennae, so to speak. She is the filter through which I see the universe. The fact is, I didn't begin to learn properly from life, or from myself, until I met her. . . . She is one of those women who help us understand the times we live in."

"What has that to do with me?"

De Troeye turned to look at him, calmly. Sardonically.

"I fear you're giving yourself too much importance now, my dear fellow."

He paused once more, leaning on his cane, and examining Max from head to toe, as though objectively weighing the dancer's good looks.

"On second thought, perhaps not," he added after a moment. "Perhaps you are giving yourself the precise amount of importance you merit."

Suddenly he moved off again, adjusting his hat over his eyes, and Max had to catch up with him.

"Do you know what a catalyst is?" de Troeye asked without looking at him. "You don't? . . . In scientific terms, it is something capable of producing chemical reactions or changes without altering the substances that produce them. . . . In simple terms, it facilitates or speeds up the development of certain processes."

Max could hear him laughing now. Quietly, almost between his teeth. As though at a funny joke only he understood.

"You seem to me like an interesting catalyst," he added. "And let me tell you something which I am sure you will agree with. . . . No woman, not even my wife, is worth more than a one-hundred-peso note or a sleepless night, unless you are in love with her."

Max stepped aside to let a woman loaded down with parcels pass by. Behind him, at the junction they had just crossed, an automobile horn blared.

"Whatever game you're playing, it's a dangerous one," Max remarked.

De Troeye's laugh grew increasingly unpleasant before trailing off, as if running out of steam. He had halted once more, and was looking at Max, slightly at an angle due to the discrepancy in their height.

"You've no idea what game I am playing. But I will pay you three thousand pesos if you agree to take part in it."

"That seems to me like a lot of money for a tango."

"It's far more than that," he said, jabbing a forefinger at Max's chest. "Will you take it or leave it?"

Max shrugged. They both knew there had never been any question about that. Not as long as Mecha Inzunza was involved.

"Barracas it is, then," he said. "Tonight."

Armando de Troeye nodded slowly. His serious expression belied the satisfied, almost cheerful tone in his voice:

"Splendid. Barracas."

—⚬—

Hotel Vittoria, in Sorrento. The afternoon sun casts a golden glow on the curtains that have been drawn across the open windows in the spacious room, with its ornate ceiling and mirrors. At the far end, in front of eight rows of chairs occupied by members of the public, a set of lights illuminates the table situated on a dais, as well as a large wooden chessboard on the wall beside the referee's table, where an assistant reproduces the moves. A solemn silence reigns inside the spacious room, broken at lengthy intervals by the whisper of a piece moving on the board followed by the immediate click of the chess clock, as each player presses his button, before noting down the move he has just made on the record sheet beside him.

Seated in the fifth row, Max Costa studies the two opponents. The Russian, dressed in a brown suit, white shirt, and green tie, leans back against his chair as he plays, head bowed. Mikhail Sokolov's broad head sinks into an excessively thick neck, seemingly constricted by his tie. Yet the coarseness of his features is softened by his watery blue eyes, which have a soft, sad expression. His thickset body and cropped fair hair give him the appearance of a gentle bear. Frequently, after making a move (he is Black at the moment), he takes his eyes off the board and stares lengthily at his hands. Every ten or fifteen minutes, he lights a fresh cigarette and in the intervals, the world champion picks his nose or gnaws on his cuticles, before becoming rapt once more, or else takes another cigarette out of the packet he keeps nearby, together with a lighter and an ashtray. In fact, Max observes, the Russian spends more time gazing at his hands, as though absorbed by them, than at the pieces.

Another click of the chess clock. On the other side of the table, Jorge Keller has just moved a white knight, and after unscrewing the cap of his fountain pen he jots down his move, which the assistant referee immediately reproduces on the wall panel. Each time one of the players moves a piece, an almost tangible thrill spreads through the audience, accompanied by expectant sighs and murmurs. They are halfway through the game.

Jorge Keller looks even more youthful when he is playing. His tousled black hair on his forehead, his blazer over his wrinkled khaki slacks, his loosely knotted narrow tie and incongruous sneakers give the Chilean a scruffy yet comforting appearance. Charming is the word. His whole demeanor suggests an eccentric student rather than the formidable chess player who in five months is to challenge Sokolov for the title of world champion. Max saw him arrive carrying a bottle of orange juice at the start of the game, when Sokolov was already waiting in his chair, then shake the Russian's hand without looking at him, set the bottle down on the table, take his place, and make his first move instantaneously, almost without glancing at the board, as if he had planned his opening gambit hours or days in advance. Unlike Sokolov, the young man does not smoke and scarcely makes any other gestures while he meditates or waits, except to reach for the orange juice, which he drinks straight from the bottle. Occasionally, while waiting for Sokolov (both men take their time to calculate each move, but the Russian usually takes longer), Keller folds his arms on the edge of the table, and lays his head on them, as if he can see with his imagination better than with his eyes. He only raises his head once his opponent has moved, as though roused by the gentle thud of the enemy piece on the board.

Everything takes place too slowly for Max. Chess seems like a boring game to him, especially at this level and with all this rigmarole. He doubts his interest would grow even if Lambertucci and Captain Tedesco were to explain to him the intricacies of each move. But the situation gives him a unique vantage point to spy from. And not just on the players. Sitting in a wheelchair in the front row, accompanied by his helper and an assistant, is the benefactor of the contest, the millionaire industrialist Campanella, disabled ten years ago after crashing his Aurelia Spider on a bend between Rapallo and Portofino. In the same row, to the left, between Irina Jasenovic and the stocky man with the grizzled beard, sits Mecha Inzunza. From where Max is sitting, if he leans slightly to one side to avoid the head of the spectator in front of him, Max can see her almost in close-up, shoulders draped in the habitual fine wool cardigan, short gray hair revealing her slender neck, her features still well defined when she turns to whisper something to the stocky man on her right. And that gentle yet determined way of tilting her head, intent upon what is going on in the game, just as in the past she was absorbed by other things, Max reflects with a look of mournful longing, by other moves, no less complex than those now unfurling before them on the chessboard on the table and the other one on the wall, where the assistant referee continues to track each move.

"Here it is," said Max Costa.

The limousine (a dark purple Pierce-Arrow with the badge of the Automobile Club on the radiator grille) stopped at the corner of a long brick wall, thirty yards from Barracas railway station. It was a moonless night, and when the chauffeur switched off the headlights the only light came from a solitary street lamp and four yellowish bulbs beneath the building's tall awning. Toward the east, over streets lined with low houses extending to the docks of the Riachuelo River, night was extinguishing the last glimmer of reddish light in the dark sky over Buenos Aires.

"What a place," commented Armando de Troeye.

"You wanted tango," Max retorted.

He had climbed out of the automobile, and, after donning his hat, was holding the door open for de Troeye and his wife. By the light of the nearby street lamp, Max saw Mecha Inzunza gather her silk shawl and glance around impassively. Although not wearing a hat or jewelry, she had on a light-colored evening dress, midheeled shoes, and long white gloves. Still overdressed for that neighborhood. She seemed unfazed by the locale, with its lurking shadows and gloomy brick footpath stretching into the darkness between the wall and the elevated iron-and-concrete railway station. Her husband, on the other hand (in a double-breasted serge suit, with a hat and cane), glanced about anxiously. The atmosphere was clearly more than he had bargained for.

"Are you sure you know this place well, Max?"

"Of course. I was born three blocks away. In Calle Vieytes."

"Three blocks? . . . Good Lord."

Max leaned toward the chauffeur's open window, to give him instructions. The man was a silent burly Italian, clean-shaven, with jet-black hair showing beneath his peaked uniform cap. The hotel had recommended him as a trustworthy, experienced driver when de Troeye had ordered a limousine. Max hadn't wanted to attract too much attention by parking outside the venue. He and the couple would walk the rest of the way, and he told the chauffeur where to wait for them, within view of the place but at a safe distance. Lowering his voice slightly, he asked the man whether he was armed. The man motioned discreetly toward the glove compartment.

"Pistol or revolver?"

"Pistol," came the brisk reply.

Max smiled.

"Your name?"

"Petrossi."

"Sorry to make you wait, Petrossi. We will only be a couple of hours, at most."

It didn't cost anything to be friendly, and was an investment for the future. At night, in a place like that, a burly Italian with a pistol was invaluable. Extra security. Max saw the chauffeur nod again, curt and professional, although in the light of the street lamp he also glimpsed a flash of appreciation. He placed his hand on the man's shoulder an instant, giving him a friendly pat before joining the de Troeyes.

"We had no idea this was your neighborhood," the composer said. "You never mentioned it."

"There was no reason to."

"And did you always live here, before you went to Spain?"

De Troeye was keen to talk, doubtless to conceal his unease, which was evident anyway from his voice. Mecha Inzunza walked between the two men, her arm looped through her husband's. She remained silent, observing everything around her; the only sound she made came from her heels clacking on the path. The three of them walked among the silent shadows of the neighborhood Max recognized at every step (the warm, moist air, the lush odor of weeds sprouting from the potholes, the muddy stench from the nearby Riachuelo), from the railway station to the squat dwellings that still preserved the old traditions of the working-class suburbs of Buenos Aires.

"Yes. I spent the first fourteen years of my life in Barracas."

"You certainly are full of surprises."

The echo of their footfalls multiplied as Max guided them through the railway tunnel toward the pool of light from another street lamp beyond the station. He turned to de Troeye.

"Did you bring the pistol you mentioned?"

Armando bellowed with laughter.

"Of course not. I was joking. I never carry a weapon."

Max nodded in relief. The idea of de Troeye walking into a dive in the slums with a gun in his pocket, despite Max's advice, had been preying on his mind.

"Just as well."

The district seemed almost unchanged since Max last went there twelve years before, despite having made several trips to Buenos Aires in between. At every moment he was retracing his own footsteps, remembering the tenement nearby where he spent his early childhood and youth, a slum like so many others in the neighborhood and the wider city. A chaotic, promiscuous place where any kind of privacy was unimaginable, crammed between the walls of a dilapidated two-story building, where people of all ages were crammed together: voices speaking Spanish, Italian, Turkish, German, or Polish. Rooms with doors that had never known a key, rented to large families or groups of single men, immigrants of both sexes who (if they were lucky) worked for the railway company Ferrocarril Sud, down at the Riachuelo docks, or in the nearby factories whose sirens sounded four times a day, punctuating the domestic routines of households where clocks were a rare possession. Women pounding wet clothes in bathtubs, swarms of children playing on the patio where the laundry hanging out at all hours was steeped in the smell of fried food or stews, which mingled with the stench from the communal latrines with their tarred walls. Homes where rats were like pets. A place where only the very young and a few youths smiled openly, the innocence of their tender years making them oblivious to the inevitable defeat life had in store for nearly all of them.

"There it is . . . La Ferroviaria."

They had paused near the street lamp. Now on the far side of the railway station, they were out of the tunnel; nearly all the houses on the dark, straight street were low-roofed, except for the few two-story buildings. One of these bore a neon sign saying *Hotel*, the last letter missing. The place they were looking for was barely visible at the end of the gloomy street: a low edifice that looked like a store, with tin walls and roof, and a small yellow lantern above the entrance. Max waited until he saw the twin headlights of the Pierce-Arrow appear to his right, as it rolled slowly to a halt fifty yards away on the corner of the next block, where he had asked the chauffeur to park. When the headlights went off, Max observed the de Troeyes and noticed that the composer was gasping with excitement, his mouth opening and closing like a fish out of water, and that Mecha Inzunza was smiling, a strange glint in her eyes. Then, pulling his hat down slightly over his eyes, he said, "Let's go," and the three of them crossed the street.

The Ferroviaria stank of cigar smoke, cheap gin, hair oil, and human bodies. Like other tango dives near the Riachuelo, during the day it was a large corner store selling foodstuffs and beverages, and by night a venue for music and dancing. It had a wooden floor that creaked underfoot, cast-iron columns, and tables and chairs where men and women sat. Opposite them, bare lightbulbs lit a zinc counter, on which several sinister-looking individuals were hunched or sprawled.

On the wall behind the bartender, who was assisted by a lanky waitress moving lazily between the tables, hung a large, dusty mirror advertising Cafés Torrados Águila and a poster from the Franco-Argentina Insurance Company with a picture of a gaucho drinking maté. To the right of the bar, next to a doorway, through which barrels of sardines in brine and boxes of noodles were visible, was a tiny podium nestled between an unlit kerosene stove and a battered-looking Olimpo pianola. On it three musicians (bandoneon, violin, and piano with left-hand keys dotted with cigarette burns) were playing a tune that sounded like a nostalgic lament, and among whose notes Max thought he recognized the tango song. "Old Rooster."

"Marvelous," breathed Armando de Troeye, in awe. "Better than I expected, perfect . . . another world."

He would have to keep an eye on him, thought Max resignedly.

De Troeye had left his hat and cane on a chair, a pair of yellow gloves was sticking out of his left-hand jacket pocket, and he had crossed his legs to reveal buttoned gaiters beneath perfectly pressed trousers. Needless to say, the Ferroviaria was a different type of world from the one he and his wife were accustomed to, and was frequented by a decidedly different clientele. There were about a dozen women, nearly all of them young, either sitting with a man or dancing with one in an area cleared of tables. They were not exactly prostitutes, Max explained in a whisper, but more like hostesses, hired to encourage men to dance with them (they received a token for each dance, which the landlord cashed in for a few cents) and to consume as much as alcohol as possible. Some of them had boyfriends, some did not. A few of the men there were in charge of the latter.

"Macs?" de Troeye ventured, repeating the word he had heard Max use on the *Cap Polonio.*

"More or less," affirmed Max. "Although not all the women here have one . . . Some are simply employed to dance, and make a living out of it the way others work in local factories or workshops. . . . Respectable tango dancers, all things considered . . ."

"Well, they don't look respectable when they dance," said de Troeye, looking around him. "Or even when they are seated."

Max gestured toward the couples entwined on the dance floor. The men, stern, solemn, exaggeratedly masculine, halted their movement in the middle of the dance (which was faster than the average modern tango) to force the woman to circle around them, without letting go, brushing against them or pressing themselves close. And whenever that happened, the woman would twist her hips furiously, sliding one leg to either side of those of the man. Tremendously sensual.

"As you can see, this is another kind of tango. Another ambience."

The waitress came over to the table carrying a pitcher of gin and three glasses. She looked Mecha Inzunza up and down, glanced indifferently at the two men, and went away again, wiping her hands on her apron. After the sudden awkward silence when they had entered (twenty pairs of eyes following them from the doorway), conversations resumed at the tables, although the blatant stares and furtive glances continued. This seemed reasonable enough to Max, who had expected it. There was nothing unusual about members of the Buenos Aires high society conducting nighttime excursions in search of some local color and low life, making the rounds of cheap cabarets or working-class cafés, but Barracas and La Ferroviaria were not part of those seedy itineraries. Nearly all of the customers here lived in the surrounding neighborhood, apart from a handful of sailors from the tugs and barges moored at the Riachuelo docks.

"What about the men?" asked de Troeye.

Max sipped his glass of gin, without looking at anyone.

"Typical, local *compadritos*, or still playing that role. Faithful to it."

"They sound almost simpatico."

"They aren't. As I told you, a *compadrito* is a working-class youngster from the suburbs, a tough guy spoiling for a fight. . . . A few are for real, the others are just trying to be or to give that impression."

De Troeye swept an arm around the room. "What about these fellows, are they for real or trying to be?"

"A mixture."

"Fascinating, isn't it, Mecha?"

De Troeye was keenly studying the men at the tables or at the bar, all of whom seemed ready for anything provided it was illegal, with their hat brims cocked over their eyes, slicked-back hair glistening down to their collars, which were turned up gangster-style, and bolero jackets with vents. Each had a glass of grappa, brandy, or gin in front of him and a lighted cheroot in his mouth, as well as the telltale bulge of a knife tucked into his waistband or down the arm of his vest.

"They look fairly dangerous," concluded de Troeye.

"Some of them might be. Which is why I advise you not to stare at them for too long, or at the women when they dance with them."

"And yet they aren't shy about staring at me," said Mecha Inzunza, amused.

Max turned to look at her. Those honey-colored eyes were exploring the room, at once curious and challenging.

"You can't expect not to be looked at in a place like this. Let's hope that's all they do."

She gave a soft, almost disagreeable laugh. A moment later she turned toward him.

"Don't scare me, Max," she said coldly.

"I don't think I am." He held her gaze with absolute calm. "I already said I doubt this kind of thing scares you."

He took out his cigarette case, offering it to the couple. De Troeye shook his head, lighting one of his own. Mecha Inzunza accepted an Abdul Pasha and inserted it into her cigarette holder, leaning over so that Max could give her a light with a match. Leaning back in his chair, Max crossed his legs and exhaled the first puff of smoke as he watched the couples dance.

"How do you tell which are prostitutes and which aren't?" Mecha Inzunza asked.

She let the ash from her cigarette drop onto the wooden floor as she observed a woman who was dancing with a stocky yet surprisingly agile man. She was young, of Slavic appearance, with blonde hair the color of old gold. She had coiled it into a bun, and her blue eyes were accentuated by mascara. She had on a red-and-white rose print blouse with skimpy undergarments beneath. Her very short skirt flapped about as she danced, occasionally revealing an extra inch of black-stockinged thigh.

"It's not always easy," replied Max, without taking his eyes off the woman. "I suppose it's a question of experience."

"Are you very experienced at telling them apart?"

"Reasonably."

The music having paused, the fat man and the blonde had stopped dancing. He was wiping the perspiration from his brow with a handkerchief, and she, without exchanging a word, sat down at a table where another couple was sitting.

"Her, for example." Mecha Inzunza gestured toward the blonde. "Is she a prostitute or a dancer, like you were on the *Cap Polonio?*"

"I don't know." Max felt a twinge of irritation. "I would have to get a little closer."

"Why don't you, then?"

He examined the tip of his cigarette as though making sure it was lit. Then he raised it to his mouth and inhaled a precise amount of smoke, exhaling it slowly.

"Later, perhaps."

The band was playing another tango, and more couples had taken the floor. A few of the men kept their left hand, the one they held their cigarette in, behind their back so that the smoke wouldn't bother their partner. Smiling contentedly, Armando de Troeye took in every detail. Twice, Max saw him take out a small pencil and jot down something in tiny, cramped writing on his starched shirt cuff.

"You were right," he said. "They dance more quickly. The movements are looser. And the music is different."

"This is the Old School Tango." Max was glad to change the subject. "They dance the way the music is played: faster and with more *cortes*. And notice the style."

"I already have. It's delightfully sluttish."

Mecha Inzunza stubbed out her cigarette fiercely in the ashtray. She seemed suddenly vexed.

"Don't be so coarse."

"I am afraid that is the word for it, my dear. Look . . . they are almost titillating to watch."

De Troeye's smile broadened into a fascinated leer. Max noticed something in the air. An unspoken language between the de Troeyes that he couldn't read, intimations and references that eluded him. Alarmingly, he seemed somehow to be included. Vaguely uneasy, and with a measure of curiosity, he wondered in what way. To what extent.

"As I explained on the ship," he said, "tango was originally a black dance. Only they danced it separated. Even in the most restrained version, when couples embrace doing those moves, it changes things a lot. . . . Ballroom tango tidied them all up, made them respectable. But, as you can see, respectability doesn't count for much here."

"Interesting," said de Troeye, listening intently to everything Max said. "Is this the true, authentic tango music?"

It wasn't the music itself that was authentic, but rather the style of playing, Max explained. These people couldn't even read a score. They played in their own way, the old way, fast and furious. As he spoke he pointed at the diminutive orchestra: three scrawny-looking men with graying hair and bushy, nicotine-stained mustaches. The youngest was the bandoneon player, who looked in his fifties. His teeth were as worn and yellow as the buttons of his instrument. At that instant, he was glancing at his fellow musicians, conferring about which piece to perform next. The fellow playing the fiddle nodded, stamped his foot several times to set the beat, the pianist began thumping the keys, the bandoneon stuttered to life with a wheeze, and they started playing "The Brush-off." The dance floor immediately filled with couples.

"There you have them," Max smiled. "The boys from the old days."

In fact, he was smiling at himself, at his own memories of the neighborhood. At the long-gone days when he would hear that music at open-air dances on Sunday mornings, or on summer nights while he played with other kids on the sidewalks, beneath street lamps still lit by gas. Seeing couples dance from a distance, and spying jeeringly on those embracing in dark doorways ("drop that bone, doggie"), and running off sniggering, listening daily to those tunes sung by men coming back from the factory, by women from the tenements huddled over laundry basins splashing soapy water. The same tunes that thugs whistled, hats pulled low to hide their faces, as they approached in pairs a lone, unwary nighttime stroller, knives glinting in the dark.

"I'd like to talk to the musicians," de Troeye proposed. "Do you think that's possible?"

"I don't see why not. When they finish playing, buy them a round of drinks. Or, better still, give them a tip. . . . Only don't flash a lot of money around. We've attracted enough attention as it is."

Couples were shuffling around the area set aside for dancing. The blonde Slavic-looking woman had taken to the floor again, this time with the man from the table she had been sitting at. Challenging, aloof, eyes fixed on the distant haze of tobacco smoke, he was making her move to the music, guiding her with subtle gestures, applying pressure with his hand resting lightly on her back, or sometimes with simple looks. Or by coming to a sudden, apparently unexpected halt, at which the woman, eyes fixed impassively on his face, would start switching her legs from side to side, at once disdainful and lascivious, pressing herself against the man as though trying to arouse his desire, twisting her hips and legs this way and that, in obedient surrender, as though accepting the intimate ritual of tango with absolute naturalness.

"If the bandoneon weren't acting as a brake," Max explained, "the rhythm would be even faster. Even looser. Bear in mind that the Old School Tango players had a flute and a guitar."

Fascinated, Armando de Troeye took notes. Mecha Inzunza was silent, transfixed by the blonde tango dancer and her partner. Several times, as they swept by, the man's eye met hers. He was a swarthy fellow in his forties, Max noted, hat tipped forward, a Spaniard or Italian with a somewhat threatening air about him. De Troeye, for his part, was nodding, thoughtful and contented. His mood was one of excitement as he began following the music with his fingers on the table, as though playing on invisible keys.

"I get it now," he said, delighted. "I understand what you mean, Max, about pure tango."

The man dancing with the blonde woman continued to ogle Mecha Inzunza each time he went by, and more insistently than before. He was a typical local compadre, or looked the part: thick mustache, tight-fitting jacket, ankle boots that moved nimbly across the wooden floor, tracing slow arabesques in between the clack of his partner's shoes. Everything about him was phony, even his mannerisms; a knucklehead with pretensions of being a tough guy. Max's experienced eye spotted the incongruous bulge of the knife on his left side, between his jacket and vest, on top of which dangled the two long ends of a white silk scarf tied with deliberate flamboyance around his neck. Out of the corner of his eye, Max also saw that Mecha Inzunza was playing along with him, holding the fellow's gaze, and his old streetwise instinct smelled trouble. Perhaps it wasn't a good idea to stay much longer, he told himself, uneasily. It seemed Señora de Troeye had mistaken La Ferroviaria for the first-class ballroom on the *Cap Polonio*.

"Calling it pure tango is an exaggeration," he said to de Troeye, forcing himself to think about the composer's last remark. "Let's just say they play in the traditional way. The old way . . . you hear the difference in rhythm and style?"

De Troeye nodded again, complacently.

"Of course. That wonderful 2/4 time, the keyboard thumping out four beats and then the countermelody . . . the initial phrases, with bass notes from the bandoneon."

They played that way because they were elderly, Max explained, and the Ferroviaria was a traditional dance venue. The nighttime crowd in Barracas was rough, ironic; they liked *cortes* and *quebradas*. Brutal embraces, leg thrusts, and provocation, like that blonde woman and her partner. If they played tango that way

at a popular Sunday gathering for families or young people, almost no one would take to the dance floor. Out of prudishness
or preference.

"Fashion," Max concluded, "is moving further and further away
from all this. Soon people will only dance that other tame, dull,
soporific tango you find in ballrooms and in the cinema."

De Troeye gave a mocking laugh. The music had stopped and
the orchestra was striking up another tune.

"Effeminate, you mean," he said.

"Possibly." Max took a swig of gin. "You could put it that way."

"There is certainly nothing effeminate about that fellow making his way over here."

Max followed de Troeye's gaze. The knucklehead had left the
blonde woman sitting at the table next to the other woman, and
was walking toward them with the traditional swagger of the Buenos Aires tough: slow, sure, measured. Stepping across the floor
with calculated grace. All that was missing, thought Max, was the
tap of cues and billiard balls in the background.

"If there's any trouble, don't stand around gaping," Max whispered hastily to the couple. "Make for the door and get in the car."

"What kind of trouble?" asked de Troeye.

There was no time for a reply. The fellow was standing before
them, motionless and serious-looking, his left hand tucked into
his jacket pocket with roguish elegance. He was staring at Mecha
Inzunza as if she were alone.

"Would you care to dance, Madam?"

Max eyed the glass pitcher of gin. In an emergency, he could
turn it into a viable weapon by smashing the lip against the table.
Only to gain time, or try to, while they made a getaway.

"I don't think . . ." he started to say in a low voice.

He was speaking to Mecha Inzunza, not the fellow who stood
waiting. But she rose to her feet with complete calm.

"Yes," she said.

She removed her gloves unhurriedly, leaving them on the table. The entire room was looking at her and her partner, who was waiting without showing the slightest impatience. When she was ready, he took her by the waist, placing his right hand on the gentle curve above her hips. She slipped her left hand over his shoulders, and without looking at each other they started to move among the other couples, heads closer than in a conventional tango, bodies acceptably far apart. Anyone would think they had danced together before, Max thought, and yet remembering the ease with which he and Mecha Inzunza had adapted to each other on the *Cap Polonio* lessened his surprise. She was certainly a very intuitive, intelligent dancer, capable of following anyone who danced well. The fellow moved with manly assuredness as he led the woman skillfully, tracing agile figures on an invisible musical stave. The couple swayed gently as she followed the rhythm of the music and the silent commands transmitted by the man's hands and gestures. All at once, the man performed a *corte*, lifting his right heel off the floor almost casually, tracing a semicircle with the tip of his shoe, at which Mecha Inzunza completed the turn with consummate ease, moving one way then the other, twice drawing closer to the man, only to pull away before becoming entangled with him once more, sliding her leg to either side of his with remarkable aplomb. She added a touch of classic lowlife elegance that was so convincing it drew gestures of approval from the onlookers at the tables.

"Good heavens," Armando de Troeye jested, "I hope they don't end up making love in front of everyone."

The remark riled Max, ruining his admiration for Mecha Inzunza's lack of inhibition on the dance floor. The man was showing off, enjoying himself, dark eyes staring into space and, beneath his mustache, mouth set in a grimace of feigned indifference, as if for him, hobnobbing with women of her class was a daily occurrence. All at once, in time to the music, he stepped to one side, came to an abrupt halt, and stamped his foot truculently. Utterly unfazed, as if they had agreed on the move beforehand, Mecha Inzunza circled around him, rubbing against one side of his body then the other, totally compliant. A gesture of female submission that seemed to Max almost pornographic.

"My God," he heard Armando de Troeye groan.

Glancing to the side, Max discovered to his astonishment that de Troeye did not look angry, but was watching the dancing couple, absorbed. Occasionally, he would take a sip of gin, and the liquor seemed to imprint a sardonic, vaguely satisfied smile on his lips. But Max hadn't much time to observe this, as the music stopped and the dance floor emptied. Mecha Inzunza strode over haughtily, escorted by the man. When she took her seat, as relaxed and composed as if she had just been enjoying a waltz, her partner gave a little nod and doffed his hat.

"Juan Rebenque, Madam," he said in a calm, hoarse voice. "At your service."

Then, barely glancing at de Troeye or Max, he wheeled around and sauntered back to the table where the two women were sitting. Watching him move away, Max knew instinctively that Rebenque—the Riding Crop—wasn't his real name, which was undoubtedly Funes, Sánchez, Roldán, but a gauchoesque moniker as outmoded as his appearance and the knife making his jacket bulge. The authentic characters he was imitating had vanished from the neighborhood fifteen or twenty years before, and, even among men like Rebenque, the revolver had long since replaced the gaucho's blade. This fellow was probably a carter who frequented these lowlife bars at night, dancing tangos, working the girls, and occasionally pulling out his antiquated knife to prove his manhood. Among men of his ilk, who were no more than neighborhood thugs, there was little sense of chivalry left, although they could still be dangerous.

"It's your turn," Mecha Inzunza said to Max.

She had just taken a lacquered powder compact out of her bag.

Tiny beads of sweat on her upper lip had pearled her soft makeup. Out of gallantry, Max offered her the clean handkerchief from his top jacket pocket.

"Pardon?" he said.

She grasped the piece of folded white linen between her fingers.

"You wouldn't want things to end like this," she replied coolly.

Max was about to say that's enough, I'll ask for the bill, and we'll leave, when he caught Armando de Troeye glancing at his wife in a way he had not seen him do before that evening, with a flash of contempt and defiance. It lasted only a moment before the mask of frivolous indifference descended once more, concealing everything. At which Max, changing his mind, turned with deliberate slowness toward Mecha Inzunza.

"Of course not," he said.

She was looking straight at him. Her pale eyes, diluted perhaps by the gin, seemed more liquid than ever in the yellow glow from the electric lightbulbs. Then she did something strange. Keeping hold of his handkerchief, she picked up one of the gloves she had left on the table before going to dance, and tucked it into Max's top pocket, arranging it deftly until it resembled an elegant white bloom. Max pushed his chair back, stood up, and walked toward the table where the man and the two women were seated.

"With your permission," he said to the man.

Rebenque looked at him with a mixture of defiance and curiosity, but Max was no longer looking at him. He had turned his attention to the blonde woman, who glanced at her older female companion (a coarse brunette) and then at the man, to see if he agreed. However, Rebenque went on staring at Max as he stood waiting politely, heels together, a faint smile on his lips, with the same careful courtesy he would have shown to any society lady at a tea dance in the Palace or the Plaza. At last, the woman stood up, embracing Max with the ease of a professional. She looked younger from close up than from a distance, despite the dark shadows under her eyes, clumsily disguised by a thick layer of foundation. She had pale, slightly almond-shaped eyes, which, along with her pulled-back hair, accentuated her Slavic look. Possibly Russian or Polish, Max thought. As he put his arm around her, he could sense the intimacy of her body, the warmth of her tired flesh, the smell of tobacco on her clothes and hair, and on her breath the last sip of grappa and lemonade. Her skin smelled of cheap cologne: Agua Florida mixed with moist talcum powder and a woman's gentle perspiration after dancing for two hours with all kinds of men.

The orchestra struck up the first bars of another tango; despite the musicians' ragged playing, Max recognized it as "Felicia." Other couples took the floor. He and the woman led off smoothly, Max allowing his instinct and experience to guide him. He realized after the first few steps that she was no great dancer, and yet she moved with a scornful, professional ease, her eyes gazing into the distance, and only occasionally glancing at his face to predict moves and intentions. Her body pressed inertly against Max, who could sense her nipples through her low-cut, cotton blouse, and obediently rotated her legs and hips around his waist in the most daring steps, guided by the music and his hands. She put no soul into her dancing, Max concluded. Like a sad but efficient robot, without energy or desire, like a prostitute who consents to the sexual act without experiencing the slightest pleasure. For a moment, he imagined her equally passive and compliant in a cheap hotel room like the one on that street, with the missing letter on the neon sign, while the mustachioed thug slipped the ten-peso payment into his jacket pocket. Taking off her clothes before lying down on a bed with used sheets and creaking springs. Acquiescing with the same air of weariness she now displayed as she performed the steps of the tango.

For some reason that he did not care to analyze, the idea excited him. What did tango danced that way signify if not the woman's submission, he reflected, amazed it hadn't occurred to him before, despite all that dancing, those tangos, those embraces. What was this old way of dancing tango, far from ballrooms and evening dress, if not an absolute, complicit surrender? An arousal of old instincts, burning ritual desires, promises made flesh for a few brief moments of music and seduction. Old School Tango. If any style of dancing was perfectly suited to a certain type of woman, it was undoubtedly this. Looking at it from that point of view made Max feel an unexpected pang of desire toward the body moving obediently in his arms. The woman must have sensed it, because her blue eyes glanced at him questioningly, before her lips resumed their impassive expression and her gaze wandered off to the remote corners of the bar. For revenge, Max performed a *corte*, one leg fixed while the other simulated a step forward then back, obliging the woman, with the pressure of his right hand on her waist, to wrap herself around him once more, and, as she brushed the inside of each thigh against his stationary leg, to return to a state of utter submission. To the silent, starkly physical moan of the woman who surrenders and cannot possibly escape.

After that figure, intentionally obscene on the part of both dancers, Max glanced for the first time toward the table where the de Troeyes were sitting. She was smoking out of her ivory cigarette holder, impassive, staring at them intently. And at that moment, Max understood that the tango dancer in his embrace was a mere pretext. An obscure truce.

4

A Woman's Gloves

I T FINALLY HAPPENS, the thing Max Costa has been waiting for with the assurance of someone preparing meticulously for the inevitable. He is sitting on the terrace at the Hotel Vittoria, near the statue of the naked woman who gazes out toward Vesuvius, having his breakfast in front of the luminous, blue-gray backdrop of the bay. Chewing contentedly on a piece of buttered toast, Dr. Hugentobler's chauffeur relishes the situation that for a few days has transported him back to the best moments of his former life, when everything was still possible, the world was there to be explored, and each day held the promise of a fresh adventure: hotel bathrobes, the aroma of good coffee, breakfast served on fine china sitting before vistas or women's faces that could only be attained with a certain amount of money or talent. Back in his element again, effortlessly resuming his old habits, Max sports a pair of Dr. Hugentobler's Persol sunglasses and is wearing his navy-blue blazer, with a silk cravat beneath the unbuttoned collar of his salmon-colored shirt. He has just set down his coffee cup and is about to replace his sunglasses with a pair of spectacles, extending an arm toward the Naples edition of *Il Mattino* on the white linen tablecloth (containing an account of yesterday's game between Sokolov and Keller, which ended in a draw), when a shadow falls across the paper.

"Max?"

An impartial observer would have admired Max's nerve: he remains for a few seconds, eyes on the newspaper, and then looks up, his expression slowly changing from hesitation through surprise to recognition. Finally, removing his spectacles, he lifts the napkin to his lips and rises to his feet.

"My God . . . Max."

The morning light causes Mecha Inzunza's eyes to sparkle, just as in the past. Faint blemishes and age spots are visible on her skin, as well as a cluster of tiny lines around her eyes and mouth, accentuated now by her astonished smile. Yet the ruthless passage of time has not succeeded in erasing the rest: her easy gestures, her sophisticated manner, the slender contours of her neck and arms, their leanness accentuated by age.

"All those years," she declares. "My God."

They are holding hands, gazing at each other. Max bows his head, raising her right hand to his lips.

"Twenty-nine, to be precise," he adds. "Since autumn nineteen thirty-seven."

"In Nice . . ."

"Yes. In Nice."

He graciously offers her a chair, and she sits down. Max beckons the waiter and after a brief consultation orders more coffee. During these moments of neutral routine Max can sense her eyes observing him. Her voice is the same, too: calm, courteous. Exactly as he remembers it.

"You've changed, Max."

He raises his eyebrows, accompanying the gesture with a wistful look: the slight, casual weariness of a man of the world.

"A lot?"

"Enough for me to have trouble recognizing you."

He leans forward slightly, politely discreet: "When?"

"Yesterday, although I wasn't sure. Or rather I thought it impossible. A vague resemblance, I told myself. . . . But this morning I saw you from the doorway. I stood watching you for a while."

Max studies her closely. Her mouth and eyes. They are identical, except for the signs of aging around them. The enamel on her teeth is less white than he remembers, no doubt affected by the nicotine of countless cigarettes. She has taken a packet of Murattis out of her cardigan pocket and is clasping it between her fingers, without breaking the seal.

"You, on the other hand, haven't changed a bit," he says.

"Don't be silly."

"I'm serious."

Now it is her turn to study him.

"You've gained a little weight," she concludes.

"More than a little, I'm afraid."

"I remember you as being taller and slimmer. . . . And I never imagined you with gray hair."

"But in your case, it suits you."

Mecha Inzunza laughs out loud, a resounding laugh that is enough to rejuvenate her. As before and as always.

"Flatterer . . . you always did know how to sweet-talk women."

"I don't know which women you are referring to. I only remember one."

A moment's silence. She smiles and looks away, contemplating the bay. The waiter arrives opportunely with the coffee and Max pours some into her cup, filling it halfway. He glances at the sugar bowl, then at her. She shakes her head.

"Milk?"

"Yes, please."

"You never used to take milk. No milk or sugar."

She seems surprised that he should remember this.

"True," she says.

Another silence, longer than the first. She continues to survey him pensively above the rim of the coffee cup as she takes small sips.

"What brings you to Sorrento, Max?"

"Oh . . . Well. I'm here on business, combined with a few days' holiday."

"Where do you live?"

He gestures toward some vague place beyond the hotel and city.

"I have a house down there. Near Amalfi. . . . And you?"

"In Switzerland. With my son. I expect you know who he is, if you're a guest at the hotel."

"Yes, I am. And I know who Jorge Keller is, naturally. Although the surname threw me off the scent."

She puts down her cup, breaks the seal on the packet of cigarettes, and takes one out. Max picks up the book of matches with the hotel crest from the ashtray, leans forward, and lights her cigarette, shielding the flame with his hands. She also leans forward, and for a moment their fingers touch.

"Are you interested in chess?"

She has settled back in her chair, exhaling the smoke, which the breeze from the bay quickly disperses. Once more that look of curiosity, fixed on Max.

"Not in the slightest," he replies, cool as can be. "Although I wandered through the room yesterday."

"And you didn't see me?"

"I probably wasn't paying much attention. I only took a quick look."

"So, you had no idea I was in Sorrento?"

Max shakes his head casually, with the old, professional aplomb.

Until a few days ago, he comments, he had no idea she had a son whose surname was Keller. Or that she even had a son. After Buenos Aires and what happened later in Nice, he lost track of her completely. Then the other war came, the big one. Half of Europe lost track of the other half. In many cases, forever.

"What I did know was what became of your husband. How he was killed in Spain."

Ignoring the ashtray, Mecha Inzunza moves her cigarette to the side so that a neat portion of ash falls on the floor. A firm, delicate tap. Then she lifts it once more to her lips.

"He never got out of prison, except to be executed." Her tone is matter-of-fact, betraying no bitterness or emotion, appropriate for speaking of something that happened many years ago. "A sad end, don't you think, for a man like that?"

"I'm sorry."

Another puff of her cigarette. More smoke dispersed in the breeze. More ash on the floor.

"Yes. I suppose that is the right word. . . . I was sorry, too."

"And your second husband?"

"An amicable divorce." She allows herself another smile. "Between two reasonable people, and on good terms. For Jorge's sake."

"Is he the father?"

"Of course."

"I imagine you've enjoyed an easy life all these years. Your family had money. Not to mention your first husband."

She nods, indifferently. She never had worries of that nature, she replies. Especially after the war ended. When the Germans invaded France, she moved to England. There she married Ernesto Keller, who was a Chilean diplomat: Max met him in Nice. They lived in London, Lisbon, and Santiago. Until their separation.

"Astonishing."

"What do you find astonishing?"

"Your extraordinary life. Your son's story."

For an instant, Max detects an unusual look in her eyes. A strange intensity: at once piercing and tranquil.

"What about you, Max . . . how extraordinary has your life been all these years?"

"Well. You know."

"No. I don't know."

He waves a hand at the terrace in an embracing gesture as if the proof lay there.

"Traveling here and there. Business . . . The war in Europe offered me some opportunities and took others away. I can't complain."

"It doesn't seem you have. Any reason to complain, I mean . . . have you been back to Buenos Aires?"

The name of that city pronounced in her even voice makes Max shiver. Warily, like someone venturing into hostile territory, he studies her face once more: the tiny lines around her mouth, the dullness of her sagging skin. She is wearing no lipstick. Only her eyes are unchanged, as they were in the tango bar in Barracas or in the other places that came afterward. In the unique shared landscape of all that he remembers.

"I've lived almost entirely in Italy," he invents on the spur of the moment. "And France and Spain."

"Business, as you say?"

"But not the same line as before." Max tries to muster the appropriate grin. "I was lucky, I raised some capital and things didn't go badly. Now I have retired."

Mecha Inzunza is no longer looking at him in the same way. A somber smile appears on her face.

"Completely?"

He stirs, ill at ease. Seemingly. The pearls he saw the day before in room 429 flash through his mind with glimmers of revenge amid soft, hazy reflections. He wonders who has more unpaid debts with the other. Her or himself.

"I don't live the way I did before, if that's what you mean."

She looks straight at him, unfazed.

"Yes, that is what I mean."

"I haven't needed to for a long time."

He says this without batting an eyelid. With complete calm. After all, he thinks, it isn't entirely untrue. In any case, she doesn't seem to be questioning that.

"Your house in Amalfi . . ."

"Yes."

"I'm glad things have gone so well for you," she says, looking at the ashtray as though seeing it for the first time. "I never thought you would lead a normal life."

"Oh, well"—he flaps his hand, fingers in the air, in an almost Italian gesture—"I never thought you would, either. I guess we all settle down sooner or later. . . ."

Mecha Inzunza has delicately put out the remainder of her cigarette in the ashtray, carefully detaching the ember. As though purposefully lingering on Max's last words.

"You mean after Buenos Aires or Nice?"

"Of course."

He can't help feeling a twinge of nostalgia. Memories come rushing back: whispered words like moans sliding over naked skin; long, graceful curves, caught in a mirror that duplicates the overcast sky outside, silhouetted against the gray window, which, like a fin de siècle French canvas, frames dripping palm trees, sea, and rain.

"How do you support yourself?"

Lost in thought (there is no pretense this time), it takes a moment for Max to hear the question, or to edge his way through to it. He is still busy rebelling inwardly at the overwhelming unfairness of the physical world: the woman's skin which he recalls with his five senses was smooth, warm, flawless. It can't possibly be the same one he sees before him now, scarred by time, he concludes with impotent rage. Someone must be accountable for such disrespect.

"Tourism, hotels, investments, that kind of thing," he says at last. "I am also on the board of a clinic near Lake Garda," he improvises once more. "I put some of my savings into it."

"Did you marry?"

"No."

She gazes with a distracted air at the bay beyond the terrace, as though ignoring Max's last response.

"I must be going now . . . Jorge is playing this afternoon, and it's hard work preparing everything. I only came down for a moment for some air while I had my coffee."

"I read that you manage all his affairs. From when he was a child."

"To some extent. I am his mother, his manager, and his secretary, arranging trips, hotels, contracts . . . that sort of thing. But he has his own team of assistants: the chess analysts with whom he prepares for each game and who accompany him everywhere."

"Analysts?"

"A challenger for the world title doesn't work alone. These games aren't improvised. You need a team of coaches and specialists."

"Even for chess?"

"Especially for chess."

They rise to their feet. Max is too much of an old hand to push things any further. Events follow their own course, and to force them is a mistake. Many men have been undone by being too clever, he reminds himself. And so he smiles the way he always did, and his closely shaven face, lightly tanned by the Naples sun, is illuminated: a broad, simple flash of white, revealing a relatively good set of teeth, despite the two crowns, half a dozen fillings, and the false incisor filling the gap made by a policeman's fist at a nightclub on Cumhuriyet Caddesi in Istanbul. That winning smile, mellowed by age, of a nice fellow in his sixties.

Mecha Inzunza studies Max's smile, which she appears to recognize. Her gaze is almost one of collusion. Finally, she hesitates. Also seemingly.

"When are you leaving the hotel?"

"In a few days. When I've finished that business I mentioned."

"Perhaps we should . . ."

"Yes. We should."

Another hesitant silence. She has thrust her hands into the pockets of her cardigan, pulling it down slightly over her shoulders.

"Have dinner with me," Max suggests.

Mecha doesn't reply to this. She is watching him, pensively.

"For a moment," she says at last, "I saw you standing before me, in that ship's ballroom, so young and handsome, in your tail-coat. . . . My God, Max, you look a mess."

He puts on a forlorn face, hanging his head with a look of worldly, exaggerated acceptance.

"I know."

"I don't mean it," she laughs suddenly as before, rejuvenated. The same loud, forthright laugh. "You look very good for your age . . . Or should I say our age. I, on the other hand . . . Life is so unfair!"

She falls silent, and Max thinks he recognizes her son's features, Jorge Keller's expression when he rests his chin on his folded arms at the chessboard.

"Yes, perhaps we should," she says eventually. "Chat for a while. But thirty years have gone by since the last time. . . . There are some places you can never return to. You said so yourself once."

"I wasn't referring to actual places."

"What then?"

Her smile has become ironic. Or rather, she looks dejected. Sincere and wistful.

"Look at me, Max. . . . Do you honestly think I am in a position to return anywhere?"

"I don't mean that kind of return," he protests, standing erect, "but rather what we remember. What we were."

"Witnesses of each other?"

Max holds her gaze without reciprocating her smile.

"Possibly. In that world we both knew."

Now there is a tender look in Mecha Inzunza's eyes. The light intensifies the familiar glimmer.

"Old School Tango," she whispers.

"That's right."

They study each other. And she almost looks beautiful again, Max concludes. The miracle of a few simple words.

"I imagine," she says, "that you came across it many times, as I did."

"Of course. Many times."

"Do you know something, Max? . . . Not once when I heard it, did I stop thinking about you."

"I can say the same: I didn't stop thinking about myself, either."

Her guffaw (oddly youthful once more) causes the people at the neighboring tables to turn their heads. For a moment, she lifts her arm, as though about to place it on his shoulder.

"The boys from the old days, you said back in that bar in Buenos Aires."

"Indeed." He sighs, with an air of resignation. "Now the boys from the old days are us."

—※—

The blunt razor wasn't giving a smooth shave. Max rinsed it in soapy water from the washbasin, then dried it on a towel and drew the blade up and down the belt he had stretched after hooking it onto the latch of the window overlooking the treetops on Avenida Almirante Brown. As he honed the blade against the leather he gazed absentmindedly at the street below. A lone automobile (carts and trams were the more common vehicles in the neighborhood of Max's boardinghouse, the Pensión Caboto, and the horse dung was only occasionally flattened by a rubber tire) was stationed next to a mule-driven cart, where a little man in a straw boater and white jacket was selling fresh brioche rolls, croissants, and burnt-sugar cakes. It was past ten in the morning, Max had not eaten breakfast yet, and the sight of the cart made his empty stomach rumble.

He hadn't had a good night. Arriving back in the small hours after accompanying the de Troeyes from Barracas to the Hotel Palace, Max had had a troubled, restless sleep. Long been familiar with that sense of unease arising from a blurred state between sleep and wakefulness, teeming with disturbing shadows. He had tossed and turned between crumpled sheets, as images distorted by his imagination assailed him suddenly, causing him to break out in a cold sweat. The most recurring image was of a landscape scattered with corpses: a hill of yellowish soil next to a wall ascending to a small fort farther up, and on the road running the length of the wall, three thousand corpses, desiccated by the weather and the sun, still bearing the marks of mutilation and torture that accompanied their deaths one summer's day in 1921. Volunteer Max Costa, 13th Company of the First Battalion of the Spanish Foreign Legion, had been nineteen at the time. Together with Boris and four other comrades, he'd made his way up the hill to the abandoned fort ("six volunteers for death" had been the order that had spurred them to advance before the rest of the company), amid the stench of rotting flesh and horrific sights, perspiring freely, dazed by the sun. Fingering his cartridge belt, his Mauser cocked, he had known with absolute certainty that only fate could save him from joining the ranks of those blackened corpses that only days earlier had been young, healthy flesh, and were now strewn along the road between Annual and Monte Arruit. From that day on, the officers in the regiment had offered their men a five-peseta piece for every Moroccan head they cut off. Two months later, in a place called Taxuda ("volunteers for death" had once again been the order), a Rif bullet ended Max's brief military career, landing him in a hospital in Melilla for five weeks. Afterward he deserted to Oran, before traveling on to Marseille, having already earned seven of those silver coins.

With the razor sharp once more, Max returned to the beveled wardrobe mirror and looked disapprovingly at the marks of insomnia on his face. Seven years had not been enough for him to lay those ghosts to rest—to drive out the demons, as the Moroccan saying went. Second Lieutenant Boris Dolgoruki-Bragation, fed up with listening to those demons, had chosen to banish them once and for all by placing the nine-millimeter barrel of a pistol in his mouth. But seven years was long enough for Max to accept their troublesome company. And so, attempting to thrust aside those unpleasant thoughts, he continued shaving as he hummed "I'm a Wild Animal": one of the tangos they had played the night before in La Ferroviaria. A few seconds later, he smiled thoughtfully at the lathered face staring back at him from the mirror. The memory of Mecha Inzunza was useful for driving out demons, or for trying to: the arrogant way she danced the tango; her words, made of silences and glints of liquid honey. As were the plans Max was devising step by step, biding his time, involving her, her husband, and the future. Ideas that were progressively taking shape, and which he appraised as he drew the steel blade carefully over his skin, still humming to himself.

Much to his relief, their foray the night before had passed without incident. After a long while spent listening to tangos played the traditional way and watching people dance (neither Mecha nor Max had done so again that evening), Armando de Troeye called the three musicians over to their table when they put down their instruments, and a decrepit piano player began to play loud, unrecognizable tangos. De Troeye had ordered something special for them to drink. The best, most expensive thing you can find, he said, passing his gold cigarette case around liberally. However, the nearest bottle of champagne, the waitress informed him cagily, after consulting the owner (a Spaniard with a waxed mustache and a loathsome visage) required a forty-block ride on tram number 17, too far at that time of night. And so de Troeye had to content himself with a few double grappas and brandies of dubious origin, a still-sealed bottle of cheap gin, and a blue glass soda siphon. They made short work of everything, including some meat pies brought as snacks, amid clouds of smoke from their cheroots.

Under normal circumstances, Max would have shown more interest in the conversation between de Troeye and the three musicians, but his thoughts were elsewhere. The bandoneon player had a glass eye and was a veteran from the days of the Hansen and the Rubia Mireya, back at the turn of the century. He assured them, following the first friendly exchanges and swigs of gin, that he couldn't read a note of music, and had never needed to. All his life he had played by ear. Moreover, what he and his fellow musicians played were authentic tangos, to be danced the old-fashioned way, fast and with *cortes* in the right places, not that smooth, ballroom style that was the rage, thanks to Paris and the cinema. As for the lyrics, they killed tango, degrading those who danced it with their obsession for making heroes of the cuckolded sucker who cried his eyes out when his woman left him for another man, or the young working girl who became a faded floozie. Authentic tango, he continued amid fresh swigs of gin and the vigorous approval of his fellow musicians, belonged to people from the working-class neighborhoods: it had a bitter sarcasm, the arrogance of ruffians and worldly women, the mocking contempt of those who thumbed their nose at life. There was no room for poets or fancy musicians. Tango was music for getting horny with a woman in your arms, or for carousing with the boys. He ought to know, he played it. In short, the tango was instinct, rhythm, improvisation, and risqué lyrics. With all due respect to the lady (his good eye glanced sideways at Mecha Inzunza), everything else was bullshit of the first order, if they would excuse his French. The way things were going, with all this starry-eyed love, sentimentality, and abandoned love nests, they would soon be singing about grieving mothers and the blind flower girl on the street corner.

De Troeye was enchanted by it all, and remained cheerful and talkative. He chinked glasses with the musicians and penciled more notes in tiny writing on his shirt cuff. The drink was beginning to show in his glassy-eyed look, occasional slurred speech, and his enthusiasm as he leaned over the table, absorbed by what they were saying. After half an hour of intense conversation, the three musicians from La Ferroviaria and the composer friend of Ravel, Stravinsky, and Diaghilev seemed as close as lifelong chums. For his part, Max kept one eye on the other patrons, who were looking over at their table with curiosity or distrust. The man who had danced with Mecha Inzunza was still staring at them, eyes squinting from the smoke of his cigar. His companion, the woman in the flowery blouse, bent casually forward to adjust her black stocking. At this point, Mecha Inzunza announced that she wanted to smoke a cigarette outside in the fresh air. Without waiting for her husband to reply, she rose and walked toward the door, heels gently tapping, as resolute and confident as when she had danced the tango a short while before. Juan Rebenque ogled her from a distance, eyes greedily taking in the sway of her hips, and only stopped to gaze at Max when he straightened his tie, buttoned his jacket, and followed the composer's wife out. As he approached the exit, Max knew without having to turn around that Armando de Troeye's eyes were also on him.

He made his way to the corner, stepping on his shadow, which the street lamp elongated across the brick pavement. Mecha Inzunza was standing there, not far from where the last of the squat dwellings with tin roofs, typical of that part of town, melted away into the dark waste ground next to the Riachuelo. As he drew closer, Max searched for the Pierce-Arrow, glimpsing it among the shadows on the far side of the street when the driver Petrossi flashed the headlights. Good man, he thought, reassured by this careful professional, with his blue uniform and peaked cap, and his pistol in the glove compartment.

By the time he reached her side, she had dropped the cigarette butt and was listening to the chorus of crickets and frogs coming from the bushes and rotting timber wharves along the river. The steel bridge at the end of the cobblestone street loomed tall in the darkness, stark against the eerie glow of the lights across the river piercing the night in Barracas Sur. The moon had not risen yet. Max came to a halt next to Mecha Inzunza and lit one of his Turkish cigarettes with a match. He could tell she was watching him in the flame's brief light. He extinguished the match and exhaled the first puff of smoke before looking at her.

"I liked your tango," she said without preamble, her face silhouetted by the distant glow.

A brief silence followed.

"I imagine," she said, "that we put into a dance what is inside us: elegance or evil."

"The same as with alcohol," Max replied softly.

"Yes."

She fell silent again.

"That woman," she finally said, "was . . ."

She broke off in midsentence. Or maybe she had said all she wished to say.

"Adequate?" he suggested.

"Perhaps."

She did not pursue the subject, nor did Max. He was smoking quietly, pondering his next moves. Possible and probable errors. Finally, he shrugged as if to conclude.

"I, on the other hand, didn't like yours."

"Really." She seemed genuinely surprised, almost offended. "I didn't think I had danced so badly."

"That's not what I meant." He couldn't help grinning, knowing she wouldn't notice. "You danced magnificently, of course."

"What, then?"

"Your partner. That isn't a very nice place."

"I understand."

"Some games can be dangerous."

A three-second silence. Then five icy words.

"What games might they be?"

He allowed himself the tactical luxury of not replying. Instead he took a last draw on his cigarette and hurled it into the distance. The ember traced a semicircle before dying in the darkness.

"Your husband seems to be enjoying the evening."

"Yes, very much," she said at last. "He is excited, because this isn't what he was expecting. He traveled to Buenos Aires with ballrooms and high society in mind . . . intending to compose tasteful, white-tie tango. I fear that meeting you on the *Cap Polonio* changed his mind."

"Forgive me, I never meant . . ."

"You needn't apologize. On the contrary: Armando is extremely grateful to you. What began as a foolish wager between him and Ravel has turned into a passionate quest. You should hear him talk about tangos, now. Old School or otherwise. All he needed was to come here and immerse himself in this ambience. He's a stubborn, obsessive creature when it comes to his work." She chuckled. "I am afraid he will be insufferable after this, and I'll end up cursing tango and whoever invented it."

She walked on a few paces, then stopped, as if the darkness seemed suddenly threatening.

"Is this neighborhood really dangerous?"

No more than any other, Max assured her. Barracas was home to humble, hardworking folk. Its proximity to the Riachuelo docks and La Boca, which was downriver, accounted for dubious places like La Ferroviaria. But farther up, street life was normal: there were tenements, immigrant families, people earning a living or trying to. Housewives in clogs or slippers, men drinking maté, entire families in robes or vests, carrying benches and wicker chairs outside to take the air after their meager supper, cooling themselves with the screens they used to fan the fire as they watched over children playing in the street.

"Over there, a block away," he went on, "is El Puentecito, the local café where my father sometimes took us to lunch on a Sunday, when business was good."

"What did your father do?"

"Different things, none of them successful. He worked in factories, owned a scrap yard, transported meat and dry goods . . . He was one of those men who are born unlucky and never manage to escape their fate. One day he grew tired of trying, and went back to Spain, taking us with him."

"Do you feel nostalgic about your old neighborhood?"

Max half-closed his eyes. He could easily conjure images of games played along the banks of the Riachuelo, among the derelict, half-submerged boats and barges, pretending he was a pirate on the murky waters. And secretly envying the son of the man who owned the Colombo limekiln, the only boy who had a bicycle.

"I feel nostalgia for my childhood," he said. "I guess the neighborhood doesn't matter so much."

Mecha walked on again, and Max followed suit. They drew close to the bridge at the end of the street, where the distant lights gently illuminated the tram tracks.

"Well"—her tone was one of compassion and perhaps condescension—"your origins were noble, however humble."

"Humble origins are never noble."

"Don't say that."

He laughed between clenched teeth. Almost to himself. Closer to the water, the chorus of crickets and frogs on the riverbank was almost deafening. The air was damper, and he noticed that she was shivering. She had left her silk shawl behind in the warehouse, draped over the back of her chair.

"What did you do after that? . . . After you returned to Spain."

"A bit of everything. I was in school for a couple of years. Then

I left home, and a friend found me a job as a bellboy at the Ritz Hotel in Barcelona. Fifty pesetas a month. Plus tips."

Mecha Inzunza, arms folded, was still shivering. Without a word, Max took off his jacket and placed it around her shoulders. As he did so, his eyes wandered briefly along her long, exposed neck beneath her bobbed hair, silhouetted against the hazy light on the far side of the bridge. For an instant, he noticed the same glow reflected in her eyes, which for a few seconds were very close to him. He noticed she had a pleasant smell, despite the smoke, the perspiration, and the stuffiness of the bar. A smell of clean skin and perfume that hadn't quite faded.

"I know everything about hotels and bellboys," he went on, fully regaining his composure. "You have before you an expert in mailing letters, working nights while resisting the lure of nearby sofas, running errands, and trudging 'round foyers and lounges calling out, 'Señor Martinez, to the telephone.'"

"Goodness." She seemed amused. "A whole other world, I imagine."

"You'd be surprised. From the outside it's difficult to see beyond the two rows of gold buttons, or the none-too-white jacket of a waiter who serves cocktails and keeps his mouth shut."

"You worry me. . . . You sound positively Bolshevik."

Max roared with laughter. He heard her laugh, too, beside him.

"It isn't true that I worry you. But I ought to."

Mecha Inzunza's white glove, which she had folded and tucked into Max's top jacket pocket when he went to dance tango with the blonde woman, shone in the dark and seemed to establish an almost intimate bond between them, he reflected, a kind of silent collusion.

"Believe it or not," he continued in a lighthearted tone, "I am also an expert on tipping. . . . Because of your social position, you and your husband are used to giving tips. But you are doubtless unaware that there are one-, three-, and five-peseta guests. All those who see themselves as blonde, brunette, tall, short, industrialists, salesmen, millionaires, or civil engineers are unaware that this is how hotel employees actually classify them. Imagine, there are even people in rooms costing over a hundred pesetas a day who tip ten centimes. . . ."

Mecha did not reply immediately, but seemed to reflect about what he had said with absolute seriousness.

"I imagine that for a ballroom dancer, tips must be important, too," she said at last.

"Of course. A lady who is happy with a waltz can slip a banknote into your jacket pocket that covers your expenses for the rest of the evening, or the entire week."

He couldn't help a note of bitterness from creeping into his voice as he explained this: a touch of resentment which, he thought, he had no reason to conceal. She seemed to be listening very carefully, and had noticed it.

"Listen, Max . . . unlike most people, men in particular, I have nothing against ballroom dancers. Or against gigolos for that matter. . . . Even in this day and age, a woman dressed by Lelong or Patou can't possibly go to restaurants or balls unaccompanied."

"Don't feel you need to humor me. I have no illusions. I lost them long ago in cold, damp boardinghouses with threadbare blankets, and only half a bottle of wine to keep me warm."

A moment's silence followed. Max knew what the next question would be an instant before she uttered it.

"And a woman?"

"Yes. Sometimes there was a woman as well."

"Give me a cigarette."

He took out his cigarette case. There were three left, he calculated almost by touch.

"Light it for me, please."

He did so. By the light of the flame he could see that she was looking straight at him. Still dazzled by the glow after he blew it out, he took a few puffs on the cigarette before placing it between her lips. She accepted it without resorting to her cigarette holder.

"What attracted you to the *Cap Polonio*?"

"The tips . . . And a contract, of course. I've been on other ships. There is a good atmosphere on the liners going to Buenos Aires and Montevideo. The journeys are long and the ladies want to enjoy themselves on board. My Latin looks and the fact that I can dance tango and other fashionable things helps. And languages."

"Which other languages do you speak?"

"French. And a smattering of German."

She had discarded her cigarette.

"Even though you started out as a bellboy, you are a gentleman. . . . Where did you learn your manners?"

Max burst out laughing. He was watching the tiny dying ember at her feet.

"From illustrated magazines: reading about the wider world, fashion, high society . . . looking around me. Observing the conversations and manners of those who possess them. The odd friend occasionally advised me, too."

"Do you enjoy your job?"

"Sometimes. Dancing isn't only a way of earning a living. It is also an excuse to hold a beautiful woman in your arms."

"And are you always so immaculately turned out, in a tailcoat or tuxedo?"

"Of course. Those are my work clothes." He was about to add: "for which I am still indebted to a tailor on Rue Danton," but stopped himself. "Whether I am dancing a tango, a fox-trot, or a Black Bottom."

"You disappoint me. I imagined you dancing lewd tangos in the seediest bars in Pigalle . . . places that only come alive after dark, when whores, ruffians, and villains parade beneath the street lamps."

"You seem familiar with the ambience."

"I already told you La Ferroviaria isn't the first shady place I have visited. Some people describe it as getting sordid pleasure from living dangerously."

"Or as my father used to say: 'He became a lion tamer and was eaten by his pupil.'"

"A sensible man, your father."

They walked back slowly the way they had come, toward the street lamp on the corner of La Ferroviaria. She seemed to move slightly ahead of him, head bowed. Enigmatic.

"And what does your husband think?"

"Armando is as curious as I am. Or almost."

Max considered the implications of the word *curious*. He thought of that Juan Rebenque fellow, standing in front of their table with the swagger of a dangerous, malicious thug, and the cold arrogance with which she had accepted the challenge. He thought, too, of her hips sheathed in her fine silk dress, gyrating around the ruffian's body. "It's your turn," she had said defiantly, deliberately, when she came back to their table.

"I know Pigalle and those places," said Max. "Although as a dancer I worked elsewhere. Until March I was at a Russian cabaret called Le Scheherazade in Rue de Liège, in Montmartre. Before that at the Kasmet and the Casanova. And at tea dances in the Ritz, as well as in Deauville and Biarritz during the high season."

"Excellent. You seem to have plenty of work."

"I can't complain. Tango has made it fashionable to be or to look Argentinian."

"Why did you end up living in France rather than Spain?"

"It's a long story. It would bore you."

"I doubt that."

"Perhaps I would bore myself."

She stopped in her tracks. The electric street lamp now illuminated her features a little better. Clear-cut lines, he noticed once again. Extraordinarily composed. Even her most banal gestures had the casual gracefulness of a master's sketch.

"Our paths might have crossed there," she said.

"It's possible, though unlikely."

"Why?"

"I told you on the ship: I would have remembered you."

She looked straight at him, without responding. A duplicated image in her steady eyes.

"Do you know what?" he said. "I admire the ease with which you accept being told you are beautiful."

Mecha Inzunza remained silent for a moment, her eyes still fixed on him. Only now it seemed that she was smiling: a faint shadow bisected by the light shining on one side of her mouth.

"I understand your success with the ladies. You are a handsome fellow. . . . Doesn't having broken a few hearts, whether of older or younger women, weigh on your conscience?"

"Not at all."

"You're right. Remorse is unusual among men when money or sex is the object, and among women when there is a man involved. . . . Besides, we are less appreciative of gentlemanly behavior and sentiments than men might think. And we often show it by falling for ruffians or ill-mannered louts."

She walked up to the bar's entrance and paused, as if she had never opened a door herself.

"Surprise me, Max. I am patient. Capable of waiting for you to astonish me."

Mustering every shred of his composure, Max reached out to open the door. Had he not known that the chauffeur was watching them from the car, he would have tried to kiss her.

"Your husband . . ."

"For God's sake. Forget about my husband."

Max's recollections of the night before at La Ferroviaria accompanied the swish of the blade on his chin. He had not yet shaved the patch of foam on his left cheek when there was a knock at the door. Heedless of his appearance (he was dressed in trousers and shoes, but with only an undershirt on top, and his suspenders were hanging down at his sides), he went to open it, and stood clutching the handle, mouth gaping.

"Good morning," she said.

She wore a loose-fitting casual dress, with a straight cut, a blue-and-white polka-dot scarf, and a cloche hat that framed her face. She was gazing with amusement at the razor in his right hand. Then her eyes moved up to meet his, first taking in the undershirt, the suspenders, and the remnants of shaving foam on his cheek.

"Perhaps this is a bad time," she said, with disconcerting calm.

By then, Max had regained enough presence of mind to respond, murmuring an apology for his state of undress before ushering her in. He closed the door, left the razor in the washbowl, pulled the coverlet over his unmade bed, slipped on a collarless shirt, and hitched up his suspenders, trying to think quickly and to calm himself as he did so.

"Forgive the mess. I had no idea . . ."

Mecha Inzunza had not uttered another word and was watching him tidy up, apparently relishing his embarrassment.

"I came to fetch my glove."

Max blinked, not understanding.

"Your glove?"

"Yes."

Still flustered, he finally realized what she meant and opened the wardrobe. The glove was still protruding from the top pocket of the jacket he had been wearing the night before. Next to that hung a gray, three-piece suit, a pair of flannel trousers, and the two evening jackets, a tuxedo and a tailcoat that he wore for work. There was also a pair of black patent leather shoes, half a dozen ties and pairs of socks (he had darned one of them that morning using a maté gourd), three white shirts, and half a dozen starched shirtfronts and cuffs. That was all. In the wardrobe mirror, Max noticed she was studying his movements, and felt ashamed that she should see how few clothes he owned. He made as if to put a jacket on over his shirt, but saw that she was shaking her head.

"Please, there's no need. It's too hot."

Closing the wardrobe, he went over and gave her the glove. She took it with barely a glance, holding it in her hand as she tap-tapped the fingers lightly against her leather bag. She remained standing, deliberately ignoring the only chair in the room, as composed as if she had been in the lounge of a hotel where she was a regular guest. Glancing around her, she took in every detail: the sun slanting through the window onto the chipped floor-tiles and the battered trunk plastered with labels from ocean liners and the odd third-rate hotel offering full board and lodging; the Primus stove on the marble-topped chest of drawers; a shaving kit, a tin of tooth powder, and a tube of Sta-Comb brilliantine arranged next to the washbowl. On the bedside table beneath a kerosene lamp (the electricity at the Caboto boardinghouse was switched off at eleven at night) were his French passport, a book of matches from the *Cap Polonio*, and a wallet, whose meager contents (seven fifty-peso and three twenty-peso notes) were, thankfully, thought Max, not visible.

"A glove is important," she said. "It shouldn't be abandoned without good reason."

She continued to look around her. Then she removed her hat very calmly, even as her eyes appeared casually to alight on Max. She tilted her head slightly to one side, and once more he could appreciate the long, graceful outline of her neck, which seemed even more exposed.

"An interesting place we went to last night . . . Armando wants to go back there."

With some difficulty, Max returned to what she was saying.

"Tonight?"

"No. We have to attend a concert this evening at the Teatro Colón. . . . Would tomorrow suit you?"

"Of course."

Mecha Inzunza sat down on the edge of the bed with perfect poise, ignoring the empty chair. She was still clasping her glove and hat, and a moment later she laid them to one side, together with her bag. Her skirt had ridden up, revealing more of her long, slender legs beneath the silk stockings.

"I once read something about women losing their gloves," she said.

She seemed genuinely pensive, as if she had never given the matter any thought before.

"Two gloves isn't the same as one," she went on. "Two would be casual neglect. One is . . ."

She left her words hanging in the air, fixing Max with her eyes.

"Deliberate?" he ventured.

"If there is one thing I like about you, it's that you could never be accused of being stupid."

Max held her bright gaze without flinching.

"And I like the way you look at me," he said softly.

He saw her frown as though considering the implications of his remark. Then Mecha Inzunza crossed her legs, placing her hands on either side of her on the coverlet. She seemed vexed.

"Really? . . . You disappoint me." There was a note of coldness in her voice. "I am afraid that sounds conceited to me. Inappropriate."

This time he did not respond. He simply stood motionless before her. Waiting. After a moment, she shrugged indifferently, as one might give up faced with an absurd riddle.

"Describe how it is I look at you," she said.

Max smiled suddenly, with apparent candor. This was his most winning expression, one he had rehearsed hundreds of times in front of mirrors in cheap hotels and seedy boardinghouses.

"It makes one pity men who have never been looked at that way by a woman."

He could scarcely conceal his dismay when Mecha Inzunza rose to her feet, as though ready to leave. He tried desperately to think what he had done wrong. To discover the offending word or gesture. But instead of collecting her things and leaving the room, she took three steps toward him. Max had forgotten that he still had shaving foam on his face, and was surprised when she reached out to caress his cheek, and, scooping up a blob of the white froth with her forefinger, deposited it on the end of his nose.

"You make a handsome clown," she said.

They flung themselves at each other, without preamble or hesitation, violently, stripping off anything that got in the way of the skin and flesh, finding their way to each other's body. As they drew back the bedcover, the woman's scent mingled with that of the man's smell left on the crumpled sheets from the previous night. An intense battle of the senses followed, a lengthy clash of pent-up passion and desire, unleashed mercilessly on both sides. Max had to summon every ounce of self-discipline as he fought on three fronts to maintain the necessary calm, controlling her responses, and muffling her cries so as not to alert everyone else in the boardinghouse to their tussle. The patch of sun from the window had slowly moved until it framed the bed, and from time to time they would rest their exhausted tongues, mouths, hands, and hips, drunk on the other's saliva and smell, their mingled perspiration gleaming under the dazzling light. And whenever that happened they would peer at each other with defiant or astonished eyes, amazed by the ferocious pleasure enveloping them, panting like a couple of wrestlers pausing during a bout, the blood throbbing in their temples, only to hurl themselves at each other once more, with the hunger of someone finally able to resolve, in an almost frenzied way, a complex personal vendetta.

For his part, during the flashes of lucidity, when he clung to particular details or thoughts that allowed him to steady himself briefly, Max was struck that morning by two remarkable things: in the throes of passion, Mecha Inzunza whispered obscenities improper for a lady; and on her warm, smooth flesh, deliciously soft in all the right places, there were bluish marks that looked like bruises left by blows.

—⁓—

It has been a while since the lights came on in their paper lanterns, after the sun had dipped behind the cliffs encircling the Marina Grande in Sorrento. In that artificial light, less precise and reliable than the one that has just gone out in a final blaze of violet where sea meets sky, the most recent traces of age on the face of the woman sitting opposite Max Costa seem to fade. The soft lights illuminating the tables at the Trattoria Stéfano eradicate all trace of the intervening years, restoring the once sharply defined, remarkably beautiful face of Mecha Inzunza.

"I could never have imagined chess changing my life in this way," she is saying. "In fact, it was my son who changed it. The chess part is purely incidental. . . . If he had been a musician or a mathematician, the result would have been the same."

It is still pleasantly warm on the seafront. Her arms are bare, and draped over the back of her chair is a lightweight cream jacket. She is wearing a long and flowing mauve cotton dress that shows off her still-slender figure in a way that seems, deliberately, to flout the fashion for short skirts and garish colors, which even women of a certain age have recently adopted. She is wearing the pearls in three strands around her neck. Sitting opposite her, Max remains motionless, showing an interest that goes beyond simple politeness. It would require close scrutiny to recognize Dr. Hugentobler's chauffeur in the calm gentleman with gray hair leaning forward slightly over the table and listening attentively. In front of him is a glass that he has barely touched, in keeping with his old habit of staying sober when the stakes are high. He is impeccably dressed in a dark double-breasted blazer, gray flannel trousers, a pale blue Oxford shirt, and a brown knitted tie.

"Or maybe not exactly the same," Mecha Inzunza continues.

"The world of professional chess is complex. Demanding. It requires extraordinary things, a special way of life. And it very much shapes the lives of the people in the players' entourage."

She pauses once more, pensive, tilting her head as she runs her finger (with its short, unpainted nail) along the lip of her empty coffee cup.

"In my life," she says at last, "I have experienced moments of radical change, upheavals that marked the beginning of new chapters. Armando's death during the Spanish Civil War was one of those. It gave me back a certain kind of freedom which I did not necessarily want, or need." She looks at Max with an ambiguous expression on her face, perhaps of resignation. "Another was when I discovered that my son was extremely gifted at chess."

"I hear you gave up your life for him."

She places her cup to one side and leans back in her chair.

"Perhaps that's a slight exaggeration. A child is something you can't explain to others. Did you ever have one?"

Max smiles, remembering very clearly her asking the same question in Nice, almost thirty years before. And he gives the same reply.

"Not that I know of. . . . Why chess?"

"Because that was Jorge's obsession since he was a child. His joy and his despair. Imagine watching someone you love with all your heart, struggling to solve a problem at once imprecise and complex. You long to help him, but you don't know how. So you try to find a person who can do for him what you cannot. Chess masters, analysts . . ."

She glances about her with a wistful smile, while Max continues to follow her every word and gesture. Farther along the tiny quayside, toward where the fishing boats are, the tables at the next restaurant, the Trattoria Emilia, are empty, and a bored-looking waiter is chatting to the female cook in the entrance. At the far end of the beach, a group of Americans can be heard laughing and talking loudly on the terrace of a third establishment, over the background voice of Edoardo Vianello singing "Abbronzatissima" on a jukebox or record player.

"It's a bit like a mother whose son is addicted to drugs. . . . When she realizes she can't stop him from taking them, she decides to supply them herself."

She is staring into the distance beyond Max and the beached fishing boats, toward the far-off lights that encircle the bay and the black slope of Vesuvius.

"It was unbearable to watch him agonizing in front of a chessboard," she goes on. "It still upsets me even now. To begin with I tried to discourage him. I'm not one of those mothers who push their children to extremes, projecting their own ambitions onto them. Quite the opposite. I tried to get him away from chess. . . . But when I realized I couldn't, that he was playing secretly and that this could come between us, I didn't hesitate."

Lambertucci, the owner, comes over to ask if they need anything, and Max shakes his head. "You don't know me," Max had instructed him that afternoon when he called to reserve a table. "I'll arrive at eight, after the captain leaves and you put the chessboard away. Officially, I've only been to your restaurant a couple of times, so avoid being familiar this evening. I want a quiet, discreet dinner: pasta with clams followed by grilled fish, and a good chilled white wine. And don't even think of wheeling out your nephew with his guitar to murder "O Sole Mio" the way you usually do. I'll explain what it's about some other time. Or maybe not."

"Sometimes after I punished him," Mecha Inzunza continues, "I would go into his room and find him lying on the bed, staring into space. I realized he didn't need to see the pieces. He was playing chess in his head, using the ceiling as a board. . . . And so I decided to support him, in every way I could."

"What was he like as a boy . . . ? I read somewhere that he started playing chess very young."

"To begin with he was a very nervous child. He would cry inconsolably if he made a mistake and lost a game. I, and later his coaches, had to force him to think before making a move. He was already showing signs of what would later become his style of play: dazzling, brilliant, and fast, always ready to sacrifice pieces when mounting an attack."

"Another coffee?" asks Max.

"Yes please."

"In Nice you used to live off coffee and cigarettes."

She gives a faint, leisurely smile.

"Those are the only old habits I hold on to. Though in moderation now."

Lambertucci arrives to take their order with an inscrutable expression and an almost exaggerated politeness, glancing sideways at Mecha Inzunza. He seems to like what he sees, and winks discreetly at Max before joining the waiter and cook from the restaurant next door, to chat about business. Every now and then, he turns his head, and Max knows what he is thinking: what is that old charlatan up to this evening? Dressed to the nines, as if it were perfectly normal, and accompanied.

"Many people think chess is all about brilliant improvisation," Mecha Inzunza says, "but they're wrong. It requires a methodical approach, exploring every possible situation in search of new ideas. . . . A great chess player memorizes the moves from thousands of his own and others' games, and tries to improve on them with new gambits or variations, studying his predecessors like someone learning languages or algebra. That is why they depend on their entourage, the assistants, coaches, and analysts I told you about this morning. Depending on the moment, Jorge may have several people in his entourage. One is his coach, Emil Karapetian, who goes everywhere with us."

"Does the Russian have assistants as well?"

"Of all shapes and sizes. He is even accompanied by an employee of the Soviet embassy in Rome. Chess is an affair of state in the USSR."

"I hear they have occupied an entire apartment house overlooking the hotel gardens. And that even the KGB is there."

"It doesn't surprise me. Sokolov has up to a dozen people in his entourage, even though the Campanella Cup is only a prelude to the world championship. . . . In a few months' time, in Dublin, Jorge will have four or five different analysts and assistants working for him. Imagine how many the Russians will have."

Max takes a small sip from his glass.

"How many do you have?"

"There are three of us here, including me. Besides Karapetian, we have Irina."

"The young woman? I thought she was your son's girlfriend."

"She is. As well as being an extraordinarily gifted chess player. She is twenty-four."

Max listened as if this were all new to him.

"Russian?"

"Yugoslav parents, but born in Canada. She played for Canada at the Olympiad in Tel Aviv, and is among the top ten or fifteen women chess players in the world. She has a grand master title. She and Emil are the core of our team of analysts."

"Do you like her as a daughter-in-law?"

"She could be worse," replies Mecha Inzunza impassively. "Like all chess players, she is complicated. There are things going on in her head that you and I will never understand. . . . But she and Jorge get along well."

"Is she a good analyst or assistant or whatever you call them?"

"Yes, excellent."

"And how does Karapetian feel about her?"

"Fine. At first he was jealous, yapping like a dog defending a bone. A girl, he muttered. That sort of thing. But she is clever. She soon had him eating out of her hand."

"And you?"

"Oh, with me it's different." Mecha Inzunza finished off her coffee. "I'm his mother, you see."

"Of course."

"My job is to watch from a distance . . . attentive yet remote."

They hear the voices of the Americans on their way toward the ramparts leading to the top of Sorrento. Afterward everything is silent. The woman gazes thoughtfully at the red-and-white-checkered tablecloth, in a way that reminds Max of a player before a chessboard.

"There are things I can't give my son," she says suddenly, looking up. "And I am not just referring to chess."

"How long will you go on for?"

"Until he no longer wants me," she replies instantly. Until Jorge no longer needs to have her near. When that time comes, she hopes she will realize and take her leave discreetly, without any fuss. She has a comfortable house in Lausanne full of books and music. A library, and a life somehow suspended, yet which she has been preparing all these years. A place to pass away peacefully when the time comes.

"That is a long way off, I assure you."

"You always were a flatterer, Max . . . an elegant scoundrel and a handsome impostor."

He bobs his head humbly, as though overcome by the back-handed compliment. How can he argue with that, his gallant gesture seems to imply. At their advanced age.

"Something I read a long time ago," she added, "made me think of you. I can't recall the exact words, but it went something like this: 'Men who have enjoyed the caresses of many women will suffer less pain and trepidation as they walk through the valley of the shadow of death' . . . What do you think?"

"Rhetoric."

Silence. She studies his face, as though attempting to recognize him despite his own appearance. Her eyes shine softly in the light of the paper lanterns.

"Why did you never marry, Max?"

"I suppose because it would have spoiled my passage through the valley of the shadow of death."

Her chuckle, spontaneous and vigorous like a young girl's, causes Lambertucci, the waiter, and the cook, who are still chatting at the restaurant next door, to turn their heads.

"You old rascal. You always were good at that type of riposte . . . swiftly making your own what belonged to others."

Max adjusts his shirt cuffs, making sure just the right amount is protruding from the jacket sleeves. He detests the recent fashion of showing almost the entire cuff, as he does tailored shirts, flashy ties, pointed collars, and tight bell-bottoms.

"During all those years, did you ever think of me?"

He asks the question gazing into Mecha Inzunza's luminous eyes. She tilts her head to one side, still observing him.

"I admit that I did. Every so often."

Max makes use of his finest attribute, flashing a dazzling smile, apparently spontaneous, which in the past had lit up his face to devastating effect depending upon the disposition of the woman to whom it was destined.

"Old School Tango aside?"

"Of course."

Mecha Inzunza has nodded her head, a tenuous smile on her lips, accepting to play along. Max is somewhat emboldened by this, and decides to push his luck, like a bullfighter cheered on by the spectators who continues to goad the bull. The blood is pumping at a steady pace through his old arteries, resolute and firm as in the distant days of adventure, with a touch of euphoric optimism similar to that provided by a couple of aspirin washed down with coffee after a sleepless night.

"And yet," he remarks with absolute calm, "this is only the third occasion we have met: on the *Cap Polonio* and in Buenos Aires in twenty-eight, and nine years later in Nice."

"I always had a soft spot for scoundrels."

"I was just young, Mecha."

His gesture is another of his favorite tricks: head bowed, oozing humility, accompanied by a wave of his left hand as though dismissing all that is superfluous. Which is everything except the woman in front of him.

"Exactly. A young, elegant scoundrel, just as I said. That's how you made your living."

"No," he protests, politely. "That's what helped me survive, which isn't the same thing. . . . Those were hard times. Aren't they always?"

As he says this he is looking at the necklace, and Mecha Inzunza notices.

"Do you remember it?"

Max adopts the expression of a gentleman who has been, or is about to be, insulted.

"Naturally I remember it."

"You certainly should." She touches the pearls momentarily. "It's the same one I had in Buenos Aires . . . and that ended up in Montevideo."

"How could I forget it." Max pauses nostalgically. "It's as magnificent as ever."

She seems no longer to be listening, caught up in her own thoughts.

"That business in Nice . . . The way you used me, Max! And what a fool I was. That second dirty trick of yours destroyed my friendship with Suzi Ferriol, among other things. And that was the last I saw of you. Ever."

"They were looking for me, remember. I had to leave. Those dead bodies . . . It would have been crazy of me to stay there."

"I remember it all. Very clearly. To the point where I realized it gave you the perfect excuse."

"That's not true. I . . ."

Now it is she who raises her hand. "Don't go down that road. You'll spoil what has otherwise been a pleasant evening."

Augmenting her gesture, she extends her arm across the table and touches Max's face, brushing it only for a moment. He instinctively kisses her fingers gently as she withdraws her hand.

"My God . . . It's true. You were the most beautiful woman I ever met."

Mecha Inzunza opens her bag, takes out a packet of Murattis, and puts one in her mouth. Leaning across the table, Max lights it with the gold Dupont that a few days ago was in Dr. Hugentobler's study. She exhales the smoke and leans back in her chair.

"Don't be a fool."

"You're still beautiful," he insists.

"Don't be an even bigger fool. Look at yourself. Even you aren't the same."

Now Max is sincere. Or possibly so.

"If things had been different, I . . ."

"It was all fortuitous. If things had been different, you wouldn't have stood a chance."

"For what?"

"You know what. To get near me."

A prolonged pause. She avoids Max's eyes and continues smoking as her gaze drifts to the lanterns, the fishermen's huts dotting the beach, the piled-up nets and beached boats on the darkening shore.

"Your first husband was certainly a scoundrel," he says.

Mecha Inzunza takes her time replying: two puffs on her cigarette and another drawn-out silence.

"Leave him out of this," she says at last. "Armando has been dead almost thirty years. And he was an extraordinary composer. Besides, he simply gave me what I wanted. Rather like I do with my son."

"I always suspected that he . . ."

"That he corrupted me? . . . Don't talk nonsense. He had his preferences, of course. Peculiar, at times. But no one forced me to play along. I had mine, too. In Buenos Aires as everywhere else, I was always in complete control over what I did. And remember, he was no longer with me in Nice. He had been killed in Spain, or was about to be."

"Mecha . . ."

He has placed his hand on hers. She pulls it away, gently.

"Don't even think about it, Max. If you tell me I was the great love of your life, I shall get up and leave."

5

An Adjourned Game

THIS ISN'T THE Buenos Aires I imagined," said Mecha.

It was hot, all the more so because of their proximity to the Riachuelo. Max had removed his hat to cool the damp sweatband, and was holding it as he walked, his free hand casually placed in his jacket pocket. They would occasionally fall in step, brushing against each other before separating again.

"Buenos Aires is many cities," he remarked. "Although basically it is two: the city of success and the city of failure."

Mecha Inzunza and Max had been lunching near La Ferroviaria, at a restaurant called El Puentecito, a fifteen-minute drive from the Caboto boardinghouse. Before that, stepping out of the Pierce-Arrow (the silent Petrossi was still driving, and not once did he look at Max in his rearview mirror), they had a drink at a bar near the railway station, leaning on the marble counter beneath a large photograph of the Barracas Football Club and a sign that said, *Please refrain from drunk and disorderly behavior and don't spit on the floor.* She had a grenadine with sparkling water and he a Cora vermouth with a dash of Amer Picon, and as they sipped their drinks amid the inquisitive glances, they heard voices speaking in Spanish and Italian belonging to men with copper chains dangling from their waistcoats, who played cards, smoking and hawking as they deposited thick gobbets of phlegm in the spittoons. It was she who insisted that Max invite her to the modest restaurant where his father used to take the family on Sundays, the one he had told her about the night before. Once there, she seemed to enjoy the dish of ravioli and the barbecued meat washed down with a bottle of rough, heady wine from the Mendoza region that a lively Spanish waiter recommended.

"I get ravenous when I make love," she had said calmly.

Exhausted accomplices, they gazed at each other lengthily during lunch, neither making any explicit reference to what had happened at the boardinghouse on Almirante Brown. Mecha was the epitome of calm (absolutely self-assured, Max noticed with astonishment) while he reflected about what it might mean for his own present and future. Those thoughts occupied him for the remainder of the meal, concealed behind the façade of his perfect manners. However, he was frequently distracted from his scheming, seized by an inner spasm at the fresh intense memory of her warm vibrant body, as she in turn peered at him over her raised glass. Pensive, as though observing with renewed curiosity the man in front of her.

"I'd like to go for a stroll," she said later in the car. "Along the Riachuelo."

She wanted to walk part of the way through the neighborhood around La Boca. She asked Petrossi to stop, and the two of them began walking on the north side of the Vuelta de Rocha, followed by the car which, with its silent chauffeur at the wheel, inched along on the left-hand side of the street. In the distance, beyond the black wooden hull and exposed timber frame of a half-submerged sailboat beside the shore (Max remembered playing there as a boy), they could see the imposing structure of the giant transporter bridge.

"I brought you a present," she said, placing a small package in Max's hands. He undid the wrapping paper to find a long leather case with a wristwatch inside: a splendid Longines, with a square, gold face, Roman numerals, and a second hand.

"Why?" he inquired.

"A whim. I saw it in a shopwindow on Calle Florida and wondered how it would look on your wrist."

She helped him set the correct time, wind it up, and fasten it. Mecha said it looked attractive. It did indeed look extremely attractive on Max's bronzed wrist, with its leather strap and gold buckle. An elegant watch that suited him. "Your hands were made to wear watches like that," she added.

"I don't suppose this is the first time a woman has given you something."

He looked at her blankly, feigning indifference.

"Possibly . . . I don't remember."

"Of course you don't. And I wouldn't forgive you if you did."

There were cafés and bars near the shore, some of which had a seedy ambience by night. Beneath the brim of her cloche hat Mecha studied the men lounging in their shirtsleeves, vests, and caps, sitting at tables in doorways, or on benches in squares, where horse-driven carts and trucks were parked. It was in such places, Max had heard it said in his house years before, that you learned the philosophy of the different races: the melancholy Italians; suspicious Jews; brutish, brutal Germans; and stubborn Spaniards, intoxicated with envy and murderous pride.

"They still step off the boats the way my father did," he said. "Eager to fulfill their dreams. . . . Many fall by the wayside, rotting like those timber boats stranded in the swamp. They begin by sending money to the wives and children they have left behind in Asturias, Calabria, Poland. . . . In the end, life wears them down, and they fade away in the squalor of a tavern or a cheap brothel. Sitting at a table, alone, in front of a bottle that never asks questions."

Mecha was looking at four washerwomen walking toward them carrying enormous baskets of damp laundry, their faces prematurely aged, their hands raw from the soap and scrubbing brushes. Max could have given each of them a name and a story, for those hands and faces, or others identical to them, were part of his childhood.

"The women have a better chance at life, the pretty ones, anyway," he added. "For a while, at least. Before motherhood wears them out, if they are lucky. Or if they are unlucky, depending on how you look at it, and they become the theme of tango songs."

His last comment had made her turn to look at him with renewed interest.

"Are there many prostitutes?"

"Just imagine." Max embraced the surroundings with a sweep of his hand. "A country of immigrants, most of them men. There are organizations that ship women over from Europe. . . . Some specialize in Russians, Romanians, and Poles. They buy them for two or three thousand pesos, and in less than a year make their money back."

He heard Mecha give a dry, humorless laugh.

"How much would they pay for me?"

He didn't reply, and they walked on in silence for a while.

"What do you want from the future, Max?"

"To stay alive as long as possible, I suppose." He shrugged, in earnest. "To have what I need."

"You won't be young and handsome forever. What about your old age?"

"I don't think about it. I have plenty to keep me busy until then."

He gave her a sidelong glance. She was observing everything as she walked, mouth slightly open, almost marveling at the newness of what she saw. Like a hunter at the ready, Max concluded, as if she wanted to imprint each scene indelibly on her memory: the brick and timber houses, with their tin roofs painted red and green bordering a rusty railway track; the honeysuckle peeping out over the patio fences and walls with broken bottles along the top; the plane trees and ceiba trees whose crimson flowers daubed the street with color. She moved languidly, studying each detail with interest, yet as easy in her manner as she had been three hours earlier while strolling naked around Max's room with the nonchalance of a queen in her bedchamber. The patch of sunlight from the window had silhouetted the flowing contours of her astonishingly supple body, casting a golden light on the soft, curly down between her thighs.

"What about you?" Max asked. "You won't be young and beautiful forever either."

"I have money. I had it before I married. . . . It's old money now, at ease with itself."

There had been no hesitation in her reply, which was calm, objective. She underlined her words with a look of disdain. "You'd be surprised how much simpler things become when you have money."

He laughed out loud.

"I think I might have some idea."

"No. I doubt you do."

They stood aside to let an ice vendor pass. He was bent double beneath the weight of the huge, dripping block on his back, cushioned by a scrap of rubber.

"You're right," said Max. "It isn't easy to put oneself in a rich man's shoes."

"Armando and I aren't rich. Simply well-off."

Max pondered the difference. They had paused next to a rail that ran alongside the path, following the Rocha bend in the river. Glancing behind him, he could see that the efficient Petrossi had stationed the car a little farther back.

"Why did you marry?"

She was looking at the boats, the barges, and the gigantic structure of the transporter bridge.

"Armando is a fascinating man . . . When I met him, he was already a successful composer. Life with him promised to be a whirlwind of excitement. Friends, concerts, travels . . . I would undoubtedly have experienced those things sooner or later. But he enabled me to do so much earlier than I expected. To leave home and to embrace life."

"Did you love him?"

"Why do you speak in the past tense?" Mecha went on looking at the bridge. "Anyway, it's a strange question, coming from a man who dances in hotels and on transatlantic liners."

Max touched the sweatband of his hat, which now was dry. He put it back on his head, tipping the brim over his right eye.

"Why me?"

She had been watching his movements, as though studying every detail with interest. Approvingly. Hearing Max's question, her eyes twinkled with amusement.

"I knew you had a scar even before I saw it."

His bewilderment seemed to amuse her, and she suppressed a smile. An hour before, without questions or comments, Mecha had caressed that mark on his skin, pressing her lips to it, licking the drops of perspiration that made his chest glisten just above the scar the bullet had left when seven years ago he had climbed the hillside with his comrades, weaving between the rocks and shrubs as the dawn mist dissolved on that Day of the Dead.

"There are men whose eyes and smiles contain something," Mecha added after a moment, as if he deserved an explanation. "Men who carry 'round an invisible suitcase, filled with heavy things."

Now she was looking at his hat, the knot in his tie, the middle button of his jacket, done up. Appraisingly.

"And also, you're good-looking and easygoing. Devilishly handsome . . ."

He didn't know why she seemed to appreciate that he said nothing.

"I like your coolheadedness, Max," she went on. "So similar to mine, in some ways."

She stood gazing at him for a moment. Spellbound. Completely still. Then she lifted her hand to stroke his chin, apparently indifferent to whether Petrossi could see her from the car.

"Yes," she said finally. "I like the fact that there's no way I can trust you."

She started walking again and Max followed, keeping level with her as he tried to assimilate all she had said. Trying hard to contain his bewilderment. They passed an old man turning the handle of an old Rinaldi barrel organ, which churned out "The Corn Cob" while the horse yoked to the cart released a copious stream of frothy urine onto the cobblestones.

"Shall we go to La Ferroviaria again tomorrow?"

"Certainly. If that's what your husband wants."

Her tone sounded different. Almost frivolous.

"I have seldom seen Armando so excited. . . . Last night, back at the hotel, he could talk of nothing else, and he stayed up very late, in his pajamas, unable to sleep, jotting things down, filling ashtrays, and humming. 'That buffoon Ravel will be eating his bolero, on toast,' he kept saying and chuckling. . . . He is terribly upset about the engagement tonight at the Teatro Colón. The League of Spanish Patriots, or some such, are holding a concert in his honor. And the evening will apparently finish with a tango show at a high-class cabaret called Les Folies Bergère. In full evening dress. Can you imagine anything more dreadful?"

"Will you go with him?"

"Naturally. You don't imagine I would let him go there on his own, with all those perfumed she-wolves on the prowl."

They would meet tomorrow, she added a moment later. If Max had no other plans, they could send the car around to Almirante Brown, at about seven. Then go for a drink, at the Richmond, for example, and dine at a nice place downtown. She had heard about a smart new restaurant called Las Violetas, if she remembered correctly. And another at the top of a tower on Calle Florida, near Pasaje Güemes.

"It isn't necessary." Max had no wish to meet Armando de Troeye on difficult territory or to engage in lengthy conversation with him. "I'll meet you at the Palace and we'll go straight to Barracas. . . . I have things to do downtown."

"It's your turn to tango this time. With me."

"Of course."

They were about to cross the street when they heard a tram bell ring behind them, and they pulled up. It went by at full throttle, the trolley pole sliding below the electric cables slung between posts and buildings, long and green, empty, save for the driver and the uniformed ticket collector, who stared at them from the platform.

"Your life is shrouded in mystery, Max. . . . That scar as well as everything else. Why you went to Paris and why you left."

An awkward topic, he thought. But perhaps she at least had a right to ask. Which she hadn't up until then.

"It's no big secret. You've seen the scar. . . . Someone shot me in Africa."

She didn't bat an eyelid. As though being shot were perfectly normal for a ballroom dancer.

"What were you doing there?"

"I was a soldier for a while, remember?"

"I am sure there are soldiers in lots of places. But why there?"

"I think I already mentioned it to you on the *Cap Polonio*. . . . It was after the slaughter at Annual, in Rif. They wanted revenge for the thousands who were slaughtered."

For a brief moment, Max wondered if it was possible to sum

up in a few sentences complex ideas likes doubt, horror, death, and fear. Clearly not.

"I thought I had killed a man," he said at last, in a neutral tone, "so I enlisted in the Spanish Foreign Legion . . . Then I discovered he wasn't dead, but by then it was too late."

"A fight?"

"Something like that."

"Over a woman?"

"Nothing so romantic. He owed me money."

"How much?"

"Enough for me to stab him with his own knife."

He noticed her eyes gleam. With pleasure, perhaps. Max thought he knew that look from a few hours earlier.

"Why the Foreign Legion?"

He screwed up his eyes, recollecting the harsh sunlight in the streets and squares of Barcelona, afraid of running into a policeman, anxious at his own shadow, and the poster on a wall outside number nine, Prats de Molló: *To those whom life has betrayed, who are out of work, who live aimlessly and without hope: Honor and pride.*

"They paid three pesetas a day," he said briefly. "And a man who changes his identity is safe in the Legion."

Mecha opened her mouth again slightly. Avid as before. Curious.

"That's good. . . . You enlist and you become someone else?"

"Something like that."

"You must have been very young."

"I lied about my age. They didn't seem to care."

"I love the idea. Do they take women?"

Afterward, she wanted to know about the rest of his life, and Max alluded briefly to a few of the steps that led him to the ballroom on the *Cap Polonio*. Oran, the Vieux Port in Marseille, the cheap cabarets in Paris.

"Who was she?"

"She?"

"The lover who taught you how to tango."

"Why do you assume she was a lover and not a dance teacher?"

"Some things are obvious, ways of dancing, for example. . . ."

He remained silent for a while, mulling it over, then he lit a cigarette and spoke a little about Boske. The barest minimum. In Marseille he had met a Hungarian dancer, who had then taken him to Paris. She bought him a tuxedo and they performed as dance partners at Le Lapin Agile and other two-bit establishments. For a while.

"Was she beautiful?"

The tobacco smoke tasted bitter, and Max automatically threw his cigarette into the oily waters of the Riachuelo.

"Yes. For a while."

He refrained from telling her more, although the images rushed back into his mind: Boske's splendid body, her black hair, bobbed in the style of Louise Brooks, her beautiful face smiling beneath straw or felt hats, amid the bustle of the Montparnasse cafés, where, with remarkable naïveté, she insisted class differences no longer existed. Always provocative and passionate in her slang-ridden Marseille accent and her gravelly voice, she was ready for anything. A dancer and occasional model, she would sit on the terrace of Le Dôme or La Closerie des Lilas on one of the wicker chairs in front of a café-crème or a glass of cheap gin, surrounded by American tourists, writers who never wrote, and painters who never painted. "*Je danse et je pose*," she would declare for all to hear, as though peddling her body in search of paintbrushes and fame. She would breakfast at one in the afternoon (she and Max rarely went to bed before dawn) in her favorite place, Chez Rosalie, where she met her Hungarian and Polish friends who supplied her with vials of morphine. Casting a greedy, calculating eye about her for well-dressed men, women in jewelry, expensive fur coats, and luxurious automobiles cruising up and down the boulevard. Just as every night she would watch the customers at the second-rate cabaret where she and Max danced graceful tangos, she in silk and he in a white tie, or clinging Apache tangos, he wearing a striped shirt and she black stockings. Always waiting for the suitable face and the decisive word. For the opportunity that never came.

"And what became of that woman?" Mecha asked.

"She got left behind."

"How far behind?"

He didn't reply. Mecha continued to look at him, admiringly.

"How did you move into high society?"

Very slowly, Max was returning to Buenos Aires. His eyes once again contemplating the streets of La Boca converging on the little square, the banks of the Riachuelo, and the Avellaneda Bridge. Mecha's face peering at him inquisitively, surprised, perhaps, by the tension in his own expression. Max blinked as if the bright daylight bothered him as much as the searing glare of Barcelona, Melilla, Oran, or Marseille. The glare of Buenos Aires stung his eyes, already dazzled by another more somber, ancient light, with Boske sprawled on their disheveled bed, her face to the wall. Her pale, naked back motionless in the gray shadows of a dawn as soiled as life itself. And Max, silently closing the door on that vision, as someone might furtively slide the lid over a casket.

"That isn't difficult in Paris," he replied simply. "The different social classes mingle a lot. People with money frequent low-life bars . . . like you and your husband at La Ferroviaria; only they don't need an excuse."

"I see. I am not quite sure how to take that."

"I had a friend in Africa," he went on, ignoring her protest. "I mentioned him to you on the boat as well."

"I remember. The Russian aristocrat with the long name. You told me he died."

Max nodded, almost relieved. It was easier for him to talk about that than about Boske, half-naked in the misty morning on Rue de

Furstenberg, about his last glimpse of the syringe, the empty vials, the glasses, bottles, and leftover food on the table, the dim half-light so close to remorse. That Russian friend, he said, had claimed he was an officer in the Tsar's army. He fought with the White Guard until the retreat at Crimea, and from there he went to Spain, where he enlisted in the Legion after an argument over a wager. He was a peculiar fellow: condescending, debonair, popular with the ladies. He had taught Max good manners, provided him with the first basic veneer (how to knot a tie, fold a pocket handkerchief, explaining which hors d'oeuvres, ranging from anchovies to caviar, should accompany a glass of iced vodka). It amused him, he once remarked, to transform a bit of cannon fodder into something that could pass for a gentleman.

"He had relatives exiled in Paris, where some made a living as hotel porters or taxi drivers. Others had managed to salvage their money, among them a cousin who owned a few tango cabarets. One day, I went to see his cousin, he hired me, and things improved. . . . I was able to buy the right clothes, to live reasonably well, and to travel a bit."

"And what happened to your Russian friend? . . . How did he die?"

This time Max's memories weren't somber. At least not in the conventional sense. His mouth twisted in a compassionate grimace as he thought of the last time he had seen Second Lieutenant Dolgoruki-Bragation, holed up in the most expensive room at the Tauima brothel with three whores and a bottle of brandy, whence, having finished with one then the others, he embarked upon life's final adventure.

"He was bored. He shot himself because he was bored."

—⚬—

Max is sitting at a table outside the Bar Ercolano, beneath the palm trees and the clock tower in Piazza Tasso, with his glasses on to read the newspapers. It is midmorning, the busiest time in the old quarter, and the occasional noise of a car exhaust pipe makes him look up from his reading. No one there today would think the tourist season was in its death throes: the tables outside Il Fauno, opposite, are all taken up by people enjoying a lunchtime drink; at the entrance to Via San Cesareo the stalls selling fish, fruit, and vegetables are crowded; and noisy swarms of Fiats, Vespas, and Lambrettas drive up and down Corso Italia. The only thing not moving are the horse-drawn carriages waiting for tourists, while their bored drivers stand in groups beneath the marble statue of the poet Torquato Tasso, chatting and smoking as they watch the women go by.

Il Mattino features a long article about the Keller-Sokolov contest, and the various matches they have played. The last ended in a draw, and apparently that puts the Russian ahead. According to the explanation Lambertucci and Captain Tedesco gave Max, each game won is worth a point, and when the opponents draw, they both mark up half a point. As things stand, Sokolov has two and half points to Keller's one and a half. An indecisive lead, the specialist reporters agree. Max has spent a while reading all this with great interest, although skipping the technical details cloaked in strange terms like the *Spanish Gambit*, the *Petrosian System*, and the *Nimzo Indian Defense*.

The newspapers all highlight the tension surrounding the contest, not so much due to the fifty thousand dollars the winner will receive but rather the political and diplomatic situation. According to what Max has just read, the Russians have held on to the international chess crown for the past twenty years, the title of world champion having been won by successive grand masters from the Soviet Union. Since the Communist Revolution, the game has become a national sport (fifty million players out of a population of two hundred-odd million, according to one of the articles), and a valuable propaganda tool beyond the Iron Curtain, to the point where every chess competition enjoys the state's full backing. As a result, according to one of the journalists, Moscow is throwing all its resources into the Campanella Chess Contest, since Jorge Keller in five months' time will be challenging Sokolov for the world title (informal capitalist heterodoxy versus rigorous Soviet orthodoxy), in what, after the thrilling prologue in Sorrento, promises to be the chess contest of the century.

Max takes another sip of Negroni and leafs through the newspaper, skimming the headlines: the Beatles plan to break up, French rock star Johnny Hallyday attempts suicide, long hair and short skirts revolutionize England. . . . The international political section refers to other revolutions: the Red Guards continue their attack on Peking, in America colored people are demanding civil rights, and a group of mercenaries is detained while attempting to intervene in Katanga. On the page, between a headline about the launch of another Gemini space mission ("USA Heads Race to Moon") and an advertisement for gasoline ("Put a tiger in your tank"), is a black-and-white image of a burly American GI, his back to the photographer, giving a piggyback ride to a little Vietnamese boy, who has turned his head and is staring distrustfully at the camera.

An Alfa Romeo Giulia goes by with the windows down, and for an instant Max thinks he recognizes the tune playing on the car radio. Looking up from the photograph of the GI and the boy (it has brought back memories of other soldiers and children, forty-five years ago), he gazes with a puzzled air at the car as it heads toward the yellow-and-white façade of Santa Maria del Carmine at the far end of the Corso Italia. Still absorbed by the newspaper, his brain takes a few seconds to identify the music his ear has already registered: the familiar strains of the popular classic, in an arrangement for orchestra with drums and electric guitar, among others, commonly known for the last forty years as the Old School Tango.

When Max halted midstep to perform the *corte*, Mecha looked into his eyes for a moment, before boldly pressing herself up against him, snaking this way and that, and sliding her thigh up and down his leg, firmly thrust forward. He stoically resisted the feel of her flesh beneath her thin crepe dress, their extraordinary intimacy, while everyone in La Ferroviaria (a dozen pairs of eyes, both male and female) seemed fixed upon them. Then Max stepped sideways, and she instantly followed with effortless grace.

"That's what I like," she whispered. "Slow and steady, don't let them think you're afraid of me."

Max placed his lips close to her right ear. Enjoying the game, regardless of the risks.

"You're quite a woman," he said.

"You ought to know."

Her proximity, the soft scent of perfume lingering on her skin, the tiny beads of sweat on her upper lip and at the roots of her hair, reawakened the desire freshly imprinted on his memory of warm, languid flesh, the aroma of sated sex and a woman's perspiration, as he felt her skin grow moist once more, the thin fabric of her dress swaying in time to the tango. It was late and the warehouse was all but empty. The three-man band was playing "Chiqué," to which only two other couples were tangoing halfheartedly, like tramcars on slow tracks: a small, chubby woman accompanied by a youth wearing a jacket and collarless shirt with no tie, and the Slavic-looking woman Max had danced with on the previous occasion. She was wearing the same floral blouse and moving with a bored expression in the arms of a fellow in a vest and shirtsleeves who could have been a docker. Occasionally, as they danced, the couples drew near to each other, and for a second the woman's blue eyes met those of Max. Indifferent.

"Your husband is drinking too much," Max said to Mecha.

"Don't interfere."

He looked nervously at the pearls she was wearing that evening, which touched the neckline of her black knee-length dress. Then, with equal unease (wearing jewelry or drinking to excess in a place like La Ferroviaria wasn't a good idea), he glanced over at the table laden with bottles, glasses, and brimming ashtrays, where Armando de Troeye sat smoking and topping up his glass with gin and soda, accompanied by Juan Rebenque, who two days before had danced a tango with his wife. Soon after they arrived, after watching them for a while, Rebenque had approached their table, his criollo mustache and black, slicked-back hair giving him a serious air, while his dark eyes flashed dangerously beneath the brim of his hat, which he never once took off. He took his time strolling over, a half-smoked cigar in the corner of his mouth, walking with that slow, rolling gait typical of the old toughs, one hand in his right pocket, knife bulging under his snug jacket with satin trim. He asked whether he might join the lady and the two gentlemen, while ordering a fresh bottle of gin and a full soda siphon from the waitress, with the authority of someone accustomed to not paying the bill. It was on him, if they had no objections, he said, looking more at Max than at Armando.

The one-eyed squeezebox player and his fellow musicians took a break, and, encouraged by de Troeye, drew their chairs around the table as Mecha and Max returned to their seats. The old pianola took up the musical baton, churning out a couple of unrecognizable tangos. After a long round of drinks and conversation, the musicians went back to their instruments, launching into "Wild Nights." Rebenque, rakishly tipping the brim of his hat even farther, suggested to Mecha they dance together. She refused, claiming she was tired, and although the *compadrón*'s smile remained impassive, he looked daggers at Max, as though he were to blame for the snub. Rebenque doffed his hat casually, rose to his feet, and went over to the blonde dancer, who stood up with a sigh, and, placing her arm over his right shoulder, started to dance resignedly. Rebenque moved in time with the music, enjoying himself, manly and serious, holding his lighted cigar behind his back, while his free hand guided his partner with apparent ease. He paused for a moment after each *corte*, then continued to sketch tangled figures on the floor, before halting his forward and backward movements once more, only to begin again. Meanwhile, the woman acquiesced with a look of apathy on her face (during one *corte*, her overly short skirt rode up to reveal almost the whole of her thigh), consenting submissively to each movement, each flourish, each hold imposed by the man.

"What do you think of her?" Mecha asked Max.

"I don't know . . . Vulgar. Jaded."

"Perhaps she is controlled by one of those shady organizations you told me about. . . . Possibly they lured her over from Russia or somewhere, with false promises."

"The white slave trade," Armando de Troeye said in a faltering voice, as he raised yet another gin to his lips with relish. The idea seemed to amuse him.

Max glanced at Mecha to see if she had been serious. After a moment's reflection he decided she hadn't.

"She looks more like she's from around here," Max replied. "And going nowhere fast."

"Vulgar, yes, but pretty," de Troeye piped up again, sniggering unpleasantly. His eyes were becoming bleary from too much drink, Max noticed.

Mecha continued gazing at the blonde woman. She was following her partner's catlike movements across the creaking floor, her body pressed against his.

"Do you like her, Max?" she asked suddenly.

Max took his time stubbing out his cigarette in the ashtray. The conversation was starting to make him ill at ease.

"She's not bad," he admitted.

"How dismissive. And yet the other night you seemed to enjoy dancing with her."

Max contemplated the smudge of lipstick on the rim of Mecha's glass, and on the ivory cigarette holder next to the smoky ashtray. He could feel the taste of that deep red in his own mouth, which had removed all trace of it on Mecha's lips as he kissed, licked, and bit her during their violent embrace the day before at the Caboto boardinghouse. Only at the end was there any hint of tenderness, when, with a final shudder, she had whispered in his ear "out, please," and he, exhausted and on the brink, had obeyed, slowly pulling out, his perspiring body pressed against hers as he gently spilled himself onto her smooth, inviting stomach.

"Do you mean she dances the tango well?" he commented, his thoughts returning to La Ferroviaria.

"She has a good body," declared de Troeye, who was watching the dancer through the glass he was holding up shakily.

"Like mine?"

Mecha had turned toward Max, half-smiling. She was directing the question at him, at once playful and supercilious. As though her husband weren't there. Or, Max concluded uneasily, precisely because he was.

"She's a different sort," Max replied, as cautiously as if he were advancing through the mist at Taxuda, bayonet at the ready.

"That goes without saying," Mecha retorted.

Max shot Armando a sidelong glance wondering how this would end (a few hours ago, the two men had spontaneously begun using the informal *tu* with each other, at de Troeye's instigation). But de Troeye only seemed interested in his gin and soda, which he had all but sunk his nose into.

"You're taller," he declared clicking his tongue. "Isn't she, Max? . . . And skinnier."

"Thank you, Armando," she said. "For being so precise."

She lifted her glass in an exaggeratedly polite toast to her husband that was bordering on the grotesque, and brimming with innuendos Max couldn't decipher. Then she fell silent. Max noticed that de Troeye would occasionally pause and stare into space, the smoke from his cigarette making him wince, apparently absorbed by musical modulations only he could hear, skillfully tapping out notes and chords on the table in a way that scarcely evoked the gestures of a man the worse for drink. Wondering how inebriated he actually was, and to what extent he merely gave that impression, Max looked at Mecha, and then at Rebenque and the blonde woman. The music had stopped, and the man had turned his back on his tango partner and was sauntering toward them, in his habitual way.

"We should go," said Max.

Between two sips, de Troeye emerged from his stupor to approve the idea.

"To another bar?"

"To bed. I imagine your tango is almost ready. . . . La Ferroviaria has nothing more to offer."

Armando protested. Rebenque, who had sat between him and Mecha, was looking at the three of them with a smile so artificial it looked as it had been painted on his face, as he tried to follow their conversation. He seemed aggrieved, perhaps because no one had praised his masterful tango with the blonde woman.

"And what about me, Max?" asked Mecha.

He turned toward her, awkwardly. Her lips were parted slightly, and her eyes flashed defiantly. He knew that in days gone by he would have been capable of killing in cold blood to have her to himself. To quell his own urgency by stripping off her dress, almost soaked through, which in the warm, smoke-filled air clung to her body like a dark skin.

"Perhaps I am not ready for bed yet," she insisted.

"We could go to La Boca," suggested de Troeye jovially, draining his gin and soda with the air of someone coming back from a distant place. "And look for something to keep us up."

"All right," she said, rising to her feet and picking her shawl up from the back of the chair, while her husband took out his wallet. "Let's take the vulgar, pretty blonde with us."

"That isn't a good idea," Max protested.

Mecha and he tried to outstare one another. What the hell are you thinking, was his unspoken question. Her disdain was response enough. Ask for more cards, or throw in your hand, her expression implied. Depending on your curiosity or your courage. You know the prize.

"On the contrary." De Troeye was counting out ten-peso notes with faltering fingers. "Inviting the young lady along is a . . . fantastic idea."

Rebenque offered to escort the dancer, as there was room for everyone in the gentlemen's big automobile, he said. He knew a good place in La Boca. Casa Margot. The best ravioli in Buenos Aires.

"Ravioli?" said de Troeye, bewildered.

"Cocaine," Max translated.

"That's right," declared Rebenque, pointedly. "You can stay awake as long as you like."

He spoke with his eye on Mecha and Max rather than her husband, as though he knew instinctively who his real opponent was. For his part, Max was wary of the ruffian's static smile, the overbearing way he called over the blonde woman (he told them her name was Melina, and she was of Polish descent), and his surreptitious glance at the wallet Armando de Troeye slipped back into his inside jacket pocket after extracting a fifty, which, together with a generous tip, he left crumpled on the table.

"Too many people," Max murmured, putting on his hat.

Rebenque must have overheard him, for he gave Max a slow, indignant smile. Sharp as a razor.

"Do you know the neighborhood, my friend?"

Max couldn't help noticing the subtle change in the way Rebenque addressed him. No longer gentleman but friend. It was clear the night had just begun.

"Somewhat," he replied. "I lived three blocks from here. A long time ago."

The other man looked Max up and down, paying special attention to his pristine cuffs. His immaculate tie.

"Yet you talk like a Spaniard."

"I worked hard to get there."

They continued studying each other in silence for a moment, with mutual distrust, while Rebenque flicked the last bit of ash from his cigar with the elongated nail on his little finger. Some situations shouldn't be hurried. A lesson both men had learned on the same streets. Max figured Rebenque must be ten or twelve years older than him. Probably one of the local youths he had seen as a little boy in a gray smock, with a satchel full of books on his back, envying their freedom to loiter outside pool halls, hitch free rides on the backs of the Southern Electricity Company trams, lie in wait like bandits for the carts selling Aguila chocolate, and filch croissants from the counter at the Mortero bakery.

"In which street, my friend?"

"Vieytes. Opposite the 105 tram stop."

"Well, I'll be damned," the other man declared. "Almost neighbors."

The blonde woman took his arm, her breasts thrust forward beneath her half-unbuttoned blouse. She wore a cheap-looking imitation Manila shawl draped over her shoulders, and was gaping at Max and the de Troeyes with renewed interest, arching her plucked eyebrows, reduced to a thin, black pencil line. It was obvious that the prospect of leaving La Ferroviaria for a while appealed to her more than the monotony of tangos at twenty cents a dance.

"Allonzenfanz," de Troeye declared cheerfully, seizing his hat and cane and making his way toward the door, staggering from the effects of alcohol.

As they stepped outside, Petrossi drove the Pierce-Arrow up and they all piled into the back. De Troeye sat on the backseat flanked by Mecha and Melina, with Max and Rebenque on the jump seats opposite. By then, Melina had understood the situation, realized who was paying for the party, and obediently followed the silent instructions Rebenque's darting eyes flashed at her through the gloom. Max observed all this, tense as a coiled spring, calculating the pros and cons, foreseeing the problems they might encounter, and the best way to escape from that dangerous territory when the time came, relatively unscathed and without a knife in the groin. As everyone from that neighborhood knew, no tourniquet could stanch a bleeding femoral artery.

—⁂—

Just after ten o'clock at night the game is adjourned. It is dark outside, and in the picture windows of the Hotel Vittoria images of the room reflected in the glass are superimposed on the lights from the villas and hotels along Sorrento's cliff top. Sitting in the audience, Max gazes at the big wooden panel reproducing the game, including the last move Sokolov made before the referee approached the table. The Russian scribbled something on his score sheet, then rose to leave the room while Keller remained behind studying the chessboard. After a while, Keller also scribbled something on his score sheet, but without moving any of his pieces, and slipped both score sheets into the same envelope, which he sealed before handing it to the referee.

And now, as Keller vanishes through a side door, the audience breaks its silence with murmurs and applause. Max stands up and glances about, puzzled, trying to determine what has just happened. He watches from a distance as Mecha Inzunza, who has been sitting in the front row between Irina Jasenovic and the burly grand master Karapetian, gets up to follow them and her son.

Max goes out into the now-noisy corridor and wanders among

the fans, listening to comments about the game, the fifth in the Campanella Chess Contest. The press office is in a small side room, and as he walks past the doorway, Max hears an Italian radio journalist relaying the game over the telephone.

"Keller seemed to be playing kamikaze chess with his black bishop move. . . . It wasn't the sacrifice of his knight that was so remarkable, but the bold advance of his bishop across a board fraught with danger. It was a deadly blow, and only Sokolov's presence of mind saved him. The Soviet Wall blocked the attack and instantly proposed a *nichiá*—a draw . . . Keller refused, and the game is set to resume tomorrow."

In another, smaller room, which appears to be out of bounds to the public, a crowd of eager fans has gathered around the open door. Inside, Max sees Keller poring over a chessboard with Karapetian, the young Jasenovic, the referee, and a handful of others, seemingly engaged in a reconstruction or breakdown of the game. Max is surprised at the difference between how long it takes for them to move during the actual game, and the speed with which Keller, Karapetian, and the girl are almost banging the pieces around the board, making and unmaking moves, considering new ones, as they discuss the merits of this or that.

"It's called a postmortem," says Mecha. He turns around to find her standing beside him, in the doorway. He didn't notice her approach.

"It sounds funereal."

She peers into the room, pensive. As is her custom in Sorrento (he knows this wasn't always the case), she dresses in a way that is unfashionable among women of any age. She is now wearing a dark skirt and loafers, and her hands remain in the pockets of an attractive, and no doubt equally expensive suede jacket. The jacket alone, Max calculates, must have cost at least two hundred thousand lire.

"It is, sometimes," she says. "Especially when Jorge loses a game.

They analyze his moves to see if he made the right ones or if there were better variations."

The clatter of pieces being moved swiftly around the board continues and occasionally they hear laughter as Keller makes a comment or joke. Then the clatter resumes, scarcely pausing even when a piece accidentally falls on the floor and the player picks it up and places it back on the board.

"I can't believe how fast they are playing."

She nods, contented. Or perhaps proud, in her quiet way. In common with all grand masters of his caliber, she explains, Jorge Keller can remember all the moves in the match, as well as all the possible variants. In fact, he is capable of reproducing from memory every game he has ever played. And most of those his opponent has played.

"At the moment, he is analyzing his moves, and those of Sokolov," she adds. "But this is for the gallery, friends, and journalists. Later, he will carry out a far more serious and complex analysis with Emil and Irina, behind closed doors."

She pauses, tilting her head slightly to one side as she contemplates her son.

"He is worried," she adds, in a different tone.

Max glances at Jorge Keller, and then at her.

"He doesn't look it," he says at last.

"He is puzzled by his opponent anticipating what he was planning with his bishop."

"I heard someone mention that just now. Something about a kamikaze bishop."

"Oh, well, people expect that from Jorge. The supposed mark of a genius . . . In fact, the move was carefully planned. He and his assistants have been preparing it for some time, in case a favorable situation arose . . . exploiting what might be a weakness in Sokolov's game when confronted with the Marshall gambit."

"I am afraid I know nothing about this Marshall fellow," Max confessed.

"What I mean is that even world champions have their weak points. It is the analysts' job to help their player discover and use them to their own advantage."

The glass door of a small adjoining room opens and the Russians appear. Two assistants lead the way, followed by the champion escorted by a dozen or so others. Behind them is a table and a jumbled chess set. Doubtless they have just carried out their own postmortem, although unlike Keller's theirs has taken place behind closed doors, witnessed only by a handful of their own journalists, now making their way to the pressroom. Sokolov, holding a lighted cigarette, passes within a few feet of Max, and his watery blue eyes meet those of his opponent's mother, to whom he directs a polite nod.

"The Russian players enjoy the advantage of being funded by their federation and supported by the state apparatus," explains Mecha. "You see that tubby fellow in the gray jacket? He is the culture and sports attaché at the Soviet embassy in Rome. . . . That one is the grand master Kolishkin, president of the Soviet Chess Federation. The tall, fair-haired man is Rostov, who almost became world champion and is now one of Sokolov's. . . . And you can be sure there are at least two KGB agents in the group."

They watch the Russians disappear down the corridor toward the foyer, headed for their delegation's apartment house overlooking the hotel gardens.

"Western players, on the other hand," she goes on, "need to win or to find some other activity that enables them to keep playing. . . . Jorge has been lucky."

"Undoubtedly. He has you."

"Well . . . that's one way of putting it."

She is still looking toward the corridor, apparently unsure about whether to add something or not. At last she turns to Max and smiles with a distracted, pensive air.

"What's the matter?" he asks.

"Nothing, I suppose. The usual in these situations."

"You look worried."

She hesitates a moment longer. At last, she makes a vague gesture with her slender, graceful hands, flecked with age spots.

"Just now, when Jorge came out, he said, 'Something isn't right.' And I didn't like the way he said it . . . or the way he looked at me."

"Well, he doesn't seem at all worried to me."

"That's the impression he gives, and wants to give. Friendly and relaxed, as you can see. As if all this took hardly any effort, when in fact you can't imagine how much effort, how many hours of study go into it. The exhausting pressure."

Her face looks weary, as if the pressure exhausts her, too.

"Come on. Let's get some fresh air."

They head down the corridor and out onto the terrace, where most of the tables are full. Beyond the balustrade, above the glow of the lantern, the dark Bay of Naples is ringed with distant, flickering lights. Max nods at the headwaiter, who seats them at a free table. Then an obsequious waiter appears out of nowhere and Max orders a couple of champagne cocktails.

"What happened today? . . . Why was the game adjourned?"

"Because they ran out of time. Each player has forty moves, or two and a half hours of play. When one of them uses up their allotted time or their forty moves, the game is adjourned until the next day."

Max leans over the table to light the cigarette she has just placed in her mouth. Afterward, he crosses his legs, trying to preserve the crease in his trousers, an instinctive habit from the old days, when an elegant appearance was still one of the tools of his trade.

"I don't understand what the sealed envelopes are about."

"Before retiring, Sokolov noted down the position of the pieces on the board in order to reproduce it tomorrow. It is Jorge's turn to move, and so, after deciding what move to make, he noted it down and gave it to the referee in a sealed envelope. Tomorrow, the referee will open the envelope, carry out Jorge's move for him on the board, set the clock in motion, and the game will recommence."

"So then it will the Russian's turn."

"Precisely."

"I expect he will have a lot to think about tonight."

"They all will," Mecha replies. "When a game is adjourned, the sealed move becomes a problem for both players. One tries to second-guess what move he has to confront, while the other wants to establish whether what he noted down was the best possible move, whether his opponent will have figured it out, and if so, will he have come up with a dangerous countermove.

"That means," she concludes, "dinner, breakfast, and lunch with a pocket chessboard next to you, working for hours on end with your assistants, thinking about it in the shower, while you brush your teeth, when you wake up in the middle of the night. . . . The chess player's worst headache is an adjourned game."

"Like ours," Max says.

Ignoring the ashtray as usual, Mecha lets the ash drop onto the floor before lifting her cigarette to her lips. As occurs whenever the light is muted, her skin appears youthful, her face radiant. Her honey-colored eyes, the same ones Max remembers, are gazing intently into his.

"Yes, in a way," she replies. "That was an adjourned game as well . . . in two parts."

In three, Max thinks. Another one is under way. But he doesn't say so.

—⟋⟍—

When the automobile came to a halt on the corner of Garibaldi and Pedro de Mendoza, a sliver of moon was piercing the night sky, competing with the glow of a street lamp shining through a tangle of branches. As he stepped out of the car, Max moved discreetly closer to Mecha, restraining her by the arm while he undid the clasp of her pearl necklace. He let it fall into his free hand before slipping it into his jacket pocket. Amid the shadows and the electric light shining in the distance, he saw her eyes open wide with surprise, and placed two fingers on her lips to silence the words she was about to utter. Then, while the others started to walk away from the car, he went up to the open window.

"Look after this," he said in a low voice.

Petrossi took the necklace without a comment. Max could only just make out his face, dimmed beneath the peak of his cap, but he thought he glimpsed a flash of complicity.

"Can you lend me your pistol?"

"Of course."

The chauffeur opened the glove compartment and placed a small, compact Browning in Max's hand, its nickel-plated barrel glinting for an instant in the dark.

"Thanks."

Max caught up with the others, ignoring the inquiring look Mecha gave him as he rejoined the group.

"Clever boy," she whispered.

As she spoke, she slipped her arm through his with perfect ease. Two steps in front of them, Rebenque was extolling the virtues of Squibb ether, available over the counter. It was heavenly, he maintained, when poured into a small glass and inhaled between drinks. Although nothing compared with Margot's raviolis. He gave a knowing laugh, now that they were all best friends. Unless, of course, the gentlemen preferred something a bit stronger.

"How much stronger?" de Troeye wanted to know.

"Opium, my friend. Or hashish, if you prefer. Morphine even . . . There's something for everyone."

And so they crossed the street, stepping gingerly over the abandoned railway tracks thick with weeds. Max could feel the reassuring weight of the gun in his pocket as he stared at Rebenque's back, and at de Troeye walking beside him, as casually as if he were strolling down Calle Florida, hat tipped back over his head, arm in arm with the blonde woman, her heels clacking. Finally they arrived at Casa Margot—a dilapidated building with an air of faded opulence next to a tiny restaurant, closed at that time of night. Above the entrance clothes were hanging on a line and the ground was strewn with prawn shells and other detritus. There was a smell of dampness, of fish bones, fish heads, and stale biscuits, as well as the swampy waters of the Riachuelo, with its tar and rusty anchors.

"La Boca's finest," Rebenque said, and Max realized he was the only one to detect the note of irony.

Once inside, everything happened without any unnecessary formalities. The establishment was a former brothel, now an opium den. As for Margot, she was a middle-aged woman of ample proportions and dyed copper-colored hair. After Rebenque whispered a few words in her ear, she bent over backward to appear courteous and accommodating. Three incongruous portraits of former Argentine rulers hung in the entrance, Max noticed, as though the previous occupants, catering to a more select clientele, had attempted to lend the bordello an air of decorum. But that was the only concession to respectability. The hallway opened out into a dark, smoky room illuminated by old-fashioned oil lamps whose fumes tainted the air. The smell of kerosene mixed with Bufach insecticide, tobacco, and hashish smoke permeated the room, along with the perspiration of half a dozen couples (some exclusively male), dancing in a slow embrace, oblivious to the music playing on the Victrola. This in turn was operated by a young Chinese man with the pointed sideburns of a screen villain, who changed the records and turned the handle. Casa Margot, Max concluded, confirming his worst fears, was a place where, at the first sign of trouble, knifes and razors would be whipped out of vests, corsets, trousers, or even shoes.

"Marvelously authentic," de Troeye said approvingly.

Mecha also seemed pleased with the place. She was studying

everything with a vague smile, eyes shining, mouth slightly open, as though breathing in that atmosphere stimulated her senses. Occasionally her eyes met those of Max, and revealed a mixture of excitement, appreciation, and promises. At such moments, Max's desire became more urgent and physical, eclipsing his anxieties about where they were and with whom. His eyes lingered pleasurably on Mecha's hips, right in front of him, as Margot led the group upstairs to a room with Turkish-style furnishings, including two green oil lamps on a low table, carpets with cigarette burns, and two large divans. A burly waiter with the air of a circus strongman brought in two bottles of alleged champagne, and two bundles of cigarettes, while the company installed themselves on the divans. All except for Rebenque, who left with Margot: to fetch food for the canaries, he said with a grin. By then Max had reached a decision, and he walked out into the corridor to wait for Rebenque, listening to the strains of "The Way to the Workshop" drifting up the stairway from the gramophone below. After a while, Rebenque reappeared carrying hashish cigarettes and six little bags, containing half-gram doses carefully folded in grease paper.

"I have a favor to ask," said Max. "Man to man."

The ruffian looked at him with sudden mistrust, trying to guess his intentions. His smile, ever-present beneath his criollo mustache, froze on his lips.

"I've been with the lady for a while," Max went on, without batting an eyelid. "And her husband likes Melina."

"So?"

"So, five is an uneven number."

Rebenque appeared to reflect for a moment about even and uneven numbers.

"Hey, my friend," he said at last. "Do you take me for a fool?"

Max was unperturbed by his brusque manner. So far. For the moment, they were simply two street dogs, one more dapper than the other, sniffing each other in an alleyway. They were agreed on that.

"It will all be paid for," he added, stressing the word *all* as he motioned toward the half-gram packages and the hashish. "This, and the other. Whatever it takes."

"The husband is a stupid Spaniard," said Rebenque, as though sharing his thoughts. "Did you see those boots? He has more dough than brains and dresses like a Frenchy."

"He'll go back to his hotel with an empty wallet. You have my word."

The last sentence seemed to please Rebenque, who looked at Max with renewed interest. In Barracas and La Boca, giving your word was something everyone understood. And people kept it more there than in Palermo or Belgrano.

"What about the lady's necklace?" the other man persisted, fingering the white scarf he wore in place of a tie. "All of a sudden she isn't wearing it."

"Perhaps she lost it. But I don't think that comes into the equation. It's a separate matter."

The ruffian went on looking him straight in the eye, still with a cold smile.

"Melina is an expensive dame. . . . Thirty pesos a night," he said with a Buenos Aires drawl, as if the thought of money thickened his accent. "A real dame."

"Of course. But don't worry. You'll be compensated."

Rebenque touched the brim of his hat, tipping it back slightly, and reached for the cigar stub tucked behind his ear. He continued to look at Max, broodingly.

"You have my word," repeated Max.

Rebenque leaned over without saying anything. He struck a match on the sole of his shoe and studied Max once more through the first puff of smoke. Max slid one hand into his trouser pocket, just below the bulk of the Browning.

"Why not have a drink downstairs?" he suggested. "Listen to some nice music and smoke a good cigar. And we'll see you later."

Rebenque was looking at his concealed hand. Or perhaps he had noticed the bulge of the pistol.

"I'm a bit short on cash, my friend. Why don't you give me something on account."

Max slowly withdrew his hand from his pocket. Ninety pesos. That was all he had left, besides the four fifty-peso notes hidden behind the mirror in his room at the boardinghouse. Rebenque pocketed the money without counting it, and in exchange handed Max the six bags of cocaine. Three pesos each, he said coolly. The hashish is on the house. They would settle up later.

"Heavy on the bicarbonate?" Max asked, looking at the cocaine.

"No more than usual." The ruffian tapped his nose with the long nail on his little finger. "But it goes in nice and smooth, like butter."

—m—

"Let Milena kiss you, Max."

Max shook his head. He was standing, jacket buttoned up, leaning against the wall between one of the divans and the open window overlooking the dark street. The fragrant smoke from the hashish drifting upward before dissolving into loose spirals made his eyes sting. He had only taken one small puff of the cigarette, which was burning down between his fingers.

"I would prefer it if she kissed your husband. She likes him more."

"That's fine by me." Armando de Troeye chuckled, draining the champagne glass he was holding to his lips.

De Troeye was sprawled on the other divan in waistcoat and shirtsleeves, cuffs rolled up over his wrists, tie pulled loose, jacket in a heap on the floor. The shades on the kerosene lamps shrouded the room in a dull, greenish light, giving the two women's skin an iridescent, oily sheen. Mecha was sitting next to her husband, leaning back languidly on the fake damask cushions, arms bare, legs crossed. She had kicked off her shoes, and from time to time would raise her hashish cigarette to her lips, inhaling deeply.

"Go on, kiss him. Kiss my man."

Melina was standing between the two divans. She had just performed a clumsy dance, supposedly in time to the music coming from downstairs, barely audible through the closed door. She was barefoot, light-headed from the hashish, her full breasts swinging beneath her unbuttoned blouse. Her black silk stockings and underwear lay scrunched up on the carpet, and after finishing her vulgar, silent dance, she was still holding her tight skirt halfway up her thighs.

"Kiss him," Mecha insisted. "On the mouth."

"Not on the mouth," Melina protested.

"Either do it or get out."

De Troeye laughed as Melina approached him, brushing a lock of blonde hair from her face as she climbed onto the divan, sat astride him, and kissed him on the mouth. In order to do so in that position, she had to hike up her skirt even farther, and the oily, green light of the kerosene lamp slid over her skin, and along her naked legs.

"You were right, Max," de Troeye said, cynically. "She does like me more."

He had slipped a hand under her blouse and was fondling a breast. Thanks to the two sachets already lying empty on the low, oriental table, de Troeye seemed to have sobered up, despite all the alcohol he must have had in his system. It only showed, Max observed with almost professional curiosity, in his slightly lumbering movements, and the way he paused midsentence, looking for a word.

"Are you sure you don't want to try?" de Troeye asked.

Max gave an evasive smile, composed yet cautious.

"Later, perhaps."

Mecha was silent, the lighted cigarette smoking between her lips, as she swung one of her legs back and forth. Max realized she wasn't looking at Melina or de Troeye, but at him. Her face was expressionless, as though the scene between her husband and the other woman meant nothing to her, or she had brought it about for his benefit. Merely so she could watch him while it was taking place.

"Why wait?" she declared all at once.

Slowly, she rose to her feet, smoothing her dress almost ceremoniously, the hashish cigarette still in her mouth; seizing Melina by the shoulders, she forced her to stand up, shepherding her away from her husband, and toward Max. Melina let herself be led, meek as a lamb, her unbuttoned blouse wet with perspiration and sticking to her pendulous breasts.

"Pretty and vulgar," said Mecha, looking straight at Max.

"I couldn't give a shit," he replied, almost tenderly.

This was the first time he had uttered a swear word in front of the de Troeyes. She held his gaze for a moment, both hands on Melina's shoulders, before thrusting her gently forward until her damp, warm chest was pressing against Max.

"Be good to him," Mecha whispered in the woman's ear. "He's a nice, local boy. . . . And a marvelous dancer."

With a dazed expression, Melina clumsily sought out Max's lips, but he turned his head away in disgust. He had thrown his cigarette out the window and was looking back at Mecha, from close up, her eyes only half visible against the greenish glow of the lamps. She seemed to be staring at him with an almost mechanical coldness, he thought. An intense, almost clinical interest. Meanwhile, the other woman had unbuttoned Max's jacket and vest, and was busy undoing his suspenders and the top button of his trousers.

"A disturbingly nice boy," Mecha added, mysteriously.

She pressed down on Melina's shoulders, forcing her to kneel in front of Max, her face level with his sex. Just then, de Troeye's voice rang out behind the two women: "What about me, damn it?"

Rarely had Max witnessed the level of contempt that made Mecha's eyes flash, before she turned to her husband, staring at him without uttering a word. I hope no woman ever looks at me like that, he said to himself quickly. For his part, de Troeye shrugged, resigned to the role of onlooker, and topped up his glass with champagne, before draining it in one go and opening another sachet of cocaine. By then, Mecha had turned back toward Max, and while Melina, still kneeling submissively, took hold of the object of the exercise with a distinct lack of enthusiasm (at least her tongue is moist and warm, Max reflected), Mecha dropped her cigarette on the carpet and drew her lips close to those of Max, barely touching them, while her eyes seemed to take on the greenish tinge of the kerosene lamp. She stood like that for a while, gazing at him from up close, her head and neck silhouetted against the gloom, her mouth less than an inch from his, while his senses became immersed in her trembling breath, the closeness of her soft, slender frame, the lingering aroma of hashish, perfume, and perspiration on her skin. It was that, and not Melina's awkward performance that quickened his desire, and when his manhood finally grew firm, pushing out through his clothes, Mecha, who appeared to have been waiting for that moment, thrust the blonde woman aside, and greedily latched onto Max's mouth, dragging him over to the divan, while behind them, her husband's gleeful laughter rang out.

—◦◦◦—

"Surely you aren't leaving already," said Juan Rebenque. "So soon."

His sinister smile hovered between them and the door, oozing hostility. He was standing in the middle of the corridor, a defiant expression on his face, hat tilted forward, hands in his trouser pockets. Every now and then, he would stare down at his shoes, as though making sure they were properly shined for the occasion.

Max, who had been prepared for this, glanced at the bulge on the left side of the man's jacket. Then he turned to de Troeye.

"How much money do you have on you?" he asked in a low voice.

De Troeye's face showed the ravages of the evening: bloodshot eyes, stubble beginning to appear on his chin, tie crooked. Melina had released his arm, and was leaning against the wall in the corridor, a bored listless expression on her face, as though all she cared about was finding a bed where she could sleep for twelve hours in one stretch.

"About five hundred pesos," murmured the bewildered de Troeye.

"Give them to me."

"All of them?"

"All of them."

De Troeye was too dazed and weary from drink to argue. He obediently fumbled for his wallet in his inside jacket pocket, and allowed Max to empty the contents coldly. As he did so, Max could feel Mecha's eyes on him (she was standing a little farther back in the corridor, her shawl draped over her shoulders, observing the scene), but he did not even glance at her. He needed to focus on far more important, dangerous things. The first of these was how to reach the car where Petrossi was waiting for them, with the least amount of trouble.

"Here you are," he said to Rebenque.

The ruffian counted the notes coolly. When he had finished, he tapped them for a moment with the fingers of one hand, pensively. Then he slipped them into his pocket and his smile broadened.

"There were other expenses," he said with an exaggerated drawl. He wasn't looking at de Troeye, but at Max. As though this were a private matter concerning the two of them.

"I don't think so," said Max.

"Well, I suggest you think again, my friend. Melina is a pretty girl, isn't she? . . . And I had to get hold of the raviolis and every-thing else (he looked barefacedly at Mecha). The lady over there, and this dupe here, they had a good time tonight, didn't they? I just want to be sure we all do."

"There's no more dough," said Max.

Rebenque seemed to pause at the last word, and he grinned even more, as though appreciating his native slang.

"What about the lady?"

"She hasn't any."

"I believe there was a necklace."

"There isn't now."

The thug slid his hands out of his pockets and unbuttoned his jacket. As he did so, the ivory handle of his knife protruded from the arm of his waistcoat.

"Then we'll have to look into that," he said, ogling the gold chain glinting beneath de Troeye's jacket. "But first I'd like to know what time it is, my watch seems to have stopped."

Max glanced at Rebenque's shirt cuffs, then his pockets.

"It doesn't look to me like you have a watch."

"It stopped working years ago. . . . Why would I carry around a broken watch?"

Max thought that it wasn't worth killing anyone for a watch. Or a pearl necklace for that matter. And yet there was something about the thug's smirking face that riled him. Too arrogant, perhaps. And too cocksure, this Juan Rebenque, because he thought he was the only one on his home ground.

"I told you I was born in Barracas, in Calle Vieytes, didn't I?"

The ruffian's smile faded, as though his criollo mustache had cast a shadow over it. What has that to do with anything, his ex-pression seemed to say. At this late stage in the game.

"You keep out of this," he replied brusquely.

The expression on his face made his sudden use of the familiar *tu* seem more intimidating. Max contemplated him at length, placing the threat in the context of where it had been made. Rebenque's manner, the hallway, the front door, the vehicle waiting in the street outside. He couldn't rule out the possibility that Rebenque had a henchman standing by, ready to lend a hand.

"As far as I remember, there was a code of honor," Max resumed, standing his ground. "People kept their word."

"Meaning?"

"When you wanted a watch, you had to pay for it."

The smile had vanished from the ruffian's face. Giving way to a menacing expression. That of a ferocious wolf, preparing to attack.

"Are you for real or a phony?"

One of Rebenque's thumbs touched his waistcoat, as if edging toward the ivory handle. Max calculated the distances instantly. He was three steps away from the ruffian's knife, which he would have to unsheathe. Max shifted almost imperceptibly to the right, so that he was facing Rebenque's left side, and better placed to defend himself with his right arm and hand. He had learned how to position himself surreptitiously in the Legion's brothels in Africa, while broken bottles and knives were flying. If there was going to be a fight, it was best to start off at an advantage.

"Oh for heaven's sake. . . . Stop all this posturing," Mecha's voice rang out behind him. "I want to go to bed. Give him the watch and let's get out of here."

This wasn't posturing, Max knew, but this was no time for explanations. Something was already sticking in Rebenque's craw, and Mecha herself was probably the cause, doubtless from the first time he saw her. Since they danced that tango. He had resented being excluded that night, and the drink he had taken while he waited hadn't helped matters. The watch, the necklace Max had entrusted to Petrossi, his ninety pesos, and the five hundred de Troeye had just parted with were mere pretexts for the knife tickling the ruffian's armpit. He wanted to show off his manliness, for Mecha's benefit.

"Leave," Max said to them, without turning around. "Go straight to the car."

Perhaps it was his tone. Or the way he was holding Rebenque's shifty gaze. But Mecha did not say another word. A few seconds later, Max noticed out of the corner of his eye that she and her husband were now standing beside him, closer to the door, their backs against the wall.

"What's the hurry, my friend?" said the ruffian. "We have all the time in the world."

I despise him because I know him right down to the soles of his shoes, thought Max. He could be me. His mistake is that he believes a tailored suit makes us different. That it erases the memory.

"Get outside," he repeated to the de Troeyes.

The ruffian's thumb drew closer to the knife. It was a few centimeters from the ivory handle when Max thrust his hand into his jacket pocket and found the warm metal of the 6.35 caliber pistol into whose chamber he had discreetly inserted a bullet before coming downstairs. Without taking the gun out of his pocket, he flipped the safety catch off with one finger. Rebenque lowered the brim of his hat, his dark, brooding eyes following Max's every move. Behind them, amid the smoky air in the back room, the gramophone started to play "Hand to Hand."

"No one leaves here," the ruffian declared brazenly.

Then he took a step forward, threatening a flash of steel in the air. His right hand was reaching into the arm of his waistcoat when Max pushed the Browning in his face. Right between his eyes.

"Since they invented this," he said calmly, "bravery is a thing of the past."

He spoke in a hushed tone, without gloating, as if this were a friendly exchange between compadres. Trusting at the same time that his hand was steady. Rebenque stared into the black hole at the end of the barrel with a serious, almost contemplative expression. Like a gambler calculating how many trump cards he held, Max reflected. Not many, he must have decided, for after a moment his fingers uncurled from around the handle of his knife.

"You wouldn't be so brave either if we were evenly matched," he said, staring straight at him, eyes flashing.

"You're quite right," said Max.

Rebenque held his gaze for a moment. Finally, he gestured with his chin toward the door.

"Beat it."

The smile had returned to his lips. As stoical as it was sinister.

"Get in the car," Max ordered Mecha and her husband, still aiming the pistol at Rebenque.

The tough did not even glance at the de Troeyes as they left—with a swift *tap-tap* of a woman's heels on the wooden floor. His eyes were still fixed on Max, brimming with ominous, implausible conjectures.

"How about it, my friend? . . . There are plenty of blades around here. Weapons for real men, you know. Someone could lend you one."

Max gave a faint, almost complicit smile.

"Another time, perhaps. I'm in a hurry now."

"What a shame."

"Indeed."

He went out into the street without haste, slowly pocketing the pistol, inhaling the cold, damp early morning air with a sense of joyous relief. The Pierce-Arrow was waiting by the entrance, engine purring, headlights on, and when Max got in, slamming the door behind him, Petrossi released the handbrake, put the car in gear, and drove off with a loud screech of tires. The jolt caused Max to fall onto the backseat, between the de Troeyes.

"My God," murmured Armando, in astonishment. "That was a very lively evening."

"You asked for Old School, didn't you?"

Sunk deep in the leather seat, Mecha burst out laughing.

"I think I'm falling in love with Max. . . . You don't mind, do you, Armando?"

"Not at all, my dear. I love him, too."

———※———

Exquisite. Superb. Those were the exact words to describe the still, sleeping body of the woman Max was contemplating in the dimly lit room, as she lay on top of the crumpled sheets. There wasn't a painter or photographer alive, he concluded, who could faithfully capture those splendid, flowing lines Mother Nature had brought together with absolute perfection to form her naked back, the clean angles of her arms as they hugged the pillow, the soft curve of her hips stretching seemingly endlessly down to her slender legs, slightly apart, revealing from behind where her pubis began. And the perfect focus for all those elongated lines and soft curves converged, exposed and vulnerable beneath her bobbed hair, was the nape of her neck, which Max had brushed with his lips before getting up, to make sure Mecha was asleep.

Almost dressed, Max put out the cigarette he had been smoking and went into the bathroom (marble and blue tiles) to knot his tie in front of the big mirror above the basin. After buttoning his vest, he went in search of his jacket and hat, which he had left in the small English-style sitting room in the enormous suite at the Hotel Palace. He found them between the lighted lamp and the mahogany sofa where Armando de Troeye lay fully clothed, starched collar unbuttoned, in his stockinged feet, curled up like a tramp asleep on a park bench. The noise of Max's footsteps made him open his eyes, and he stirred groggily on the red velvet upholstery.

"What's going on, Max?" he asked, his tongue thick with sleep.

"Nothing. Petrossi still has Mecha's necklace and I'm going to fetch it."

"Good boy."

De Troeye closed his eyes and turned over. Max stood staring at him for a moment. His contempt for the man was almost as intense as his astonishment at what had happened during the past few hours. He felt a sudden urge to give the man a brutal, ruthless beating, and yet, he concluded coldly, that would not solve anything. Other, more pressing thoughts were on his mind. He had been reflecting about them at length as he lay motionless, beside Mecha's spent, sleeping form. His recent memories and sensations crashed past like boulders swept along by a torrent: crossing the hotel foyer while propping up de Troeye, the night porter giving them the key, going up in the elevator and arriving in the room, the grunts and stifled giggles. And then, de Troeye watching with the glassy stare of a startled animal as his wife and Max tore their clothes off, colliding in an urgent, shameless embrace, kissing each other's mouths and flesh, inching backward toward the bedroom, where, not even bothering to close the door, they flung themselves on the bed and he plunged into her with a frenzy that seemed more like an act of revenge than of passion, or love.

Max closed the door very quietly behind him and emerged into the corridor. The carpet muffled his footsteps, and he went past the elevator—descending the broad, marble staircase instead, as he pondered his next moves. He had lied about Petrossi still having Mecha's necklace. After getting out of the car at the hotel entrance, Max had asked the chauffeur to wait in order to drive him back to the Caboto boardinghouse. He had given Petrossi his pistol back, retrieved the pearls, and without Mecha or her husband seeing, had slipped them into his own pocket. They had been there all along, and there they still lay, bulging beneath Max's fingers as he felt the left inside pocket of his jacket. He crossed the lobby, greeted the night porter with a raise of his eyebrows, and went outside. He found Petrossi snoozing in the car beneath a street lamp, cap beside him on the seat over a folded edition of *La Nación*, head reclining against the leather rest. He sat up when Max tapped on the window with his knuckles.

"Drive me to Almirante Brown, please. . . . No, don't put the hat on. Leave it. You can go home afterward."

They didn't exchange a word during the journey. From time to time, in the glow of a passing street lamp reflected off the façade of a building or a wall, and with the gray dawn light creeping in, Max glimpsed the chauffeur's silent gaze in the rearview mirror and their eyes met. When the Pierce-Arrow came to a halt in front of the boardinghouse, Petrossi got out to open the door for Max, who stepped out of the car, hat in hand.

"Thank you, Petrossi."

The man looked at him impassively.

"You're welcome, sir."

Max took a step toward the entrance then stopped in his tracks, turning back.

"It was a pleasure to meet you," he said.

Max couldn't be sure in that hazy light, yet he had the impression Petrossi was smiling.

"On the contrary, sir, the pleasure was all mine."

Now it was Max's turn to smile.

"That's a fine Browning. Take good care of it."

"I'm glad it came in handy."

A look of bewilderment flashed across the chauffeur's face as Max removed his Longines wristwatch.

"It isn't much," he said, giving it to him. "But I have no money on me."

Petrossi turned the watch over in his hands.

"It isn't necessary," he protested.

"I know. And that makes it even more so."

—⁂—

Two hours later, after packing his suitcase and hailing a cab outside the Caboto boardinghouse, Max Costa boarded the steamer linking the two banks of Río de la Plata. Not long afterward, having breezed through Customs and Immigration, he arrived in the city of Montevideo. The police investigation, which a few days later retraced the ballroom dancer's steps in the Uruguayan capital, suggested that on the journey over from Buenos Aires, Max had met a Mexican woman, a professional singer at the Teatro Royal Pigalle, and had spent the night with her in a luxury room at the Victoria Plaza Hotel. The following morning he had disappeared leaving behind his luggage and a large bill (for the room, various services, dinner with champagne and caviar), with which the furious Mexican woman was confronted when a hotel clerk roused her. He was carrying the mink coat Max had bought her the previous afternoon at the most expensive furrier in Montevideo. Since he had no money on him at the time, he had asked for it to be delivered to the hotel the next day, when the banks opened.

By that time, Max had already bought his passage on a liner, the *Conte Verde*, sailing under the Italian flag to Europe with a stopover Rio de Janeiro. Three days later he disembarked in the Brazilian city, where the police lost all trace of him. The last thing they were able to discover was that, before leaving Montevideo, Max had sold the pearl necklace to a Romanian jeweler, a known receiver of stolen goods, who owned an antique store in Calle Andes. The man, called Troianescu, admitted in his statement to the police that he had paid three thousand pounds sterling for the pearls (two hundred perfect specimens)—just over half their market value. But the young man who sold them to him in Café Vaccaro, introduced to him by a friend of a friend, seemed eager to close the deal. An agreeable fellow, by the way. Well dressed and courteous. With a pleasant smile. Had it not been for the two hundred pearls, and the hurry he was in, Troianescu would have taken him for a perfect gentleman.

6

The Promenade des Anglais

FTER DINING AT the hotel, they go out for a stroll, making the most of the mild weather. Mecha has introduced Max to the others ("A dear friend, from longer ago than I care to remember"), and he has effortlessly blended in, with the composure he always possessed when confronting any situation—that likable spontaneity, a mixture of politeness and discreet ingenuity, which had opened so many doors for him in the past, when each day was a challenge and a fight for survival.

"So, you live in Amalfi?" Jorge Keller asks.

Max's calm is faultless.

"Yes. On and off."

"It's a beautiful place. I envy you."

A pleasant young man, Max concludes. In good shape, like those all-American college boys who win trophies, only with the polish of a good European education. He has removed his tie, rolled up his sleeves, and, his jacket slung over one shoulder, he scarcely fits the idea people usually have of an aspiring world chess champion. He seems unconcerned about the adjourned game. During dinner he was relaxed and entertaining, sharing jokes with Karapetian, his mentor and trainer. When it was time for dessert, Karapetian insisted on withdrawing to analyze the variants of the sealed move, in advance of the work he and Irina Jasenovic would resume with Jorge Keller the following day after breakfast. It was Karapetian who, before retiring, suggested they go for a stroll. It'll do you good, he told his protégé. And clear your head. Go and enjoy yourself for a while, and take Irina with you.

"How long have you two been together?" asked Max after Karapetian had left.

"Too long." Keller sighed, with the mischievous air of someone talking about his teacher the moment his back is turned. "Meaning at least half my life."

"He listens to Emil more than he does to me," Mecha added.

The young man burst into laughter.

"You are just my mother. Emil is my jailer."

Max looked at Irina Jasenovic, wondering to what extent she might be the key to that dungeon. She wasn't exactly pretty, Max reflected. Attractive, perhaps, with her youthfulness, that miniskirt that evoked swinging London, and those big, brown, almond eyes. She appeared quiet and sweet-natured. A bright girl. She and Keller seemed more like friends than lovers—communicating through gestures and exchanging glances behind the grown-ups' backs, as though chess were a shared transgression. A clever, complicated piece of mischief.

"Let's have a drink," Mecha suggests. "Over there." They have been chatting as they make their way down Calle San Antonino and Via San Francesco toward the gardens of the Hotel Imperial Tramontano. On a bandstand lit by lanterns and surrounded by bougainvillea, palms, and magnolias, a band is performing to an audience of about thirty people dressed in polo shirts, miniskirts, and jeans, with sweaters draped over their shoulders. They are seated at tables around the dance floor, close to the cliff top, with the dark backdrop of the bay and the lights of Naples flickering in the distance.

"I don't remember my mother ever mentioning you. . . . Where did you two meet?"

"On a liner bound for Buenos Aires, in the late twenties."

"Max was the ship's ballroom dancer," Mecha adds. "His job was to dance with the ladies and young women, and he did it rather well . . . he played an important part in the famous tango my first husband composed."

The young Keller responds with indifference to this information. Either he has no interest in tango, Max deduces, or he dislikes the allusion to his mother's previous married life.

"Oh, that," he says, coldly. "Tango."

"What do you do now?" Irina asks.

Dr. Hugentobler's chauffeur puts on a suitable face, halfway between convincing and evasive.

"I'm in business," he replies. "I have a private clinic in the north."

"That's not bad," Keller comments. "From tango dancer to owning a clinic and a villa in Amalfi."

"With periods in between that weren't always prosperous," Max points out. "A lot can happen in forty years."

"Did you ever meet my father? Ernesto Keller?"

A vague gesture, as though scouring his memory.

"It's possible. . . . I'm not sure."

Max's gaze meets that of Mecha.

"You met him on the Riviera," she says calmly. "During the Spanish Civil War, at Suzi Ferriol's house."

"Yes. That's right . . . Of course."

The four of them order refreshments: two soft drinks, a mineral water, and a Negroni for Max. While the waiter comes back with a full tray, there is a roll of drums and a clash of cymbals, two electric guitars start up, and the singer (an elderly fellow wearing a toupee and a sequined jacket), imitating the voice of Gianni Morandi, launches into "Fatti Mandare Dalla Mamma." Jorge Keller and Irina exchange a brief kiss and get to their feet, moving agilely among the other dancers to the lively rhythms of a twist.

"Extraordinary," says Max.

"What is extraordinary?"

"Your son. His manner. The way he handles himself."

Mecha looks at him ironically.

"You mean the aspiring world chess champion?"

"Yes, him."

"I see. I imagine you were expecting a pale, awkward youth with a chessboard for a brain."

"Something like that."

Mecha shakes her head. Don't be misled, she tells him. The chessboard is there. He may not give that impression, but he is still playing the adjourned game. What makes him different from other players, perhaps, is the way he deals with it. Some grand masters are like monks, withdrawing from everything and everyone around them. But not Jorge. His style of play is precisely a projection of the game of chess onto the world and life. "Beneath his deceptively normal exterior, full of energy," she says finally, "he has a conception of space and objects entirely different from yours, or mine."

Max nods, looking at Irina Jasenovic.

"What about her?"

"She's a strange girl. Even I can't understand what goes on inside her head. There is no doubt she is a great player. Resourceful, intelligent . . . and yet I can't tell how much of her behavior comes from her, or whether it is her relationship with Jorge that defines everything. I have no idea what she was like before."

"I never thought women could make good chess players. I always assumed it was a man's game."

"Well, you're mistaken. There are plenty of women grand masters, most of them from the Soviet Union. The trouble is very few make it to the world championships."

"Why?"

Mecha takes a sip of her drink and reflects for a moment. Emil Karapetian has a theory about that, she says at last. Playing the odd game of chess isn't the same as competing in a world tournament or championship. That requires sustained effort, extreme concentration, and tremendous emotional stability. It is far more challenging for women, who are often subject to hormonal fluctuations, to maintain that level of stamina. Things like motherhood and periods can upset that balance that is so crucial in a grueling chess tournament, which can last weeks or even months. That is why so few women reach a high level.

"And you agree with him?"

"To some extent, yes."

"What about Irina?

"Absolutely not. She insists there is no difference."

"And your son?"

"He agrees with Irina. He says it is a question of attitudes and habit. He believes things will change a lot in the coming years, in chess as in everything else . . . that things are already changing, with the youth revolution, the moon within our reach, music, politics, and everything else."

"I am sure he is right," affirms Max.

"You say that as if you weren't sorry."

She looks at him, her interest piqued. His words sounded more like a provocation than a casual remark. He responds with a wistful expression.

"Every time has its moment," he says in a restrained voice. "And its people. Mine finished a long time ago, and I can't stand drawn-out endings. They are undignified."

Mecha looks younger when she smiles, he notices, as though it smoothed her wrinkles. Or perhaps it is that knowing glimmer in her eyes, which is identical now to the way he remembers it.

"You still know how to turn a good phrase, my friend. I often wondered where you picked them up."

The former ballroom dancer makes a dismissive gesture, as if the answer were obvious.

"Here and there, I suppose. . . . After that, it is a question of using them at the right moment."

"Well, you haven't forgotten your good manners. You are still the perfect *charmeur* I met forty years ago, on that dazzling white liner. I notice you didn't include me in your speech about bygone eras just now."

"You are still so vibrant. I only have to see you with your son and the others."

His first sentence sounds almost resentful, and Mecha looks at him, thoughtfully. Perhaps with a sudden wariness. Max feels his façade weaken momentarily, and he plays for time, reaching across the table to fill her water glass. When he leans back in his chair, he is once more fully in control. Even so, she continues to watch him intently.

"I don't understand why you talk like that. The bitterness in your voice. Things haven't gone badly for you."

Max makes a vague gesture. This is also a way of playing chess, he tells himself. Possibly he has spent his whole life doing that and nothing else.

"Perhaps world-weariness is the right description," he replies cautiously. "A man has to know when it is time to quit smoking, drinking, or living."

"Another well-turned phrase. Who said that?"

"I forget." Max is smiling now, once again on safe ground. "It might even have been me. I am too old to know for sure."

"And are you too old to know for sure when to quit a woman? . . . There was a time when you were expert at it."

He looks at her with a deliberate mixture of tenderness and reproach. But Mecha shakes her head, rejecting his attempt at complicity.

"I don't know what it is you regret so much," she goes on. "Or what you pretend to regret. You led a dangerous life. You could have ended up very differently."

"Penniless, you mean?"

"Or in prison."

"I have been in one or two," he admits. "Not often or for long, but I have been there."

"I'm amazed you managed to turn your life around. How did you do it?"

Once again Max pulls an ambiguous face that embraces every imaginary possibility. The smallest detail can often wreck the best cover.

"I had a couple of lucky breaks after the war. Friends. Business opportunities."

"And the odd wealthy woman, perhaps?"

"I don't think so . . . I forget."

At that moment, the man Max once was would have created a timely pause, lighting a cigarette with easy elegance. But he no longer smokes, and besides, the gin in his Negroni has upset his stomach. So he does his best to look impassive, wishing he could dissolve a teaspoon of liver salts in a glass of warm water.

"Don't you feel any nostalgia for those days, Max?"

She is looking at Jorge and Irina, who are still dancing beneath the lanterns in the park. To a rock number, this time. Max watches them move on the floor then stares at the leaves, yellowing in the darkness, or lying shriveled on the ground, next to the tables.

"I feel nostalgia for my youth," he replies, "or rather for what was attainable because of it. . . . On the other hand, I have found that autumn brings calm. At my age it makes me feel safe, far removed from the shocks of spring."

"Don't be so ridiculously polite. Say *our* age."

"Never."

"Idiot."

A pleasant silence, once more conspiratorial. Mecha reaches into her jacket pocket for some cigarettes, leaves the packet on the table without lighting one.

"I know what you mean," she says at last. "I feel the same. One day I realized there were more unpleasant people around, hotels were no longer as elegant, and traveling was less fun. Cities were uglier, and men more ill-mannered, less attractive . . . and then the war in Europe swept away the last remnants."

She falls silent again for a moment.

"Fortunately, I had Jorge," she adds.

Max nods absentmindedly, reflecting on what she has said. He doesn't say so, but she is mistaken. At least in his case. His problem isn't nostalgia for the good old days, but rather something far more clichéd. He spent most of his life struggling to survive in that milieu, to adapt to a world, which, when it collapsed, would end up dragging him down as well. And when that happened, he was too old to start again: life had ceased to be a vast hunting ground abounding in casinos, expensive hotels, transatlantic liners, and luxurious railway trains, where an ambitious young man's fortunes could be decided by the way he parted his hair or lit a cigarette. Hotels, traveling, cities, ill-mannered, unattractive men, as Mecha had said, with remarkable precision. The old Europe of dance halls and palaces, Ravel's "Bolero," and the "Old School Tango" could no longer be contemplated through a champagne glass.

"My God, Max . . . You were a handsome devil. That composure, so refined and roguish at the same time."

She gazes at him intently, as though scouring his aged features for the attractive youth she once knew. Tamely, with an air of graceful stoicism (on his lips the gentle expression of a man who has accepted the inevitable), he submits to her examination.

"An exceptional story, don't you think?" she says at last, softly. "You and me . . . Us, the *Cap Polonio*, Buenos Aires, Nice."

Perfectly calm, without uttering a word, Max leans forward slightly, seizes her hand, and kisses it.

"What I said the other day was not true," says Mecha, rewarding the gesture with a dazzling smile. "You look very good for your age."

He shrugs with the right amount of modesty.

"Now that *is* untrue. I'm just another old man who has experienced love and loss."

Her guffaw rouses a few stares from the neighboring tables.

"You old rogue. That's not yours, either."

Max holds her gaze.

"Prove it."

"You looked thirty years younger when you said that. Did you put on that same blank face when the police questioned you?"

"What police?"

They both laugh now. Max, as well, a lot. With pure pleasure.

"You really do look good," he says. "You were . . . you are the most beautiful woman I have ever seen. The most elegant and the most perfect. You seemed to walk through life with a spotlight following your every movement, illuminating you continuously. Like those screen idols who seem to embody the myths they themselves created."

Mecha's face has suddenly grown serious. A moment later he sees her smile halfheartedly. As though from a long distance away.

"The spotlight faded long ago."

"That is untrue," Max protests.

"Listen, that's enough. We are two old hypocrites, lying to each other while the youngsters dance."

"Would you care to dance?"

"Don't be foolish. Old, presumptuous, and foolish."

The rhythm of the music has changed again. The singer with

the toupee and the sequined jacket is taking a rest, and the band strikes up an arrangement of "Crying in the Chapel"; the couples on the dance floor embrace. Jorge Keller and Irina also dance like that. The young woman rests her head on his shoulder, her arms folded around his neck.

"They seem to be in love," Max remarks.

"I don't know if that is the right word. You should see them poring over a chessboard together, analyzing a game. She can be ruthless, while he paces up and down like an angry tiger. . . . Emil Karapetian often has to step in and mediate. But the arrangement seems to work."

Max is gazing at her again, intently.

"What about you?"

"Oh, well. As I said before, I am the mother. I stay on the sidelines, watching. Ready to meet their needs. Taking care of practical things . . . But I always know my place."

"You could live your own life."

"And who says this isn't my own life?"

She taps her fingers gently on the packet of cigarettes. At last she takes one and Max obligingly lights it for her.

"Your son is very much like you."

Mecha exhales a puff of smoke and looks at him with sudden wariness.

"In what way?"

"His physique, obviously. Tall and slim. There is something in his eyes when he smiles that reminds me of you. . . . What was his father, the diplomat, like? Honestly, I scarcely remember anything. He was a pleasant, charming fellow, wasn't he? That dinner in Nice. Little else."

She listens intently, hidden behind coils of smoke that dissolve in the delicate breeze from the sea nearby.

"You could be his father. . . . Did you never think of that?"

"Don't talk nonsense. Please."

"It isn't nonsense. Just think for a moment. Jorge's age. He's twenty-eight. . . . Doesn't that suggest anything?"

Max moves uneasily in his chair.

"Look. It could have been . . ."

"Anyone? Is that what you were going to say?"

All at once, she seems vexed. Sullen. She puts out her cigarette brusquely, crushing it in the ashtray.

"Don't worry. He isn't your son."

Despite everything, Max can't get the idea out of his head. He carries on thinking, fretting. Making absurd calculations.

"That last time, in Nice . . ."

"Oh, damn you, Max . . . To hell with you and with Nice."

—∙∙∙—

The morning was chilly but splendid. Outside the window of the room at the Hôtel de Paris, Monte Carlo, the branches on the trees swayed, shedding the first leaves of autumn in the mistral that had been blowing for days through cloudless skies. Max (hair slicked back, skin perfumed by a face rub) finished dressing, paying careful attention to every detail of his attire. After buttoning his vest he pulled on the jacket belonging to the seven-guinea, three-piece Cheviot wool suit, tailor-made five months before at Anderson & Sheppard of London. He tucked a white handkerchief in his top pocket, checked that his red-and-gray-striped tie was straight, glanced at the shine on his brown leather shoes, and began distributing among his pockets the objects laid out on the chest of drawers: a Parker Duofold pen, a tortoiseshell cigarette case (the initials on this one were his) stocked with twenty Turkish cigarettes, and a wallet containing two thousand French francs, a private membership *carte de saison* for the casino and another for the Sporting Club. His gold-plated Dunhill cigarette lighter was on the small breakfast table over by the window, on top of a newspaper whose main headline announced the latest news from the Spanish

Civil War: "Franco's Troops Attempt to Win Back Belchite." Max slipped the lighter into his pocket, dropped the newspaper in the wastepaper basket, picked up his felt hat and Malacca cane, and went out into the corridor.

He saw the two men as he skipped down the last few steps of the magnificent staircase beneath the glass-domed foyer. They had their hats on and were sitting on one of the sofas on the right, next to the entrance to the bar. His first thought was that they were policemen. At thirty-five (it was seven years since he had stopped working as a ballroom dancer in luxury hotels and on transatlantic liners), Max possessed a well-developed professional instinct for detecting dangerous situations. A glance at the two men was enough to tell him this was one: when they saw him appear, they had exchanged a few words, and were now looking at him with visible interest. In order to avoid an awkward scene in the foyer (a possible arrest, although in Monaco he had a clean slate), Max walked toward them with a casual air, as if he was heading for the bar. The moment he drew level with them, the two men rose to their feet.

"Mr. Costa?"

"Yes."

"My name is Mauro Barbaresco, and my friend here is Domenico Tignanello. Could we have a little chat?"

The one who had spoken (in fluent Spanish but with an Italian accent) had broad shoulders, a hooked nose, and bright eyes. He was wearing a gray, somewhat tight-fitting suit, the trousers sagging at the knees. His companion was small and thickset, a southerner, with a melancholy expression and a big mole on his left cheek; he wore a dark, pin-striped suit (crumpled, with shiny elbows, Max noticed), a tie that was too wide, and scuffed shoes. Both men must have been in their late thirties.

"I only have half an hour. Then I have an engagement."

"That will be sufficient."

The smile of the man with the hooked nose seemed too friendly

to be reassuring (Max knew from experience that a friendly policeman was more dangerous than a hostile one). However, if those
two were on the side of law and order, he concluded, it wasn't in
the traditional way. On the other hand, the fact that they knew
his name wasn't so remarkable. He was registered in Monte Carlo
under the name of Máximo Costa, and his Venezuelan passport
was valid and authentic. He also had a bank account containing
four hundred and thirty thousand francs in a branch of Barclays,
and another fifty thousand in the hotel safe, to guarantee that he
was a respectable, or at any rate solvent client. And yet, he had a
bad feeling about those two. His nose was trained to detect trouble,
and he sniffed it now.

"Could we invite you for a drink?"

Max peered inside the hotel bar. Emilio, the waiter, was preparing a cocktail behind the counter, and various guests were sipping
their drinks, ensconced in leather armchairs between walls adorned
with etched glass and varnished wood panels. Max decided this
wasn't the ideal place to hold a conversation with the two men, and
gestured toward the revolving door leading out into the street.

"Let's go to the Café de Paris, opposite."

They crossed the square in front of the casino, where the doorman, who had a good memory for tips, nodded at Max. The wind
from the north had turned the nearby sea a deeper shade of blue,
and the mountains along the coastline with their abrupt grays and
ochers loomed more vividly in that extensive landscape of villas,
hotels, and casinos that was the Riviera: a boulevard sixty kilo-
meters long inhabited by nonchalant waiters waiting for diners,
leisurely croupiers waiting for gamblers, fast women waiting for
wealthy men, and smart hustlers, like Max, waiting for the chance
to profit from it all.

"The weather is turning," the man named Barbaresco said to his
companion, looking at the sky.

For some reason that he didn't pause to analyze, Max thought the man's words sounded like a threat, or a warning. At any rate, they strengthened his conviction that trouble lay ahead. Trying to keep a cool head, he chose an outside table beneath the awnings, in a quiet corner of the terrace. On the left was the imposing façade of the casino, and on the far side of the square were the Hôtel de Paris and the Sporting Club. The three of them sat down, and the waiter came over. True patriots, Barbaresco and Tignanello ordered Cinzanos. Max ordered a Riviera cocktail.

"We have a proposition for you," the man with the hooked nose said.

"When you say *we*, to whom are you referring?"

Barbaresco took off his hat and ran his hand over head. It was bald and tanned, and together with his broad shoulders gave him a healthy, athletic appearance.

"We are middlemen," he replied.

"Acting for whom?"

A tired smile. Barbaresco stared at the red drink the waiter had put in front of him, but did not touch it. His glum friend had picked his up and was lifting it to his lips, gingerly, as though nervous of the lemon slice floating inside.

"All in good time," replied Barbaresco.

"Very well," said Max, poised to light a cigarette. "Let's hear your proposition."

"A job here in the South of France. Handsomely rewarded."

Max lowered his lighter and stood up calmly, motioning to the waiter to bring the bill. He had enough experience of agitators, informers, and undercover policemen not to want to prolong the situation.

"It has been a pleasure, gentlemen. . . . As I told you earlier I have a prior engagement. Good day."

The other two remained in their seats, unflustered. Barbaresco plucked an identity card out of his pocket, and showed it to Max.

"This is serious, Mr. Costa. Official business."

Max looked at the card. It bore a photograph of its holder next to the acronym SIM.

"My friend has an identical one. Isn't that right, Domenico?"

His companion nodded silently, as though instead of referring to his identity card Barbaresco had asked if he had tuberculosis. Tignanello had also removed his hat, revealing a shock of glossy black curls that accentuated his southern looks. Sicily or Calabria, Max surmised. With all the melancholy of his people stamped on his face.

"And are they authentic?"

"As authentic as the sacred host."

"Be that as it may, your jurisdiction ends in Ventimiglia, am I right?"

"We're just passing through."

Max sat down again. Like all readers of newspapers, he knew about Italy's territorial ambitions since Mussolini had seized power. They wanted to restore the old border in the South of France as far as the Var River. He was equally aware that with the atmosphere created by the Spanish Civil War, as well as the political tensions throughout Europe and the Mediterranean, that whole strip of coast was teeming with German and Italian spies. He also knew that SIM was short for Servizio Informazioni Militare, Italy's foreign secret service.

"Before getting down to business, Mr. Costa, allow me to tell you that we know everything about you."

"How much is everything?"

"I'll let you be the judge of that."

Following this preamble, Barbaresco drank his vermouth (three long sips resembling pauses) as he gave a remarkably accurate account, lasting approximately two minutes, of Max's career in Italy over the past two years. Besides other minor incidents, this included the theft of jewelry belonging to an American woman named Howells from her apartment on Via del Babuino in Rome;

another theft, this time from a Belgian woman at the Grand Hotel, also in Rome; a safecracking at Villa Bolzano, owned by the Marquesa Greco de Andreis; and the theft of jewelry and money belonging to the Brazilian soprano Florinda Salgado from her suite at the Hotel Danieli in Venice.

"I did all that?" Max remarked calmly. "You cannot be serious."

"Yes, I'm perfectly serious."

"With all those crimes, all that evidence against me, it seems odd I was never arrested."

"No one said anything about evidence, Mr. Costa."

"Ah."

"The truth is, none of the suspicions about you have ever been officially confirmed."

Crossing his legs, Max finally lit his cigarette.

"You have no idea how relieved I am to hear it. . . . Now, tell me, what is it you want from me?"

Barbaresco turned his hat around in his hands. Like his companion's, they looked meaty, with stubby nails. And dangerous, too, no doubt, if the need arose.

"There's a bit of business," he said. "A problem we need to solve."

"Here in Monaco?"

"In Nice."

"And where do I come in?"

"Despite your Venezuelan passport, you are of Argentinian and Spanish origin. You are well connected socially, and move easily in certain circles. In addition, you have never been in trouble with the French police, even less so than with our own. That gives you a respectable cover. . . . Isn't that right, Domenico ?"

The other man nodded again with his usual apathy; he seemed accustomed to his colleague doing all the talking.

"And what do you expect me to do?"

"Employ your skills to our advantage."

"I have many different skills."

"What interests us"—Barbaresco looked again at the other man as though seeking his agreement, but Tignanello did not utter a word or make a gesture—"is your ability to infiltrate the lives of your victims, in particular wealthy women. On a few occasions, you have also shown an impressive ability to scale walls, break in through windows, and open safes. This last fact surprised us until we had a conversation with an old acquaintance of yours, Enrico Fossataro, who answered a few of our questions."

Max, who was putting out his cigarette, remained unimpressed. "I don't know the man."

"How strange, because he speaks very highly of you. Isn't that right, Domenico? He describes you, word for word, as a decent fellow and a true gentleman."

Max's expression remained inscrutable, even as he smiled inwardly at the memory of Fossataro: a tall, lithe individual with impeccable manners who had once worked for a company called Conforti, which manufactured safes, before he decided to use his knowledge to break them open.

They had met in the café at Hotel Capşa in Bucharest in 1931, pooling their skills on several lucrative occasions. It was Fossataro who showed Max how to use a diamond tip to cut through windows, how to avail himself of the various locksmith's tools, and how to crack a safe. Enrico always prided himself on behaving with a certain degree of honor, causing his victims the least possible distress. "You rob the rich, but you don't ill-treat them," he used to say. "They are generally insured against theft, but not against wickedness." Before his social rehabilitation (like many of his compatriots he ended up joining the Fascist Party) Fossataro was a legend among the fashionable European underworld. An avid reader, he had on one occasion, in Verona, called a halt halfway through a break-in, leaving everything as he had found it, after discovering that the owner of the house was Gabriele D'Annunzio. And then there was that famous night when, having knocked out its nanny with a an ether-soaked handkerchief, Fossataro proceeded to give the baby its bottle as it lay awake in its cradle, while his accomplices burgled the house.

"In other words," Barbaresco concluded, "besides your social graces, and your gigolo ways, you are a shameless scoundrel. What the French delicately refer to as a *cambrioleur*, a thief, albeit of the gentlemanly variety."

"Am I supposed to look surprised?"

"That won't be necessary, we take no credit for knowing about you. We have the entire state apparatus at our disposal. As I am sure you are aware, the Italian police force is one of the most efficient in Europe."

"On a par with the Gestapo and the NKVD, I believe, as regards efficiency."

Barbaresco frowned.

"You are no doubt thinking of OVRA, the fascist secret police. But my colleague and I are *carabinieri*. Do you understand? We are attached to the military police."

"That makes me feel a whole lot better."

Barbaresco remained silent. For a few seconds, his displeasure at the irony of Max's remark was palpable. Finally he seemed content to let it pass.

"A prominent figure in the world of international finance is in possession of some documents that are important to us," he explained. "For complicated reasons relating to the situation in Spain, they are currently being kept in a house in Nice."

"And you want me to get them for you?"

"Precisely."

"To steal them?"

"No, not to steal them, to recover them. So as to return them to their rightful owner."

Beneath his apparent indifference, Max was becoming increasingly curious.

"What documents are they?"

"You'll find out in good time."

"And why me, exactly?"

"I told you before, you move easily in those circles."

"Who do you take me for? Rocambole?"

For some unknown reason, the name of the fictional adventurer caused Tignanello to break into a smile, and his mournful expression lifted for an instant as he scratched the mole on his cheek. Afterward, he continued gazing at Max with the expression of someone who is always expecting bad news.

"This is espionage. You are spies."

"You make it sound so melodramatic," said Barbaresco, trying unsuccessfully to put the crease back in his trousers by pressing them between finger and thumb. "In fact, we are simple employees of the Italian state, with daily allowances and expense accounts and that sort of thing." He turned to his companion, "Isn't that right, Domenico?"

Max didn't find it so straightforward. At least not his part in it.

"Spying in times of war is a capital offense," he said.

"France isn't at war."

"But she could be soon. The outlook is bleak."

"The documents we want you to recover relate to Spain. . . . The worst thing they could do is deport you."

"But I don't want to be deported. I like it here in France."

"I assure you, the risks are negligible."

Max looked at one, then the other with genuine surprise.

"I thought secret agents used their own recruits for this kind of job."

"That's precisely what we are trying to do now," said Barbaresco, smiling benignly. "To recruit you. How else do you suppose we find people? They don't simply walk up to us and say: 'I want to be a spy.' Some are persuaded by patriotism, others by money. You don't appear to sympathize with either side in the Spanish Civil War. In fact, I'd say you don't care one way or the other."

"The truth is, I am more Argentinian than Spanish."

"That must explain it. In any case, patriotism aside, the only other motive is money. And in that area you have proven to have firm convictions. We have been authorized to offer you a reasonable sum."

Max laced his fingers together, resting them on the knee of his crossed leg.

"How reasonable?"

Barbaresco leaned across the table, lowering his voice.

"Two hundred thousand francs in the currency of your choice, plus an advance of ten thousand francs for expenses in the form of a check from the Crédit Lyonnais, Monte Carlo. I can give you the check right now."

Max gazed with absentminded professional fondness at the jewelry shop next door. The owner, a Jew called Gompers with whom Max occasionally did business, would every afternoon repurchase from the gamblers at the Casino the majority of the jewels he had sold them that very morning.

"I have several ongoing matters to deal with. This would mean putting them on hold."

"We believe that the amount we are offering is more than enough to compensate you."

"I need time to think it over."

"There isn't any time. You only have three weeks in which to sort this out."

Max looked from right to left, taking in the façades of the casino, the Hôtel de Paris, and the adjacent Sporting Club, and the permanent column of gleaming Rolls-Royces, Daimlers, and Packards parked around the square, their drivers standing in groups chatting beside the steps. Only three nights earlier, in those very places, Max had enjoyed a double slice of luck: an Austrian lady (ex-wife of an artificial leather manufacturer from Klagenfurt), no longer in her prime, though still beautiful, with whom he had a rendezvous of four days' time aboard Le Train Bleu, and a *cheval* in the Sporting Club, when the little ivory ball landed in number 26, winning Max eighteen thousand francs.

"Let me put it a different way. I am very happy working alone. I do as I choose, and it's never occurred to me to work for any government, whether it be fascist, national-socialist, Bolshevik, or run by Fu Manchu."

"Of course, you are free to refuse." Barbaresco's expression belied his words. "But you ought to bear in mind a couple of things. Your refusal would upset our government. Isn't that right, Domenico? . . . And the police authorities would doubtless be forced to reconsider their attitude toward you, if for any reason you decided to set foot on Italian soil."

Max made a swift calculation. Being unable to enter Italy would mean having to forsake the eccentric American ladies in Capri and on the Amalfi coast, the bored Englishwomen in their rented villas on the outskirts of Florence, and the nouveau-riche Germans and Italians, who left their wives unattended in Cortina d'Ampezzo and the Venice Lido while they haunted the bars and casinos.

"And not only that," Barbaresco went on. "Italy enjoys excellent relations with Germany and other European countries. Not forgetting Franco's more than likely victory in Spain. As you know, police forces can be more efficient than the League of Nations. And they sometimes work together. If one country were to show a keen interest in you, others would soon be alerted. And if that were the case, the territory in which you claim to work alone and do your own thing could become exasperatingly small. Am I making myself clear?"

"You are," Max replied calmly.

"Now imagine the opposite scenario. The future possibilities. Good friends everywhere, and a vast hunting ground . . . not to mention the money you'll earn from this."

"I'll need more details. To see for myself whether what you're proposing is at all possible."

"You'll be given that information the day after tomorrow, in Nice. You have a room reserved for you for three weeks at the Negresco: we know that's where you like to stay. It's still a good hotel, isn't it? Although we prefer the Ruhl."

"You will be at the Ruhl?"

"No such luck. Our superiors believe that luxury should be reserved for celebrities like yourself. We'll be in a small, rented house near the port. Isn't that right, Domenico? . . . Spies in tailcoats with gardenias in their buttonholes only exist in movies. Like the ones by that Englishman, Hitchcock, and fools like him."

—m—

Four days after the conversation in the Café de Paris, sitting beneath an awning outside La Frégate opposite the Promenade des Anglais in Nice, Max (in white cotton twill trousers and a double-breasted navy blue jacket, his cane and panama hat on the adjacent seat) was squinting against the intense glare from the bay. All around was a blaze of luminous buildings in whites, pinks, and creams, and the reflection off the water was so bright that the crowd strolling along the seafront resembled a line of anonymous backlit shadows.

It was barely noticeable that summer was over, he thought. The street sweepers had a few more fallen leaves to sweep up, and at dawn and dusk the landscape acquired the pearly gray hues of autumn. And yet the orange trees were still heavy with fruit, and the mistral kept the sky cloudless and the sea indigo blue, while the walkway overlooking the pebbly beach across from the line of hotels, restaurants, and casinos was filled with people every day. Unlike in other towns along the coast, where luxury boutiques were already closing and the hotel beach huts were being dismantled, in Nice the *saison* continued into winter. Despite the arrival of paid vacations, which, after the victory of the Popular Front in France, had seen a wave of tourists flock south (one and a half million workers had enjoyed cheap train tickets that year), Nice had kept its perennial inhabitants: wealthy pensioners, English couples with dog included, elderly ladies who concealed the ravages of time beneath wide-brimmed hats and Chantilly lace veils, or Russian families, who, forced to sell off their luxury villas, hung on in modest downtown apartments. Not even at the height of the season did Nice pretend to be a resort: the naked backs and espadrilles that abounded in nearby tourist destinations were frowned upon there. And more often than not the American tourists, rowdy Parisians, and middle-class Englishwomen passing themselves off as distinguished ladies glided through without stopping on their way to Cannes or Monte Carlo, as did the German and Italian businessmen who plagued the Riviera, the new rich who had prospered under the Nazi and fascist regimes.

One of the figures silhouetted against the light stood out among the others, and as it drew closer to the table and to Max, it began to acquire features as well as an aroma of Worth perfume. By then, Max had already risen to his feet, adjusting his tie, and with a luminous smile as dazzling as the light flooding everything around him, he extended both hands in greeting.

"Good God, you look ravishing, Baroness."

"Flatteur."

Asia Schwarzenberg sat down and removed her sunglasses. After ordering a whiskey with Perrier water, she gazed at Max with her big, almond-shaped, slightly Slavic eyes. Max gestured toward the menu on the table.

"Shall we go to a restaurant or would you prefer a light lunch?"

"A light lunch here will be fine."

Max browsed the menu, which had on the back a Matisse drawing of the Palais de la Méditerranée with some palm trees along the Promenade.

"Foie gras and Château d'Yquem?"

"Perfect."

The baroness smiled, revealing a set of pearl-white teeth, her incisors stained with the ubiquitous red lipstick she left on everything from cigarettes to the rims of glasses and the shirt collars of men she was kissing good-bye. But, perfume aside (in Max's opinion Worth made perfect clothes but their scents were too musky), that was her only indulgence. Unlike the bogus titles many international gold diggers paraded around the Riviera, Baroness Anastasia von Schwarzenberg was the genuine article. A brother of hers, a friend of Prince Yusupov, was among Rasputin's assassins, and her first husband was executed by the Bolsheviks in 1918. Her title, however, came from her second marriage to a Prussian aristocrat who died of a heart attack in 1923, bankrupted after his horse Marauder lost the Grand Prix de Deauville by a head. With no other source of income, although well connected, Asia Schwarzenberg, who was tall, slender, and graceful, had modeled for some of the largest fashion houses in France. The old, bound editions of *Vogue* and *Vanity Fair* still found in the reading rooms of transatlantic liners and luxury hotels were full of sophisticated photographs of her by Edward Steichen or the Seebergers. And the fact is that, despite being almost fifty, she still looked stunning in clothes (a dark blue bolero jacket over baggy cream-colored trousers, which Max's trained eye identified as Hermès or Schiaparelli).

"I need an introduction," he said.

"Man or woman?"

"A woman. Here in Nice."

"Difficult?"

"Somewhat. A lot of money and social standing. I want to join her circle."

The baroness listened attentively, with finesse. Weighing up the possible benefits, Max supposed. Besides selling antiques, claiming they belonged to her Russian family, for many years she had made a living from her contacts, obtaining invitations to parties, villa rentals, a reservation at an exclusive restaurant, or an article in a fashion magazine. On the Riviera, Baroness Asia Schwarzenberg was a kind of society go-between.

"I won't ask what you are up to," she said, "because I can usually imagine."

"It's not so simple this time."

"Do I know her?"

"You'd have no difficulty even if you didn't. But tell me, Asia Alexandrovna, is there anyone you don't know?"

The foie gras and champagne arrived, and Max deliberately left off talking while they sampled them, without the baroness showing any impatience. She and Max had dallied briefly five years before, when they met on New Year's Eve at the embassy in Saint Moritz. Things didn't go any further because they both realized at the same time that the other was a penniless gold digger. And so they had stayed up until dawn, breakfasting on cake and hot chocolate at Hanselmann's, she in a gold lamé gown under her mink coat, and he still formal in his tailcoat. Since then, their relations had been friendly and mutually advantageous, neither encroaching on the other's territory.

"You were photographed together this summer in Longchamps," Max said at last. "I saw the picture in *Marie Claire*, or another of those magazines."

The baroness was genuinely surprised, arching her meticulously plucked eyebrows.

"Susana Ferriol?"

"Yes, her."

The baroness's wicker chair creaked slightly as she leaned back, crossing her legs.

"You are talking big game, darling."

"Why do you think I came to you?"

Max had opened his cigarette case and was offering it to her. He leaned forward to light her cigarette then lit his own.

"It's not a problem as far as I am concerned," said the baroness, puffing thoughtfully on her cigarette. "I've known Suzi for years. What exactly do you need?"

"Nothing in particular. The chance to visit her home."

"Is that all?"

"Yes. The rest is my business."

A cloud of smoke. Slow. Cautious.

"I have no wish to know about the rest," she added. "But I warn you she is not a woman of easy virtue. I've never known her to take a lover . . . although, what with the war in Spain, everything has been turned upside down. People are constantly coming and going, refugees and everyone else. . . . Utter chaos."

That word, *refugees*, was ambiguous, thought Max. It conjured up images of poor people, their photographs published in the foreign press: weathered peasant faces, tears trickling down their furrowed cheeks, families fleeing the bombing, filthy children sleeping on top of wretched bundles of clothes, the misery and despair of those who had lost all but their lives. And yet, many of the Spaniards who sought refuge on the Riviera had nothing in common with those people. Comfortably installed in a climate that resembled their own, they would take villas, apartments, or hotel rooms, bask in the sun, and dine at expensive restaurants. And not only on the Riviera. Four weeks earlier, while Max was preparing a coup that didn't work out as planned, he had met several of those exiles in Florence, an aperitif in Casone followed by dinner in Picciolo or Betti. For those who had managed to flee, and still possessed bank accounts abroad, the Civil War was no more than a temporary inconvenience. A distant storm.

"Do you know her brother, Tomás Ferriol?"

"Of course I do," she said, and raised a warning finger. "Watch out for him."

Max recalled his most recent conversation, that morning, with the two Italian secret service men at Café Monnot in Place

Masséna, next to the municipal casino. The two men had abstemiously ordered lemonades, and Tignanello sat there gloomily silent as in Monte Carlo, while Barbaresco gave Max the promised details of the job they wanted him to do. Susana Ferriol is the key person, Barbaresco had explained. Her villa at the foot of Mont Boron is a kind of private office for her brother's secret business. It is also where Tomás Ferriol stays whenever he comes to the Riviera, and he keeps the documents in the safe in his study. Your job is to infiltrate their circle of friends, size up the situation, and obtain what we need.

Asia Schwarzenberg continued to observe Max closely, as though weighing his chances. She didn't look willing to lay a five-franc bet on him.

"Ferriol," she went on, after a brief pause, "isn't the sort of man who will tolerate anyone fooling around with his little sister."

Max calmly acknowledged the warning.

"Is he here in Nice?"

"He comes and goes. I bumped into him a few times about a month ago. Dining at La Réserve, and then at a party in the Antibes villa that Dulce Martínez de Hoz rented this summer. But he spends most of his time traveling between Spain, Switzerland, and Portugal. He has close ties with the Nationalist government in Burgos. They say, and I believe it, that he continues to bankroll General Franco. Everyone knows he financed the early stages of the military insurrection in Spain . . ."

Max was looking beyond the tables at the cars parked alongside the pavement and the figures strolling continuously up and down the Promenade. Sitting at a nearby table was a couple with a skinny, cinnamon-colored dog with a noble bearing. The young woman had on a flimsy dress and a silk turban hat and was pulling at the dog's leash to stop it from licking the shoes of the man at the next table, who was busy filling his pipe and staring at the sign above the Thomas Cook travel agency.

"Give me a couple of days," the baroness said. "I have to find the right strategy."

"I don't have much time."

"I'll do what I can. I suppose you will cover my costs."

Max nodded absentmindedly. The man at the nearby table had lit his pipe and was looking at them, perhaps inadvertently, and yet it made Max feel uncomfortable. There was something familiar about that stranger, he decided, although he couldn't pin it down.

"It won't be cheap," the baroness went on. "You have set your sights high with Suzi Ferriol."

Max looked back at her.

"How high? . . . I was thinking six thousand francs."

"Eight thousand, darling. Everything is so expensive these days."

The man with the pipe appeared to have lost all interest in them, and was smoking as he watched the figures strolling along the Promenade. Max took out the envelope he had prepared from his inside jacket pocket, and, using the table as a shield, added another thousand francs from his wallet.

"I'm sure you'll make do with seven thousand."

"Yes, I'll make do," the baroness said with a grin.

She slipped the envelope into her bag and took her leave. Max stood waiting while she moved away, then paid the bill, put on his hat, and made his way between the tables, passing the man with the pipe, who appeared not to notice him. A moment later, on the last of the three steps leading from the terrace to the pavement, he remembered. He had seen the man that morning, sitting outside Café Monnot having his shoes shined, while Max was talking to the two Italian secret agents.

"There's a problem," Mecha blurts out.

They have been strolling for a while, chatting idly, near the San

Francesco cloister and the gardens of the Hotel Imperial Tramontano. The late-afternoon sun is sinking behind the cliffs overlooking the Marina Grande on their left, casting a golden glow on the
haze above the bay.

"A serious problem," she adds after a moment.

She has just finished her cigarette, and after loosening the
ember on the iron safety rail, she throws the remains over the side.
Her tone of voice and manner surprise Max, and he studies her
motionless expression from the side. She narrows her eyes, staring
obstinately at the water.

"That move of Sokolov's," she says at last.

Max continues to look at her, puzzled. Not knowing what she
is talking about. The adjourned game ended yesterday in a draw. A
half-point for each player. That is all he knows.

"Bastards," mutters Mecha.

Max's bewilderment gives way to alarm. Her tone is one of
disdain, with a hint of anger. Something he has never seen in her
before, he concludes. Although perhaps that isn't entirely true.
Voices from a distant shared past bubble up gently out of nowhere.
Max has already experienced this. In another world, another life.
That cold, polite disdain.

"He already knew the move."

"Who did?"

Hands thrust into the pockets of her cardigan, she shrugs as if
the answer was obvious.

"The Russian, of course. He knew the move Jorge was going to
make."

It takes a moment for the words to sink in.

"Are you telling me . . . ?"

"That Sokolov was prepared. And this isn't the first time."

A long, stunned silence.

"But he is the world champion," Max says, struggling to digest
the information. "Surely it's only normal for these things to happen."

Mecha looks away from the bay and fixes him with a silent gaze. There is nothing normal, her eyes are saying, about these things happening or being done in this way.

"Why are you telling me this?" he asks.

"You in particular?"

"Yes."

She lowers her head, pensive.

"Because I might need your help."

Max is the one who is stunned now, and he rests his hand on the cliff-top rail. There is an unsteadiness about his gesture, like the sudden awareness of an unexpected, almost threatening, attack of vertigo. The social life Dr. Hugentobler's chauffeur has invented in Sorrento has a specific purpose, which doesn't involve Mecha Inzunza needing him. On the contrary.

"What for?"

"All in good time."

He tries to gather his thoughts. To plan what to do in this unknown situation.

"I wonder . . ."

Mecha Inzunza cuts across him, calmly.

"I have been asking myself these past few days what you might be capable of."

Her voice as she speaks is soft, and she holds his gaze, as though watching for him to reply in kind.

"With regard to what?"

"To me."

A casual gesture of protest, barely expressed. This is the reformed Max, the successful Max, who now acts a little offended. Dismissing any conceivable doubts about his reputation.

"You know perfectly well . . ."

"Oh no I don't."

She has stepped away from the rail and is strolling beneath the palm trees toward the cloister. After an almost theatrical pause,

Max follows and draws level with her, walking alongside her in reproachful silence.

"I honestly don't know," Mecha repeats, pensive. "But that isn't my main concern."

Max's curiosity gets the better of his pretense at wounded pride. He politely extends an arm to steer his companion clear of a pair of voluble Englishwomen taking photographs of each other.

"Is this about your son and the Russians?"

Mecha doesn't reply straightaway. She has come to a halt at the corner of the convent, in front of a small archway leading to the cloister. She appears to hesitate about whether to keep walking, or to say what she then says: "He has an informant. Someone on the inside who is telling them how Jorge prepares his games."

Max blinks in astonishment.

"A spy?"

"Yes."

"Here in Sorrento?"

"Where else?"

"But that's impossible. There is only you, Karapetian, and Irina . . . unless there is someone you haven't told me about."

Mecha shakes her head.

"No one. Just the three of us."

She walks under the archway and Max follows her. After crossing the gloomy corridor, they step into the greenish luminosity of the deserted cloister, amid the columns and pointed stone arches that surround the trees in the garden. There was that sealed move, Mecha explains in hushed tones. The one her son placed in the envelope and handed to the referee after the game was adjourned. The whole of that night and the next day were spent going over the move and its consequences, examining each of Sokolov's possible responses. Jorge, Irina, and Karapetian carried out a systematic analysis of all the variants, preparing countermoves for each one. They all agreed that, after studying the board for no less than twenty minutes, Sokolov would most likely respond by taking a pawn with a bishop. This would give Jorge the chance to lay a trap with his knight and queen, and Sokolov's only way out would be a risky move with his bishop—a kamikaze style of play that was typical of Keller but not of his conservative opponent. When the referee opened the envelope and played the sealed move, Sokolov, as predicted, walked straight into the trap by taking the pawn with his bishop. After which Keller played his knight and queen as agreed. And then, without batting an eyelid, analyzing for only eight minutes something it had taken Keller, Irina, and Karapetian all night to come up with, Sokolov played the risky variant with his bishop. The very move they were sure he would never attempt.

"Could it be a coincidence?"

"There are no coincidences in chess. Only right and wrong moves."

"Are you saying Sokolov already knew what your son was planning and how to counter it?"

"Yes. Jorge's idea was quite obscure and brilliant. Not the most logical move. Impossible to fathom in eight minutes."

"And couldn't there be other people involved, an employee at the hotel, for example? Or hidden microphones?"

"No. I've checked. It's an inside job."

"Really? Goodness me. Then it's either Karapetian or the girl."

Mecha remains silent, contemplating the trees in the little garden.

"That's incredible," says Max.

She turns toward him, almost brusquely, a mixture of astonishment and scorn on her face.

"Why incredible? It's simply part of life, with its customary betrayals." Her expression has grown suddenly dark. "That should come as no surprise to you, of all people."

Max chooses to sidestep her comment.

"I suppose it must be Karapetian."

"It could equally well be Irina."

"Are you serious?"

She replies with a cold, halfhearted smile that lends itself to a host of different interpretations.

"Why on earth would Jorge's trainer or his girlfriend betray him?" asks Max.

Mecha makes a weary gesture, as though disinclined to spell out the obvious. Then she lists the various possible motives in an impassive voice: personal, political, financial, adding a moment later that the reasons for the betrayal are immaterial. There will be time enough to find that out. The important thing is to protect her son. The Sorrento tournament is reaching its halfway mark, and the sixth game will be played tomorrow.

"All this, and the world title just around the corner. Imagine the damage. The devastation."

The two Englishwomen taking photographs have just entered the convent. Mecha and Max move away from them, through the cloister.

"If our suspicions hadn't been aroused, we would have been sold down the river long before we got to Dublin."

"Why are you confiding in me?"

"I told you before," she said, with the same icy smile. "I might need your help."

"I don't see how. Chess isn't my . . ."

"This isn't just about chess. I also said, all in good time."

They have come to a halt once more. Mecha leans back against one of the columns, and Max feels a stab of his old fascination. Despite the years that have passed, Mecha Inzunza retains the stamp of her former beauty. She isn't as splendid as she was thirty years ago, and yet she still reminds him of a serene gazelle, harmonious and agile in her movements. Realizing this, Max gives a gentle, melancholy smile. By staring at her so intently, he has miraculously conflated the features of the woman before him with those of the person he remembers: one of those unique creatures for whom, in a now distant past, sophisticated high society became a willing accomplice, a resigned servant, and a brilliant stage. The magic of all her former beauty blossoms once more before his astonished eyes, almost triumphant amid the drooping flesh, skin blemishes, and other signs of aging.

"Mecha . . ."

"Be quiet. Don't."

He remains silent for an instant. We weren't thinking about the same thing, he concludes. Or so it seems.

"What will you do about Irina, or Karapetian?"

"My son spent last night mulling it over, and we discussed it this morning. . . . A decoy move."

"Decoy?"

The Englishwomen are approaching through the garden, and so Mecha lowers her voice to a whisper. It involves planning a particular move or series of moves in order to check your opponent's response, she explains. Depending on what Sokolov does, it might be possible to deduce whether one of his analysts has warned him beforehand.

"Is it foolproof?"

"Not completely. The Russian might conceal the fact that he already knew by pretending to be flummoxed or in difficulty. Or even work the problem out by himself. But it could give us a clue. Sokolov's own self-confidence might also be of some use. Have you noticed how condescending he is toward Jorge? My son's youth and audacity infuriate him. That may be one of the world champion's weak points. He thinks he has this sewed up. And now I am beginning to understand why."

"Who will you try this out on, Irina or Karapetian?"

"Both. Jorge has come up with two theoretical innovations, two new ideas for the same, very complex, position, which have never been put into practice by any grand master. They both relate to one of Sokolov's favorite opening gambits, and Jorge intends to use them to lay his trap. He will ask Karapetian to analyze one, and Irina the other, but insist they don't discuss the problem with each other on the pretext of avoiding contamination."

"And then by playing one or the other he will unmask the traitor. Is that the idea?"

"Roughly speaking, yes. Although it isn't quite that simple. Depending on Sokolov's response, Jorge will know which of the two moves he was prepared for."

"You seem very sure that Irina doesn't suspect what your son is up to. To share a bed is to share intimacies."

"Is that the voice of experience talking?"

"It's the voice of common sense. For men and women."

You don't know Jorge, she replies, a faint smile on her lips. His ability to be secretive, where chess is concerned. His mistrust of everything and everyone. His girlfriend, his trainer. Even his mother. And that is on a normal day. Imagine what he is like now, with this worry hanging over him.

"Amazing."

"No. Just chess."

Now that he has at last understood, Max reflects calmly on the possibilities: Karapetian or the girl, secrets that survive pillow talk, suspicion and betrayal. Life's lessons.

"I still don't know why you are telling me about this. Why you confide in me. We haven't seen each other for thirty years. I am practically a stranger."

She has stepped away from the column, drawing her face nearer to his. She almost brushes against his cheek as she whispers, and for a moment, despite all the years, the ravages of time and old age, Max feels the murmur of the past, as a shudder of excitement passes through him at the closeness of Mecha's body.

"The decoy move for Irina and Karapetian isn't the only one we have planned. Failing all else, there is another, which an analyst with a sense of humor might call the *Inzunza Defense* or the *Max Variant*. And that, my dear, will be played by you."

"Why me?"

"You know why. Or perhaps not. Perhaps you are so stupid that you really don't know."

7

Of Thieves and Spies

THE BAY OF Angels was still a deep shade of blue. The high rocks beneath the chateau of Nice offered protection from the mistral wind, which barely riffled the water on that part of the shoreline. Leaning against the parapet wall at Rauba-Capeù, Max turned his gaze from the white sails of a sloop moving away from the port and looked at Mauro Barbaresco, standing next to him with his jacket unbuttoned, his necktie loosened, hands thrust in the pockets of his crumpled trousers, hat tipped back on his head. He had dark shadows under his eyes, and his face needed the attentions of a barber.

"There are three typewritten letters," he was telling Max. "They're in a folder Ferriol keeps in the safe in his study at his sister's villa. No doubt there are other documents in there. But we're only interested in the letters."

Max glanced at the other man, Domenico Tignanello, who

had the same disheveled appearance as his colleague. He was standing a few yards away, leaning with a weary air against the door of a dilapidated black Fiat 514 with French plates and a dirty mudguard, gazing gloomily up at the monument to the dead of the Great War. Both men looked as if they had spent an uncomfortable night. Max imagined them lying awake, earning their meager salary as small-time spies, tailing someone (possibly him), or driving through the night from the nearby border, chain-smoking in the glare of the headlights along the twisting black ribbon of asphalt, bordered by streaks of white paint on the trees lining the road.

"Don't take the wrong letters," Barbaresco went on. "We want those three and no others. Double-check before taking them, and make sure you put the file back where it was. The longer it takes Ferriol to find out they're missing, the better."

"I need an exact description."

"You'll recognize them easily from the official seal. They were written between July twentieth and August fourteenth of last year, a few days after the military uprising in Spain." Barbaresco paused for a moment, wondering how much more he should reveal. "They are signed by Count Ciano."

Max listened impassively to this information as he tucked his cane under his arm and reached into his pocket for his cigarette case. He gently tapped a cigarette against the lid and placed it between his lips without lighting it. Like everyone else, he knew who Count Galeazzo Ciano was. Newspaper headlines carried his name, and his face often appeared among the pages of illustrated magazines and newsreels. Swarthy, good-looking, and elegant, always in uniform or wearing evening dress, Il Duce's son-in-law (he was married to Mussolini's daughter Edda) was minister of foreign affairs in the fascist government.

"It would help if I knew more. What is in these letters?"

"You don't need to know much. They contain secret communiqués about preliminary military operations in Spain, as well as expressing my government's sympathy for the patriotic uprising of Generals Mola and Franco. For reasons that are of no concern to us or to you, the letters must be retrieved."

Max listened carefully.

"Why are they here?"

"Ferriol was in Nice last year, around the time of the uprising. He stayed at the villa in Boron and used Marseille airport as the connection for the various trips he made in a private airplane between Lisbon, Biarritz, and Rome. It's quite normal for him to receive personal correspondence here."

"I assume the letters must be compromising. For him or someone else."

Barbaresco ran his hand over his unshaven cheeks in a gesture of impatience.

"You aren't paid to make assumptions, Costa. Besides any technical considerations that might help you do your job, what is in the letters is none of your concern. Or ours, for that matter. Just use your skills to find the best way to obtain them."

With these last words Barbaresco signaled to his colleague, who stepped away from the car and walked leisurely toward them. He had taken an envelope out of the glove compartment in the car and was looking askance at Max.

"Here's the information you asked for," said Barbaresco. "It includes a plan of the house and another of the garden. The safe is a Schützling, installed in a cupboard in the main study."

"When was it made?"

"Nineteen thirteen."

Max was holding the sealed envelope in his hands. Without opening it, he slipped it into his inside jacket pocket.

"How many servants in the house?"

Lips sealed, Tignanello raised five fingers.

"Five," Barbaresco specified. "Maid, housekeeper, chauffeur, gardener, cook. Only the first three live in. Their rooms are on the top floor. There's also a guard in the lodge at the entrance."

"Any dogs?"

"No. Ferriol's sister can't stand them."

Max calculated how long it would take him to open a Schützling. Thanks to the instruction of his former colleague Enrico Fossataro, the former ballroom dancer boasted two Fichets and a Rudi Meyer on his curriculum, not to mention half a dozen safes with more conventional locks. Schützlings were Swiss-made, and had a slightly antiquated mechanism. If conditions were ideal and he used the right technique and made no mistakes, he would need an hour at most. However, the problem wasn't time, but rather how to get at the safe and work calmly and without interruption.

"I shall need Fossataro."

"Why?"

"Keys. The safe has a combination and a traditional lock. Tell him I need a full set of double-bitted keys."

"A full set of what?"

"He'll know what I mean. And I'll need another advance. My costs are mounting."

Barbaresco remained silent, as if he hadn't heard Max's last words. He glanced at his colleague, who was once more leaning against the Fiat, gazing up at the monument to the dead. An enormous white urn set in an arched niche in the rocky wall, and below it the inscription *La ville de Nice à ses fils morts pour la France*.

"It brings back sad memories for Domenico," Barbaresco said. "He lost two brothers at Caporetto."

Barbaresco had removed his hat and was running his hand over his bald head in a weary gesture. Then he looked at Max.

"Were you never a soldier?"

"Never."

Max stared straight at him. Barbaresco seemed to be studying him, turning his hat over in his hands as if that helped him discover whether Max was telling the truth. Perhaps being in the army leaves its stamp on you, reflected Max. Like the priesthood. Or prostitution.

"I was," said Barbaresco after a moment. "In Isonzo. Fighting the Austrians."

"How interesting."

Barbaresco shot Max another probing, suspicious glance.

"The French were our allies in that war," he added after a moment's silence. "That won't be the case in the next one."

Max raised his eyebrows with the right amount of ingenuousness.

"Will there be a next one?"

"You can be sure of that. All that English arrogance together with the stupidity of the French . . . and the Jews and communists plotting behind the scenes. Do you see what I am saying? It can only end badly."

"Of course. Jews and communists. Thank heavens for Hitler. Not to mention Mussolini."

"You can be sure. Fascist Italy . . ."

Barbaresco broke off, as though suddenly wary of Max's calm approval. He glanced at the entrance to the old port and the lighthouse on the end of the jetty, then took in the sweep of the beach and the city, which stretched beyond Rauba-Capeù beneath the green hills speckled with pink and white villas.

"This city will be ours again one day." He narrowed his eyes, darkly.

"I have no objection to that," said Max. "In the meantime, I need more money."

A further silence. Not without an obvious effort, Barbaresco slowly emerged from his patriotic dreams.

"How much?"

"Another ten thousand francs. Or the equivalent in your currency, I don't mind. This is an expensive town."

Barbaresco responded with an evasive gesture.

"We'll see what we can do. Have you met Susana Ferriol yet? Have you found a way of getting close to her?"

Cupping his hands, Max lit the cigarette, which for a while he had been holding between his fingers.

"I'm invited to dinner there tomorrow evening."

A look of genuine admiration flashed across Barbaresco's face.

"How did you pull that off?"

"It doesn't matter." Max exhaled a puff of smoke that was instantly swept away by the breeze.

"Once I have staked out the house, I'll report back to you."

Barbaresco smirked, glancing obliquely at Max's immaculately pressed, tailored suit, Charvet shirt and tie, and shiny leather Scheer shoes purchased in Vienna. Max thought he detected a simultaneous glint of respect and envy in his eyes.

"Well, be quick about reporting back and doing the job. Time is running out, Costa. And that is bad." He put on his hat and nodded in the direction of his partner. "For Domenico and myself. As well as for you."

—ᴍ—

"The Russians have much more at stake in Sorrento than a prize," says Lambertucci. "What with the cold war, the nuclear arms race, and the rest of it, why not throw chess into the mix as well?"

The muffled strains of Patty Pravo singing "Ragazzo Triste" on the radio reach them from the kitchen, muffled by a multicolored plastic strip curtain. At one of the tables near the door, a dejected Captain Tedesco (he lost both games to Lambertucci that afternoon) is gathering the chess pieces up off the board while Lambertucci pours three glasses of red wine from a carafe.

"The Kremlin," continues Lambertucci, setting the glasses down on the table, "wants to show that their grand masters are superior. Thereby proving that the Soviet Union is, too, and will end up winning a political and, if necessary, a military victory over the West."

WHAT WE BECOME / 239

"Is it true?" Max asks. "Are the Russians better at chess?" Max (in his shirtsleeves, collar undone, jacket draped over the back of his chair) is paying careful attention to what is being said. Lambertucci puts on a smug expression in homage to the Russians.

"They have every reason to show off. They have bribed the International Federation, which is safely in their pocket. . . . As we speak, only Jorge Keller and Bobby Fischer pose them any real threat."

"And they will eventually succeed," says Tedesco, who has closed the box containing the chess pieces and is sipping his wine. "Those unorthodox youngsters play a new, more imaginative game. They are forcing the dinosaurs to leave the confines of their habitual positional play and venture into unknown territory."

"In any event," says Lambertucci, "up until now they have had the upper hand. Tal, who was Latvian, was beaten by Botvinnik, who lost a year later to Petrosian, who was Armenian. All Russians. Or Soviets, to be more precise. And now Sokolov is world champion. Another Russian, and then another. Moscow doesn't want that to change."

Max raises his glass to his lips and looks outside. Beneath the bamboo canopy, Lambertucci's wife is laying out checkered tablecloths and candles in empty wine bottles, for customers who, given the lateness of the season, are unlikely to arrive at that time in the afternoon.

"And so," Max says cautiously, "spying might be usual practice in these instances. . . ."

Lambertucci brushes away a fly that has landed on his forearm and rubs his old Abyssinian tattoo.

"Absolutely," he confirms. "Every competition is fraught with a web of conspiracies worthy of a spy movie. The players are under immense pressure. If a top-class Soviet player becomes champion, he will enjoy a privileged lifestyle, but if he loses, he risks reprisals. The KGB is unforgiving."

"Remember Streltsov," say Tedesco. "The soccer player."

The carafe is passed around the table again as Tedesco and Lambertucci explain what happened to Streltsov. One the best players in the world, on a par with Pelé, his career was destroyed because he broke the rules by refusing to leave his local team, Torpedo, to join Dynamo Moscow, the unofficial KGB team. He was tried on some trumped-up charge and sent to a Siberian labor camp. When he returned five years later, his sporting career was over.

"Those are their methods," concludes Lambertucci. "And Sokolov must be going through the same thing with all those analysts, advisers, bodyguards, and calls from Khrushchev urging him on, assuring him the proletarian paradise is cheering him on. He may give the impression of being calm when he is playing, but still waters run deep."

Tedesco nods in agreement.

"But in spite of all this, their players manage to stay focussed and perform well. That's the real Soviet miracle."

"Does it include cheating?" Max asks, casually.

Tedesco gives a one-sided grin, screwing up his good eye.

"It certainly does. Anything from the silliest ploys to the most elaborate trickery."

He goes on to list a few. At the last world championship, when Sokolov was playing Cohen in Manila, a Soviet embassy employee sat in the front row taking flash photographs in an attempt to put the Israeli off his game. It was also rumored that during the olympiad in Varna, the Russians planted a parapsychologist in the audience with the aim of distracting Sokolov's opponents telepathically. And apparently when he was defending his title against the Yugoslav Monfilovic, his advisers slipped him instructions with the yogurts they ate during the game.

"But the best story of all," he concluded, "is the one about Bobkov, a player who defected from the Soviet Union during the Reykjavík tournament: they managed to infect his underwear in the laundry room at the hotel with the bacterium that causes gonorrhea."

Now is the time, thinks Max, to cut to the chase.

"What if," he suggests nonchalantly, "one of the opponent's analysts were a spy?"

"Analysts?" Lambertucci looks at him, intrigued. "My word, Max, you *are* getting technical."

"I've been reading about it."

It does happen sometimes, they confirm. There was a notorious case involving an English analyst called Byrne. He was working for the Norwegian Aronsen, who played Petrosian shortly before Petrosian lost the title to Sokolov. Byrne confessed to having leaked information about Aronsen's game with Petrosian to some alleged Russian bookmakers who were placing two-thousand-ruble bets on each game. It was later discovered that the information had in fact been passed on to the KGB, and in turn to one of Petrosian's assistants.

"Could something like that be going on here in Sorrento?"

"Considering what is at stake between now and the world title, anything is possible," says Tedesco. "Chess isn't always confined to a board."

Lambertucci's wife comes in with a broom and dustpan, and turns them out while she airs the room and sweeps between the tables. They drain their glasses and step outside. Beyond the tables and the bamboo canopy, Dr. Hugentobler's Rolls-Royce Silver Cloud flaunts its silver-plated angel on the cherry-red hood.

"Is your boss still away?" asks Lambertucci, admiring the vehicle.

"For now."

"I envy you. What do you think, Capitano? A spot of work and then time off, until the boss gets back."

The three men laugh together as they walk along the jetty to the harbor, where a fishing boat has just come in, attracting a crowd of passersby eager to see their catch.

"What's so special about Keller and Sokolov?" Lambertucci asks Max. "And why the sudden interest in chess?"

"The Campanella contest has aroused my curiosity."

Lambertucci winks at Tedesco.

"The Campanella contest and possibly a certain lady you dined with here the other night."

"Who didn't seem to be the housekeeper." Tedesco chortles.

Max glances at Tedesco, who grins archly. Then he turns to Lambertucci again.

"You told him already?"

"Of course. Who else am I to confide in? Besides, I never saw you look so dapper. And there was I, pretending we'd never met. . . . God knows what you were up to!"

"You did your best to find out by eavesdropping."

"It was all I could do not to laugh out loud, watching you play the lothario at your age. You reminded me of Vittorio De Sica when he puts on aristocratic airs."

They are standing on the quayside, near the fishing boat. As the crew unloads the crates, a breeze sweeps through the nets and lines piled on the quayside, wafting the smells of fish, salt, and tar.

"You're like a pair of old washerwomen with your gossip."

Lambertucci nods, brazenly.

"Skip the introduction, Max. Get to the point."

"She is, or was, an old acquaintance. That's all."

The two amateur chess players exchange a knowing look.

"She also happens to be Keller's mother," Lambertucci parries. "And don't pull that face; we saw her photograph in the newspapers."

"This has nothing to do with chess. Or with her son. . . . I told you, she's an old acquaintance."

Max's last words elicit a skeptical look from both men.

"An old acquaintance," says Lambertucci, "who sparks off a half-hour discussion about Russian chess players and the KGB."

"A fascinating subject, it has to be said," Tedesco remarks. "So, no complaints."

"All right. Let's drop it, shall we?"

Lambertucci nods, still in a teasing mood.

"If you insist. We all have our little secrets, and this is your affair. But it will cost you. . . . We want tickets to watch the games in the Vittoria. But we can't afford them. Now you have connections, that changes the situation."

"I'll do what I can."

Lambertucci takes a last draw on his cigarette, which is burning down to his fingers. Then he throws it into the water.

"Aging is a tragedy. She was a beautiful woman, wasn't she? You only have to look at her."

"Yes." Max watches the cigarette end bobbing on the oily water below. "They say she was very beautiful."

—⁓—

Through a picture window open on to the Mediterranean, the midday sun cast a light on the Jetée-Promenade—a splendid edifice opposite Hôtel Ruhl, resting on piles dug into the seabed and offering a view of the coastline, the beach, and the Promenade des Anglais, as if the observer were in a boat anchored a few yards offshore. The restaurant window, adjacent to Max's table, overlooked the Bay of Angels to the east, and gave a clear view of the towering castle in the distance, the port entrance, and beyond, Le Cap de Nice with the Villefranche road meandering through its craggy greenery.

He saw the shadow before the man. The first thing he sensed was the smell of English tobacco. Max was leaning over his plate, finishing his salad, when a waft of pipe smoke reached him and the floor creaked slightly as a dark shape loomed on the bright patch. He glanced up and encountered a polite smile, a pair of round, tortoiseshell spectacles, and a hand—the one holding the pipe (the other was clutching a crumpled panama hat)—pointing toward the empty chair across the table from Max.

"Good afternoon. . . . Might I sit down here for a moment?"

The oddness of the request, made in perfect Spanish, took Max by surprise. Still holding his fork in midair, he stared at the stranger (the intruder, to be more precise), racking his brains for a reply to this impertinence.

"Of course not," he said at last. "I mean of course you can't."

The man hesitated, as if he had been expecting a different response. He hadn't stopped smiling but looked somewhat flustered and pensive. He wasn't very tall, Max thought, and calculated that if he stood up, he would be a head higher. The man had a neat, inoffensive appearance, accentuated by his spectacles, and the brown suit he wore with a waistcoat and bow tie, all of which seemed to hang loosely from his bony, delicate-looking frame. His hair was parted in the middle, seemingly with a ruler, dividing his black, slicked-back hair into two precise halves.

"I fear I got off to a bad start," the stranger said, smiling doggedly. "Please forgive my clumsiness, and give me another chance."

At which, casually, without awaiting a response, the man walked away a few paces and then returned. Suddenly he no longer seemed so innocuous, thought Max. Or so fragile.

"Good afternoon, Mr. Costa," he said calmly. "My name is Rafael Mostaza and I have something important I wish to discuss with you. If you'll allow me to sit down, we can talk more easily."

The smile was identical, only now Max observed an additional, almost metallic glint, behind his spectacles. Max had set his fork down on his plate. Having regained his composure, he leaned back in the wicker chair, wiping his mouth with his napkin.

"We have mutual interests," the other man went on. "In Italy as well as here in Nice."

Max looked at the waiters in their white aprons standing far off, next to the potted plants beside the entrance. There was no one else in the restaurant.

"Do sit down."

"Thank you."

When the strange fellow ensconced himself in the chair and began emptying his pipe, tapping the bowl lightly against the window frame, Max realized where he had seen him before. In fact, he had seen the man twice in the past few days: once while he was talking to the Italian agents at Café Monnot, and again when he was lunching with Baroness Schwarzenberg on the terrace of La Frégate, opposite the Promenade.

"Please, carry on eating," the man said, shaking his head at one of the waiters, who was walking toward them.

Leaning back in his chair, Max studied him with veiled unease.

"Who are you?"

"I just told you. Rafael Mostaza, commercial traveler. Call me Fito, if you prefer. Everyone else does."

"And who is everyone?"

The man winked, without replying, as if they shared an amusing secret. Max had never heard the name before.

"A commercial traveler, you say."

"Just so."

"What sort of commerce?"

Mostaza's smile broadened slightly. He seemed to wear it with the same ease he wore his bow tie: openly, pleasantly enough, and possibly a little loose. Yet the metallic glint remained, as though the lenses in his glasses chilled his gaze.

"All commerce is related nowadays, don't you think? But never mind about that. What's important is the story I am about to tell you. A story involving the financier Tomás Ferriol."

Max registered the name calmly as he raised his glass of wine (a splendid burgundy) to his lips. He replaced it on the exact spot where it had left an indentation on the white tablecloth.

"I beg your pardon. Whom did you say?"

"Oh, come now. Believe me, it is an interesting story. Allow me to tell it to you."

Max touched the wineglass, without picking it up this time. Despite the open window, he felt suddenly flushed. Uncomfortable.

"You have five minutes."

"Don't be grudging. Listen first, and you'll see how you grant me more time."

In a hushed voice, occasionally biting down on his unlit pipe, Mostaza began his tale. Tomás Ferriol, he said, was among the group of monarchists who, the year before, had supported the military uprising in Spain. In fact, it was Ferriol who bore the initial cost, and had continued to finance the rebels. It was common knowledge that his immense fortune had turned him into the rebels' unofficial paymaster.

"Admit it," Mostaza broke off, pointing the stem of his pipe at Max, "my story is beginning to intrigue you."

"Perhaps."

"I told you. I'm good at telling stories."

Mostaza resumed his tale, saying that Ferriol's opposition to the Republic wasn't simply ideological: he had made several failed attempts to reach an agreement with successive republican governments. But they didn't trust him, and they were right. In 1934, a judicial investigation would have sent him to prison had he not used his money and influence to avoid a sentence. After that, his political position could be summed up in the words he pronounced at a private dinner among friends: "The Republic, or me." And that was what he had been doing for the past year and a half: destroying the Republic. Everyone knew he had bankrolled the July uprising. After a meeting held in San Juan de Luz with a messenger sent by the conspirators, Ferriol had paid out of his own pocket, through an account at the Kleinwort bank, for the plane and the pilot that flew Franco from the Canary Islands to Morocco. And while that plane was in the air, five Texaco oil tankers on course to deliver twenty-five thousand tons of crude to the Spanish state oil company Campsa changed direction and headed to the area under rebel control. The order conveyed by telegram said, *Don't worry about payment.* Tomás Ferriol had footed the bill and was continuing to do so. It was estimated that in fuel alone he had already given the rebels a million dollars.

"But this isn't only about fuel," Mostaza resumed after pausing for a moment so that Max could assimilate the information. "We know Ferriol had a meeting with General Mola at his headquarters in Pamplona in the early days of the uprising. During that meeting Ferriol showed Mola a list of guarantees he had signed, totaling six hundred million pesetas. Interestingly, true to Ferriol's style, he didn't give or offer Mola any money. He simply showed him his solid credentials as a guarantor. Proposing to bankroll everything. And that included using his commercial and financial contacts in Germany and Italy."

Mostaza fell silent, sucking on his unlit pipe, his eyes fixed on Max, as a waiter came to take away Max's empty plate while another arrived with the second course—entrecôte *à la niçoise.* The square of light had moved up from the floor onto the white tablecloth. The brightness was now illuminating Mostaza's face from below, revealing an ugly scar Max hadn't noticed before on the left side of his neck, below the jaw.

"The conspirators," Mostaza went on, after the waiters had left, "also needed aircraft. Tactical air support, to transport the Moroccan rebel troops to the peninsula, and for bombing raids. Four days after the uprising, General Franco sent a message to the German High Command via their military attaché to France and Portugal, asking for ten Junker aircraft. Ferriol took care of the Italians." Mostaza leaned forward slightly, resting his elbows on the table. "Do you see how the different strands come together?"

Max had forced himself to carry on eating normally, but he was finding it hard. After two mouthfuls, he placed his knife and fork side by side on his plate, at the precise angle of five o'clock. Then he wiped his mouth with his napkin, rested his starched cuffs on the edge of the tablecloth, and looked straight at Mostaza, without saying a word. "The Italian offer," his interlocutor went on, "went through the Foreign Minister, Count Ciano. Initially in a private conversation he and Ferriol had in Rome, then via an exchange of letters detailing the operation. Italy had twelve Savoia Marchetti aircraft on standby in Sardinia, and Ciano, after consulting with Mussolini, promised they would be in Tetuán at the rebels' disposal by the first week of August, pending receipt of a million pounds sterling. Neither Mola nor Franco had that much money, but Ferriol did. And so he advanced part of the sum and guaranteed the remainder. On July 30, the twelve aircraft took off bound for Morocco. Three went down over the sea, but the others arrived in time to transport the Moroccan troops and legionnaires to the peninsula. Four days later, the Italian merchant vessel *Emilio Morlandi*, which was chartered by Ferriol and had left La Spezia carrying ammunition and fuel for those aircraft, docked in Melilla.

"I told you the Italians wanted a million pounds for their aircraft, but Ciano is a man with a lavish lifestyle. Extremely lavish. His wife, Edda, is Il Duce's daughter, and while that brings many advantages, it also incurs a great deal of expense. Do you follow?"

"Perfectly."

"Good, because now we get to the part where you come in."

A waiter came to remove Max's plate, almost untouched. He sat motionless, his hands resting on the edge of the table, staring at Mostaza.

"And what makes you think I have anything to do with this?"

The other man did not reply at once. He was gazing at the bottle of wine laying in its raffia basket.

"What are you drinking, if you don't mind me asking?"

"Chambertin," Max replied impassively.

"Which year?"

"Nineteen eleven."

"And the cork held up?"

"Yes it did."

"Splendid . . . I'd like to try some, if I may."

Max signaled to the waiter, who brought over another glass and filled it. Mostaza set his pipe down on the table and studied the wine in the light, admiring the intense red of the burgundy. Then he raised the glass to his lips, savoring the wine with visible pleasure.

"I've been tailing you for some time," he blurted, as though suddenly remembering Max's question. "Those two Italian fellows . . ."

He broke off, leaving it up to Max to imagine exactly when one trail had led to another.

"Then I found out as much as I could about you."

Mostaza resumed his narrative. Hitler and his government detested Ciano. For his part, Ciano, who was no fool, had always favored Italy keeping its distance from some of Berlin's ambitions. And he was still of that opinion. Which is why, being a cautious man, he kept several secret safe-deposit boxes in suitable locations. For political reasons, a large account he held at an English bank had to be moved, and his money was currently in continental banks, mainly Swiss.

"Ciano demanded four percent commission for the Savoia Marchetti deal. Forty thousand pounds. Almost a million pesetas, guaranteed by Ferriol at the Société Suisse in Zurich until it was paid with gold confiscated from the Banco de España in Palma de Mallorca. What do you say to that?"

"It's a lot of money."

"More importantly," Mostaza said after taking another sip of wine, "it's a major political scandal."

Despite his composure, Max was no longer bothering to conceal his interest.

"I see," he said. "Once the information is made public, you mean."

"Precisely." Mostaza placed his finger on the stem of his glass to prevent a drop of wine from running down onto the tablecloth. "The people who told me about you, Mr. Costa, said you were a good-looking, clever fellow. I couldn't care less about your looks. I am, on the whole, a man of conventional tastes. But your intelligence speaks for itself."

He paused, savoring another mouthful of burgundy.

"Tomás Ferriol is a sly fox," he went on, "and he wanted everything in writing. There were time pressures, this was a safe deal, and Ciano's commissions are no secret in Rome. His father-in-law knows about them, and raises no objections providing things are done discreetly, as they have been up until now. And so Ferriol contrived to generate written evidence of the aircraft deal, which included three letters where Ciano, in his own handwriting, mentions the four percent commission. You can imagine the rest."

"Why do they want those letters back now?"

Mostaza contemplated his nearly empty glass with a satisfied expression.

"There could be numerous reasons. Tensions within the Italian government, where Ciano's position is currently contested by other fascist families. Perhaps Ciano is simply being cautious about the future, now that a rebel victory in Spain isn't unthinkable. Or he wants to divest Ferriol of evidence that he could use as diplomatic leverage. The fact is, Ciano wants those letters, and you have been hired to get them."

It was all so glaringly obvious that Max set aside his original misgivings.

"I still have a question, which I may also have posed to others. Why me? Surely Italy has spies of its own."

"The way I see it is simple." Mostaza had picked up his pipe, and, after taking out an oilcloth pouch, he proceeded to fill the bowl, tamping the tobacco down with his thumb. "We are in

France. The international situation is delicate. You are a man with no political affiliation. Stateless, in a sense."

"I have a Venezuelan passport."

"Not meaning to boast, but I can buy a dozen of those things. Moreover, you have a criminal record, proven or not, in several European and South American countries. . . . If something went wrong, you would be arrested. In which case they could deny everything."

"And whose side are you on in all this?"

Mostaza, who had fished out a box of matches and lit his pipe, looked at Max, almost with astonishment, through the first puffs of smoke.

"Well. I thought you would have guessed that by now. I work for the Spanish Republic. I am one of the good guys. Assuming there are any in a situation of this kind."

A casual reader (on ocean liners, trains, and in hotels) of serialized fiction published in illustrated magazines, Max associated the word *spy* with sophisticated international adventuresses and sinister men skulking around under cover of darkness. Hence his surprise at the easy way Fito Mostaza offered to accompany him back to his hotel, enjoying an agreeable (Mostaza's choice of adjective) stroll along the Promenade. Max raised no objection, and for part of the way they chatted like two acquaintances about nothing in particular, just like all the other people coming and going at that time of day between the hotels on one side and the beach on the other. And so, puffing calmly on his pipe, Mostaza finished explaining the details of the affair, while answering the questions occasionally posed by Max (who despite the apparently relaxed situation, did not lower his guard).

"In brief: we will pay you more than the fascists. Not to mention the Republic's debt of gratitude."

"For what that's worth," Max allowed himself to comment, ironically.

252 / Arturo Pérez-Reverte

Mostaza gave a soft, almost good-natured laugh, jaw clenched. The scar below his chin gave his laughter an ambiguous quality.

"There is no need to be spiteful, Mr. Costa. After all, I represent the legitimate Spanish government. You know, democracy versus fascism."

Swinging his cane, the former ballroom dancer cast a sidelong glance at Mostaza. The man looked even smaller and more delicate when he was moving on his feet, and if it weren't for his spectacles, he would seem like a jockey in civvies. However, in Max's profession one automatic reflex was to classify men and women by what they didn't say. In his shadowy world, a conventional word or gesture was as valueless, in terms of useful information, as the expression on the face of an experienced cardsharp who knows his adversary's hand. These were the codes Max had learned over the years. And the three quarters of an hour he had spent in Fito Mostaza's company were enough to tell him that the man's friendly tone, his likable openness when he claimed to be one of the good guys, could be more deceptive than the surliness of the two Italian agents. Whom, as a matter of fact, Max was surprised not to have seen skulking behind a newspaper on a bench along the Promenade, tailing them only to discover, with understandable annoyance, that Fito Mostaza was upsetting their plans.

"Why not steal the letters yourselves?"

Mostaza walked on a few steps without replying. Then gave a shrug.

"Do you know what Tomás Ferriol would say? That he isn't interested in buying politicians before they are elected, because it is cheaper to buy them once they are in power."

He fell silent, puffing vigorously on his pipe and leaving behind him a trail of tobacco smoke.

"We are in a similar situation," he said at last. "Why organize an expensive, risky operation when we can take advantage of one that is already under way?"

With that, Mostaza continued walking, laughing softly as before. He seemed pleased with the way the conversation was going.

"The Republic doesn't have money to burn, Mr. Costa. The peseta is depreciating fast. There is an almost poetic justice in the fact that Mussolini will be the one paying most of your fee."

Max was contemplating the Roll-Royces and Cadillacs parked outside the Palais de la Méditerranée's impressive façade, among the line of expensive hotels that seemed to stretch along the gentle sweep of the Bay of Angels into infinity. There was nothing in that part of Nice to challenge the wealthy visitor's comfortable view of the world. There were only hotels, casinos, bars, the magnificent beach, the nearby city center with its cafés and restaurants, and the luxury villas in the surrounding hills. Not a single factory or hospital. The workshops, the humble dwellings of domestic servants and laborers, the prison and the cemetery, even the demonstrators who had begun clashing in the street of late under the watchful eyes of the gendarmes, singing "The Internationale" or "The Marseillaise" and handing out copies of *Le Cri des Travailleurs*, or shouting "death to the Jews," were a long way from there. In neighborhoods where the majority of those strolling along the Promenade des Anglais would never set foot.

"And what is to stop me from refusing your offer? Or informing the Italians about your proposal?"

"Nothing whatsoever," admitted Mostaza evenly. "You see how far we are willing to play fairly, within reason. Without resorting to threats or blackmail. It is entirely up to you whether you collaborate or not."

"What if I don't do as you ask?"

"Ah, that's another matter. If you refuse, you must understand that we will do our best to influence the course of events."

Max doffed his hat to two familiar faces (a Hungarian couple in the room next door to his at the hotel) who had just walked past.

"If that isn't a threat . . ." he whispered sarcastically.

Mostaza responded with an exaggerated sigh of resignation.

"This is a complicated game, Mr. Costa. We have nothing against you personally, unless your actions put you in the enemy camp. Otherwise, you will enjoy our full support."

"In the form of more money than the Italians, you said."

"Of course. Providing the sum isn't astronomical."

They continued strolling along the Promenade, where a continuous flow of stylish people passed them by: men in midseason tailor-made suits, beautiful, haughty women walking pedigree dogs.

"This is a curious city," Mostaza remarked, confronted by two smartly dressed ladies with a borzoi on a lead. "Full of women who are inaccessible to most men. You and I are the exception, of course. . . . The difference is that I have to pay, and for you it is the other way around."

Max glanced about: women, men, it made no difference. These were people for whom, in short, carrying five one-thousand-franc notes around in their wallet was nothing out of the ordinary. The cars with their shiny chrome rolled along the road's surface, in perfect harmony with the glittering landscape of which they were a part. The entire Promenade was one long hum of purring engines and carefree conversations, of blithe, expensive well-being. I worked hard to get where I am, Max thought angrily. To move with ease in these comfortable surroundings, far away from those squalid neighborhoods smelling of rotten food, which in places like this have been banished to the outskirts. And I'll see to it that no one sends me back there.

"But don't imagine that this all boils down to who pays more or less," Mostaza was saying. "My bosses think, I suppose, that my personal charm plays a part. My job is to persuade you. To convince you that working for thugs like Mussolini, Hitler, and Franco isn't the same as working for the legitimate Spanish government."

"Skip that bit."

Mostaza laughed the same way he had before. Softly, jaw clenched.

"Very well. Let's leave ideology out of it and focus instead on my personal charm."

He had come to a halt and was emptying his pipe, tapping it gently against the handrail between the Promenade and the beach. Afterward he slipped it into his jacket pocket.

"I like you, Mr. Costa. . . . Despite your shady profession, you are what the English would call a decent chap. Or at least, you give that impression. I have been looking into your past for some time, as well as watching the way you behave. It will be a pleasure to work with you."

"What about the competition?" Max protested. "The Italians might grow angry. Understandably."

Mostaza responded with a sharp smile, no more than an instant and none too pleasant. A predatory glare. The scar on his neck seemed to grow deeper in the brightness of the walkway.

"I can't give you an answer now," said Max. "I need time to think it over."

Mostaza's round spectacles flashed twice beneath his panama hat as he nodded understandingly.

"I'll make sure you get it. You reflect about it calmly, while continuing to deal with your fascist friends. In the meantime, I will follow your progress discreetly, from a distance. Far be it from us, as I said before, to force the issue. We prefer to believe in your common sense and your good conscience. There is no hurry. You can give me your answer at any time, even at the last moment."

"Where can I find you, if necessary?"

Mostaza flapped his hands, in a vague gesture that might have referred to their present location, or the South of France in general.

"During the next few days, while you are making up your mind, I have other business in Marseille. So I shall be coming and going. But don't worry. I'll be in touch."

He proffered his hand, waiting for Max to reciprocate the gesture, which he did, encountering a firm, frank grip. Too firm, he told himself. Too frank. Then Fito Mostaza hurried away. For a few moments, Max watched the small, agile figure, swerving in and out of the passersby with surprising ease. After that, all he could see was the man's light-colored hat moving amid the crowd, and soon he lost sight of him completely.

—⁓—

The day dawns clear and sunny, as on previous mornings, and the Bay of Naples is vivid with blues and grays. The waiters move around the terrace of the Hotel Vittoria carrying trays laden with coffeepots, rolls, butter, and jam among the metal tables decked with white tablecloths. At the table in the western corner of the stone balustrade, Max Costa and Mecha Inzunza are having breakfast. She is dressed in a suede jacket, dark skirt, and Belgian loafers, while he is sporting his preferred morning attire since he has been staying at the hotel: flannel trousers, a dark blazer, and silk neckerchief. His gray hair, meticulously groomed, is still damp from the shower.

"Have you found a solution to the problem yet?" he asks.

They are alone at the table, and the adjacent ones are empty. Even so, she lowers her voice.

"It's possible. We'll find out this afternoon whether it has worked or not."

"Irina and Karapetian aren't suspicious?"

"Not at all. The pretext of avoiding any contamination between them has worked for the moment."

Pensive, Max spreads a pat of butter onto a triangular piece of toast. They had met by chance. She was reading a book, which is now lying on the table (*The Quest for Corvo*: he doesn't recognize the title) between her empty coffee cup and an ashtray bearing the hotel crest and containing two Muratti cigarette butts. She was closing her book and stubbing out the second cigarette when he stepped through the glass door of the Liberty lounge and went over to greet her, whereupon she invited him to take a seat.

"You said I would be doing something."

She gazes intently at him for a moment, scouring her memory. Finally she leans back in her chair with a grin.

"The Max variant? . . . All in good time."

He takes a bite of toast and sips his coffee.

"Are Karapetian and Irina already working on those ideas Jorge came up with?" he asks, after patting his lips with his napkin. "Those decoy moves you mentioned?"

"They are. Separately, as we planned. The two of them think they are analyzing the same situation, but they aren't . . . Jorge keeps insisting they don't exchange ideas because he doesn't want any contamination to occur."

"Who has made more progress?"

"Irina. And that is good for Jorge, because the thought that it could be her is more abhorrent to him. . . . And so in his next game, he will try out that new variant, to clear up any doubts as soon as possible."

"What about Karapetian?"

"He has asked Emil to do a more in-depth analysis, because he plans to keep that one for Dublin."

"Do you think Sokolov will fall into the trap?"

"Probably. The idea is to make him play with the Keller touch, sacrificing pieces and launching bold, penetrating, brilliant attacks."

Just then, Max glimpses Karapetian in the distance, a couple of newspapers in his hand, heading for the lounge. He points him out to Mecha, who follows the grand master with a vacant expression.

"It'll be sad if it's him," she says.

Max can't help looking surprised.

"You'd prefer it to be Irina?"

"Emil has been with Jorge since he was a boy. He owes a great deal to Emil. We both do."

"But the two youngsters . . . I mean, what about love and all the rest of it?"

Mecha looks down at the ground strewn with the ash from her cigarettes.

"Oh, that," she says.

Then, without pausing, she starts talking about the next step, assuming Sokolov takes the bait. They don't intend to expose the informant, if it does turn out to be one of these two. With the world title challenge in Dublin coming up, it is better to give the information to the Soviets, so that Sokolov doesn't suspect they have been onto him since Sorrento. After Dublin, of course, whoever turns out to be the spy will never work with Jorge again. There are ways to get rid of people with or without a scandal, as appropriate. This has happened before: a French analyst was talking too much at the tournament in Curaçao, where Jorge was playing Petrosian, Tal, and Korchnoi. On that occasion it was Emil Karapetian who exposed the infiltrator. In the end they agreed to fire him without anyone suspecting why.

"He could also have been a scapegoat," Max points out. "A ploy by Karapetian to divert suspicion away from himself."

"I thought of that," she said, solemnly. "And so did Jorge."

And yet, her son owes his teacher so much, she goes on to say a few moments later. Jorge was thirteen when she persuaded Karapetian to work with him. They have been together for fifteen years, playing on pocket chessboards everywhere they go, on trains, in airports and hotels. Preparing for games, studying gambits, variants, attacks, and defenses.

"For more than half his life I have watched them eat breakfast together, playing blindfold chess, going over plans they made during the night, or improvising."

"You'd prefer it to be her," Max says gently.

Mecha seems not to have heard his remark.

"He wasn't a remarkable child. People have this idea that great chess players are more intelligent than the rest of humanity, but that isn't true. Jorge was only exceptional in his ability to concentrate on several different things at once; the Germans have a long word for it ending in *verteilung*, and to think abstractly about number series."

"Where did he and Irina meet?"

"At the tournament in Montreal, a year and a half ago. She was dating Henry Trench, a Canadian chess player."

"And what happened?"

"She and Jorge met at a party held by the organizers, and they spent all night sitting on a park bench talking about chess. Then she left Trench."

"She seems to be good for him, don't you think? Keeps him sane in situations like this."

"She plays her part," Mecha admits. "But Jorge isn't an obsessive player. He isn't the type to let the uncertainties and tensions of a long game get to him. His sense of humor and a certain amount of detachment help. One of his pet expressions is "I'm not going to let this drive me crazy." That attitude keeps him from becoming neurotic. As you say, it helps him to stay sane."

She pauses for a moment, head tilted to one side.

"Yes, I imagine Irina does play a part in that," she says at last.

"If his girlfriend is passing information to the Russians, I imagine that would affect his concentration. His performance."

Mecha isn't concerned about that aspect of the problem. Her son, she explains, is capable of working with the same intensity on several different things, apparently simultaneously, without losing sight of the main issue: chess. His ability to focus is astonishing. He might seem to be daydreaming, and all of a sudden he blinks, grins, and is with you again. That capacity he has to go off and come back is the most remarkable thing about him. Without these flashes of normality, his life would be very different. He would become an eccentric or a depressive.

"That's why," she adds after a pause, "as well as being capable of superhuman concentration, he can also become absorbed by things other than the game he is playing. Like playing a different game in his head. Thinking calmly about the infiltrator, about a trip or a film. Solve another problem, or make light of it. Once, when Jorge was small, he sat in front of the chessboard analyzing a move for twenty minutes without budging or making a sound. And when his opponent started to show signs of becoming impatient, he looked up and said, 'Ah, is it my turn to move?'"

"You still haven't told me what you think. Whether you believe she is the one passing on information."

"I told you. It could equally be Irina or Karapetian."

He raises his eyebrows, acknowledging the difficulty.

"She seems to be in love."

"Heavens, Max." She looks at him ironically, almost with surprise. "Am I hearing things? Since when did love get in the way of betrayal?"

"Give me one good reason why Irina would sell him to the Russians?"

"That question doesn't become you either. Why would Emil?"

She has raised her eyes, impassively, and Max follows the direction of her gaze. Three floors up, beneath the arches on the patio of the adjacent building, Jorge and Irina are leaning out, contemplating the view. They are both wearing white bathrobes and look as if they have just got up. She has her arm looped through his and her head is resting on his shoulder. After a moment, they notice Max and Mecha, and wave to them. He waves back while she remains motionless, staring at them.

"How long did your marriage to his father, the diplomat, last?"

"Not long," she says after a brief silence. "Although I tried my hardest. I suppose having a child made a difference. At some point in her life every woman becomes a victim of her womb or her heart. But none of that was possible with Ernesto. He was a good man, made unbearable not by his many qualities, but because he refused to give any of them up."

She breaks off, a curious smile playing across her face. She rests her hand on the tablecloth, next to the stain left by a drop of coffee. The blemishes on the back of her hand resemble the stain. Liver spots marking the years on her loose skin. Suddenly, the memory of that firm, warm flesh thirty years ago becomes hard for Max to bear. Masking his unease, he leans across the table and checks how much coffee is left in the pot.

"That was never your problem, Max. You always knew . . . Oh, hell. I often wondered where you got all that composure. That watchfulness."

He makes as if to pour her some more coffee, but she shakes her head.

"So handsome," she adds. "My God, you were handsome. A watchful, handsome scoundrel . . ."

Embarrassed, Max studies the inside of his empty coffee cup.

"Tell me more about Jorge's father."

"I already told you, I met him in Nice, at that dinner party at Suzi Ferriol's house. Don't you remember?"

"Vaguely."

With a weary air, Mecha slowly withdraws her hand from the tablecloth.

"Ernesto was terribly polite and distinguished, but he lacked Armando's talent and imagination. One of those men who use others as a pretext to talk about themselves. What they say might interest you, but they don't need to know that."

"Are a lot of men like that?"

"You never were. You were always a good listener."

Max graciously acknowledges the compliment, with calculated modesty.

"Tricks of the trade," he confesses.

"That fact is, things went wrong between us," she goes on, "and

I ended up behaving with the spiteful resentment we women often resort to when we are in pain. Actually, I suffered very little, but he didn't need to know that, either. More than once, he tried to escape from what he referred to as the mediocrity and failure of our marriage. And, like most men, he only got as far as other women's vaginas."

It didn't sound vulgar coming from her, Max noticed. Like so many other things imprinted on his memory. He had heard her use stronger words in the past, with the same, almost surgical coolness.

"I got a lot further, as you know," Mecha resumes. "I am referring to a particular kind of immorality. Immorality as a conclusion. As an acknowledgment of morality's sterile, passive injustice."

Once again, she gazes, with indifference, at the ash on the floor. Then she looks up at the waiter, who informs them that the breakfast service is about to close, and asks if they would like anything else. Mecha stares at him as though she hasn't understood the question, or was far away. Finally she shakes her head.

"Actually, I failed twice," she says when the waiter has left. "As an immoral wife with Armando and as a moral wife with Ernesto. Fortunately for me, my son came along and changed everything. I was given another possibility. A third way."

"Do you remember your first husband more?"

"Armando? How could I forget him. His famous tango has haunted me all my life. As it has you, in a way. And it lives on."

Max looks up from his empty coffee cup again.

"I eventually found out what we still didn't know in Nice," he says. "That they killed him."

"Yes. In a place called Paracuellos, just outside Madrid. They dragged him from the prison and took him there to shoot him," she says, with an imperceptible shrug, accepting tragedies that occurred too far back in time, the scars conveniently healed. "A group of men dragged poor García Lorca out and made a martyr of him. Another lot did the same to my husband. Which of course turned him into a hero. And made his music famous."

"Did you never go back to Spain?"

"To that sad, embittered country reeking of the sacristy and run by black marketeers and mediocre ruffians? No. Never." She looks toward the bay and gives a sarcastic smile. "Armando was cultured, educated, a freethinker. A creator of marvelous things. If he were still alive, he would have despised those military butchers and their blue-shirted thugs with pistols on their belts, just as he would the numbskulls who killed him."

She pauses, then gazes at him, inquisitively.

"What about you? What was your life like during that time? Is it true you returned to Spain?"

Max puts on a suitably serious face as he casts his mind back over those heady days: all those people with new money greedy for luxury, hotels returned to their previous owners, newly rebuilt towns and cities, businesses flourishing under the protection of the new regime: rich pickings for those who knew where to look. Max's cautious expression is his way of glossing over years of exploits and possibilities, vast sums of money changing hands, there for the taking by anyone with the courage or talent to go after it: the black market, women, hotels, trains, borders, refugees, worlds collapsing amid the ruins of the old Europe, one war following another, even more bloodthirsty one, with the feverish conviction that when it was all over, nothing would be the same.

"Once or twice. I went back and forth between Europe and the Americas during the Second World War."

"You weren't afraid of U-boats?"

"Terrified, but I had no choice. Business, you know."

She smiles, almost benevolently.

"Yes, I know . . . Business."

He tilts his head, with deliberate candor, conscious she is watching him. They both know that the word is a simplification, although

Mecha has no idea to what extent. The truth is that during the war in Europe the Iberian peninsula was an extremely lucrative hunting ground for Max Costa. With his Venezuelan passport (he paid a great deal of money to acquire that nationality, which guaranteed him immunity in almost any situation), he employed his easy manner in restaurants, dance halls, tea dances, bars, and cabarets, in winter and summer resorts—frenetic hubs of social life frequented by beautiful women and men with fat wallets. By that time Max had honed his professional skills to an extraordinary extent. The result was a run of resounding successes. The era of failure and decline, the disasters that would cast him into the pit of despair, were a long way off. The new Spain, under Franco, was generous: a string of profitable deals in Madrid and Seville; an elaborate three-way swindle between Barcelona, Marseille, and Tangiers; an extremely wealthy widow in San Sebastián; and a jewelry heist that began in the Estoril casino and ended successfully in a villa in Sintra. During that episode (the lady concerned, not overly attractive, was cousin to the would-be heir to the throne, Juan Carlos of Bourbon), Max started dancing again, furiously. Even to Ravel's "Bolero" and the "Old School Tango." And he must have danced devilishly well, for, once it was all over, the victim was the first to clear his name with the Portuguese police. Max Costa couldn't possibly be a suspect, she swore to them. He was far too much of a gentleman.

"Yes," Mecha says distractedly, glancing back up at the balcony where the two youngsters are no longer standing. "Armando was different."

Max knows she isn't really talking about Armando. She is thinking about the Spain that killed him, the country she never wanted to return to. Still, he feels a pang of resentment. A trace of old anger toward a man whose company he kept for only few days: on board the *Cap Polonio* and in Buenos Aires.

"So you said. He was cultured, imaginative, and a freethinker. I haven't forgotten the bruises on your body where he hit you."

She notices the tone in his voice and gives him a disapproving look. Then she turns toward the bay, in the direction of Vesuvius's dusky cone.

"That was a very long time ago, Max. It's tasteless of you."

He doesn't reply. He is content to look at her. Narrowing her gaze against the sun's glare has increased the number of fine wrinkles around her eyes.

"I married very young," Mecha adds. "And Armando made me delve into my dark, inner places."

"In a way, he corrupted you."

She shakes her head before replying.

"No. Although *in a way* might hold the clue. It was all there before I met him. He merely placed a mirror in front of me. Guided me to those inner places. Or perhaps not; perhaps his role was simply to show them to me."

"And you did the same with me."

"You liked looking, as much as I did. Remember those hotel mirrors?"

"No. I liked to look at you looking."

A sudden burst of laughter makes her sparkling eyes appear young again. Her face is still turned toward the bay.

"You wouldn't let go, my friend. You weren't that sort of fellow. On the contrary. Always so clean, despite your dirty tricks. So wholesome. So conscientious and true to your lies and betrayals. A good soldier."

"For God's sake, Mecha. You were . . ."

"It doesn't matter anymore what I was." She has turned abruptly to face him, all of a sudden serious. "But you are still a charlatan. And don't look at me like that. I know that look too well. Better than you could imagine."

"I'm being honest," Max protests. "I never thought I mattered to you."

"Is that why you left Nice as you did? Without waiting to see what happened? My God. As stupid as the others. That was your mistake."

She has leaned back in her chair. She remains like that for a moment, as though searching for a precise memory in the aged face of the man before her.

"You were living in enemy territory," she says at last. "In the midst of an ongoing war: I could see it in your eyes. In situations like that we women realize that men are mortal, passing through, returning from some front or other. And we are just that little bit more willing to fall in love with you."

"I never liked wars. Men like me are usually on the losing side."

"It doesn't matter anymore," she says coldly. "But I'm glad you haven't lost your easy smile. That elegance you have maintained, like the last square at Waterloo. You remind me very much of the man I forgot. You have aged, and I don't mean physically. I suppose that happens to everyone who attains a degree of certainty. Do you have many certainties, Max?"

"Not many. Only that men doubt, remember, and die."

"That must account for it. Doubt is what keeps people young. Certainty is like a malignant virus that infects us as we get older."

"Memory, you said. Men remember, then they die."

"At my age, yes." He nods. "That's all."

"What about doubts?"

"Not many. Only uncertainties, which isn't the same."

"What do I remind you of?"

"Women I forgot."

She seems to sense his irritation, because she tilts her head slightly, observing him with interest.

"You are lying," she says at last.

"Prove it."

"I will . . . I promise you I will. Just give me a few days."

—⁂—

He sipped his gin fizz and looked around at the other guests. Almost everyone had arrived, and there were no more that twenty or so. It was a black-tie dinner: the men in tuxedos, the majority of women in low-backed dresses. Not much jewelry, and discreet in almost every case, polite conversations that took place largely in French or Spanish. They were friends and acquaintances of Susana Ferriol. There were a few refugees from Spain, but not the kind habitually shown in the newsreels. The rest belonged to the international set, permanent residents of Nice and the surrounding areas. The aim of the dinner was for the hostess to introduce the Colls, a Catalan couple, to her friends. The Colls had managed to flee from the republican zone. Luckily for them, aside from their apartment in Barcelona in a building designed by Gaudí, a tower in Palamós, and a few factories and warehouses that had been requisitioned by the workers, the Colls had sufficient funds in European banks to keep them going until things returned to normal. Minutes before, Max had overheard Mrs. Coll (full hips and big eyes, small and feisty) explaining breathlessly to several of the other guests how she and her husband had hesitated at first between Biarritz and Nice, finally opting for the latter because of its mild climate.

"Dear Suzi was kind enough to find a villa for us to rent. Right here, in Boron. The Savoy isn't bad, but nothing compares to having your own place. And with the Blue Train, Paris is only a step away."

Max deposited his empty glass next to one of the picture windows that looked out onto the illuminated environs of the house: the circular, gravel driveway lined with leafy plants; the cars lined up beneath the palm trees and cypresses, gleaming under the street lamps; the chauffeurs gathered around the glowing tips of their cigarettes to the side of the stone steps (Max had arrived in the Chrysler Imperial belonging to Baroness Schwarzenberg, who was at present sitting in the main room conversing with a Brazilian movie actor). Beyond the trees in the garden, Nice was a glittering arc around the dark stain of the sea, with the tiny prong of the Jetée-Promenade like a jewel encrusted in its side.

"Another cocktail, sir?"

Max shook his head, glancing about as the waiter moved away. A small jazz band was playing in the main hall, welcoming the guests amid the scent from the myriad flowers arranged in blue and red glass vases. Dinner was in twenty minutes. In the dining room, visible through a glass door, twenty-two places were laid. According to the seating list propped on a lectern outside, Mr. Costa was near the far end of the table. After all, he was only invited as Baroness Schwarzenberg's companion, which counted for very little in society. When he was introduced to her, Susana Ferriol had addressed him with the precise smile and the appropriate words expected of an efficient hostess who knew how to behave (how nice to meet you, I'm so glad you could come), before inviting him in, introducing him to some of the other guests, guiding him toward the waiters, and forgetting about him for the moment. Susana Ferriol (Suzi to her friends) was dark-haired and extremely thin, almost as tall as Max, with a hard, angular face, from which shone a pair of intense black eyes. Her choice of evening dress was unconventional: she wore a flowing white trouser suit with a silver pinstripe that accentuated her thinness, and Max would have wagered his pearl cuff links that somewhere stitched into the lining was a Chanel label. Tomás Ferriol's sister weaved in and out of her guests, affecting a sophisticated languor of which she was doubtless overly conscious. As Baroness Schwarzenberg had remarked, leaning back against the car seat on the way, elegance could be acquired through money, education, hard work, and intelligence, but wearing it with ease, my dear (the glow from the street lamp lit up her spiteful smile), required crawling around on genuine Persian rugs from birth. For at least two generations. And the Ferriols' extreme wealth only went back one (their father had begun building his fortune during the Great War selling contraband tobacco in Mallorca).

"There are exceptions, of course. And you are one of them, my friend. I don't know many men who can cross a hotel foyer, light a woman's cigarette, or discuss wine with a sommelier the way you do. And I was born when Leningrad was still called Saint Petersburg. Imagine the things I have seen, and what I see now."

Max took a few steps, glancing around the room with the stealth of a hunter. Although the villa was a typical turn-of-the-century building, the interior was functional and simple, in accordance with the latest fashion: clean, straight lines; bare walls, save for an occasional modern painting; furniture made of steel, polished wood, leather, and glass. The former ballroom dancer's sharp eye, practiced in the art of survival, took in every detail of the house and its guests. Clothes, jewelry, trinkets, conversation. Tobacco smoke. With the excuse of taking out a cigarette, Max paused between the main hall and the entrance to take a look at the staircase leading up to the next floor. According to the plans he had studied in his room at the Negresco, on the other side were the library and the study Ferriol used when he was in Nice. Getting into the library was simple: the door was open, and on the far wall the books with their gilded covers shone on the shelves. He took a few more paces, cigarette case open in his hand, then came to a halt once more, pretending to listen to the five musicians in evening dress playing a slow swing ("I Can't Get Started") amid some potted plants, near a glass door that gave onto the garden. Max finally lit his cigarette as he leaned against the library door close to where a French couple were speaking in hushed tones (the woman was blonde and attractive, and her eye shadow was too thick). He glanced inside the room and discovered the study door, which according to the information he had was usually locked. Getting in wouldn't be difficult, he concluded. Everything was on the ground floor and there were no bars. The safe was built into a cupboard in the wall, next to a window. He would need to see it from the outside, but this window was a possible entry point. Another was the glass door where the musicians were playing, which gave onto a patio. A diamond tip or a screwdriver for the window, a picklock for the study door. An hour inside, and with a little luck the job would be done. That part of it, at least.

He had been loitering on his own for too long in the entrance, and that wasn't good. He took a puff on his cigarette and glanced about with an indolent air. The last guests were arriving. He had already spoken with a few people, exchanged the customary smiles and pleasant words. Appropriate gestures for the ladies, and an apparently sincere friendliness toward their husbands and companions. After dinner, a few couples would decide to dance. This generally gave Max the almost perfect opportunity (especially with the married women who got into difficulties, and this smoothed his path as well as spared the need for conversation). However, that evening he wasn't about to venture into such dangerous territory. He couldn't afford to draw attention to himself. Not there. Not with what was at stake. And yet, as he walked around, from time to time he sensed women staring at him. An occasional whispered comment: who is that handsome fellow, and so forth. Max, who was thirty-five then, had been interpreting those kinds of looks for fifteen years. Everyone attributed his presence there to a probable liaison with Asia Schwarzenberg, and it suited him that they think that. He decided to join a woman and two men chatting on a steel-and-leather sofa. The woman and one of the men were sitting; the other man was standing. Shortly after he had arrived, Max had exchanged pleasantries with the seated man—a rather stocky fellow with a thin, blond mustache, closely trimmed hair, and a friendly face. He had given Max his card: Ernesto Keller, Chilean Vice-Consul in Nice. The woman also looked familiar, but not from that evening. An actress, Max seemed to remember. Spanish as well. Beautiful and serious. Conchita something. Monteagudo, perhaps. Or Montenegro.

For an instant, still motionless, Max caught sight of his reflection in a large mirror with a thin, oval frame hanging above a narrow, glass table: the vivid white of his shirt between black silk lapels, his handkerchief poking out of his top pocket, and the meticulous strip of starched cuff emerging from each sleeve of his waisted tuxedo; a hand casually placed in his right trouser pocket, the other half-raised clutching his smouldering cigarette, and revealing a glimpse of the gold strap and casing of his eight-thousand-franc, slim-line Patek Philippe wristwatch. Then he looked down at the brown-and-white diamond carpet beneath his patent leather shoes, and thought (as he still often did) about his friend and fellow legionnaire, Lieutenant Boris Dolgoruki-Bragation. About what he would have said or how he would have laughed, between glasses of brandy, at seeing Max dressed that way. From the child playing on the banks of the Riachuelo in Buenos Aires, or the soldier climbing, rifle at the ready, amid desiccated corpses up the charred slopes of Mount Arruit, Max had come a long way before stepping onto that carpet in the Riviera villa. And there was still a difficult stretch to cover between him and the closed door awaiting him at the far end of the library, as unfathomable as fate itself. He took a short, precise draw on his cigarette, while also deciding that the risks and hazards of some paths never entirely vanish (he felt another pang of anxiety as he remembered Fito Mostaza and the two Italian spies). And that, in fact, the only truly simple day in his life was the one he managed to leave behind each night as he drifted into an always restless, uncertain sleep.

Then he smelled a woman's soft perfume close by him. He recognized it instinctively as Arpège. And when he turned around (nine years had passed since Buenos Aires), he found Mecha Inzunza standing before him.

8

La Vie Est Brève

Y OU STILL SMOKE those Turkish cigarettes," she remarked. She was gazing at him, with curiosity rather than surprise, as though attempting to fit together disparate fragments: his well-tailored evening suit, his features. The glow from the nearby electric lamps seemed suspended in her eyes, spilling over the ivory-colored satin evening gown that hugged her shoulders and hips, illuminating her naked arms and back above the plunging line of the dress. Her skin was bronzed, and she wore her hair in the latest style, a few inches longer than in Buenos Aires, with a slight wave, parted and pulled back from her face.

"What are you doing here, Max?" she said, after an instant. It wasn't so much a question as a conclusion, and the meaning was clear: this couldn't possibly be happening. The man Mecha Inzunza had met on the *Cap Polonio* could not have made his way naturally to that house.

"I demand to know. . . . What are you doing here?"

There was a harshness in her insistence. And Max, who, after his initial shock (mixed with waves of panic) was starting to regain his composure, realized that remaining silent would be a grave mistake. Suppressing the urge to withdraw and protect himself (he felt like a raw clam having just received a squirt of lemon), he gazed at those luminous eyes, while contriving to refute everything with a smile.

"Mecha," he said.

Her name and the smile were simply ways to gain time. He was thinking on his feet, or trying to. Without success. He glanced discreetly to either side of him, to see if their conversation had aroused anyone else's interest. She noticed this, for her gleaming eyes hardened beneath her eyebrows plucked in two finely penciled brown lines. She is just as ravishing, Max thought absurdly. More compact, more womanly. He looked at her slightly open mouth, painted bright red (it still appeared less angry than expectant), and then his gaze descended to her neckline. Suddenly he noticed the necklace: splendid pearls with a soft, almost muted glow, in three strands. It was either an exact replica of the one he had sold nine years before, or it was the same one.

That was probably what saved him, he would later conclude. His expression of surprise when he saw the pearls. The sudden flash of triumph in her eyes when she seemed to read his thoughts as if he were transparent. Her initial look of disdain giving way to irony and finally suppressed amusement that caused her throat and lips to quiver as though about to laugh. She had raised a hand (in the other she was holding a snakeskin baguette bag) and her long, slender fingers, with nails painted the same shade as her lips, and adorned with a simple, gold wedding ring, came to rest on the pearls.

"I recovered the necklace a week later, in Montevideo. Armando went to fetch it for me."

The image of her husband stood out for an instant among Max's memories. Since Buenos Aires, he had seen him in photographs in illustrated magazines, even a few times on newsreels in the cinema, his famous tango playing in the background.

"Where is he?"

He glanced about uneasily as he spoke, wondering how Armando de Troeye's presence might complicate matters. But he was relieved when he saw her shrug, gloomily.

"He isn't here. . . . He's far away, now."

Max was a resourceful fellow, toughened by the many scrapes he had gotten into over the years. More than once, his calm under pressure had saved him from disaster by the skin of his teeth. Just then, while he was trying to think quickly, the awareness that revealing his unease might bring him uncomfortably close to a French prison gave him added resolve. A way of regaining control of the situation, or of limiting the damage. Ironically, he thought, the necklace can save me.

"The necklace," he said.

He spoke without knowing what he would say next. Simply another attempt to gain time, to establish a defensive point. But it was enough. She touched the pearls again. There was no incipient laughter this time; instead she recovered her look of defiance. Her triumphant smile.

"The Argentinian police were extremely helpful when my husband reported the pearls missing. They put him in contact with their Uruguayan counterparts, and Armando traveled to Montevideo to recover the necklace from the man you had sold it to."

Max had finished his cigarette, and was holding the smouldering end in his fingers, looking around purposefully for somewhere to put it. Finally he stubbed it out in a heavy, crystal ashtray on a nearby table.

"Have you given up dancing, Max?"

He turned to face her, at last. Looking straight into her eyes with as much serenity as he could muster. And he must have done so with sufficient aplomb, because, after posing the question in a sour voice, she continued to contemplate him, then nodded in silent affirmation of some thought he was unable to make out. As though at once surprised and amused by the man's composure. His cool audacity.

"I live a different kind of life," he said.

"The Riviera isn't a bad place to do that in. How do you know Suzi Ferriol?"

"I came here with a friend."

"Which friend?"

"Asia Schwarzenberg."

"Ah."

The guests were beginning to head toward the dining room. The young blonde who had been speaking in French walked past, leaving a whiff of cheap perfume in her wake, followed by her companion who was studying his pocket watch.

"Mecha. You are . . ."

"Leave it, Max."

"I've heard that tango. A thousand times."

"Yes. I imagine you have."

"I'd like to explain a few things to you."

"Explain?" Her eyes flashed once more. Two golden darts. "That doesn't sound like you. When I saw you, I thought you might have improved somewhat over time. I prefer your cynicism to your explanations."

Max thought it wiser to say nothing. He remained by her side, erect and apparently relaxed, four fingers of his right hand thrust into his jacket pocket. Then he saw her smile faintly, as though laughing at herself.

"I was observing you for a while," she said, "before I came over."

"I didn't see you. I'm sorry."

"I know you didn't see me. You were concentrating, pensive. I wondered what you were thinking about. What you were doing here, and what you were thinking about."

She isn't going to give me away, Max decided. Not tonight, anyway. Or not until after the coffee and cigarettes. And yet, despite that momentary certainty, he knew he was on treacherous ground. He needed more time to think. To figure out whether Mecha Inzunza's arrival on the scene would make things difficult for him.

"I recognized you at once," she was explaining. "I just wanted to decide what to do."

She pointed toward a flight of stairs on the other side of the entrance that led to the upper floors. At its foot were large fig trees in pots and a table where a waiter was clearing away empty glasses.

"I noticed you as I came down the stairs, because you didn't sit. You were one of the exceptions. Some men sit, others stand. I usually mistrust the latter."

"Since when?"

"Since I met you. . . . I scarcely recall having seen you sit. Not on the *Cap Polonio* or in Buenos Aires."

They walked a few paces toward the dining room, pausing in the doorway to check their places on the seating plan. Max kicked himself for having failed to check beforehand all the names around the table. And there she was: *Mrs. Inzunza.*

"And what are you doing here?" he asked.

"I live nearby, because of the situation in Spain. I rent a house in Antibes, and I occasionally visit Suzi. We've known each other since high school."

Inside the dining room, the guests were taking their places around the table, where the silver cutlery lay shining on the tablecloth beside candelabra with red, green, and blue spirals of glass. Susana Ferriol, who was attending to her guests, glanced at Mecha and Max with a look of faint consternation—surprised to see him (Max was sure his hostess wouldn't have remembered his name) conversing with her friend.

"What about you, Max? You still haven't told me what brings you to Nice. Although I think I can imagine."

He smiled. A world-weary, affable smile. Calculated to the millimeter.

"Perhaps your imaginings are mistaken."

"I can see you've perfected that smile." She was looking him up and down now with a mixture of scorn and admiration. "What else have you been busy perfecting all this time?"

—⚬—

He spots Irina Jasenovic from a distance, near Sorrento cathedral: sunglasses, patterned miniskirt, flat sandals. She is looking in the window of a clothes store on Corso Italia. Max stays close by, watching her from the other side of the street until she continues walking toward Piazza Tasso. He isn't following her for any particular reason; he simply feels the need to observe her discreetly, now that he knows she might be secretly linked to the people on the Russian player's team. Curiosity, perhaps. A desire to get closer to the center of the intrigue. He has already managed to do that with Emil Karapetian, whom he came across after breakfast in one of the small lounges at the hotel, surrounded by newspapers, his ample frame ensconced in an armchair. The sum of their encounter was a polite exchange of greetings, a comment about the mild weather, and a brief chat about how the games were going, which prompted Karapetian to leave the newspaper open on his lap (even where chess is concerned, he seems averse to conversations requiring anything more than monosyllables), and speak for a moment, somewhat diffidently, with the courteous, gray-haired gentleman with the friendly smile, who it seems is an old acquaintance of his protégé's mother. And when Max finally stood up, leaving Karapetian in peace, with his nose once more buried in his newspaper, the only conclusion he drew was that the Armenian has a blind belief in Jorge's superiority over his Russian opponent, and that regardless of the outcome of the Sorrento contest, he is certain that in a few months' time Keller will be the world champion.

"He is the chess of the future," he concluded, encouraged by Max, in what was his longest monologue in the entire conversation. "After his contribution to the game, the Russian's defensive tactics will smell of mothballs."

Karapetian doesn't seem like a traitor, is Max's conclusion. Certainly not a man who would sell his former disciple for thirty pieces of silver. And yet, life has taught Dr. Hugentobler's chauffeur, to his own detriment and to that of his fellow men, how flimsy the ties are that prevent human beings from lying or betraying. How easy it is, moreover, for the traitor who is still undecided to receive a final push, a helping hand, from the very person he is about to betray. No one is immune to this, he concludes with almost dispassionate relief as he strolls along the Corso Italia, keeping his distance from Jorge Keller's girlfriend. Who can look themselves in the eye in a mirror and say, *I have never betrayed*, or *I will never betray*?

The young woman has sat down at one of the tables outside the Fauno bar. After reflecting for a moment, Max saunters across to her and strikes up a conversation. Before doing so, he instinctively glances around. Not because he is expecting Soviet spies to be lurking behind the palm trees in the square, but because that kind of vigilance is part of his old training. I may be a mangy, toothless old wolf, he tells himself perversely, but that doesn't mean my hunting grounds are any less fraught with peril.

Memories of young women, he thinks as he sits down. What he has retained. What he knows. She is a generation or several generations younger, he concludes, looking down at her miniskirt, her bare knees, as he orders a Negroni and talks about the first thing that comes into his head.

"Sorrento is a nice town. . . . Have you been to Amalfi yet?

What about Capri?" Old, tried and tested smiles, polite gestures rehearsed and deployed a thousand times. "There are fewer tourists at this time of year. . . . I promise, you won't be disappointed."

Not particularly pretty, he notices again. Nor ugly. Just young-looking, fresh-faced, like an ad for Peggy Sage. In brief, the allure of a twenty-something-year-old for whoever finds twenty-something-year-olds alluring. Irina has taken off her sunglasses (oversized, white frames), and the only makeup she is wearing is the thick black eyeliner around her big, expressive eyes. Her hair is tied back in a ribbon that has the same op-art pattern as her skirt. A plain face, friendly looking now. Chess doesn't confer character, Max reflects. On either men or women. A superior intellect, a mathematical brain, a prodigious memory can just as easily produce an ordinary smile, an anodyne word, a vulgar gesture as the men and women for whom such things are as habitual as the course of life itself. Even chess players are no more intelligent than the rest of us mortals, he had heard Mecha Inzunza say a couple of days earlier. Theirs is simply a different kind of intelligence. Wirelesses that pick up different frequencies.

"I never imagined Mecha looking after her son in this way, among the chess-playing world," Max said, testing the ground. "My memory of her is very different. From before all this."

Irina appears interested. She leans forward, resting her elbows on the table, next to a glass of Coca-Cola with ice cubes floating in it.

"Is it a long time since you two last met?"

"Many years," he says. "And our friendship goes back even further."

"What a lucky coincidence, both of you being here in Sorrento."

"Yes. Very lucky."

The waiter brings his drink. The young woman gazes at Max, intrigued, while he raises his glass to his lips.

"Did you ever meet Jorge's father?"

"Briefly. Just before the war." He sets the glass down gently on the table. "Actually, I knew her first husband better."

"De Troeye? The musician?"

"That's right. The one who composed the famous tango."

"Ah, of course. The tango."

She gazes at the horse-drawn carriages stationed in the square, awaiting prospective customers. The drivers idling in the shade beneath the palm trees.

"That world must have been fascinating. Those clothes, that music. Mecha said you were an exceptional dancer."

Max waves his arm in a gesture that is midway between a polite protest and dismissive modesty. He learned it thirty years back, from one of Alessandro Blasetti's films.

"I wasn't bad."

"And what was she like then?"

"Elegant. Very beautiful. One of the most attractive women I ever met."

"It feels strange to think of her like that. She's Jorge's mother."

"And how is she as a mother?"

A silence. Irina touches the ice in her glass with her finger, but doesn't drink.

"I'm not the best judge of that."

"Too possessive?"

"She shaped him, in a way," Irina says, after remaining silent for a moment. "Without her sacrifices, Jorge wouldn't be what he is. Or what he could become."

"Do you mean he would be happier?"

"Oh, no, please. Nothing of the sort. Jorge is a happy man."

Max nods, politely, while he takes another sip of his drink. He needn't dig far to remember happy husbands whose wives, in another life, deceived them with him.

"She didn't want to create a freak, the way some mothers do," Irina adds after a while. "She always did her best to bring him up like a normal boy. Or at least to make that compatible with chess. And she succeeded, to some extent."

She says these last words hurriedly, glancing around the square, as though afraid Mecha Inzunza might appear at any moment.

"Was he really a gifted child?"

"Just imagine. He learned to write at the age of four from watching his mother, and by the time he was five he knew all the countries and capital cities in the world by heart. She realized his potential very early on, but also the potential dangers. And she worked hard to avoid them."

Her face seems to tense for a moment when she says the word *hard*.

"She still does," Irina adds. "Constantly . . . as if she is afraid he will fall into the abyss."

She doesn't say *an* abyss, but rather *the* abyss, Max notices. The noise of a Lambretta backfiring as it passes close by appears to make her jump.

"And she is right," she adds, gloomily, almost in a whisper. "I have seen many people fall into it."

"Surely you exaggerate. You're young."

She gives a brisk, almost savage smile that seems to age her by ten years. Then her face relaxes again.

"I've been playing chess since I was six," she says. "I have seen many players end badly. They become caricatures of themselves, away from the chessboard. Being the best requires an inhuman effort. Especially if you never make it."

"Did you once dream of being the best?"

"Why do you speak in the past tense? I still play chess."

"I'm sorry. I had no idea. I assumed that an analyst was similar to the team of bullfighters in Spain whose job it is to assist the matador. I didn't mean to offend you."

She gazes down at Max's hands. The age spots. His clipped, manicured nails.

"You don't know what it is to lose."

"Excuse me?" Max stifles a chuckle. "I don't know what?"

"It's obvious from your appearance."

"Ah."

"Sitting in front of the chessboard and seeing the consequences of a tactical error. How easily your talent and your chances go up in smoke."

"I understand . . . but appearances can be deceptive. Failure isn't exclusive to chess players."

She seems not to have heard him.

"I also knew all the countries and capital cities in the world by heart," she says. "Or the equivalent. But things don't always turn out the way they should."

She is smiling now, almost valiantly. For her respectable audience. Only a young girl can smile like that, Max reflects. Sure of the effect it will have.

"It's difficult, being a woman," she adds, her smile fading. "Even now."

The sun, whose rays have been moving from table to table across the terrace, lights up her face. Squinting, she puts on her dark glasses.

"Meeting Jorge gave me a fresh opportunity. To experience all this at close hand."

"Do you love him?"

"Do you think your age gives you the right to ask impertinent questions?"

"Of course. There have to be some advantages."

Silence. The noise of the traffic. A distant horn blast.

"Mecha says you were a very handsome man."

"I'm sure it's true. If she says so."

The sun is touching Max now, and he can see his reflection in the girl's big dark glasses.

"Oh, yes," she says impassively. "Of course I love Jorge."

She crosses her legs, and Max looks for a moment at her bare knees. Her flat leather sandals reveal the arch of her foot and her toenails painted dark red, almost purple.

"Sometimes I watch him playing," she goes on, "moving a piece, taking risks the way he does, and I think I love him madly. . . . Other times I see him make a mistake, something we have prepared together, which he decides to change at the last moment, or hesitates over. . . . And at that moment I detest him."

She falls silent for a moment, as though pondering the truth of what she has just said.

"I think I love him more when he isn't playing chess."

"That's normal. You're young."

"No. Youth has nothing to do with it."

The silence that follows is so long that Max assumes their conversation is over. He calls the waiter's attention, asking for the bill with a snap of his fingers.

"Do you know something?" Irina suddenly blurts out. "Every morning, when Jorge is playing in a tournament, his mother comes down to breakfast ten minutes early, to make sure everything is ready for when he arrives."

Max thinks he notices a tone of displeasure. A tinge of resentment. He has an ear for such things.

"So what?" he murmurs.

"So, nothing." Irina moves her head and Max's reflection bobs up and down in her dark glasses. "He goes down, and there she is with everything ready: orange juice, fruit, coffee, toast. Waiting for him."

—⁕—

The red and green lights on a boat sailing out of Nice harbor advanced slowly between the dark stains of the sea and sky, against the flashes from the lighthouse beyond. Separated from the port by the dark hill of the castle, the city encircled the Bay of Angels like a luminous strip, curving slightly southward, from which a few specks of light have detached themselves, to drift up toward the nearby hills.

"I'm cold," Mecha Inzunza said with a shiver.

She was sitting behind the wheel of a car she herself had driven there, in her shimmering gown, her embroidered silk shawl with long tassels wrapped around her shoulders. From the passenger seat, Max leaned toward the dashboard, slipped off his jacket, and draped it over her. In his shirtsleeves and skimpy vest, he, too, could feel the dawn chill seeping through the closed roof of the convertible.

Mecha rummaged in her bag in the dark. He heard her crumple an empty pack of cigarettes. She had finished them after dinner, and then smoking with him there in the car. It felt like an eternity ago, Max reflected, since he had taken his place at the dining table, next to an extremely thin, middle-aged Frenchwoman who designed jewelry for Van Cleef & Arpels, and the young blonde with the cheap perfume: a singer and actress named Elvira Popescu, who turned out to be an amusing tablemate. During dinner, Max gave his attention to both women, although he ended up chatting more with the actress, who was delighted that the attractive, elegant gentleman on her left was from Argentina (I'm crazy about tango, she declared). The younger woman giggled a lot, especially when Max gave a discreet imitation of the different ways screen actors like Leslie Howard or Laurence Olivier lit a cigarette or held a glass. A good raconteur, he told a funny story that made the older lady smile, and even lean toward them with interest. Each time the young actress laughed, Max disguised his unease as he felt Mecha Inzunza observing him from the other end of the table, where she was sitting next to the fair-haired, mustachioed Chilean gentleman. Over dessert, he saw her drink two cups of coffee and smoke four cigarettes.

After that, everything happened as it should have. Without

forcing the issue, she and Max avoided each other when all the guests left the dining room. Later, while he was chatting to the Colls, the young actress, and the Chilean diplomat, their hostess approached the group, informing the baroness that a dear friend of hers, who had come there unaccompanied, was feeling unwell and was preparing to return to her house in Antibes, and would she mind awfully if Max accompanied her, for they had just discovered they were old acquaintances. Max confirmed that this was true and agreed to the request. After first hesitating, almost imperceptibly, for an instant, Asia gave her consent. Of course she didn't mind, she declared, charmingly cooperative, before observing wittily that Max was the perfect companion for any woman feeling under the weather, or even in perfect health. There were sympathetic smiles, apologies, and thanks all around. The baroness gave Max a long, knowing look (how do you do these things, she seemed to be saying, admiringly) while Susana Ferriol glanced at him out of the corner of her eye with fresh and barely concealed curiosity as she shepherded him toward the entrance where Mecha Inzunza was waiting, enveloped in her shawl.

After formally taking their leave, they walked outside, where, instead of a large, chauffeur-driven limousine, Max was surprised to find a small Citroën 7C two-seater with its engine running, which an attendant had just parked at the front of the house. Mecha paused beside the open car door, and began to touch up her makeup with the lipstick and mirror she had fished out of her bag, in the light of the lanterns illuminating the steps and the circular driveway. Afterward, they climbed into the car and she drove in silence for five minutes, Max gazing at her profile in the glare of the headlights reflecting off the walls of the villas. The car stopped near the sea, at an overlook close to Le Lazaret, amid pines and agaves. From there they could make out the flashing lighthouse, the harbor entrance, the dark mass of the hill beneath the castle, and the lights of Nice in the distance. Then she switched off the engine and they talked. They continued to do so, between lengthy silences, as they smoked in the dark, scarcely able to see in the dimness of distant lights or the glow of cigarettes. Without looking at each other.

"Give me one of your Turkish ones, please."

She hadn't lost the ease of tone and manner he had so admired on board the *Cap Polonio*, typical of young women of her generation, brought up on movies, novels, and illustrated women's magazines. But nine years later she was no longer a girl. She must have been thirty-two or thirty-three, Max calculated, looking back. A couple of years younger than him.

"Of course. Forgive me."

He took his cigarette case from his inside jacket pocket, felt for a cigarette, and lit it with his Dunhill. Then, without extinguishing the flame, he exhaled the first puff of smoke and placed the cigarette directly between her lips. Before snapping the lighter shut, he was able once again to make out her silent profile facing the sea, just as it had been earlier when it was lit up by the intermittent beams from the lighthouse.

"You haven't told me where your husband is."

He had been turning the question over in his mind all evening. Despite the passage of time, a slew of memories was washing over him. Far too many intense images. Armando de Troeye's absence somehow distorted the situation. Made everything feel incomplete. Still more unreal. The tip of Mecha's cigarette glowed twice before she spoke again.

"He's in prison in Madrid. They arrested him a few days after the military uprising."

"Despite his fame?"

She gave a bitter laugh. Almost silent.

"Because of it, you ought to say. Have you forgotten what Spain is like? The paradise of envy, barbarity, and treachery."

"Still, it seems absurd. Why Armando? I didn't think he was active in politics."

"He never took sides. He has as many Republican friends on the left as he does monarchist friends on the right. Add to that the jealousy over his international fame. And finally some statements he made in *Le Figaro* about the chaos and lack of authority in the Republican government, which brought him a few more enemies. As if that weren't enough, the head of the secret service is a communist, and a composer, as mediocre as they come. Need I say more?"

"I thought Armando's fame would ensure your safety. Influential friends, success abroad . . ."

"That's what he thought. And so did I. But we were wrong."

"Were you there?"

Mecha nodded. The military uprising took place when they were in San Sebastián, and when Armando de Troeye saw which way the wind was blowing, he convinced her to cross the border into France. They had planned to meet up in Biarritz, but before that, he said he wanted to drive to Madrid to deal with a few family matters. They arrested him shortly after he arrived. Denounced by the concierge.

"Have you heard from him?"

"Only a letter written three months ago from the Model Prison. As far as I know he is still there. I've made appeals through friends, and Picasso and the Red Cross are doing what they can. We are attempting a trade-off with another prisoner in the nationalist zone, but so far without result. And that worries me. There is a lot of talk about executions on both sides."

"Do you have enough funds to keep up this lifestyle?"

"We saw what was coming in Spain, so Armando took precautions. And I know the right people who will make sure things remain as they should until this madness is over."

Max stared at the flashing lighthouse, without saying a word. His mind was on people whose money protected them, and what he understood by things remaining as they should, from the point of view of Susana Ferriol's dinner guests. He thrust the thought aside, experiencing the familiar age-old pang of dim resentment. In fact, he concluded, the idea of Armando de Troeye betrayed by his concierge and marched off to prison by left-wing militias wasn't so absurd, given the way the world was. Someone occasionally had to pay the price in the name of, or on behalf of, the right people. And it wasn't such a high price. Even so, Mecha wasn't far off the mark when she described the situation in Spain as madness. Traveling on his Venezuelan passport, Max had visited Barcelona on business a few months earlier. Five days had been enough for him to witness the sorry spectacle of the Republic plunging into chaos: Catalan separatists, communists, anarchists, Soviet agents, all protecting their own interests, killing one another miles from the battlefront. Settling scores with more ferocity than when fighting the fascists. Envy, barbarity, and treachery, Mecha had said with clearheaded precision. The diagnosis was correct.

"Fortunately, I have no children," she was saying. "It's hard to flee with them in your arms when Troy is burning. Do you have children?"

"Not as far as I know."

A brief silence. Rather cautious, he thought he noticed. He anticipated her next question.

"And you didn't marry, either?"

He smiled to himself. Mecha couldn't see his face.

"Not as far as I know."

She didn't laugh at his joke, and another silence followed. The lights in Nice shimmered on the still, dark water beneath the parapet wall.

"I thought I saw you once, from a distance. Three years ago, at the Longchamps racetrack. . . . Is that possible?"

"Yes," he lied. He had never been to Longchamps.

"I asked my husband for the binoculars, but it was too late. I lost you."

Max was gazing into the darkness toward the now invisible hills around Le Lazaret. Susana Ferriol's villa stood out in the distance, amid the shadows of the pine trees. He would have to approach from there, he thought, the day he made his move. From the sea, it should be fairly easy to climb over an unobtrusive part of the wall. In any event, he would need to look at everything more closely in daylight. Make an exhaustive study of the terrain. Find the way in, and more importantly the way out.

"My memories of you are strange, Max . . . the Old School Tango. Our brief adventure."

Gradually he returned to her words. To her profile in the darkness.

"That tune has haunted me for years," she was saying. "I hear it everywhere."

"I imagine your husband won his wager with Ravel."

"Do you really remember that?" She seemed surprised. "The tango versus the bolero? It was terribly amusing. And Ravel was a good sport. The night of the premiere in the Salle Pleyel in Paris, he admitted defeat and invited us to dinner at Le Grand Véfour, with Stravinsky and a few other friends."

"Your husband composed a magnificent tango. It's perfect."

"In fact all three of us created it. Have you ever danced to it?"

"Many times."

"With other women, naturally."

"Of course."

Mecha leaned her head against the seat.

"What happened to my white glove? Do you remember? You used it as a handkerchief in your jacket. Did I ever get it back?"

"I think so. I don't recall keeping it."

"What a shame."

She was holding her cigarette in the hand resting on the steering wheel, and each beam from the lighthouse illuminated curls of smoke drifting upward.

"Do you miss your husband?" Max asked.

"Sometimes." Mecha hadn't replied immediately. "But the Riviera is a good place to be. A sort of foreign legion that only allows in people with money; Spanish fugitives from one side or the other or both, Italians who dislike Mussolini, rich Germans fleeing the Nazis. . . . What most bothers me is not having been able to go to Spain for over a year. That cruel, stupid war."

"There is nothing to stop you from traveling to the nationalist zone if you want. The border at Hendaye is still open."

"When I say cruel and stupid, that goes for both sides."

The tip of her cigarette glowed once more. Then she rolled down the window and flung it into the darkness.

"In any event, I was never dependent on Armando."

"You mean only for money?"

"I see that your fine clothes can't mask your impertinence, my dear."

He knew that she was looking at him, but he kept his eyes fixed on the distant glimmer of the lighthouse. Mecha shifted restlessly in her seat, and once again Max felt her closeness. Warm, he remembered. Slender, soft, and warm. He had been admiring her naked back at Susana Ferriol's house, the low-cut ivory-colored satin dress, her bare arms, the curve of her neck as she tilted her head, her gestures as she spoke to thc other guests, her pleasant smile. Her sudden seriousness when, from the far end of the table or of the main hall, she became aware of his eyes on her and turned her gaze on him.

"I was a young girl when I first met Armando. He had experience, and imagination."

A violent rush of remembered images jostled in Max's mind. A surfeit of sensations, he reflected. He preferred the word *sensations* to *emotions*. He did his best to collect himself. To listen to what she was saying.

"Yes," Mecha went on. "Armando's imagination was the best thing about him. To begin with."

She had left the window open to the night breeze. After a moment, she rolled it back up.

"He used to tell me about other women he had known," she resumed. "For me it was like a game. A challenge. It excited me."

"He also beat you. The bastard."

"Don't say that. . . . You don't understand him. It was all part of the game."

She stirred again, and Max could hear the soft rustle of her dress against the leather seat. When they were leaving Susana Ferriol's place, he had lightly touched her waist as he politely ushered her first through the main door, before going in front of her down the steps. During that tense moment, absorbed by the strangeness of the situation, he had not noticed his sensations (or perhaps they were emotions after all, he decided). Now, in the shadowy intimacy of the car, as he remembered the way her evening dress hugged her hips, he felt an all too real, overwhelmingly physical desire. An astonishing hunger for her skin, her flesh.

"We ended up progressing from word to deed," she was telling him. "Watching and being watched."

He returned to her words as though from a long way off, and for a while he didn't realize that she was still talking about Armando de Troeye. About their strange relationship, to which on at least two occasions Max had been a witness and an unexpected participant in Buenos Aries.

"I discovered, or he helped me discover those dark excesses. Desires I never imagined in myself. . . . And that fueled his own."

"Why are you telling me this?"

"Now, you mean? Today?"

She fell silent for a moment. Apparently surprised by his interruption, or his question. Her voice sounded sad when she spoke again.

"That last night, in Buenos Aires . . ."

She broke off, abruptly. Opening the door, she stepped out of the car and walked beneath the shadows of the pine trees until she reached the parapet wall overlooking the rocks and the sea. Max stayed where he was, apprehensive, before finally joining her.

"Promiscuity," he heard her say. "An ugly word."

Outside in the night air, the twinkling lights in Nice were smothered at regular intervals by the flashing lighthouse. Mecha gathered the tuxedo jacket around her, revealing the tassels of her light shawl. Max shivered in his shirtsleeves and vest. Without a word, he took a step toward her, prizing the lapels of the jacket out of her hands, and reached into the inside pocket for his cigarette case. As he rummaged around, he inadvertently brushed her breast, hanging free beneath her silk shawl and satin gown. Mecha did nothing to stop him.

"Money made it all easy. Armando could afford to buy me anything. Any situation."

Max tapped his last cigarette against the lid of the cigarette case. He had seen enough that last night in Buenos Aires to have no trouble imagining to what situations she was referring. The momentary flare of the lighter illuminated the pearl necklace close to his hands cupped around the flame.

"Thanks to Armando, I discovered pleasures that drew out my pleasure," she added. "Made it more intense. Dirtier, perhaps."

Max shivered, uncomfortable. He didn't want to hear about this. And yet, he concluded with irritation, he had taken part in it himself. He had been a necessary collaborator, or accomplice: La Ferroviaria, Casa Margot, the blonde tango dancer, Armando de Troeye soused in alcohol and cocaine, slumped on the sofa at the Hotel Palace while they coupled shamelessly before his bleary eyes. Even now, the memory of it aroused his desire.

"And then you came along," Mecha had continued, "on that dance floor that swayed to the ship's roll. With your winning smile. And your tangos. Appearing on cue. And yet . . ."

She moved, withdrawing in the distant glow of the lighthouse, its beam circling over the rocks at Le Lazaret and the walls of the villas closest to the sea.

"What a fool you were, my dear."

Max leaned over the parapet wall. This wasn't the conversation he had expected that evening. No recriminations or threats, he noted. He had spent part of the time preparing to confront that other matter, but not this. Anticipating the understandable rage and recriminations of a wronged, and therefore dangerous, woman, but not the strange melancholy that imbued Mecha Inzunza's words and silences. It struck him that the word *wronged* was inappropriate. At no moment had Mecha felt wronged. Not even when she had awoken that morning in the Hotel Palace in Buenos Aires to find him gone and her pearl necklace missing.

"That necklace . . ." he began to say, falling silent as he became conscious of his own awkwardness.

"Oh, for God's sake," she said with infinite disdain. "I would throw the damned thing into the sea this instant, if there were anything left to prove."

All at once, the taste of tobacco turned sour on Max's tongue. At first he was taken aback, mouth half-open as though in midsentence, then he was overcome by a strange and sudden tenderness. So like remorse. He would have moved closer to Mecha to stroke her hair, had he been able. Had she let him. And he knew she wouldn't.

"What do you want, Max?"

A different tone now. Harder. Her moment of vulnerability had lasted only the space of a few words, he reflected. With an unease unlike the one he habitually experienced, and which up until then he would have deemed impossible in him, he wondered how long his own would last. The warm throb he had noticed a moment ago.

"I don't know. We . . ."

"I wasn't referring to us." Her wariness had returned. "I'm asking you once more what you are doing here, in Nice. At Suzi Ferriol's house."

"Asia Schwarzenberg . . ."

"I know who the baroness is. You couldn't possibly be involved. She isn't your type."

"She's an old acquaintance. There are such things as coincidences."

"Listen, Max. Suzi is my friend. I have no idea what you are up to, but I hope it doesn't involve her."

"I am not up to anything. With anyone. I told you I live a different kind of life now."

"Good. Because I won't hesitate to turn you in at the slightest suspicion."

He laughed between gritted teeth. Unsure.

"You wouldn't do that," he ventured.

"Don't run the risk of finding out. This isn't the dance floor on the *Cap Polonio*."

He took a step toward her. Compelled by a sincere desire, this time.

"Mecha . . ."

"Don't come near me."

She had slipped out of his jacket, letting it drop to the ground. A dark pool at Max's feet. The white shawl withdrew very slowly, ghostlike, amid the shadows of the pine trees.

"I want you out of my life and the lives of the people I know. As of now."

As Max stood up clutching his jacket, he heard the engine of the Citroën start up, and the beam of the headlights cast his shadow against the parapet wall. Then the car drove off toward Nice with a screech of tires on the stony ground.

—⚉—

The walk back to the hotel along the road from Le Lazaret to the port was long and tedious, and Max turned up the collar of his tuxedo against the early morning chill. Amid the shadows on the Cassini quayside, he was fortunate enough to find a coach, the driver asleep on his seat. Beneath the folded tarpaulin top as they climbed the hill at Rauba-Capeù, Max was lulled by the sway of the vehicle, aware of the horses' hooves on the firm tarmac while a ribbon of violet slowly separated the dark shadows of sea and sky. This is also the story of my life, he reflected, part of it anyway: searching in the early hours for a taxi, smelling of a woman or a wasted night, or both. In contrast with the sparse lighting in the port and the city's outskirts, as they came around the hill where the castle was, Max glimpsed the distant curve of street lamps illuminating the Promenade des Anglais, which seemed to stretch away into infinity. When they reached Les Ponchettes, he felt hungry and wanted a cigarette, so he paid off the driver and walked under the arches on the Cours Saleya, where the detritus from the flower market had a cemetery smell. He continued beneath the dark boughs of the young plane trees until he found a café that opened early.

He bought a pack of Gauloises for twelve francs and ordered a cup of coffee and a piece of bread with a bowl of hot milk. He sat beside a window overlooking the street, smoking while the shadows outside faded to gray, and a couple of street cleaners connected a hose with a big, brass nozzle sluicing the ground after sweeping up the wilted stems and petals. Max reflected about the night's events and those that would take place during the coming days, doing his best to minimize the effect Mecha Inzunza's sudden appearance might have on his plans, and on his life. In order to regain control over his actions and feelings, he attempted to focus on the practical side of what awaited him, on confronting unforeseen dangers and possible variants. This was the only way, he told himself. To face his unease, the risk of making mistakes that could end in disaster. He thought of the Italian secret agents, of the man who called himself Fito Mostaza, and he wriggled uncomfortably in his chair, as if the early morning chill were seeping into his bones through the windowpane. There was too much at stake, he thought, for him to allow the memory of Mecha Inzunza and its consequences to cloud his judgment. For the untimely alliance of what had taken place nine years ago and that very night to weaken his resolve, when he needed it to remain firm for so many reasons.

He considered briefly the possibility of fleeing. Going back to the hotel, packing his bags, and heading for new hunting grounds, in the hope of better times. As he pondered this alternative he glanced about, in search of ideas. He was looking for old certainties, useful assurances in a colorful profession and a life fraught with risk. There were two travel posters fixed to the wall with thumbtacks, one advertising the French railway, the other the Riviera. Max stared up at them thoughtfully, a cigarette hanging from his lower lip, eyes screwed up. He was fond of trains (he preferred them to transatlantic liners or the exclusive, closed society of commercial air travel), with their endless offer of adventure, life suspended between one station and the next, the possibility of establishing lucrative relationships, the sophisticated clientele of the dining car. Smoking as he lay on a narrow bunk in the sleeping car, alone or with a woman, listening to the sound of the wheels running along the tracks. He recalled one of his most recent journeys on a night train (the Orient Express from Istanbul to Vienna), climbing out at four one chilly morning in Bucharest, after dressing discreetly and quietly closing the door of his compartment that gave onto the corridor, leaving behind his suitcase and a fake passport in the conductor's safekeeping, carrying with him two thousand pounds' worth of jewelry bulging in his overcoat pockets. As for the other poster, he contemplated it with a grin. He recognized the place where the artist had made his illustration: a viewpoint amid a stand of pines overlooking Golfe-Juan and the plot of the land that, eighteen months before, for a generous commission and in partnership with an old Hungarian friend called Sandor Esterházy, Max had helped to sell to a wealthy American (Mrs. Zundel, owner of Zundel & Strauss, Santa Barbara, California). During the course of an intimate relationship fueled by roulette, tangos, and moonlit nights, he had persuaded her to part with four million francs for it, failing to mention one crucial detail: the hundred-yard-wide strip of coast between Mrs. Zundel's land and the sea belonged to someone else, and wasn't included in the sale.

He wouldn't leave, he decided. The world was becoming too small, and the words *far away* were increasingly meaningless. Here was no worse than anywhere else; it was better even, having a mild climate and ideal neighbors. If war did break out in Europe, it would be a good place to weather the storm, or make money out of it. Max knew the Riviera like the back of his hand, he had no record here, and besides, wherever he went he would find policemen, risks, dangers. Every opportunity had a price, he decided. A roulette wheel to play. And that included Ciano's letters to Ferriol, Fito Mostaza's sinister smile, and the troubling seriousness of the Italian spies. And, in the last few hours, like an unsolved puzzle, Mecha Inzunza.

> *La vie est brève*
> *Un peu de rêve*
> *Un peu d'amour*
> *Fini! Bonjour!*

Max hummed to himself, absentmindedly. Fatalistic. No one said it would be easy to leave behind the tenement in Barracas, the hillside in Africa strewn with corpses where even the hyenas weren't in a laughing mood. There was a certain sort of man (and Max was one of them) who had no choice but to follow paths of no return. Unknown journeys on a one-way ticket. Holding that thought, he drained his coffee cup and rose to his feet, as his old professional poise, forged from within, came flowing back. Maurizio, the receptionist at the Hotel Danieli in Venice, who had seen some of the world's wealthiest men and women stand in front of his counter and ask for their key, had said to him once, as he pocketed the generous tip Max had just given him: "Women are the only worthwhile temptation, don't you agree, Mr. Costa? Everything else is negotiable."

A few dreams,
A little love . . .

Max left the café, hands in his pockets, a fresh cigarette in his mouth, and strolled along the wet pavement reflecting the gray dawn light until he reached the tram stop. Being happy feels good, he told himself. And realizing that you are when you are. Cours Saleya no longer smelled of rotting flowers, but of damp cobblestones and saplings dripping with morning dew.

—⚅—

Sitting among the audience, beneath the cherubs and blue skies painted on the ceiling of the main hall in the Hotel Vittoria, Max is following the game on the board on the wall where the players' moves are being reproduced. Since the last click of the chess clock (Jorge Keller's thirteenth move) the silence has been absolute. Besides the soft main light illuminating the dais upon which the table, two chairs, chessboard, and two players are situated, the rest of the room is almost in darkness. Outside, the evening is closing in, and the branches of the trees on the cliff top bordering the road down to the harbor, visible through the large picture windows, are tinged with a red glow.

Max hasn't managed to grasp the details of the game taking place before his eyes. He is aware, because Mecha Inzunza has explained it to him, that Jorge Keller, who is playing black, has to complete certain moves with his pawns and bishops in preparation for other, more risky and complex ones. That will be when the possible preplanned responses might start, depending on the information Sokolov has received from Irina, assuming she is the source. If so, after Keller sacrifices that pawn, Sokolov should expect Keller's bishop (which Max thinks is the one to the left of the white pieces on the board) to mount a dangerous attack on his knight. In which case, to fend off the attack, Sokolov should respond by moving one of his white pawns forward two squares.

"Those two squares would give Irina away," Mecha had told him that afternoon, when they met in the foyer before the game commenced. "Any other move would point the finger at Karapetian."

On Max's right, Captain Tedesco, his one good eye on the panel showing the placement of the pieces, is smoking a cigarette, using a paper cone for an ashtray. From time to time, at Max's request, he leans over to comment on a move or position. On his other side, fingers interlaced, twirling his thumbs, Lambertucci (who has put on a jacket and tie for the occasion) is closely following the progress of the game.

"Sokolov has complete control over the center of the board," Tedesco says in a hushed voice. "I think Keller can only change the situation if he frees his bishop."

"And will he?"

"I've no idea. Those guys can think many more moves ahead than I."

Lambertucci, who hears what his friend is saying, agrees, also in a whisper: "Keller is preparing for one of his typical attacks. And, yes. If he manages to advance, he can do a lot of damage with his bishop."

"What about the black pawn?" Max asks.

The other two men study the board then look at him, puzzled.

"Which black pawn?" says Tedesco.

Max is more focused on the players than on the board, where unknown forces are at play, the workings of which he doesn't understand. Sokolov, a cigarette burning down between his nicotine-stained fingers, tilts his blond head dolefully, studying the position of the pieces with his watery blue eyes. Facing him, Jorge Keller, tie loosened, jacket draped over the back of his chair, has just stood up (Max has noticed that he often does this when there is a long wait, to stretch his legs) and walked a few paces, hands in his pockets, a dreamy expression on his face, contemplating the floor as though measuring it out with long strides in his sneakers. When the game started, he walked in purposefully, without looking at anyone, holding his customary bottle of orange juice. He extended his hand to his opponent, who remained seated, put the bottle down on the table, and watched Sokolov make his opening gambit before moving one of his pawns. Mostly, he sits motionless, head resting on his arms, which are folded in front of the board, occasionally taking a swig of his orange juice out of the bottle, or standing up and walking a few paces, as he is doing now. The Russian hasn't left his seat once. Leaning back in his chair, gazing continuously down at his hands, as if the board were superfluous, he plays with tremendous calm: relaxed, unperturbed, living up to his nickname, the Soviet Wall.

The soft thud of felt on wood, followed by the click of the chess clock as Sokolov presses the button setting off his opponent's timer, bring Keller back to the board. A restrained, almost inaudible murmur sweeps around the room. Keller looks at the black pawn Sokolov has just taken, lined up next to the others. Instantly reproduced on the panel by the referee's assistant, the Russian's move seems to open the way for one of Keller's bishops, hitherto blocked.

"This doesn't look good," murmurs Tedesco. "I think the Russian has made a mistake."

Max glances at Mecha, who is sitting in the front row, but he can only see her cropped, silvery hair, her head completely still. Beside her, he sees Irina's face from the side. Her eyes aren't on the panel, but rather on the board and the players. Next to Irina, Emil Karapetian is watching, mouth half-open, absorbed. The other end of the first row, and part of the second row, is taken up by the entire

Soviet delegation—more than fifteen of them by Max's count. As he studies them one by one (fusty-looking clothes by Western standards, white shirts, thin ties, lighted cigarettes, inscrutable faces) he can't help wondering how many of them work for the KGB. Or whether any of them do.

Less than five minutes after his opponent's last move, Keller moves his bishop forward next to a white pawn and knight.

"Here we go," Tedesco whispers, excitedly.

"This is it," adds Lambertucci. "But notice how cool the Russian is. He doesn't bat an eyelid."

Another brief murmur from the audience, and then complete silence. Sokolov is thinking, unflustered except for the fact that he has lit a cigarette, staring more intently at the board now. Possibly at the white pawn, which Max knows holds the key to what could happen. And just as Keller, after a long swig of orange juice, starts to stand up again, Sokolov advances his pawn two squares. He does so abruptly, aggressively, almost slamming his hand down on the clock, as if to pin his opponent in his chair. And it works. Keller pauses in midmovement, looks at the Russian (their eyes meet for the first time during the game), and, very slowly, sits down again.

"Almost instantaneous," murmurs Tedesco, admiringly, as he realizes the significance of the move.

"What's happening?" asks Max.

Tedesco doesn't reply immediately; he is following the players' rapid, almost violent exchange of pieces. Bishop takes pawn, knight takes bishop, pawn takes knight. *Clack, clack, clack.* The chess clock clicking every three or four seconds, as if it had all been carefully rehearsed. And perhaps it had, Max concluded.

"The white pawn forced the exchanges, stopping the bishop's attack," Tedesco explains finally.

"Dead in its tracks," Lambertucci confirms.

"And Sokolov was quick to see it. Like lightning."

Keller is still holding the last piece he has captured from

Sokolov. He places it on one side of the board, next to the others, takes a long swig of orange juice, and tilts his head forward slightly, as though momentarily weary after a prolonged exertion. Then, with apparent indifference, he turns toward his mother, Irina, and Karapetian, his face blank. Still with a doleful air, Sokolov slides his elbows farther over the table, leaning toward Keller and moving his lips, whispering something to him.

"What's happening now?" Max asks.

Tedesco shakes his head as if the game were over.

"I imagine he is offering him *nichiá* . . . a draw."

Keller studies the board. He doesn't seem to be listening to the Russian. His face gives nothing away. He could be thinking about whether there is another possible move, Max concludes. Or about something else. The woman who has betrayed him, for example, and why. At last Keller nods, and, without looking at his opponent, shakes his hand as both men stand up. A few feet away from her son, Mecha Inzunza hasn't moved for several minutes. For his part, Karapetian remains with his mouth half-open, perplexed. Between them, Irina is staring at the board and the empty chairs, impassive.

9

The Max Variant

MECHA INZUNZA STOPS at a kiosk on Via San Cesareo and buys some newspapers. Max is standing beside her, one hand in the pocket of his gray blazer, watching her leaf through them in search of the section reporting on yesterday's game. Below the four-column headline "Draw in the Sixth, in Il Mattino," there is a photograph of the players as they leave the table: the Russian is staring blankly at Keller, whose head is turned, as if he were preoccupied by something other than the game, or looking at someone behind the photographer.

"It's been a difficult morning," Mecha remarks as she folds the newspaper. "Emil, Jorge, and Irina are still together conducting a postmortem."

"Isn't she suspicious?"

"Not in the slightest. Hence the postmortem. Emil can't understand why Jorge played the way he did yesterday. When I left, Irina was criticizing him for accepting a draw."

"A cynical ploy?"

They are walking down the street. Mecha has put the newspapers in a large canvas-and-leather bag she is carrying on her shoulder over a suede jacket and a patterned silk scarf with autumnal hues.

"Not entirely," she says. "Jorge could have gone on playing, but he didn't want to take any more risks. The discovery that Irina is working for Sokolov rather unsettled him. . . . Perhaps he didn't trust himself to resist the pressure until the end. So he accepted the Russian's offer."

"He did well to stick it out. He looked calm up on the podium."

"Jorge has nerves of steel. He was prepared for this."

"What about when he's with the girl? How good an actor is he?"

"Better than she. And, do you know something? With him there's no pretense, no hypocrisy. You or I would have grilled her then sent her packing. In fact, I would happily have strangled her. . . . I still have an overwhelming urge to do just that. But there he is, poring over a chessboard with her, analyzing and retracing moves, asking her advice with complete naturalness."

The street is long and narrow, and where the stores have set up their wares outside it becomes even more restricted. Every now and then, Max slows his pace to allow others through.

"Isn't this too big a blow?" he asks. "Will he be able to concentrate and carry on playing as before?"

"You don't know Jorge. For him, this coolheadedness is logical. He's still playing. Sometimes the game takes place in a hotel, sometimes elsewhere."

They walk through patches of light and shade, illuminated in places by the yellowish light reflecting off the tall façades of the buildings. Stores selling leather goods, souvenirs, groceries, and fruit and vegetables jostle with fishmongers and salumerias, the smells of which mingle with the leather and spices. Laundry has been hung out to dry from the balconies.

"He hasn't said a word about this," Mecha resumes, after a brief pause, "but I am certain that now, in his head, he is playing two opponents, Sokolov and Irina. A kind of simultaneous chess."

She falls silent again, gazing idly at a store selling women's fashions (hippie-style, Positano linen).

"Later," she goes on, "when he has finished here in Sorrento, Jorge will look up from the chessboard and really analyze what happened. The emotional side. That will be the tough moment for him. Until then, I'm not worried about him."

"Now I understand Sokolov's confidence," Max remarks. "His almost arrogant attitude in the last few games."

"He made a mistake. He should have waited longer before making his move. Made some effort at dissimulating. Not even the world champion could take less than twenty minutes to grasp the full complexity of that situation and make the right decision. And it only took him six."

"Impetuosity?"

"Vanity, I suppose. With a longer analysis, Sokolov might conceivably have reached the same conclusion on his own, and that would have made us doubt Irina's guilt. But I imagine Jorge riled him."

"You mean he got up every five minutes in order to provoke him?"

"Of course."

They are near the Sedile Dominova loggia, where half a dozen tourists are listening to a guide giving explanations in German. Sidestepping the group, they turn left into the narrow gloom of Via Giuliani. Ahead of them, the red-and-white bell tower of the Duomo looms, outlined against the intense light. The clock shows eleven twenty in the morning.

"I never imagined a world champion making that kind of mistake," Max observes. "I assumed they were less . . ."

"Human?"

"Yes."

Everyone makes mistakes, she responds. And after a few paces, she adds thoughtfully, "My son exasperates him." The pressure of the buildup to the world championship is intense, she goes on to explain. Jorge's apparent frivolity, his walks around the table, the way he makes chess look so effortless. The Russian is the exact opposite: conscientious, methodical, cautious. The sort who sweats blood. But yesterday, despite his habitual calm, the world champion, who has his title, his government, and the International Chess Federation behind him, couldn't control his urge to teach the contender a lesson, to cut down to size the spoiled brat of the capitalist world, and the Western press. He moved his pawn just as Jorge was about to leave the table again. You're going to stay right where you are, his gesture was saying. Sit still and keep thinking.

"In the end, they're only human," she says, as if to herself. "They feel hate and love the way we all do."

She and Max are walking side by side. Occasionally, their shoulders brush.

"Or maybe not." Mecha tilts her head to one side for a moment as if she had noticed a flaw in her own argument. "Maybe it is different for them."

"How about Irina? Is she behaving normally?"

"With utter shamelessness," she snorts, her voice suddenly hard. "Completely at ease in her role of faithful collaborator and enamored young girl. If it weren't for what we know, I would believe she was innocent. . . . You haven't a clue how good women are at pretending when the stakes are high!"

Max does know, but says nothing. He is content to pull a silent face as he remembers women on the telephone to their husbands or lovers from a hotel room, sprawled naked on or under the sheets, leaning back against the very pillow where he is resting his head listening to them in admiration. Perfectly calm, without a catch in their voice, conducting clandestine relationships that have lasted days, months, or years. Under similar circumstances, any man would have given himself away in seconds.

"I wonder whether this kind of betrayal is a punishable offense?"

"To whom would we report it?" She laughs again, skeptically. "To the Italian police? The International Chess Federation? This is a private arena. If we had solid evidence, we could raise a scandal, and possibly annul the contest if Jorge were to lose. But even if we did have proof, we would gain nothing. We would simply poison the atmosphere during the five-month run-up to the world championship. And Sokolov would stay where he is."

"Does Karapetian know about Irina yet?"

Jorge spoke to him last night, Mecha confirms. And he didn't appear all that surprised. These things happen, he said. Remember, he has come across cases of spying before. Emil is a calm, pragmatic man. And he isn't in favor of throwing the girl out on her ear.

"He and Jorge agree that we should let Irina and the Russians think they have the upper hand. Pass on doctored information through her, prepare false opening moves. Use her rather like a double agent without her knowing."

"Only they'll catch on in the end," Max ventures.

"They might be able to keep up the deception for a couple of more games. They have played six already, two wins to Sokolov, one to Jorge, and three draws, so the Russian is only one point ahead. They still have four left to play. That offers interesting possibilities."

"What could happen?"

"If we prepared the right kind of traps and Sokolov walked into them, the deception would work once, maybe twice. They might put it down to a mistake, a slip, or a last-minute change of tactic. The second or third time they would start to smell a rat. If we made it too obvious, they would assume that Irina was working with Jorge, or that we were manipulating her. . . . But there's another way: we don't make full use of what we know, we ration the doctored information through Irina, and take her with us to Dublin."

"Can you do that?"

"Of course. This is chess. The art of lying, assassination, and warfare."

They weave through the traffic on Corso Italia. Scooters and cars, exhaust fumes. Max takes Mecha's hand as they cross to the other side. When they reach the pavement, Mecha stays close to him, casually taking his arm. They gaze at their reflection, side by side, in a store window cluttered with television sets. After a moment, she gently lets go of Max's arm, as nonchalantly as she had taken it.

"The important thing is the world championship," she continues very calmly. "This is merely a preliminary skirmish, a probing of the challenger in a kind of unofficial final. It would be wonderful to reach Dublin with the Russians still thinking they can count on Irina. Imagine Sokolov finding out there that we have been controling his spy since Sorrento. . . . What a splendid coup. A fatal blow."

"Will Jorge be able to withstand all that pressure? Being around her for the next five months?"

"You don't know my son. His coolheadedness when it comes to chess. Irina is just another piece on the board now."

"And what will you do with her afterward?"

"I don't know." Once more, there is a hard, metallic tone in her voice. "And I don't care. Of course we will expose her once the world championship is over. Whether privately or publicly remains to be seen. Irina is finished as an international chess player. She might as well crawl into a hole for the rest of her life. I'll do everything in my power to make life unbearable for the little bitch wherever she tries to hide."

"I wonder what made her do it? How long she has been working for Sokolov."

"My dear . . . where Russians and women are concerned there is no way of knowing."

She says this with a joyless, almost unpleasant laugh. Max responds with a elegant, good-natured gesture.

"It's the Russians who interest me," he explains. "I know less about them than I do about women."

She bursts out laughing at his remark.

"Good God, Max. You may no longer look the part, but you're still an incorrigible womanizer. An old-school gigolo."

"I wish I were." He is laughing now, too, straightening Dr. Hugentobler's silk cravat beneath his open shirt collar.

"They could have gotten to Irina early, as part of a long-term strategy," says Mecha, returning to the subject. "Or they may have recruited her later on, with money or other inducements. A girl like Irina, who has a flair for chess, could, with the backing of the Russians who control International Chess Federation, have a future. And she is as ambitious as the next person."

They are in front of the cathedral's iron gates, which are open.

"It isn't easy playing second fiddle," she remarks. "And the chance not to is tempting."

Bells start to ring in the stone belfry. Mecha looks up, covering her head with her scarf as she crosses the threshold. Max follows, and together they penetrate the huge empty nave, his slow footfall echoing on the marble floor.

"What will you do?"

"I'll help Jorge, as always . . . to play. To win here and in Dublin."

"That will have an end, I suppose."

"What?"

"You always being at his side."

Mecha gazes up at the ornate ceiling. The light seeping through the windows illuminates the golds and blues around the biblical scenes. At the other end of the church, the sanctuary lamp shines in the gloom.

"We'll know that when we come to it."

They circle the columns and walk down one of the side aisles, taking a look at the chapels and the oil paintings. The air is musty and smells of warm candle wax. In a niche in the wall, above some lighted candles, there are votive offerings from sailors, tin and wax effigies.

"Five months is a long time," Max insists. "Are you sure Jorge will be able to keep up the deception?"

"Why not?" She looks at him with what appears to be genuine surprise. "Isn't that exactly what Irina has been doing?"

"I'm talking about his feelings as well. They share the same room. The same bed."

A strange expression. Distant. Almost cruel.

"I told you before. He isn't like us. He lives in a compartmentalized world."

A priest emerges from the sacristy, and crosses himself before the main altar after looking at them curiously. Mecha lowers her voice to a whisper as they walk back the way they came, toward the exit.

"When it comes to chess, Jorge is able to view things with extraordinary detachment. As if he were walking in and out of different rooms, without taking anything from one to the other."

The sun dazzles them as they cross the threshold. Mecha lets her scarf fall onto her shoulders and ties it loosely around her neck.

"How will the Russians treat Irina when this all comes out?" Max asks.

"That's not my concern. . . . But I hope they throw her in the Lubyanka prison, or somewhere equally ghastly, and then send her to Siberia."

She has walked through the gates, ahead of Max, and is hurrying down Corso Italia, as if she had remembered some urgent matter. Quickening his pace, he draws level with her.

"Which brings us," he hears her say, "to the Max variant."

With these words, she pulls up abruptly, and Max can't help

but gaze at her, uneasily. Then, astonishingly, she moves her face so close that she almost brushes his shoulder. Her eyes have the hardness of amber now.

"There's something I want you to do for me," she whispers. "Or, more precisely, for my son."

—⁂—

The black Fiat ground to a halt in Place Rossetti, next to the tower of the Cathédrale Sainte-Réparate, and three men climbed out of it. Max, who had heard the engine and glanced up from the pages of *L'Éclaireur* (workers demonstrations in France, show trials and executions in Moscow, concentration camps in Germany), watched from beneath his hat brim as they strolled toward him, the taller, skinnier one flanked by the other two. While they were making their way over to his table on the corner of Rue Centrale, Max folded his newspaper and called to the waiter.

"Two Pernods with water."

The three men stood looking down at him. Mauro Barbaresco, Domenico Tignanello, and in the middle, the tall, skinny fellow dressed in a stylish chestnut-brown, double-breasted suit and a gray taupe Borsalino hat, tilted rakishly over one eye. The collar of his blue-and-white broad-striped shirt was fastened with a gold pin below his tie. He was holding a small, leather bag in one hand, the sort physicians use. For a long time, Max and he studied each other, with a solemn expression. The four men, one seated and the others standing, remained silent until the waiter came over with the drinks, removing Max's empty glass from the table and replacing it with the two Pernods, two glasses of ice water, two teaspoons, and some sugar lumps. Max balanced a teaspoon across one of the glasses, placed a sugar lump on it, and began decanting the water so that it trickled with the dissolved sugar into the greenish liquid. Then he set the glass down opposite the tall, skinny man.

"I assume," he said, "you take it the same way you always did."

The other man's face seemed to grow gaunter as he smiled, revealing a row of yellow teeth and receding gums. Then he pushed his hat back, sat down, and raised the glass to his lips.

"I don't know what your friends would like," Max commented, as he repeated the same procedure with his glass. "I've never seen them drink Pernod."

"Nothing for me," Barbaresco said, taking a seat as well.

Max savored the strong, sugary anisette. Tignanello remained standing, glancing around with his usual air of melancholy mistrust. Responding to a gesture from his colleague, he moved away from the table and walked over to the newspaper stand, from where, Max assumed, he could keep a discreet watch over the square.

Max looked again at the tall, skinny man. He had a long nose and big, sunken eyes. He had aged since the last time they met, Max thought. But he still had the same smile.

"I hear you're a fascist now, Enrico," he said softly.

"In times like these a man has to do something."

Mauro Barbaresco leaned back in his chair, as though he wasn't sure he was going to like this conversation.

"How about we get on with it," he suggested.

Max and Enrico Fossataro carried on looking at each other while they drank. Finally, Fossataro raised his glass, as though in a toast, before draining it. Max did likewise.

"If you agree," he said, "we can dispense with discussions about how long it has been, how much we've aged, and all that."

"Very well." Fossataro nodded.

"What are you up to these days?"

"Life isn't so bad. I have an official post in Turin. Civil servant in the Piedmont government."

"Politics?"

"Public Security."

"Ah."

Max smiled at the image of Fossataro in an office. The fox

guarding the chicken coop. The last time they met was three years ago on a job they did together, in two parts: a villa in the hills around Florence and a suite at the Hotel Excelsior (Max provided the charm offensive at the hotel, while Fossataro employed his skills at the villa under cover of darkness), with a view over the Arno and the Piazza Ognissanti where a group of Blackshirts were marching, intoning the "Giovinezza" before beating some poor wretches to death.

"A Schützling," Max said simply. "From 1913."

"They already told me: a stylish imitation wood box, with false moldings around the locks. Do you remember the house on Rue de Rivoli? Belonging to that English redhead you took to Le Procope for dinner?"

"Yes. But you were in charge of the hardware that time. I had my hands full with the lady."

"That doesn't matter. It's an easy one."

"I don't suppose there's any point in me asking you to do it. Not now."

The other man revealed his teeth once more. His dark, sunken eyes had a plaintive air.

"I tell you, those safes are easy as pie. They have a trigger lock, a triple combination, and the key." He reached into his jacket pocket and pulled out some drawings copied from a blueprint. "I have the diagrams here. You'll get the hang of it in no time. Are you working by day or at night?"

"At night."

"How long do you have?"

"Not long. I need a quick method."

"Can you use a drill?"

"No tools. There are people in the house."

Fossataro wrinkled his brow.

"Manually, it'll take you an hour at least. Do you remember the Panzer in Prague? It nearly drove us crazy."

Max grinned. September 1932. Half the night perspiring in a woman's bed, next to a window looking out over the dome of St. Nicholas, until she fell asleep. Fossataro working noiselessly on the floor below by torchlight, in her absent husband's study.

"Of course I remember."

"I brought a list of the original combinations for this model, which might save you time and effort." Fossataro reached down for the leather bag sandwiched between his legs and handed it to Max. "And I brought a set of a hundred and thirty double-sided keys, also straight from the factory."

"Goodness . . ." The bag was heavy. Max set it on the ground, by his feet. "How did you get hold of those?"

"You'd be surprised what a government position can do."

Max fished his tortoiseshell cigarette case out of his pocket and placed it on the table. Fossataro opened it without asking and took a cigarette.

"You look good, Max," he said, snapping the case shut and motioning toward Barbaresco, who was following their conversation in silence. "My friend Mauro here tells me things are going well for you."

"I can't complain." Max had leaned forward to offer Fossataro a light. "Or rather, I couldn't, up until recently."

"These are difficult times, my friend."

"Don't I know it."

Fossataro took a few drags on his cigarette and gazed at it with satisfaction, marveling at the quality of the tobacco.

"These two aren't so bad," he said, pointing toward Tignanello, who was still posted beside the kiosk, then gesturing to include Barbaresco. "Of course, they can be dangerous. But who can't? I've had fewer dealings with the sad southerner, but Mauro and I once worked together, isn't that so?"

Barbaresco said nothing. He had taken off his hat and was running his hand over his bald, bronzed head. He looked tired, as though he wanted their chat to end. It occurred to Max that he and his colleague always looked tired. Maybe that was one thing Italian spies had in common, he concluded. Could it be that their English, French, and German counterparts were more enthusiastic about their work? Possibly. Faith can move mountains, people often said. It must a useful thing to have in some lines of work.

"That's why he came to me when they were considering you for this job," Fossataro went on. "I told them you were a good sort, and popular with the ladies. That you look the part in evening clothes, and can outshine the professionals on any dance floor. . . . I also told them that if I had your good looks and gift for the gab, I would have retired years ago: I wouldn't mind walking some millionairess's poodle."

"Perhaps you talked to them too much." Max smiled.

"That's possible. But consider my situation. *Credere, obbedire, combattere* . . . Duty to the fatherland, and all that."

A silence ensued, which Fossataro used to blow a perfect smoke ring.

"I suppose you know, or have guessed, that Barbaresco isn't Mauro's real name."

Max glanced at the Italian spy, who was listening impassively.

"It doesn't matter what my name is," he said.

"Quite so," Max agreed evenly.

Fossataro blew another smoke ring, less perfect than the first, before continuing:

"Italy is a complex country. The good thing is that we always manage to reach an understanding among ourselves. *Guardie e ladri* . . . Cops and robbers. And that's as true before Mussolini as during his time and after, assuming there is an after."

Barbaresco was still listening with a blank expression, and Max started to warm toward him. Returning to his comparisons between spies, he imagined holding that same conversation with an Englishman, who would have been filled with patriotic indignation, or a German, who would have looked at them with contemptuous mistrust, or a Spaniard, who, after agreeing vigorously with every-thing Fossataro said, would have gone running to denounce him, in order to ingratiate himself with someone, or because he envied the tie he was wearing. Max opened his cigarette case and offered it to Barbaresco, who shook his head. Behind him, Tignanello had gone to sit down with a newspaper on one of the wooden benches in the square, as if his legs were aching.

"You've made some good connections, Max," Fossataro was saying. "If all goes well, you'll have new friends. In the right camp. It is good to think about the future."

"The way you have."

It was a seemingly throwaway remark, made while Max was lighting a cigarette, but Fossataro looked at him intently. Moments later, he wore the melancholy smile of someone with an unshakable belief in the limitless stupidity of mankind.

"I'm growing old, my friend. The world we knew, the one that sustained us, is doomed. And if another war breaks out in Europe, it will sweep everything away. You agree, don't you?"

"I do."

"Then put yourself in my place. I am fifty-two years old. Too old to be breaking locks and tiptoeing round other people's houses in the dark. What's more, I've spent seven of those behind bars. I'm a widower, with two unmarried children. There's nothing like it for encouraging a man to be a patriot. Making him raise his arm in the Roman salute to anyone they put in front of him. Italy has a future, we are the good guys. There are jobs, we're constructing buildings, sports stadiums, battleships, and we give the communists castor oil and a kick up the backside (here, to lighten the tone of his discourse, Fossataro winks at Barbaresco, who continues to listen, stony-faced). And it feels good to have the *carabinieri* on my side for a change."

Two smartly dressed women went by, heels clattering as they

walked down Rue Centrale: hats, bags, narrow skirts. One of them was very pretty, and for a moment her eyes met Max's. Fossataro stared at them until they turned the corner. Never mix sex with business, he had heard Max say in the old days. Except when sex makes business easier.

"Remember Biarritz?" Fossataro said. "That affair at the Hôtel Miramar?"

The memory brought a smile to his lips, making him look younger for a moment, enlivening his gaunt face.

"How long ago was that?" he went on. "Five years?"

Max nodded. Fossataro's contented expression brought back memories of wooden rails along the seafront, beach bars with punctilious waiters, women in pajama suits with narrow waists and flared trousers; naked, suntanned backs; familiar faces; parties with film stars, singers, people from the business and fashion worlds. Like Deauville and Cannes, Biarritz offered rich pickings in summer, plenty of opportunities for those who knew where to look.

"The actor and his girlfriend," Fossataro remembered, still grinning.

Then he proceeded to tell Barbaresco, with great eloquence, how in the summer of 1933 Max and he had planned a sophisticated job involving a movie actress called Lili Damita, whom Max had met at the Chiberta golf course, and with whom he had spent three mornings on the beach, three afternoons at the bar, and three evenings on the dance floor. On the all-important evening when Max was supposed to take her dancing at the Hôtel Miramar while Fossataro broke into her villa and made off with cash and jewelry to the tune of fifteen thousand pounds, her boyfriend, a famous Hollywood actor, arrived unannounced at the hotel, having walked off a set in the middle of filming. However, Max was lucky on two counts. Firstly, the jealous boyfriend had drunk too much on the journey there, and when his betrothed stepped out of a taxi on Max's arm, the punch he aimed at the elegant seducer's jaw missed its target because he lost his balance. And secondly, Enrico Fossa-taro was ten yards away from the scene, at the wheel of a hired car, ready to drive off to burgle the villa. When he saw what was going on, he climbed out of the car, walked over to the group, and, while Lili Damita squawked like a mother hen watching her chick being slaughtered, he and Max calmly gave the American a systematic beating, as the hotel receptionists and bellboys looked on with sat-isfaction (the actor, who habitually drank too much, was unpopular with the staff), out of revenge for the fifteen thousand dollars that had just slipped through their fingers.

"And do you know who the fellow was?" Fossataro was still talking to Barbaresco, who by then had pricked up his ears. "None other than Errol Flynn!" He laughed out loud, clapping Max on the arm. "You have before you the two fellows who gave Captain Blood a drubbing!"

—w—

"Do you know what the book is, Max? In chess. Not a book, *the* book."

They are in the gardens of the Hotel Vittoria, strolling along one of the side paths that runs like a tunnel between the varieties of trees, bright patches of sunlight filtering through their branches. Beyond the trellises laden with vines, seagulls are wheeling above the cliffs of Sorrento.

"A player is the sum of all his or her games and analyses," Mecha Inzunza goes on to explain. "Hundreds of hours of study go into each move on the board, countless strategies and variants, the result of working with a team or alone. A grand master can remember thousands of things: moves made by his predecessors, games played by his opponents. All of it, regardless of memory, is kept as a record."

"A kind of manual?" Max asks.

"Exactly."

They are making their way back to the hotel, unhurriedly. A few bees are hovering around the oleanders. As they penetrate farther into the garden, the traffic sounds behind them on Piazza Tasso grow more distant.

"A chess player can't travel or function without his or her personal papers," she continues. "What they are able to carry with them from place to place. A grand master's book contains the work of a lifetime: opening moves and variants, studies of opponents, analysis. Usually kept as notebooks or files. In Jorge's case, eight thick leather-bound notebooks, containing seven years' worth of annotations."

They linger in the rose garden, where a tiled bench encircles a table blanketed with leaves.

"A player is defenseless without that book," Mecha adds, placing her bag on the table and sitting down. "Not even someone with the most prodigious memory can retain everything. There are things in Jorge's book without which it would be hard for him to play Sokolov: previous games, analyses of his attacks and defenses. Years of work. Imagine, for example, that the Russian doesn't like playing the king's gambit, an opening based on the sacrifice of a pawn. And that Jorge, who has never used the king's gambit, considers doing so at the Dublin championship."

Max is standing in front of her, listening attentively.

"All that would be in Jorge's book?"

"Of course. What a disaster if it fell into Sokolov's hands. All that work for nothing. His secrets and analyses in his opponent's possession."

"Couldn't the book be rewritten?"

"It would take a whole lifetime. Not to mention the psychological blow: the knowledge that your opponent is aware of all your strategies, your thoughts."

She looks behind Max, who turns, following the direction of her gaze. The apartment house occupied by the Soviet delegation is close, only thirty feet away.

"Don't tell me Irina has given Jorge's book to the Russians . . ."

"No. Thank goodness. Otherwise he would be finished against Sokolov, here and in Dublin. This is something else."

A brief silence. Mecha fixes Max with her glittering gaze as the sunlight spills through the trellis.

"This is where you come in," she says, in a strange, mysterious voice, a faint smile on her lips.

Max raises his hand as though demanding silence in order to make out a note or some obscure sound.

"I'm afraid . . ."

He pauses for a second, unable to go on, and Mecha interrupts, impatiently. She has opened her bag and is riffling through it.

"I want you to get hold of the Russian's book for my son."

Max's jaw drops. Literally.

"I'm not sure I understand."

"Then I'll spell it out for you." She extracts a pack of Murattis from her bag and puts one in her mouth. "I want you to steal Sokolov's notebook with all his openings in it."

She has uttered these last words with tremendous calm. Max's hand reaches automatically for his lighter, but he freezes.

"And how do I do that?"

"By walking into the Russian's apartment and taking it."

"Just like that."

"Just like that."

A buzzing of bees, close by. Oblivious to them, Max is staring at Mecha. With an overwhelming desire to sit down.

"Why would I do that?"

"Because you've done it before."

He sits down beside her, still in shock.

"I've never stolen a Russian chess book."

"But you've stolen lots of other things," says Mecha, who has plucked a box of matches from her bag and is lighting her own cigarette. "One of them mine."

Max removes his hand from his pocket and rubs his chin. What is this foolishness, he thinks, completely at a loss. What the hell is he getting into, or are they getting him into?

"I'm no longer a . . . I don't do that anymore."

"But you know how to. Remember Nice."

"That's absurd. Nice was nearly thirty years ago."

Mecha says nothing. She smokes, watching him very calmly, as though everything had been said and the ball was in his court. She's enjoying this, he realizes with sudden horror. She finds this situation and Max's bewilderment amusing. And yet she's deadly serious.

"Are you suggesting I break in to the Soviet delegation's apartments, find Sokolov's chess book, and hand it over to you? And how am I to do that? How on earth do you propose I do that?"

"You have the knowledge and the experience. You'll find a way."

"Look at me." He touches his face as he leans over, as if it weren't plain to see. "I'm not the man you remember from Buenos Aires or from Nice. I have . . ."

"Things to lose?" She looks at him from very far away, disdainful and unfeeling. "Is that what you are trying to tell me?"

"I stopped taking certain kinds of risk a long time ago. I live peacefully, without any problems with the law. I am fully retired."

He stands up abruptly, ill at ease, and takes a few paces around the arbor. Gazing nervously at the yellow walls (suddenly they look menacing to him) of the apartment house occupied by the Russians.

"Besides, I'm too old for this game," he adds, genuinely despondent. "I haven't the strength, or the heart for it."

He has turned toward Mecha, who remains seated, smoking calmly as she watches him.

"Why should I do it?" he protests. "Give me one good reason why I should expose myself to such danger at my age."

She opens her mouth to speak, but stops herself almost instantaneously. She stays like that for a few seconds, pensive, her cigarette smoking between her fingers, studying Max. At last, with infinite scorn and sudden vehemence, as though venting a long-pent-up rage, she puts out the cigarette on the marble tabletop.

"Because Jorge is your son. Stupid."

He had gone to see her in Antibes, concealing his desire to explain himself beneath the guise of caution. It was dangerous, he told himself, for her to be on the loose over the next few days. In case some remark or secret she might confide to Susana Ferriol placed him at risk. It was easy enough finding her address. A brief telephone call to Asia Schwarzenberg, who made a few inquiries, and two days after his meeting with Mecha Inzunza, Max was stepping out of a taxi outside the gates of a villa surrounded by laurel bushes, acacias, and mimosas, near La Garoupe. He walked across the garden down a beaten earth driveway, where the Citröen two-seater was parked, bordered by cypress trees whose dark foliage contrasted with the calm, shimmering surface of the sea beyond. The house was a bungalow built on a small, rocky outcrop, with a broad terrace and a sunny veranda beneath wide arches, overlooking the garden and the bay.

Mecha Inzunza didn't look surprised. She welcomed him with unnerving ease after the maid who had opened the door vanished in silence. She was wearing a Japanese, silk pajama suit with a narrow waist, which accentuated her slender lines, discreetly hugging her hips. She had been watering the plants in one of the inside patios, and her bare feet left damp traces on the black-and-white tiles as she led Max through to the living room. It was decorated in the safari style that for the past few years had been all the rage on the Riviera: folding chairs and tables, built-in shelves, glass and chrome everywhere, with a couple paintings on otherwise bare walls, in a house that was beautiful, uncluttered, and simple, and in which only the very rich could afford to live. Mecha poured him a drink; they smoked and tacitly agreed to engage in polite chitchat, as though their recent encounter at Susana Ferriol's dinner party, and subsequent farewell, had been the most normal thing in the world. They discussed the villa she had rented while the conflict in Spain dragged on, how ideal it was to spend the winter there, the mistral, which made the skies a cloudless blue. Afterward, when they had run out of small talk, and the conversation was beginning to pall, Max proposed they have lunch somewhere nearby, at Juan-les-Pins or Eden Roc, and continue chatting. Mecha responded to his suggestion with a lengthy silence, then repeated the last word he had said under her breath with a contemplative air. Finally, she told Max to pour himself a drink while she changed to go out. I'm not hungry, she said. But a walk would do me good.

And there they were, strolling amid the grove of pines rooted in the sand, the rocks and clumps of seaweed on the shore in the shimmering midday sun, the azure waters of the bay open to the skies, and the sandy beach stretching as far as the old city wall. Mecha had changed out of her pajamas into a pair of black trousers and a blue-and-white-striped sailor's top. She wore sunglasses (and a hint of eye shadow beneath the dark lenses) and her sandals crunched on the gravel alongside Max's brown brogues. He was in shirtsleeves, hair slicked back, hatless, his jacket folded over his arm, and his sleeves turned up twice over his bronzed wrists.

"Do you still dance tangos, Max?"

"Occasionally."

"Even the Old School Tango? I don't suppose you've lost your touch."

He looked away, uncomfortable.

"Things aren't the way they used to be."

"You mean you no longer need to dance for money?"

He chose not to reply. He was thinking of her swaying in his arms that first time in the ballroom on the *Cap Polonio*. The sun illuminating her slender body in the room at the boardinghouse on Almirante Brown. Her mouth and her greedy, searching tongue when she thrust the tango dancer aside at the dive in Buenos Aires. Her husband's dazed expression, eyes bleary with drink and drugs, his salacious laughter as they copulated in front of him, there and later on in the hotel room, where they met in a hungry embrace, obscene in their nakedness and utter abandon. He was thinking, too, of the countless times he had remembered that scene over the nine years that had gone by, whenever an orchestra struck up the first bars of the melody composed by Armando de Troeye, or he heard it playing on a radio or phonograph. That tango (the last time he had danced to it was five weeks before, at the Carlton in Cannes with the daughter of a German steel manufacturer) had followed Max halfway around the world, and it always gave him a feeling of emptiness, absence, or loss, an intense, physical yearning for Mecha Inzunza's body. Her luminous eyes, open wide, staring at him from close up, frozen with pleasure. Her delicious flesh, always warm and moist in his memory, which he recalled so vividly, and which was close to him once more—still so unbelievably, so strangely close.

"Tell me about your life," she said.

"Which part?"

"This one." She made a gesture that seemed to embrace him all. "The part you've been cultivating all these years."

Max began to talk, cautiously, discreetly, and without going into detail. Skillfully mixing fact and fiction, weaving together amusing anecdotes and interesting situations that obscured the checkered parts of his life. With that natural ease he had, adapting his genuine past to that of the person he was pretending to be at that moment: a wealthy businessman, socialite, habitué of trains, transatlantic liners, and luxury hotels in Europe and South America, perfected over time and from consorting with distinguished or wealthy people. He spoke without knowing whether she believed him or not, but in any case did his best to avoid any reference to the clandestine nature of his true activities, or their consequences: to the brief spell in a Havana jail, which ended happily in his release, or his minor brush with the law in Kraków following the suicide of a wealthy Polish furrier's sister, or the shot that missed its target in the doorway of a gambling den in Berlin, involving a bungled sting during an illegal card game. Nor did he mention the money he had made and spent with identical ease during those years, or the emergency funds he kept in Monte Carlo, or his long, invaluable association with the safebreaker Enrico Fossataro. Nor, of course, did he mention the pair of professional swindlers, a husband and wife, he had encountered at the Chambre d'Amour bar in Biarritz, during the autumn of '31. Their brief association ended when the wife (a melancholy, attractive Englishwoman named Edith Casey, who specialized in fleecing wealthy widowers) took it upon herself to strengthen her ties with Max, to the point where her husband took exception. He was a cultivated yet brutish Scotsman, who called himself McGill or McDonald, and whose more or less justified jealousy brought to an end a year of mutually lucrative activities, following an unpleasant scene in which, to the couple's surprise (they had always considered him a peace-loving young gentleman) Max had been forced to resort to a couple of dirty tricks he had learned during his time in the Legion in North Africa. He had left McGill or McDonald or whatever his real name was laid out on the carpet of a room in the Hôtel du Golf de Deauville, with a bloody nose, while Edith Casey hurled insults at him as he fled along the corridor and vanished from their lives.

"What about you?"

"Oh . . . Me."

She had been listening to him attentively, in silence. Now she shrugged in response to Max's question, smiling beneath her dark glasses.

"High society. Isn't that what they call it in the illustrated magazines?"

He would have reached over to take off her sunglasses so that he could see the expression in her eyes, but he didn't dare.

"I never understood the way your husband . . ."

He fell silent, but she said nothing. The dark glasses reflected Max, inquisitively. Waiting for him to finish his sentence.

"The way he . . ." he started to say, before pausing again, ill at ease. "I don't know. You and he."

"And third parties, you mean?"

A silence. Drawn out. Cicadas were singing in the pines.

"Buenos Aires wasn't the first time, or the last," Mecha finally said. "Armando had his own way of looking at life. At relationships between the sexes."

"A strange one, in any case."

A joyless laugh. Sharp. She raised her hands slightly to express surprise.

"I never thought of you as a prude, Max. . . . Nobody would have said so in Buenos Aires."

She was drawing with her foot in the sand. What looked like a heart, he decided. But she finally erased it when she seemed to be tracing an arrow that pierced it.

"It started as a provocative game. A challenge to upbringing and morality. Then it became part of all the rest."

She took a few paces toward the shore, amid the clumps of seaweed, until she appeared framed by the dazzling turquoise of the water.

"It happened gradually, from the very beginning. The morning of our honeymoon, Armando contrived to have the waitress who brought our breakfast discover us naked in bed, making love. We laughed like crazy."

Shielding his eyes with his hand, Max strained to make out her face against the light. But all he could see was her silhouette against the shimmering bay as she continued to tell her story, in a monotonous, almost jaded voice.

"We took a friend home once, after a dinner party. An Italian musician, terribly handsome and languorous with curly hair. D'Ambrosio he was called. Armando arranged things so that the Italian and I made love in front of him. He only joined in after watching closely for a long time, with a smile and a strange glint in his eye. With that special propensity he had for mathematical elegance."

"Did you always . . . enjoy it?"

"Not always. Especially not at the beginning. A conventional Catholic upbringing isn't something you forget overnight. But Armando liked to push the boundaries . . ."

Max felt his tongue sticking to the roof of his mouth. The sun was sweltering and he was thirsty. And strangely uneasy, too, an almost physical malaise. He was tempted to sit down where he stood, at the risk of ruining his immaculate trousers. He wished he hadn't left his hat behind at the villa. Yet he knew it wasn't the sun, or the heat.

"I was very young," she went on. "I felt like an actress going out onstage seeking the audience's approval, hoping people will applaud."

"You were in love. That explains a lot."

"Yes . . . I suppose I did love him in those days. A lot."

She had tilted her head as she said that, reflecting. Then, she glanced around, as though looking for an image or word. Possibly an explanation. Finally, she seemed to give up, and gave a resigned, ironical shrug.

"It took me a while to realize that it wasn't just him. I had my own dark places. I would never have gone that far, otherwise. Not just to please him. Sometimes he hit me. Or I hit him. Once, in Berlin, he made me sleep with two young waiters from a bar in Tauentzienstrasse. That night he didn't even touch me. He would usually come to me, when the others were done, but on that occasion he just sat there smoking and watching until it was over. That was the first time I really enjoyed feeling I was being observed."

She had told the story in a neutral tone, without inflection. She could have been reading out of a pharmacist's leaflet, thought Max. And yet she seemed interested in the effect her words had on him, he was surprised to notice. In a rather cold, clinical way. As if she were an anthropologist. The contrast with his own tumultuous emotions was as stark as all that light clashing with the dark outline of her shadow. This woman aroused jealousy in him, he realized, more alarmed than astonished. This was a strange, unfamiliar despair he had never experienced before. Of violent, unsatisfied desire. Animal resentment and rage.

"Armando groomed me," she was saying. "With a methodical patience that characterized him, he showed me to use my mind in sex. Its immense power. The physical side is only part of it, he used to say. The necessary, inevitable embodiment of everything else. It is a question of harmonies."

They came to a halt momentarily. Returning to the path between the beach and the pines, and Mecha slipped off her sandals, taking Max's arm with complete naturalness.

"Afterward, I would go to bed and listen to him working at the piano in his studio until dawn. And I admired him even more."

Max managed to detach his tongue from the roof of his mouth. "Do you still use your mind?"

His voice had sounded hoarse. Dry. It had almost hurt to speak. "Why do you ask?"

"Your husband isn't here." He made a sweeping gesture that embraced the bay, Antibes, and the rest of the world. "And I don't think he will be coming back soon. With his mathematical elegance."

He stared at Mecha with an aggressive wariness.

"You want to know if I sleep with other men? Or women? When he isn't around? Yes, I do, Max."

I don't want to be here, he thought, surprising himself. Not in this light that dulls my judgment. Dries up my thoughts and my mouth.

"Yes," she repeated. "I do, sometimes."

She had paused once more, outlined against the glare of the beach. The soft sea breeze ruffled her hair across her skin, lightly bronzed by the southern French sun.

"Just like Armando," she said in an inscrutable voice. "Or you yourself."

In the lenses of her dark glasses, the coastline, the clump of pines, and the beach with the azure sea were reflected. Max watched her carefully, his eyes lingering on the curve of her shoulders and her torso beneath the striped shirt, slightly damp under the arms where she had perspired. She was even more beautiful than in Buenos Aires, he concluded, almost despondently. If that were possible. She must be thirty-two now; the perfect age when a woman becomes fully formed. Mecha Inzunza was one of those seemingly unattainable women whom men dreamed about in the bowels of ships or the trenches at a battlefront. For thousands of years, they had killed, waged war, and razed cities for women like her.

"There's a place near here," she said suddenly. "Pension Semaphore . . . close to the lighthouse."

He looked at her, confused at first. Mecha pointed to a path on their left leading through the pine trees, past a white villa surrounded by palm trees and agaves.

"It offers cheap lodgings for tourists. There's a small outdoor restaurant under the shade of a magnolia tree. They rent rooms."

Max was a calm man. His nature and life itself had made him what he was. It was this calm that allowed him to stand firm and keep his mouth shut, motionless in front of her. Lest a clumsy word or gesture sever the tenuous thread from which everything was hanging.

"I want to go to bed with you," Mecha said abruptly, in response to his silence. "And I want that to happen now."

"Why?" he managed to speak, at last.

"Because during the past nine years you have often been in my mind, if you get my meaning."

"In spite of everything?"

"In spite of everything." She grinned. "Pearl necklace included."

"Have you been there before?"

"You ask too many questions. And they are all stupid."

She had raised a hand, placing her fingers on Max's dried lips. A soft caress, filled with strange promise.

"Of course I have," she said after a moment. "And it has a room with a big mirror on the wall. Perfect for watching."

—⁜—

The blind was made of wooden slats. The afternoon sun seeping in cast strips of light and shade on the bed and over Mecha's body as she slept. Lying beside her, trying not to wake her, Max turned to study her face, touched by a ray of sunlight, mouth half-open, nostrils flaring slightly as she breathed softly, and her naked breasts with their dark nipples and tiny drops of perspiration glistening between the strips of light. And the surface of her taut skin, descending toward her belly and forking at her thighs, covering her sex, from which his seed oozed silently onto the sheet with the smell of their bodies and the gentle perspiration of their prolonged embraces.

Raising his head slightly from the pillow, Max contemplated their motionless forms in the huge mirror on the wall, with its silver backing tarnished through age and neglect, like the rest of the cheap furnishings: a chest of drawers, a bidet and washbasin, a dusty lamp and some twisted electric cables fastened to the wall with porcelain insulators, a faded travel poster proposing, rather unconvincingly (a yellow sunset and a few purple pine trees), a visit to Villefranche. One of those rooms, in short, which seemed to cater to commercial travelers, fugitives from justice, would-be suicides, or lovers. Without her sleeping beside him and the shafts of sunlight falling through the blinds, Max would have found it depressing, reminiscent of other places where he had stayed out of necessity rather than choice. And yet, from the moment they crossed the threshold, Mecha seemed delighted by the squalid room that had no running water, and the sleepy landlady who handed them the key in exchange for forty francs, without asking for their identity papers or posing any questions. The moment the door was closed, Mecha's voice had grown hoarser, and she had started to perspire. Max was surprised when, while he was commenting on the pleasant view, which, with the window open, he said, compensated for the gloomy décor, she walked up to him, mouth half-open as if she were breathless, interrupting his deliberate observations, slipping her striped blouse over her head, to reveal her breasts, paler than the rest of her skin exposed to the sun.

"You're so handsome, it hurts to look at you."

Her upper body was completely naked, and she raised one hand, pushing his chin with her finger to turn his head so that she could see him better.

"I'm not wearing my necklace today," she whispered after a moment.

"What a shame," he parried.

"You're a scoundrel, Max."

"Yes . . . sometimes."

Everything happened afterward in a complex yet orderly sequence of flesh, saliva, caresses, and essential moistness. From the moment she kicked off her last piece of clothing and lay on the bed, from which he had removed the coverlet, Max realized she was already unusually aroused, ready to receive him instantly. That room in a boardinghouse, he concluded, seemed to work miracles. And yet there was no hurry, he told himself, determined to keep his cool. And so he attempted to draw out their foreplay, aware that his desire, swelling painfully in every nerve and muscle (grating his clenched teeth, gasping with suppressed desire and rage) might jeopardize everything. They couldn't settle nine years in thirty minutes. And so he employed every ounce of self-control and experience to prolong the caresses, the collisions, the almost extreme violence she insisted on sometimes (she punched him twice while he attempted to take her), the groans of pleasure and breathless gasps in between caresses, two or twenty different ways of kissing, licking, and biting. Max had forgotten about the mirror on the wall, but she hadn't. And finally he discovered her peering into it, head turned to the side, while he was busy with her body and her mouth, watching herself and him. Max turned his head, too, and saw himself there, engaging in what looked like a savage duel, back arched over her, arms tensed so that the muscles and tendons seemed about to burst as he struggled to immobilize her, and also to hold back, while she writhed with animallike ferocity, biting and hitting out at him until, all at once, eyes fixed on him in the mirror, awaiting his reaction, she yielded, clasping him at last, or anew, his flesh vibrant with pleasure, slowly abandoning herself to the age-old ritual of complete surrender. And after Max had watched himself and watched her in the mirror, he had turned once more to look at her close up, the real image just two inches from his eyes and lips, glimpsing a flicker of disdain in her honey-colored gaze and a defiant smile on her mouth that belied it all; his apparent dominance and her own submission. Then Max's will finally deserted him, and like a vanquished gladiator he sank his face into Mecha's neck, losing all sense of his surroundings, and slowly, intensely, defenseless at last, he spilled his seed into the dark warmth of Mecha Inzunza's belly.

10

The Click of Ivory

MAX HASN'T HAD a good night. I've certainly known better ones, he thought to himself in the morning as he emerged from an uneasy sleep. He was still thinking about this as he ran the Braun electric razor over his chin, contemplating his tired face in the mirror of the hotel bathroom, the bags under his eyes, the signs of recent anxiety added to the ravages of time and life, not to mention last-minute failures and fresh doubts, just when he thought everything was almost settled, or he had settled everything, when it was too late to start applying new labels to old experiences. Several times during his fretful night, tossing and turning between sleep and wakefulness, he imagined he could hear his old certainties plummet like a pile of plates crashing noisily to the floor. The sum of his eventful life, which until only a few hours before, he thought he had salvaged from his successive misadventures, was a kind of worldly indifference, which he assumed with gallant serenity. And now this last bastion of calm fatalism, a mind-set that until the previous day was his sole asset, has been smashed to smithereens. Sleeping peacefully, with the serenity of a tired old marathon runner, has been the one remaining privilege that, prior to his last conversation with Mecha Inzunza, Max believed he could still enjoy at his age, without life snatching it away from him.

His first impulse, the old instinct when faced with the smell of danger, was to flee: to put an immediate end to that absurd, mean-ingless affair (he detests the word *romance* and refuses to call it that) and return to his duties at Villa Oriana before things become too complicated and the ground gives way beneath his feet. To put on the face of a good loser and forget what went before, acknowledge what is, and accept what can never be. And yet, there are impulses, he concludes. Instincts and interests that in some cases lead men astray but in others cause the ball to land in the appropriate slot on the roulette wheel. Paths that, contrary to what elementary prudence might suggest, are impossible to avoid when they present themselves. When they beckon with answers to questions that have never been posed.

One such answer could lie in the billiard room at the Hotel Vittoria. Max has been looking for it for a while, and is surprised to find it there of all places. Emil Karapetian directed him to it when Max asked if he had seen Jorge Keller. They met a moment ago on the terrace: Karapetian and Irina were having breakfast together so normally (she greeted Max with a friendly smile) that it is obvious the young analyst has no idea her connection to the Russians has been discovered.

"Billiards?" Max was surprised. Somehow this didn't fit with the image he had of a chess player.

"It's part of his training," Karapetian explained. "Sometimes he runs, or goes for a swim. Other times he shuts himself away and practices cannon shots."

"I'd never have thought it."

"Neither did we," replied Karapetian, shrugging his broad shoulders with a sour expression. "But that's Jorge for you."

"And he plays by himself?"

"Nearly always."

The billiard room is on the main floor, past the reading room: a mirror duplicates the light from a window overlooking the terrace; there is a scoreboard with a cue rack, and a long, narrow metal lamp hangs above the billiard table. Hunched over it, Jorge Keller is playing one cannon shot after another, accompanied only by the soft sound of the cue's cushioned tip and the balls clicking against each other with almost monotonous precision. Standing in the doorway, Max watches the chess player: he is completely focused, and scores a perfect cannon each time, stringing them together mechanically, as though each triple cannon of the ivory balls set up the next shot on the green baize, in a sequence that, if he so wished, could last forever.

Max scrutinizes the young man, intent upon taking in every last detail, noticing anything he might have missed on earlier occasions. At first, simply out of an innate self-preservation, he rummages in his memory for the long-distant, hazy features of Ernesto Keller, the Chilean diplomat he had met in the autumn of 1937 at Susana Ferriol's dinner party. He recalls a fair-haired, distinguished-looking, affable fellow, and tries to make the image fit with the appearance of the young man who, for all official purposes, is his son. Then he tries to match this memory with that of Mecha Inzunza, the way she looked twenty-nine years ago, the part of her that has been genetically passed down to her son, who is now standing still beside the table, studying the position of the balls and chalking his cue. Slender, tall, and upright. Like his mother, of course. But like Max too, in his youth. They resemble each other in looks and build. And it's true, Max concludes with a sudden sinking feeling, that the mop of thick, black hair falling across Jorge's brow as he leans over the rail is as unlike that of his mother (from the *Cap*

Polonio Max remembers hers as light brown, almost dark blonde) as it is that of the man whose name he bears. If Jorge wore his hair slicked back the way Max did when his was still as luxuriant and dark, it would be identical to the hair he used to run his hand over, when he was Jorge's age, smoothing it before walking slowly in time with the rhythms of the orchestra, gently clicking his heels, and, with a smile on his lips, inviting a woman onto the dance floor.

It can't be true, he decides irritably, thrusting the idea aside. He doesn't even know how to play chess. He is furious with himself for remaining there, lurking in the doorway, searching for himself in the young man's features. That sort of thing only happens in movies, plays, and radio soap operas. If it were true, surely he would have felt something the first time he saw him, or spoke to him, some inner vibration, a sign, a tremor. An affinity, perhaps. Or a simple memory. How could a man's natural instinct remain oblivious to such an important truth? To these supposed facts. "The call of the blood," as they used to refer to it in old melodramas about millionaires and orphans. Only Max has never heard such a call. Not even now, blinded by a painful belief in some inexplicable mistake, an uneasy foreboding that troubles him as nothing ever has before. None of this can be true. Regardless of whether Mecha is lying or not (and she most likely is), this is sheer, dangerous nonsense.

"Good morning."

He easily engages Jorge in conversation, despite everything. He has never found that difficult in any situation, and billiards isn't a bad topic. Max can play reasonably well from his days in Barcelona, when as a bellhop he would gamble his three-peseta tips on a game of thirty-one and on Spanish pool in the billiard room of a dive bar in the Barrio Chino. Women hovering in the doorway; pimps with tie pins and braces, skin gleaming with sweat and cigarette smoke beneath the greenish light projected onto the baize by lampshades soiled with flies, holding lighted cigarettes as they cued up; the sound of cannon shots and an occasional entreaty or curse, which often had more to do with what was going on outside: the players would fall silent as they listened for the sound of feet running in rope sandals, police whistles, stray shots from a union man's pistol, the noise of rifle butts slamming against the ground.

"Do you play billiards, Max?"

"A little."

Jorge has a good face in profile, accentuated by the lock of hair falling across his brow that gives him an even more relaxed, easy-going air. And yet the smile with which he greets the new arrival is at odds with his distant look, concentrated on his next shot and the successive combinations of the three ivory balls.

"Grab a cue, if you want."

He's a good player, Max decides. Systematic and sure of himself. Perhaps being a chess player is about that: the ability to see the whole or the space, the concentration. The fact is, Jorge can play a sequence of cannons with astonishing ease, as if he were able to calculate several shots in advance.

"I didn't know you were good at billiards as well."

"Actually I'm not. Doing this isn't the same as playing against an opponent, off three cushions."

Max walks over to the rack and chooses a cue.

"Shall we keep going for the highest run?" the young man suggests.

"If you want."

Jorge nods and continues playing. With a series of smooth cue actions he shoots one cannon after another off one cushion, always contriving to leave the balls as close to each other as possible.

"It's a way of concentrating," he says, without looking up from the table. "Of thinking."

Max watches him, intrigued.

"How many shots can you see in advance?"

"How funny you should ask." Keller smiles. "Is it that obvious?"

"I know nothing about chess, but I imagine it must be similar. Seeing moves or seeing cannons."

"I can see at least three." He points at the balls, the angles, and the cushions. "There and there, perhaps five."

"Is billiards really similar to chess?"

"Not similar. But they do have things in common. Faced with each situation there are several possibilities. I try to determine how the balls will move, and make that happen. As with chess, it's a question of logic."

"Is this how you train?"

"Training is too big a word for it. It helps me exercise my brain with the least amount of effort."

Jorge stops after missing an easy cannon. It's clear he has done so out of politeness: the balls aren't very far apart. Max levels his cue and leans over the table; he shoots and the ivory balls gently collide. Five times the red ball rolls to and from the cushion, tracing a precise angle with each contact.

"You aren't bad yourself," Jorge comments. "Have you played much?"

"A bit. More when I was young than now."

Max has missed the sixth cannon. Keller chalks his cue and hunches over the table.

"Shall we play off three cushions?"

"All right."

The balls collide more forcefully. Keller plays four cannons in a row. With the last, he deliberately places Max's cue ball in a difficult position.

"I knew your father." Max studies the three balls carefully. "A long time ago. On the Riviera."

"We didn't live with him for long. My mother got divorced quickly."

Max gives the cue ball a sharp tap, sending it in the opposite direction to the others.

"When I met him you weren't born yet."

Keller doesn't answer. He remains silent while Max makes a second cannon, and, faced with the difficulty of a third, chooses instead to leave his opponent's cue ball in an awkward position in a corner.

"Irina . . ." Max starts to say.

Keller, who is raising the butt of his cue for a piqué shot, pauses and looks at Max as though wondering how much he knows.

"Your mother and I go back a long way," Max explains.

Keller moves his cue back and forth a few times, nearly touching the ball, as though hesitating to take the shot.

"I know," he says. "Since Buenos Aires, with her previous husband."

Finally he shoots, shakily, and misses. He gazes at the table for a moment before turning toward Max, sullenly. As though holding him responsible for his blunder.

"I don't know what my mother has told you about Irina."

"Very little . . . or just enough."

"She must have her reasons. But as far as I'm concerned, it's none of her business. Just as your conversations with my mother are no concern of mine."

"I didn't mean to . . ."

"Of course. I know you didn't mean to."

Max studies Keller's hands: long, slender fingers. The nail on his index fingers slightly rounded like his.

"When you were a boy, did she . . ."

Keller raises his cue, interrupting him.

"May I be frank with you, Max? My whole future is in the balance here. I have problems of my own, both professional and personal. And suddenly you come on the scene, someone my mother had never spoken to me about. And with whom, for reasons I'm unaware of, she has an unexpected rapport."

Keller leaves his last words hanging in the air, and looks at the billiard table as if he has just remembered it is there. Max picks up the red ball, absentmindedly feeling the weight of in his hand, before replacing it where it was.

"Has she told you nothing about me?"

"Very little: an old friend, from the tango days . . . that sort of thing. I have no idea whether you were lovers or not back then. But I know her, and I know when someone is special to her. It doesn't happen often." Although it isn't his turn, Keller leans over the table and strikes the cue ball. It rebounds off three cushions before producing a perfect cannon. "The day my mother bumped into you, she was awake all night. I could hear her pacing up and down. . . . The next morning, her bedroom reeked of tobacco, and the ashtrays were full of cigarette ends."

The ivory balls kiss gently. Concentrating, Keller tosses his hair back, slides the cue along his hand on the baize, then shoots again. He never gets agitated, Mecha told Max the last time they spoke about him. He has no negative emotions and doesn't know what it is to feel sad. All he does is play chess. And that he gets from you, Max, not from me.

"You can understand my misgivings," the young man says. "I've got more than enough on my plate at the moment."

"Listen. I never meant to . . . I'm simply a guest here. This is an extraordinary coincidence."

Keller appears not to be listening. He is studying the cue ball, which has ended up in an awkward position.

"I don't mean to be rude. You're a nice enough guy. Everybody likes you. And as I said, albeit in a roundabout way, my mother seems very fond of you. But there's something that doesn't convince me. Something I don't like."

The shot, hard this time, gives Max a start. The balls scatter all over the place, striking the cushions and ending up in an impossible position.

"Perhaps it's your way of smiling," Keller adds. "With your mouth, I mean. Your eyes appear to be somewhere else."

"Well, your smile is similar."

No sooner has Max spoken than he regrets his remark. To hide his frustration at his own clumsiness, he pretends to study the balls intently.

"That's why I said it," Keller says, evenly. "It's as if I'd seen that smile before."

He remains silent for a moment, reflecting seriously about what he has just said.

"Or possibly," he goes on, "it's the way my mother looks at you sometimes."

Concealing his unease, Max leans over the table, strikes the three cushions, and misses the shot.

"Melancholy?" Keller chalks his cue. "A complicit sadness? Could that be how to put it?"

"Perhaps. I don't know."

"I dislike that look my mother gives you. How can sadness be complicit?"

"I don't know that either."

"I'd like to know what happened between you. Although this isn't the time or the place."

"Ask her."

"I have. . . . All she says is: 'Ah, Max.' When she clams up, there's no way of making her talk."

Abruptly, as if he has suddenly lost interest in the game, Keller puts the chalk down on the rail of the table. Then he walks over to the rack on the wall and replaces his cue.

"We were talking about seeing cannons or moves just now," he says after a moment. "And that's been my problem since I first saw you: there's something about your game I don't trust. I'm already threatened from all directions. . . . I'd ask you to stay out of my

mother's life, but that would be going too far. It's not for me to say.
And so I'll ask you to stay out of mine."

Max, who has put down his own cue, lifts his hands in a gesture
of polite protest.

"I never meant to . . ."

"I believe you. I do. But it makes no difference. . . . Keep away
from me, please." Keller points at the table as if his contest with
Sokolov were taking place right there. "At least until this is over."

———

Toward the east, beyond the lighthouse in Nice harbor and Mont
Boron, scattered clouds gathered over the sea. Leaning forward to
light his pipe out of the wind, Fito Mostaza exhaled a few puffs of
smoke, glanced up at the hazy sky, and winked at Max from behind
his tortoiseshell spectacles.

"The weather's about to break," he said.

They were standing below a statue of King Charles Felix,
near the iron guardrail along the edge of the road with a view
over the harbor. Mostaza had asked Max to meet him at a small
café, which was closed when Max arrived, and so he was waiting
on the road, looking at the boats moored along the dockside, the
tall buildings in the background, and the huge sign advertising
Galeries Lafayette. At a quarter past, he saw Mostaza's small,
agile figure strolling toward him up the hill from Rauba-Capeù,
hat casually tipped back on his head, jacket open over the same
shirt and bow tie, hands in his trouser pockets. Seeing the café
was closed, Mostaza had shrugged with silent resignation and
reached into his pocket for his tobacco pouch. He proceeded to
fill his pipe as he positioned himself beside Max, glancing about
with vague curiosity, as if to confirm what Max had been looking
at while he waited.

"The Italians are getting impatient," Max said.

"Have you seen them again?"

Max was certain Mostaza already knew the answer to his own question.

"We had a brief chat yesterday."

"Yes," Mostaza conceded after a moment, between puffs. "That's what I thought."

He was contemplating the moored boats, as well as the packages, barrels, and crates piled up next to the railway line that ran alongside the quays. Finally, without taking his eyes off the harbor, Mostaza turned his head.

"Have you made up your mind yet?"

"What I have done is to tell them about you. About your proposal."

"That's only natural." A philosophical smile appeared around Mostaza's pipe stem. "You're covering your back as best you can. I appreciate that."

"How nice to find you so understanding."

"We're all human, my friend. With our fears, our ambitions, our cautiousness . . . How did they respond to the revelation?"

"They didn't. They listened carefully, looked at each other, and we changed the subject."

Mostaza nodded, approvingly.

"Good lads. Professionals, needless to say. I wouldn't have expected any less. . . . It's a pleasure to work with people like that. Or against them."

"I admire all this fair play," Max remarked sarcastically. "The three of you could meet up, come to some agreement, or stab each other in a friendly way. It would make my life a lot easier."

Mostaza burst out laughing.

"All in good time, my friend . . . Meanwhile, tell me, what have you decided in the end? Fascist dictatorship or Republic?"

"I'm still thinking it over."

"Very well. But you're running out of time. When do you plan to break into the house?"

"In three days' time."

"Any particular reason why?"

"A dinner party at someone's house. I know Susana Ferriol will be out for several hours."

"What about the servants?"

"I'll worry about them."

Mostaza was looking at Max while sucking on his pipe, as though gauging the significance of each reply. Finally, he removed his spectacles, pulled the handkerchief out of the top pocket of his jacket, and began polishing them energetically.

"I'm going to ask you a favor, Mr. Costa. . . . Whatever you decide, tell your Italian friends that in the end you have decided to work for them. Tell them as much about me as you can."

"Are you serious?"

"Perfectly."

Mostaza held his spectacles up to the light and put them on again, satisfied.

"There's more," he added. "I actually want you to work for them. Fair and square."

Max, who had reached for his cigarette case and opened the lid, paused in midmovement.

"You mean I should hand the documents over to the Italians?"

"That's right," Mostaza replied, calmly holding Max's astonished gaze. "It's their operation, after all. They're paying for it. I think it only fair, don't you?"

"What about you?"

"Oh, don't worry. I'm my own boss."

Max put the case back in his pocket without taking a cigarette. He had lost all desire to smoke, or to be in Nice, for that matter. Which part of the trap is most lethal? he was thinking. Where in this spider's web will I be ensnared? Or eaten alive?

"Did you ask me here to tell me that?"

Mostaza touched Max's elbow lightly, drawing him closer to

the railing separating them from the sheer drop into the harbor.

"Come here. Look," he said almost tenderly. "Down there is Quai Infernet. Do you know who Infernet was? The officer in command of the *Intrépide* during the Battle of Trafalgar. He refused to flee with Admiral Dumanoir and went on fighting until the end. Do you see that merchant ship moored there?"

Max said he could (it was a black-hulled freighter with two blue stripes on its smokestack). Mostaza went on to give a brief history of that ship. The *Luciano Canfora* was carrying war matériel intended for Franco's troops: ammonia salts, cotton, tin and copper ingots. It was scheduled to set sail for Palma de Mallorca in a few days' time, and it was more than likely Tomás Ferriol who had paid for the cargo. The whole thing had been set up, Mostaza added, by a group of Francoist secret agents based in Marseille who had a shortwave radio station on a yacht moored in Monte Carlo.

"Why are you telling me this?" asked Max.

"Because you and the *Luciano Canfora* have things in common. The shipping agents think it is going to sail to the Balearic Islands, unaware that unless things go badly wrong, its next port of call will be Valencia. I am currently busy persuading the captain and his chief engineer that they will benefit more all 'round if they work for the Republic. . . . As you can see, Mr. Costa, you aren't the only cause of my sleepless nights."

"I still don't understand why you're telling me this."

"Because it's true . . . and because I'm sure that, in a fit of cautious honesty, you'll pass it on to your Italian friends at the first opportunity."

Max removed his hat, and ran his hand through his hair. Despite the clouds gathering over the sea and the easterly breeze, he felt suddenly, uncomfortably hot.

"You're joking, of course."

"Not at all."

"Wouldn't that endanger your operation?"

Mostaza pointed his pipe at Max's chest.

"My dear friend, this is all part of the same operation. Keep watching your back and let me take care of the dirty work. . . . All I ask is for you to continue being what you are: a nice fellow loyal to everyone who approaches him, who is trying to get out of this situation as best he can. No one is going to blame you for anything. I'm sure the Italians will appreciate your forthrightness as much as I do."

Max looked askance at him.

"Have you ever thought they might try to kill you?"

"Of course I have." Mostaza laughed between gritted teeth, as if it were all obvious. "In my line of work, it's one of the added risks."

Then he fell silent for a moment and contemplated the *Luciano Canfora* before turning to Max.

"The problem in this sort of mess," he went on, fingering the scar below his jaw, "is that sometimes it's the other people who die. And, in one's own modest way, one can be as dangerous as the next man. Has it never occurred to you to be dangerous?"

"No, not really."

"That's a shame." Mostaza studied him with renewed interest, as though glimpsing a quality he hadn't noticed before. "I can see something in your nature, you know? A certain predisposition."

"I get by quite well being peaceful."

"Has it always been so?"

"You only have to look at me."

"I envy you. Truly. I'd like to be like that, too."

Mostaza took a couple of unrewarding puffs on his pipe, then removed it from his mouth, examining the bowl with a frown.

"Do you know something?" he went on. "Once I sat up all night in a first-class compartment, chatting with a distinguished gentleman. An extremely pleasant fellow, moreover. You remind me of him. We hit it off well. At five o'clock in the morning, noticing the time, I decided I knew enough and stepped out into the corridor to smoke a pipe. Then someone waiting outside entered the compartment and shot the pleasant distinguished gentleman in the head."

He had fished out a box of matches and was relighting his pipe, absorbed by the process.

"It must be marvelous, don't you think?" he said finally, shaking the match to put it out.

"I don't know what you mean."

Mostaza looked at him with interest, exhaling thick puffs of smoke.

"Do you know anything about Pascal?" he asked unexpectedly.

"About as much as I know about spies," Max confessed. "Probably less."

"He was a philosopher. He wrote about the power of flies. They win battles."

"I don't understand."

Mostaza's face broke into a benevolent smile, at once ironic and melancholy.

"I envy you, believe me. How reassuring to be that third man surveying the scene with indifference. To believe yourself far removed from your fascist friends and from me. Intent upon being honest with everyone, not taking sides, and then sleeping peacefully. Whether alone or in company is no concern of mine. But peacefully, all the same."

Max was edgy, exasperated. He felt the urge to punch that cold, absurdly knowing smile, an arm's length from his face. But he was aware that, despite the fragile appearance of its owner, that smile wasn't the kind to let itself be punched easily.

"Listen," he said, "I'm going to be rude."

"Don't worry, go ahead."

"I couldn't give a damn about your war, your ships, and your letters from Count Ciano."

"I admire your bluntness," Mostaza conceded.

"I don't care if you admire it or not. Do you see this watch? This suit made in London? Do you see my tie purchased in Paris? I worked hard to achieve all this. To wear it with ease. I sweated blood to get where I am. . . . And now that I've arrived, a whole bunch of people, in one way or another, are intent upon making things difficult for me."

"I understand. . . . Your coveted, lucrative Europe is drooping like a fading lily."

"Then give me time, damn you, to enjoy it a little."

Mostaza appeared to reflect calmly about that.

"Yes," he said. "Perhaps you're right."

Clutching the rail, Max leaned out above the harbor, as though seeking to breathe in as much of the sea air as possible. To clear his lungs. Beyond La Réserve, he could make out Susana Ferriol's house on the rocky shoreline, in the distance, amid the ocher-and-white villas dotting the green hillside of Mont Boron.

"You and they have embroiled me in something I don't like," Max added after a moment. "And all I want is to get it over with. To be rid of you all."

Mostaza tutted sympathetically.

"Well, I've got bad news for you," he replied. "Because you can't get away from us. We are the future, like machines, airplanes, red flags, black, blue, or brown shirts. . . . You arrived too late for a party that is already doomed." He pointed with his pipe toward the clouds gathering over the water. "A storm is brewing not far from here. That storm will sweep everything away, nothing will ever be the same again. Those fancy ties you bought in Paris will be of little use to you then."

—⚬—

"I don't know whether Jorge is my son," says Max. "Actually, I've no way of knowing."

"Of course not," replied Mecha Inzunza. "You only have my word for it."

They are sitting at a table on the terrace of a bar on the Piazzetta in Capri, next to the cathedral steps and the clock tower looming above the road that winds up from the harbor. They arrived midafternoon, in the little ferryboat that takes half an hour from Sorrento. It was Mecha's idea. "Jorge is resting," she said, "and it's been years since I went to the island." She invited Max to go with her.

"During that time, did you . . ." he starts to say.

"Go with other men, you mean?"

Max doesn't reply immediately. He watches the people sitting at the other tables or strolling past, backlit by the setting sun. Snatches of conversation in English, Italian, or German reach them from the adjacent tables.

"The other Keller was around then," he adds as though concluding a convoluted line of reasoning. "Jorge's official father."

Mecha gives a scathing laugh. She is playing with the ends of the silk scarf tied at her neck, over a gray sweater and black slacks that hug her long legs, skinnier now than twenty-nine years ago. She is wearing a pair of black Pilgrim shoes without buckles, and the leather and canvas shoulder bag is hanging from the back of her chair.

"Listen, Max. I'm not asking you to accept paternity, not at this time of your life and mine."

"I don't intend . . ."

She raises her hand, silencing him.

"I can imagine what you intend or don't intend. I was merely answering your question. Why should I do it, you asked. Why should you should run a risk with the Russians by stealing their book?"

"I'm too old for these tricks."

"Perhaps."

Mecha reaches absentmindedly for her wineglass on the table, next to Max's. He looks once more at her skin sagging with age, like his own, and the blemishes on the back of her hand.

"You were more interesting when you took risks," she adds, wistfully.

"And a lot younger," Max replies, unflinching.

She gazes at him, sardonically.

"Have you, or we, changed so much? Don't you feel the old tingling in your fingertips anymore? Your heart beating faster than usual?"

She contemplates the graceful look of resignation he gives her by way of a reply: a gesture in keeping with the navy-blue sweater draped with deliberate casualness over the shoulders of his white cotton polo shirt, the gray linen trousers, and his white hair combed back like in the old days, with an immaculate side part.

"I wonder how you did it," she adds. "What stroke of luck allowed you to change your life . . . and what her name was. Or their names. The women who footed the bill."

"There weren't any women." Max tilts his head, uneasily. "Just luck. As you said."

"An easy life."

"Yes."

"The one you always dreamed of."

"Not exactly. But I can't complain."

Mecha looks over at the steps leading from the Piazzetta to the Palazzo Cerio, as though searching for a familiar face among the crowd.

"He *is* your son, Max."

A silence. She drains her glass, with short, almost thoughtful sips.

"I'm not trying to make you pay for anything," she says after a moment. "You aren't responsible for his life or mine. . . . I was merely giving you a valid reason for helping him."

Max pretends to busy himself with smoothing out his trousers, so as not to appear troubled.

"You will do it, won't you?"

"His hands, perhaps," he concedes, at last. "His hair looks like mine, too. . . . And something about the way he moves."

"Don't keep dwelling on it, please. Take it or leave it. But stop acting so pathetic."

"I'm not pathetic."

"Yes you are. A pathetic old man, desperately trying to rid himself of a sudden, unwanted burden. When there is no burden."

She has risen to her feet, seizing her bag. She looks up at the clock tower.

"There's a vaporetto leaving at six forty-five. Let's take a last stroll."

Max puts on his glasses to read the bill. Then he returns them to his trouser pocket, pulls his wallet out, and leaves two thousand-lira notes on the table.

"Jorge never needed you," says Mecha. "He had me."

"And your money. An easy life."

"You sound almost disapproving, my dear. Although if memory serves, you were always chasing money. And now that you appear to have it, you aren't hurrying to give it up."

They walk over to the parapet wall. Lemon groves and vineyards slope down toward the cliff tops, tinged red with the light streaking the Bay of Naples. The disk of the sun begins sinking into the sea, throwing into relief the distant island of Ischia.

"And yet you missed your chance twice. . . . How could you have behaved so stupidly toward me? So clumsy, and so blind?"

"I was too busy, I suppose. Trying to survive."

"You were impatient. Incapable of waiting."

"You were heading in a different direction." Max chooses his words carefully. "To places where I felt uncomfortable."

"You could have changed that. You were a coward . . . although in the end you succeeded, unintentionally."

She shivers for a second as if she were cold. Max offers her his sweater, but she shakes her head. With her silk scarf she covers her short gray hair, fastening it under her chin. Then she stands beside him leaning over the parapet wall.

"Did you ever love me, Max?"

Taken aback, Max doesn't reply. He gazes obstinately at the red-tinged water trying silently to separate the word *regret* from the word *melancholy*.

"Oh, what a fool I am." She touches his hand in a fleeting caress. "Of course you did. You did love me."

Desolation is another word for it, he decides. A kind of damp, hidden lament for all that was and is no more. For the warmth and the body that are unreachable now.

"You don't know what you've missed all these years," Mecha goes on. "Seeing your son grow up. Seeing the world through his eyes, as he began to open them."

"Assuming it's true, why me?"

"You mean, why did I choose you?"

She doesn't reply straightaway. The church bell has chimed, its sound echoing over the island's hills. Mecha glances up at the clock once more, turns away from the parapet wall, and begins walking toward the terminus of the funicular railway that runs from the Piazzetta down to the marina.

"It happened," she says when he sits down beside her on a bench inside the funicular, where they are the only passengers. "That's all. Then I had to decide, and I decided."

"To keep him."

"To keep him, yes. All to myself."

"And the father . . . ?"

"Oh, yes. The father. As you say, he was convenient. Useful, at first. Ernesto was a good man. Good for the boy . . . But then that need diminished."

With a slight judder, the funicular descends between banks of vegetation and views of the sunset over the bay. The remainder of the short journey passes in silence, broken in the end by Max.

"I spoke to your son this morning."

"How funny." She seems genuinely surprised. "We had lunch together and he didn't mention it."

"He asked me to stay away from him."

"What did you expect? He's an intelligent lad. His instinct doesn't only work for chess. He senses something ambiguous about you. Why you're here, and all the rest. Actually, I think he senses it through me. He couldn't care less about you. It's my attitude toward you that puts him on guard."

By the time they reach the harbor, the sun has gone down and the marina has taken on grayish tones and shadows. They walk along the quayside, watching the fishing boats moored nearby.

"Jorge can feel there's a special bond between us," says Mecha.

"Special?"

"Old. Misguided."

After saying this, she falls silent for a moment. Max walks beside her, not daring to say a word.

"You asked me a question just now," she says at last. "Why do you think I wanted to keep that child?"

Now Max is the one who remains silent. He looks to one side, then the other, finally smiling nervously, admitting defeat. And yet she continues to stare at him intently, awaiting his reply.

"The truth is, you and me . . ." he ventures.

Another silence. Mecha watches him as the light fades and everything around them seems to die slowly.

"Ever since that first tango we danced in the ship's ballroom," Max says at last, "ours was a strange relationship."

Mecha is still staring at him, with a look of such utter contempt now that he almost has to force himself not to look away.

"Is that all? Strange, you say? . . . For God's sake, Max. I've been in love with you ever since we danced that tango . . . almost my whole life."

—〰—

Night was also drawing in twenty-nine years before, over the bay in Nice, while Max Costa and Mecha Inzunza walked along the Promenade des Anglais. The sky was overcast, and the last rays of light were fading fast among the dark clouds, fusing the line between the sky and the rough sea crashing onto the pebbly beach. The odd heavy raindrop, presaging a downpour, splashed on the ground, giving a forlorn look to the motionless palm fronds.

"I'm leaving Nice," said Max.

"When?"

"In three or four days. As soon as I've finished some business here."

"Will you be coming back?"

"I don't know."

She said nothing more about it. She was walking steadily in her high heels, despite the damp ground, hands in the pockets of a gray raincoat with the belt pulled tight, accentuating her slender waist. Her hair was swept up under a black beret.

"Will you stay in Antibes?" asked Max.

"Yes. Probably all winter. At least for as long as the situation in Spain lasts, and while I'm awaiting news of Armando."

"Have you heard anything?"

"No."

Max hooked his umbrella over one arm, then removed his hat and shook the raindrops off before putting it on again.

"At least he's still alive."

"He was a few weeks ago. Now, I don't know."

The Palais de la Méditerranée had just switched on its lights. As though responding to a general signal, the street lamps suddenly came on along the wide sweep of the Promenade, casting alternate light and shadows on the façades of the hotels and restaurants. Opposite the Hôtel Ruhl, beneath the covered walkway to La

Jetée-Promenade where a uniformed doorman was standing guard, three young men in evening dress were hanging around, trying their luck with the cars that pulled up and the women who stepped out of them on their way inside, where music was playing. Clearly none possessed the hundred francs that was the price of admission. All three men looked at Mecha, quietly covetous, and one of them went over to Max to cadge a cigarette. He smelled of cheap cologne. Extremely young and rather handsome, he looked Italian and was dressed like the others in a double-breasted jacket, tapered at the waist, a starched collar, and a bow tie. The suit looked hired and the shoes were somewhat scuffed, but the young man behaved with a self-assurance and almost insolent swagger that made Max smile. Max came to a halt, unbuttoned his Burberry, took out his tortoiseshell cigarette case, and offered it to the young man, open.

"Take a couple more for your friends," Max suggested.

The youth looked at him with vague unease. Then he plucked out three cigarettes, thanked him, glanced once more at Mecha, and went to join the others. Max went on walking. Out of the corner of his eye, he saw her looking at him, amused.

"Old memories," she said.

"Indeed."

As they moved away, the tune playing on the Jetée-Promenade came to an end, and the orchestra struck up another melody.

"I don't believe it." Mecha laughed, linking arms with Max. "You staged the whole thing for me . . . gigolos included."

Max laughed as well, just as astonished: the strains of the Old School Tango wafted over from the casino dance hall, competing with the sound of the surf on the pebbles.

"Would you like to go in and dance to it?" he jested.

"Don't even think about it."

They strolled along. Listening.

"It's beautiful," she said, when they could no longer hear the tango. "Far better than Ravel's piece."

They walked for a while in silence. Then Mecha gave Max's arm a squeeze.

"Without your contribution, that tango wouldn't exist."

"On the contrary," he said. "I'm sure your husband would never have succeeded in composing it without you. It's your tango, not his."

"What nonsense."

"I danced with you, remember. In that corner dive in Buenos Aires . . . I haven't forgotten how he looked at you. How we all did."

It was completely dark outside by the time they crossed the bridge over the Paillon. On their left, beyond the gardens, Masséna Square was lit up by street lamps. A tram passed close by, between the dense, shadowy trees, scarcely visible but for the sparks from the trolley pole.

"Tell me something, Max." She was fingering her neck beneath her raincoat. "Had you always planned to take the necklace, or were you improvising as you went along?"

"I was improvising," he lied.

"You're lying."

He looked straight at her with complete candor.

"No I'm not."

There was almost no traffic: the odd horse-drawn carriage went by, hood up, lantern burning, rolling over wet leaves, and occasionally they were dazzled by the moist, hazy lights of a car. They crossed the road carelessly, leaving the Promenade behind them, and turned down a side street near Cours Saleya.

"What was that dive called again?" asked Mecha. "The tango place."

"La Ferroviaria. Next to Barracas station."

"Do you think it's still there?"

"I don't know. I never went back."

Heavy raindrops were once more falling onto Max's hat. Still not enough to warrant opening his umbrella. The couple quickened their pace.

"I'd like to listen to music again in a place like that, with you. . . . Are there places like that in Nice?"

"You mean, seedy?"

"No, silly, I mean special. Perhaps a little sleazy."

"Like that boardinghouse in Antibes?"

"For example."

"With or without a mirror?"

She responded by forcing him to stop in his tracks and lower his head. Then she kissed him on the lips. A fleeting yet forceful kiss, thick with remembrances and immediate purpose. Max was seized by an urgent desire.

"Of course," he said calmly. "There are places like that everywhere."

"Name one."

"Here, the only one I know is Lions at the Kill. A nightclub in the old part of town."

"I love the name." Mecha made as if to rub her hands together, knowingly. "Let's go there right now."

Max took her arm, forcing her to walk on.

"I thought we were going to dinner. I reserved a table at Bouttau, next to the cathedral."

Mecha pressed her face into his shoulder, almost bringing him to a halt.

"I can't stand that restaurant," she said. "The chef always comes out to greet the diners."

"What's so bad about that?"

"A lot of things. Everything started to go wrong the day dressmakers, hairdressers, and cooks began fraternizing with their customers."

"And tango dancers," Max added, chuckling.

"I have a better idea," she proposed. "Let's have a snack at La Cambuse: oysters and a bottle of Chablis. And afterward you can take me to that nightclub."

"As you like. But before we go in, put your necklace and bracelet away in your bag. We don't want to tempt fate."

They were near to a street lamp in Cours Saleya when she looked up at him. Her eyes glinting like copper or tin.

"Will the boys from the old days be there, too?"

"I'm afraid not." Max smiled, wistfully. "Only the ones from today."

—⬩—

Lions at the Kill wasn't a bad name, but it promised more than it offered. There were bottles of cheap champagne in ice buckets; dark, dusty corners; a singer of indeterminate gender with a gravelly voice who dressed in black and imitated Edith Piaf; and, after ten o'clock, some striptease acts. The ambience was fake and self-conscious, somewhere between late Apache and tired Surrealist. The tables were taken up by a few American and German tourists mistakenly expecting to find some excitement, a few sailors from nearby Villefranche, and three or four individuals, with pointed sideburns and dark, pin-striped suits, who looked like movie gangsters, and whom Max suspected were employed by the owner to give the place atmosphere. Halfway through the second striptease act (a plump Egyptian woman with large, pale, quivering breasts), Mecha yawned and said she'd had enough, so Max asked for the bill, paid two hundred francs for the bottle they had scarcely touched, then once more they found themselves outside.

"Is that all there is?" Mecha seemed disappointed.

"Here in Nice, yes. Almost."

"Take me to the almost, then."

Max responded by opening his umbrella, while signaling the end of the street. The rain was dripping from the eaves. They were in Rue Saint-Joseph, near the crossroads and the hill up to the castle. Two women were standing close to the only streetlight, sheltering beneath the small awning of a closed florist shop. One of the women stepped back into a doorway when she saw them, but the other stood her ground as they approached. She was skinny and tall. Dressed in a short jacket with a Persian lamb collar and a close-fitting, dark, midlength skirt. The skirt hugged the clean curve of her hips, accentuating her slender legs, which seemed even longer in her high, wedge shoes.

"She's pretty," said Mecha.

Max studied the woman's face. In the light of the street lamp she looked young behind the dark stain of her painted lips. She wore thick eye shadow beneath eyebrows that were a penciled line, barely visible below the narrow brim of her dripping hat.

"Perhaps she is," Max conceded.

"She has a nice body, supple. Almost elegant."

They had drawn level with the woman who was looking at them: a professional, fleeting glance aimed at Max, which turned to blank indifference the moment she realized he and his companion were arm in arm. An inquisitive look followed, sizing up Mecha by her clothes and appearance. The raincoat and beret didn't give much away, but Max noticed her instantly taking in Mecha's shoes and handbag, as though reproaching her for not caring about ruining them in that rain.

"Ask her how much she charges," whispered Mecha.

She had leaned toward Max as she spoke, almost fervently, her eyes still fixed on the woman. He looked at Mecha uneasily.

"It's none of our business."

"Ask her."

The woman had overheard their exchange (which was in Spanish), or was guessing. Her eyes moved from him to her, seeming to understand. A smile, somewhere between disdainful and expectant, played on her dark red lips. Mecha's bag and shoes had stopped being important. Marking limits or distances.

"How much?" Mecha asked her, in French.

With professional discretion, the woman replied that it depended on them. On the time, and the gentleman's preferences. Or those of the lady. She had stepped to one side to shelter from the rain, moving out of the light after looking over the couple's shoulder, her hand resting on her hip.

"Doing it with him while I watch," Mecha said, with icy calm.

"Don't even think about it," Max protested.

"Be quiet."

The woman mentioned a figure. Max looked again at her long, slender legs, beneath the clinging skirt. He felt aroused, in spite of himself. Not so much by the prostitute, as by Mecha's attitude. For a brief moment he imagined a room somewhere nearby rented by the hour, a bed with soiled sheets, him penetrating that skinny, supple body while Mecha, naked, watched them attentively. Turning to her afterward, still moist from the other woman, to penetrate her in turn. To find himself once more inside that pure, natural, perfect body he could feel palpitating hungrily on his arm.

"Bring her with us," Mecha demanded suddenly.

"No," said Max.

—⁓—

In the Negresco, as the rain came drumming on the windowpanes, they came together in a frantic, passionate embrace that was like a combat: hungry, silent—except when they moaned, hit each other, or cried out, a silence made of avid, taut flesh and warm saliva, alternating with sudden, lewd curses, which Mecha whispered in Max's ear with obscene zeal. The memory of the tall, thin woman accompanied them throughout, as intensely as if she had been there watching or being watched, obeying their bodies saturated with perspiration and desire, locked in a fierce embrace.

"You would whip her while thrusting in and out of her," Mecha whispered breathlessly, licking the sweat from Max's neck. "Bite her back, tear her flesh. Yes. Making her scream."

In a moment of extreme violence, she punched Max's face until his nose bled, and when he tried to stanch the blood that was spotting the sheets, she continued to kiss him furiously, hurting him even more, her nose and mouth caked in his blood, like a frenzied wolf devouring its prey, pulling it apart with its teeth; meanwhile, clasping the iron bars of the bedstead, Max tried to find a way of controlling himself on the verge of the abyss, forced to grit his teeth to repress a howl of animal anguish, as old as time itself, arising from deep inside him. Holding back as best he could the overwhelming desire, past the point of no return, the longing to plunge into the empty, soulless, desolate void of that woman dragging him to the verge of madness and oblivion.

"I feel like a drink," she said later, putting out a cigarette.

Max thought that was a good idea. They slipped their clothes on over skin reeking of flesh and sex, and descended the wide staircase to the circular foyer and the wood panel bar, where Adolfo, the Spanish waiter, was closing up. The frown on his face relaxed when he saw who was approaching. For Adolfo had long considered Max a member of that select brotherhood, never officially defined, not even by their financial status, whom, out of habit or instinct, barmen, taxi drivers, headwaiters, florists, shoeshine boys, hotel receptionists, and other personnel essential to the smooth functioning of high society, could recognize at a glance. And there was a reason for all that goodwill. Max was aware that with the kind of life he led, such accomplices in the servant world could be invaluable, and he contrived at every opportunity to strengthen those ties, with a skillful mixture (which anyway came naturally to him) of easy amiability, thoughtfulness, and generous tips.

"Three West-Indians, Adolfo. Two for us and one for yourself."

Although the barman was willing to prepare one of the tables (he had turned the bronze appliqué wall lights back on for them) they settled for two bar stools beneath the wooden balustrade of the floor above, sipping their drinks in silence, very close, gazing into each other's eyes.

"You smell of me," she said. "Of us."

It was true. Pungent, very physical. Max smiled, his head tilted, a broad strip of white flashing across his tanned skin, where a stubble was beginning to show. Despite having powdered her face before coming down, Mecha had red marks on her chin, neck, and mouth from chafing against it.

"You're a handsome devil."

She touched his nose, which was still bleeding slightly, and then left a red fingerprint on one of the small embroidered napkins on the bar.

"And you are a dream," he said.

He took a sip of his drink: chilled, perfect. Adolfo had an extraordinary talent for making cocktails.

"I dreamt about you when I was a little boy," he added, wistfully.

It sounded sincere, and it was. Mecha looked at him intently, lips parted, breathing with quiet agitation. Max had placed his hand on her waist, and could feel the perfect curve of her hip beneath the mauve fabric.

"Nothing in life comes free," she jested, folding the napkin away.

"Well, I hope I've already paid, otherwise the bill will be ruinous."

She placed her fingers on his lips, silencing him.

"*Goûtons un peu ce simulacre de bonheur,*" she said.

They were quiet again. Max was relishing the cocktail and her closeness, his physical awareness of her skin and flesh. The silence associated with their recent pleasure. This wasn't a simulacrum of happiness, he told himself. He felt truly happy, lucky to be alive, to have encountered no further obstacle on the path that had led him there. That long, perilous, interminable path. The thought of leaving her felt like an unbearable wrench. Verging on fury. He wished he could be far away from the two Italians and Fito Mostaza. He wished they were all dead.

"I'm hungry," said Mecha.

She was looking at Adolfo in the way of someone used to having everybody, servants included, at her beck and call. Accepting her abrupt tone as part of his job, the barman apologized, adding that everything was closed at that time of night. But, he said, after hesitating for a moment, if the lady and gentleman would come with him, he could fix up a little something for them. Then, with a knowing look, he switched off the lights and beckoned them to follow him through the back door, down a poorly lit staircase into the basement. They went after him hand in hand, enjoying the unexpected adventure, and made their way down a long corridor toward the deserted kitchen. On a table next to a stack of shiny pots and pans was a cured Spanish ham (all the way from the Alpujarras, Adolfo declared proudly as he removed the cloth that was draped over it).

"Are you any good with a knife, Mr. Max?"

"First rate. I was born in Argentina, you know."

"Then start slicing, if you don't mind. I'm going to fetch you some burgundy."

No sooner had they returned to the room than Max and Mecha tore off their clothes again, coming together with renewed urgency, as if for the first time. They spent the rest of the night in semislumber, embracing whenever they awoke, each responsive to the other's insistent desire. Finally, as the first light of dawn began to filter through the window, they plunged into a deep, exhausted sleep. They lay calmly side by side until Max opened his eyes and, without looking at his watch, went over to the window, where a pale light and the sound of the still-falling rain penetrated through the curtains. A lone dog was scampering across the pebbly beach. Through the windowpane, speckled with raindrops running into tiny trickles, the sea was a misty gray sheet, while along the Promenade the palm fronds drooped mournfully toward the glistening tarmac. Max turned to gaze once more at the beautiful, naked woman asleep facedown amid the rumpled sheets, and he knew that this dull blue light, smeared by the autumn rain, was a sign that he was about to lose her forever.

—∞—

According to information from the hotel receptionist, Spadaro, Mikhail Sokolov occupies the penthouse in the apartment building housing the Soviet delegation. His spacious apartment has a balcony from which—above the centenary pines, beyond the main hotel buildings along the cliff top—he has a view over the entire Bay of Naples. That is where the world champion resides and prepares his chess games together with his team of helpers.

Sitting beneath an ivy-covered bower with a pair of antique Wehrmacht Dienstgläser that Captain Tedesco has lent him, Max is studying the apartment building while pretending to bird-watch. And what he sees is far from encouraging: entry by the conventional route seems impossible. He spent the afternoon convincing himself of this, and told Mecha about it after dinner, sitting in that same spot in the garden.

"Sokolov's entourage occupies the lower floors," Max explained, pointing toward the lit windows. "There is a single staircase and elevator in the lobby from which to access all floors. I've made a few inquiries and they always have a man on guard. No one can get into Sokolov's apartment without being seen."

"There has to be some other way," insisted Mecha. "There's a game this afternoon."

"Too soon, I'm afraid. I still don't know how to do it."

"They play again the day after tomorrow, and it'll be dark when they finish. You'll have time, then. And closed doors were never a problem for you. Haven't you got . . . I don't know. Tools? A picklock or something?"

There were years of professional poise in the way Max shrugged his shoulders.

"The problem isn't the locks. The one downstairs is a modern

Yale, easy to pick. The one to his suite is probably even simpler, the old, conventional type."

He fell silent, gazing up at the gloomy building with a worried look. Like a mountaineer contemplating the difficult part of a rock face.

"The problem is getting up there," he said. "How to get past those damned Bolsheviks without being seen."

"*Bolshevik*." She chuckled. "No one uses that word anymore."

A flash. Mecha was lighting a cigarette. The third since they had been in the garden.

"You have to try, Max. You did it before."

A silence. The faint odor of tobacco wafting through the air.

"In Nice, remember," she said. "At Suzi Ferriol's house."

Funny, he thought. Or ironical. That she should use that as an argument.

"Not only in Nice," he replied calmly. "But I was half the age then that I am now."

He remained silent for a moment, calculating even the unlikeliest probabilities. In the silence of the garden they could hear distant music coming from a bar on Piazza Tasso.

"What if they catch me . . ."

His words hung gloomily in the air. In fact, he was scarcely aware of having said them out loud.

"They would undoubtedly rough you up," she admitted.

"That doesn't bother me so much." He smiled to himself, uneasily. "But I've been thinking about it. What scares me is going to jail."

"How odd, to hear you say that."

She seemed genuinely astonished. He shrugged.

"It always scared me, but now I'm sixty-four."

In the distance, the music was still playing. Fast, modern. Too faint for Max to be able to recognize the tune.

"This isn't like in the movies," he went on. "I'm not Cary Grant, playing the guy in that absurd caper about a hotel thief. There aren't any happy endings in real life."

"You were much more handsome than Cary Grant, silly."

She had taken his hand and was pressing it between hers: thin and slender. And warm. Max was still listening to the music in the distance. Of course, he concluded pulling a face, it wasn't a tango.

"Do you know something? You're the one who reminded me of that woman, that actress. Or she reminded me of you: slim, refined. You still look like her. Or she looks like you."

"He's your son, Max. Be sure of that, at least."

"Perhaps he is," he replied. "But look."

He had lifted her hand, inviting her to touch his face. To feel the effects of time.

"There could be another way in." Her touch feels like a caress. "Maybe you should look again tomorrow, in daylight. And you'll find it."

"If there was another way." He was barely listening to her. "If I was younger, more agile. Too many 'ifs,' I'm afraid."

Mecha withdrew her hand from his face.

"I'll give you everything I have, Max. However much you want."

He turned to look at her, astonished. He could make out the shape of her face in the darkness, silhouetted against the distant lights and the glowing tip of her cigarette.

"You're joking, of course," he said.

The silhouette moved. Two shiny copper-colored eyes glinting at Max. Her gaze fixed on him.

"Yes, I'm joking." Twice the glowing tip burned more brightly. "But I will, I would give you everything."

"Including a cup of coffee at your place in Lausanne?"

"Of course."

"And the pearl necklace?"

Another, lengthy silence.

"Don't be silly."

The glowing tip dropped to the ground, and went out. She was clasping his hand again. The distant music in the square had stopped.

"I'll be damned," he said. "You make me feel like a foolish lover. You make the years fall away."

"That's the idea."

He hesitated slightly. Only slightly, now. His mouth throbbed from keeping back what he was about to confess.

"I don't have a penny, Mecha."

She waited a few seconds.

"I know."

Max had the breath knocked out of him. He was shocked and speechless.

"How do you know?" Something burst inside him, a wave of panic. "What do you know?"

He wanted to snatch his hand away, sit up straight. Run away from there. But she restrained him gently.

"I know you don't live in Amalfi, but here in Sorrento. That you are employed as a chauffeur at a house called Villa Oriana. I know things haven't gone well for you in the last few years."

Thank goodness I'm sitting down, Max thought, his free hand leaning on the bench. Otherwise I'd have keeled over. Like an idiot.

"I made some inquiries the moment you turned up at the hotel," Mecha said at last.

Bewildered, Max tried to make sense of his thoughts and feelings: humiliation, shame. Mortification. All those days keeping up a pointless charade, making a fool of himself. Pirouetting like a clown.

"You've known from the start?"

"More or less."

"And why did you play along?"

"Several reasons. Curiosity, at first. It was fascinating to recognize the old Max: the man of the world, deceitful and amoral."

She paused for a moment. She was still holding his hand in hers.

"Besides, I like being with you," she said at last. "I always have."

Max freed his hand and rose to his feet.

"Do the others know?"

"No. Only me."

He needed some air. To breathe deeply, rid himself of conflicting emotions. Or possibly he needed a drink. Something strong. Which would shake up his guts until they turned inside out.

Mecha remained seated, perfectly calm.

"If Jorge weren't involved, under different circumstances . . . well. It would have been fun. To spend time with you. See what you were after. How far you intended to go."

She fell silent for a moment.

"What was your plan?"

"I'm not sure now. To relive the old days?"

"In what way?"

"In every way, perhaps."

She stood up slowly. Almost laboriously, Max thought.

"The old days died. They went out of fashion, just like our tango. Dead, like your boys from the old days, like you yourself. Like the two of us."

She clung to his arm the way she had twenty-nine years before, that night they had gone to Lions at the Kill, in Nice.

"It's flattering," she added. "To see you come alive again because of me."

She had taken his hand and was raising it gently to her lips. A sweet kiss. Her voice sounded like laughter.

"To pretend to look at you again the way I once did."

—⁓—

The sun already is high in the sky. Max continues to study the apartment block next to the Hotel Vittoria, the binoculars pressed against his eyes. He has just walked around the outside of the building, looking closely at the entrance leading to the main gate, and has now positioned himself among some bougainvilleas and lemon trees, in order to examine the other side. Nearby is a small pond, and a little pavilion with a bench. He approaches the pavilion, and from there inspects the part of the building that was hidden before. He now has a clear view of the whole of the front, including Sokolov's balcony, the red-tiled cornice and the surrounding gutter, above which he spots a lightning rod. Gutters and lightning rods require maintenance, someone to go up and check they are in working order, Max says to himself. With a flash of optimism, he scours every inch of the façade. And what he sees there brings back his old, youthful smile, which seems to erase the ravages of time from his face: a metal ladder set into the wall and ascending from the garden.

Replacing the binoculars in their case, Max passes close to the building, as if taking a stroll. When he reaches the bottom of the ladder, he looks up. The metal has rusted, leaving orange marks on the wall, but the rungs look sturdy enough. The bottom one is near the ground, above a flower bed. The distance up to the roof is forty meters, and the rungs are quite close together. The amount of effort required seems reasonable: ten minutes to climb up in the dark, taking every kind of precaution. It might be a good idea, he thinks, to carry a snap hook and harness to secure himself halfway up, and to take a rest, if he gets too exhausted. Apart from that, he wouldn't need much equipment: a small rucksack, some mountaineering rope, a few tools, a flashlight, and the right clothing. He looks at his watch. The shops in the center of town are already open, along with the hardware store in Porta Marina. He'll need some sneakers as well, and black shoe polish to dye everything with.

Just like in the good old days, he reflects, turning his back on the building and walking away through the garden. He is excited to be doing something again, or by the imminence of action. That old, familiar flutter of doubt, calmed by a drink or a cigarette, when the world was still a hunting ground for the clever and intrepid. When life had an aroma of Turkish cigarettes, cocktails in the lounge bar of a Palace Hotel, a woman's perfume. Of pleasure and danger. And now, remembering that, Max has the impression that each step he takes is lighter, that he has regained his agility. But the best of all isn't that. When he looks in front of him, he discovers that his shadow has come back. The sun piercing the tops of the pine trees is projecting it onto the ground, steady and elongated, as it was before. Joined to his feet, where it had been in the past. Timeless, with no signs of aging, or fatigue. And, having recovered his shadow, the former ballroom dancer laughs out loud the way he hasn't laughed for many years.

II

The Ways of a Wolf

THE RAIN WAS still falling on Nice. Amid the murky grayness enveloping the old city, clothes hung from the balconies like the tatters of tragic lives. His raincoat buttoned up to the neck and with opened umbrella, Max Costa crossed Place du Jésus, avoiding the rain-pocked puddles, heading for the cathedral steps. Mauro Barbaresco was there, leaning against the locked gates, hands in the pockets of his oilskin sleek with rain, watching Max curiously from beneath the soggy brim of his hat.

"It's tonight," said Max.

Without uttering a word, Barbaresco began to walk toward Rue Droite. Max followed him. There was a bar on the corner, and two doors down, a dark tunnel-like entrance. They crossed an interior patio and climbed two flights of wooden stairs that creaked beneath their feet. On the second-floor landing, Barbaresco opened a door and ushered Max through. Max left his umbrella propped against the wall, removed his hat, and shook off the water. The house, dark and uninviting, stank of boiled vegetables and damp, soiled clothing. A corridor led to the kitchen door, then another door, which was ajar, revealing a bedroom with an unmade bed, and finally a sitting room with two old armchairs, a sideboard, and a dining table with the remains of breakfast on it. Seated at the table, vest undone, shirtsleeves rolled up above his elbows, Domenico Tignanello was reading the funnies in *Le Gringoire*.

"He says he's doing it tonight," said Barbaresco.

Tignanello's gloomy expression appeared to brighten a little. He gave a nod of approval, put the newspaper down on the table, and with a gesture offered Max the coffeepot standing next to a couple of dirty cups, an oil cruet, and the remains of some toast on a plate. Max declined the offer as he undid his raincoat. A dim light was seeping through the open window, casting the corners of the room in shadow. Barbaresco, removing his oilskin, went over to the window, framed in the murky square of light.

"What news of your Spanish friend?" he asked, after he had taken a good look outside.

"He isn't my friend, and I haven't seen him again," Max replied calmly.

"Not since your meeting at the harbor?"

"That's right."

Barbaresco had draped his oilskin over the back of a chair, oblivious to the drops of water pooling on the floor.

"We've made some inquiries," he said. "Everything he told you is true: the nationalist radio station in Monte Carlo, his attempts to redirect the *Luciano Canfora* to a Republican port . . . The only thing we haven't been able to establish, for the moment, is his identity. Our organization has no record of any Rafael Mostaza."

Max gave him the blank stare of an impassive croupier.

"I suppose you could follow him. I don't know . . . take his photograph, or something."

"Maybe we will." Barbaresco smirked. "But to do that we'd need to know when your next meeting with him is."

"There's nothing planned. He turns up and asks me to meet him whenever he pleases. Last time he left a note at the reception desk of the Negresco."

Barbaresco stared at him in astonishment.

"He doesn't know about you breaking into Susana Ferriol's house tonight?"

"He knows, but he said nothing."

"Then how does he plan to get the documents?"

"I haven't the faintest idea."

Barbaresco exchanged a bewildered glance with his colleague before looking back at Max.

"Curious, don't you think? That he doesn't mind you telling us everything? That he even encourages it. And that he hasn't shown up today."

"Perhaps," Max conceded coolly. "But it isn't my job to find out these things. You're the spies."

He took out his cigarette case, contemplating the open box, as though which cigarette he chose was what mattered just then. Finally he placed one in his mouth and put the case away, without offering it to the two men.

"I suppose you know your job," he said at last, flicking his lighter.

Barbaresco walked to the window and looked outside. He appeared anxious, as if he had fresh cause for concern.

"It certainly isn't normal. Showing one's hand like that."

"Maybe he's trying to protect him," Tignanello suggested.

"Protect me? . . . From whom?"

Domenico Tignanello quietly contemplated the hair on his arms. Silent once more, as though the effort of opening his mouth had exhausted him.

"From us." Barbaresco replied, for him. "From his people. From yourself."

"Well, when you find out, let me know." Max calmly exhaled a puff of smoke. "I have other things to think about."

Barbaresco sat down in one of the armchairs. Pensive.

"We're not being set up, are we?" he said at last.

"By Mostaza or by me?"

"By you, of course."

"How would I do that? I have no choice in all this. But if I were in your shoes, I'd try to locate this fellow. Clear things up with him."

Barbaresco exchanged further looks with his colleague, before glancing resentfully at Max's suit, visible beneath his open raincoat.

"Clear things up . . . you make it sound refined."

Those two, Max thought, always looked as if they'd emerged from a sleepless night, with their crumpled clothes, bloodshot eyes ringed with dark shadows, and their stubbly faces. They probably had.

"Which brings us to the important bit," Barbaresco added. "How do you propose to enter the house?"

Max looked down at Barbaresco's damp shoes, the soles split at the toes. With all that rain, his socks must be drenched.

"That's my concern," he replied. "What I need to know is where we're going to meet so that I can hand over the letters, assuming I get them. Assuming everything goes well."

"This is a good place. We'll be here all night, waiting. And there's a telephone in the bar downstairs. One of us can stay there until it closes, in case there's a change of plan. . . . Will you be able to get into the house without any problem?"

"I imagine so. There's a dinner party at Cimiez, near the old Hôtel Régina. Susana Ferriol is one of the guests. That'll give me plenty of time."

"Do you have everything you need?"

"Yes. The keys Fossataro brought are perfect."

Tignanello slowly raised his eyes, fixing them on Max.

"I'd like to see how you do it," he said unexpectedly. "How you open that safe."

Max arched his eyebrows, surprised. A flash of interest seemed to light up the swarthy southerner's taciturn face, making him look almost friendly.

"So would I," Barbaresco said. "Fossataro told us you were good at it. Cool, calm, and collected, he said. With safes and with women."

Those two made him think of something, Max told himself. He associated them with an image he couldn't quite visualize. Which mirrored their appearance and manner. But he couldn't pin it down.

"You'd be bored watching," he said. "In both cases, it's slow, routine work. A question of patience."

Barbaresco grinned. He seemed to like Max's reply.

"We wish you the best of luck, Costa."

Max gazed at them at length. He had finally found the image that had eluded him: two soaking wet dogs in the rain.

"Yes," he said, reaching into his pocket for his cigarette case again, and offering it them, open. "I expect you do."

—∙∙∙—

She shows up in midafternoon, while Max is preparing the equipment for his nocturnal foray. Hearing the knock he looks through the peephole, slips on his jacket, and opens the door. Mecha Inzunza is standing there, a smile on her face, hands in the pockets of her knitted cardigan. A gesture which, as though time had stood still (although it could be Max confusing the past and the present), reminds him of that distant morning, almost forty years ago, at the Caboto boardinghouse in Buenos Aires. When she went to see him on the pretext of picking up the glove she herself had tucked into his top pocket, like some strange white flower, before he danced a tango at La Ferroviaria. Even her manner as she enters the room and walks around (calm, curious, slowly glancing about) resembles that other way she once had: tilting her head in order to survey Max's simple, orderly world; pausing in front of the open window with its view over Sorrento; or suddenly losing her smile as she glimpses the objects which he, with the meticulousness of a soldier preparing for combat (and the ambivalent pleasure of reliving, through that old campaign ritual, the thrill of uncertainty in the face of his imminent mission), has laid out on the bed: a small rucksack, a flashlight, a thirty-meter length of nylon mountaineering rope, already knotted, a tool bag, some dark clothes, and a pair of sneakers, which he has dyed with shoe polish that afternoon.

"Good Lord," she exclaims. "You're really going to do it."

She says this pensively, with admiration, as though until that moment she hadn't quite believed in Max's promises.

"Of course," he says simply.

There is nothing artificial or forced about his tone. Nor is he seeking that day to cover himself in glory. Ever since he made his decision, and found a way of implementing it, or thought he had, he has found an inner calm. A professional fatalism. His old ways, the gestures that before were a sign of youthful vigor, have in the last few hours restored an astonishing sense of self-assurance. A past, renewed feeling of pleasurable peace, where the risks of the exploit, the dangers of a blunder or a stroke of misfortune, dissolve in the face of the intensity of what is to come. Even Mecha Inzunza, Jorge Keller, or Mikhail Sokolov's chess book aren't in the forefront of his mind. What matters is the challenge Max Costa (or whoever he was in the past) has thrown down to the aging man with gray hair who gazes back at him occasionally from the mirror.

She is still watching him intently. With a different kind of expression, Max thinks he notices. Or perhaps one he had considered impossible.

"The game starts at six," she says at last. "If all goes well, you'll have two hours of darkness. More, with any luck."

"Or less?"

"Possibly."

"Does your son know I'm doing this?"

"No."

"What about Karapetian?"

"He doesn't know, either."

"How are things with Irina?"

"They've prepared an opening gambit with her, which Jorge won't use, not all of it anyway. The Russians will think he has changed his game plan at the last moment."

"Won't that make them suspicious?"

"No."

She runs her fingers over the mountaineering rope, as though it suggested unusual situations she hadn't thought of before. All of a sudden she seems anxious.

"Listen, Max. It's true what you said just now. The game could finish sooner than we envisage—if there's an unexpected stalemate, or one of them resigns. In which case, you run the risk of still being there when Sokolov and his people return."

"I understand."

Mecha seems to hesitate further.

"If things go wrong, forget about the book," she says at last. "Just get out of there as quickly as you can."

He looks at her gratefully. He likes hearing her say that. This time, the old fraud in him can't resist adjusting his lips into an appropriate, stoical smile.

"I trust it will be a long drawn-out game," he says. "Complete with postmortem analysis, as you call it."

She looks at the tool bag. It contains half a dozen implements, including a diamond glass cutter.

"Why are you doing this, Max?"

"He's my son," he replies without thinking. "You said so yourself."

"You're lying. You couldn't care less if he's your son or not."

"Perhaps I'm indebted to you."

"You? Indebted?"

"I may have loved you back then."

"In Nice?"

"Always."

"You have a strange way of showing it, my friend . . . then as well as now."

Mecha has sat down on the bed, next to Max's equipment. All of a sudden, he feels the urge to explain once more what she already knows full well. To let some of his old bitterness float up to the surface.

"You never wondered how those without money see the world, did you? What life looks like when they open their eyes in the morning."

She gazes at him in surprise. There is no trace of harshness in Max's tone, more a certain coldness. Detachment.

"You were never tempted," he goes on, "to wage a private war against those who sleep peacefully without worrying about what they will eat the next day. Against those fair-weather friends who come to you when they need you, flatter you when it suits them, then don't let you hold your head up high."

Max has stepped over to the window and is pointing at the view of Sorrento and the luxury villas dotted over the green slopes of Punta del Capo.

"I was certainly tempted," he goes on. "And there was a time when I thought I could win. That I could stop being buffeted about in this absurd carnival . . . and feel the touch of real leather in luxury cars, drink champagne out of crystal glasses, embrace beautiful women . . . Everything you and your two husbands have enjoyed from the beginning, due to simple, stupid chance."

He pauses for a moment, turning to look at her. From there, in that light, sitting on the bed, she looks almost beautiful again.

"That's why it never mattered in the slightest whether I loved you or not."

"I was willing to give you all that."

"Yes, you could allow yourself that luxury, as well. But I had other, more pressing things to attend to. Love wasn't at the top of my list."

"What about now?"

He walks over to her with an air of resignation.

"I told you two days ago. I failed. I'm sixty-four now, I'm tired, and I'm scared."

"I understand . . . yes, of course. You're doing this for yourself. For the same reasons that brought you to this hotel. Not even because of me."

Max has sat down beside her, on the edge of the bed.

"It is because of you," he says. "Although in a roundabout way. Because of what you were and what we became. What I was."

She looks at him almost tenderly.

"How did you live during those years?"

"Those years of failure? . . . By withdrawing gradually to where I am now. Like a defeated army that keeps fighting even as it slowly is routed."

For a moment, out of simple habit, Max feels the urge to accompany his words with a heroic half-smile, but he stops himself. It's not necessary. Besides, everything he has said is true. And he knows she knows that.

"The postwar years were good to me," he continues. "Everything then was about business, reconstruction, fresh opportunities. But it was an illusion. Other people arrived on the scene. A different kind of scoundrel. Not better, but more uncouth. Rudeness even became profitable, depending on where you were. I found it hard to adapt and I made a few mistakes. I trusted the wrong people."

"Did you go to jail?"

"Yes, but that wasn't the problem. My world was disappearing.

Or had already disappeared, when I had scarcely touched it with my fingertips. And I didn't realize."

He talks about this for a while longer, sitting very close to Mecha who is listening attentively. Ten or fifteen years summed up in a few words: the brief, unbiased chronicle of a downfall. The communist regimes put an end to his old stomping grounds in Central Europe and the Balkans, he explains, and so he tried his luck again in Spain and South America, without success. He had another chance in Istanbul, where he entered into a partnership with a man who owned bars, cafés, and cabarets, but that also ended badly. Then he spent some time in Rome, as a sort of elegant hustler, an older escort for American tourists and two-bit foreign screen actresses, accompanying them to Strega and Doney on Via Veneto, the restaurant Da Fortunato next to the Pantheon, Rugantino's in Trastevere, or shopping on Via Condotti, on commission.

"My last relatively lucky stroke was a few years back, in Portofino," he concludes. "Or that's what I thought it was. I got my hands on three and a half million lira."

"From a woman?"

"It doesn't matter where. I had it. Two days later, I checked into a cheap hotel in Monte Carlo. I had a hunch. That same evening I went to the casino and filled my pockets with chips. I started off winning, and decided I was on a roll. I lost twelve bets in a row and left the table quaking."

Mecha is staring at him. Astonished.

"You lost everything there, just like that?"

Max's old-man-of-the-world smile comes to his aid, knowing and accepting.

"I still had two chips of fifteen thousand francs each, so I went to a roulette table in another room to try to win some of it back. The ball was already rolling, and there I was, clutching my chips, unable to decide. Finally, I did, and I lost it all. . . . Six months after that I was in Sorrento working as a chauffeur."

His smile has gradually faded. Now his lips are set in an expression of infinite desolation.

"I told you I was tired. But I didn't say how tired."

"You said you were scared as well."

"Less so today. I think."

"Did you know that your age corresponds exactly to the number of squares on a chessboard?"

"I hadn't realized."

"Well it's true. That could be a good sign, don't you think?"

"Or a bad one. Like the story of my last roulette game."

Mecha remains silent for a moment. Then she cocks her head, staring down at her hands.

"Once, fifteen years ago, in Buenos Aires, I saw a man who looked just like you. He had the same walk, the same gestures. I was sitting in the Alvear bar with some friends, and I saw him come out of an elevator. . . . Much to the astonishment of my friends, I grabbed my coat and ran after him. For about fifteen minutes I genuinely thought it was you. I followed him all the way to La Recoleta, and saw him go into La Biela, the automobile club café on the corner. I went in after him. He was sitting by one of the windows, and as I walked past, he looked at me . . . and I saw that it wasn't you. I kept walking, left through the other door, and went back to my hotel."

"Is that all?"

"Yes. Except that I thought my heart was going to explode."

They look at each other closely, with a calm intensity. In the past, in another life, he thinks, leaning on the bar in an exclusive cocktail lounge, this would be the time to order another drink or to kiss. She kisses him. Very softly, moving her face slowly toward his. On the cheek.

"Take care tonight, Max."

The arc of electric street lamps along the Promenade des Anglais was gradually disappearing in the rearview mirror, encircling the hazy darkness of the Bay of Nice. Having passed Le Lazaret and La Réserve, Max stopped the car at the coastal viewpoint and switched off the windshield wipers and headlights. The rain falling through the pines drummed onto the hood of the Peugeot 201 he had hired that afternoon. He checked his watch in the light of a match and sat smoking a cigarette while his eyes grew accustomed to the dark. The road skirting Mont Boron was deserted.

Finally he was ready. He discarded the cigarette and climbed out of the car, the heavy tool bag slung over his shoulder and a package under his arm. His hat was dripping as he did up all the buttons on the dark, oilcloth raincoat he wore over all-black clothes, a sweater and slacks, apart from a pair of canvas, rubber-soled Keds, usually comfortable, which became sodden after only a few paces. He made his way along the road, hunched beneath the rain, and when he reached the first villas, barely visible in the dark, he stopped to get his bearings. There was a single, misty circle of light nearby from an electric street lamp opposite a house with a high wall. Max avoided it by leaving the road and following a winding path below, feeling his way through the agaves and bushes for fear he might lose his footing and plunge into the water, which the tide was casting onto the rocks below. Twice he pricked his fingers on some briars, and when he sucked the wounds, he tasted blood. The rain was hindering him, but by the time he left the path to climb back up to the road, it had abated. The light was behind him now, faintly illuminating the corner of a stony wall. And thirty feet away, Susana Ferriol's house loomed, ominously.

He squatted at the foot of the brick wall, beneath the dark shadows of some palm fronds. Inside the package was a blanket, and, hugging it and the bag to him, he scaled the slippery tree trunk. The distance between the trunk and the wall was less than three feet, but before making the leap, he folded the blanket in two and threw it on the top of the wall, which was lined with shards of glass. He felt the now-harmless pieces of glass underneath the blanket as he landed, letting himself drop to the other side, rolling to minimize the force of the impact and to protect his legs. He stood up soaking wet and brushed off some of the water and mud. A distant speck of light glowed amid the trees and shrubs in the garden, illuminating the main gates, the porter's lodge, and the circular driveway leading up to the front door. Steering clear of the lighted area, Max made his way around to the back of the house. He stepped cautiously, not wanting to make too much noise splashing in puddles or walking into flower beds and flowerpots. With the rain and the mud, he thought, he was going to leave tracks all over the place, inside and outside the house, including those of the Peugeot 201 at the nearby viewpoint. He was still brooding about that, as he removed his raincoat and hat in the shelter of a small porch, beneath the window he was planning to force open. It didn't matter how late Susana Ferriol returned from her dinner party in Cimiez, she was bound to notice the intrusion. Even so, with any luck, by the time the police arrived and saw his trail, he would be far away from there.

—∞—

Night has just fallen over Sorrento. The moon isn't out yet, and this facilitates Max's plan. When he comes down from his room at the Vittoria with a large travel bag, wearing an evening jacket over his dark clothing, the concierge, busy sorting correspondence and putting it into the various pigeonholes, scarcely notices him. The foyer and steps leading to the garden are deserted, for everyone is attending the Keller-Sokolov game in the main hall. Once outside, Max passes a van belonging to the Italian state television, and casually walks down the path through the garden toward the main gate on Piazza Tasso. Halfway along, when he can see the traffic lights and street lamps in the square, he veers off to one side, and heads for the pavilion where a few days earlier he had been spying on the apartments occupied by the Russian delegation. The building is in darkness, save for the lamp above the main entrance and a single lit window on the second floor.

Max is aware of his heartbeat. It feels too fast. Racing as if he had swallowed ten cups of coffee. In fact, what he took half an hour earlier—convinced that in the next few hours he would need something to boost his energy and help clear his head—was a couple of Maxiton tablets, purchased without a prescription but with a suitably respectable smile at a pharmacy on Corso Italia. Even so, as he takes deep breaths and stays still, trying to calm down, the enveloping night, the challenge he has set himself, inescapable age tightening his chest and hardening his arteries, he is seized by an almost unbearable anguish. An anxiety bordering on panic. Now, amid the lonely shadows of the garden, each stage of his plan seems like an act of folly. He pauses for a moment, overwhelmed, until the riot of heartbeats appears to calm a little. He must decide, he thinks at last, whether to turn back or press ahead. Because he hasn't a lot of time. With a sigh of resignation, he unzips the bag and takes out the rucksack; he opens it, slipping off his outdoor shoes and replacing them with the sneakers colored with black polish. He also takes off his jacket, and together with the shoes bundles it in the bag, which he hides among some bushes. Now he is dressed entirely in black, and he ties a dark silk scarf around his head to cover the lightness of his gray hair. He then fastens a loop of rope around his waist with a snap hook and harness in case he feels weak during the ascent. How ludicrous I must look in this getup, he thinks to himself, frowning ironically. Playing the cat burglar at my age. Good God. If Dr. Hugentobler could see me now, his esteemed chauffeur, scaling walls. Then, resigning himself to the inevitable, Max slings the rucksack over his shoulders, looks right, then left, steps out from behind the pavilion, and heads for the building, keeping to the darkest shadows cast by the lemon and palm trees. All at once, the beam from the headlights of a car that has just driven through the main gates toward the hotel illuminate him among the bushes. This makes him withdraw to the safety of the shadows. A moment later, when the light has died away, and he has calmed down, he emerges from his hiding place and reaches the Russians' building. There, at the foot of the wall, everything is pitch-black. He gropes for the first rung. When he finds it, he checks the rucksack is secure on his back, hoists himself up, gaining a purchase on the wall with his feet, and extremely slowly, pausing on each rung to conserve his energy, he begins his ascent to the roof.

—m—

In Nice, the Schützling safe (large, painted brown) was exactly as Enrico Fossataro had described it. Concealed inside a built-in mahogany cupboard in one of the study walls, it was resting on the floor surrounded by shelves lined with books, files, and papers. The safe looked daunting: a steel door with no visible keyhole or combination lock. Max examined it for a moment with the beam of light from the flashlight. There was a thick, Oriental rug next to the base, which would muffle the clinking sound of the keys if he had to try them out one by one. He shone the light on the watch on his left wrist and checked the time. This was going to be a slow job, the sort that required a fine touch and a lot of patience. He moved the flashlight again to illuminate the trail of water and mud across the parquet floor and the carpet, marking his path from the window, which he had closed behind him after forcing it open with a screwdriver. Those dirty tracks were a setback, although fortunately the window was in the study, and so everything, including his muddy footprints, was confined to the same space. Providing the door to the library remained closed, there wouldn't be a problem. And so he went over to it, cautiously, and made sure it was locked.

He stood still, listening for a moment, until the sound of blood rushing through his ears subsided and he could hear more clearly.

The rain would disguise some of the sounds he made while working on the safe, but could also mask until it was too late other sounds that might alert him to someone approaching the study. In any event, there was little danger at that hour: the cook and gardener had gone home, the governess was resting upstairs, and the chauffeur must have been at the wheel of the car, waiting for Susana Ferriol in Cimiez. Only the maid would be on the ground floor: according to the information Max had obtained, she usually stayed up listening to the radio in a small room off the kitchen until her mistress returned. He took off his hat and raincoat, placed the bag containing the tools on the rug, and spread his hand on the cold metal of the safe.

The locks on a Schützling were hidden beneath a molding that framed the door like a painting. After he exerted the correct amount of pressure, the molding moved aside, exposing the mechanism: four keyholes placed vertically, the top one requiring a simple key, the three others fitted with an additional combination lock. Max needed to open the bottom three first, and that would take time. He set to work, positioning the flashlight properly, selecting a key from the bunch he had in his tool bag, then proceeding to try it out in each of the three locks, to see which *sang* more: which was more responsive and transmitted the sounds of the inner mechanism more audibly. His sodden trousers and shoes were making him shiver with cold, hampering him, and his hands, scratched by briars on the path, were slow to find the necessary delicacy of touch. After trying every number from 0 to 19 on each combination, he went for the one at the bottom. He began slowly turning the dial, first to the left then to the right, repeating the same procedure on the other two. Once he had located what he thought was probably the right position, he went back to the first combination lock. Everything depended on the utmost precision now, and the cuts on his fingers had not only slowed him down but had smeared the key with some blood. Noticing those barely perceptible vibrations required a sensitive touch, and he cursed himself for not having thought to wear gloves outside. Finally, he came across the right combination. He glanced at his watch: twenty-four minutes for the most difficult one. Enrico Fossataro would have been three times as fast, but things were going better than expected. With a smile of satisfaction, he relaxed his hands momentarily before inserting the key in the second combination lock. Fifteen minutes later, all three combination locks were correctly aligned. Then he turned off the flashlight and paused for a rest. He lay sprawled on his back on the carpet for a few minutes, using the opportunity to listen to the silence in the house. During that time he tried to think of nothing, except the safe in front of him. The patter of rain outside had stopped, and inside nothing moved. He found himself craving a cigarette. Sitting up with a sigh, he rubbed his legs, numb from cold beneath his wet trousers and shoes, and went back to work.

It was all a question of patience now. If these were the right keys, one of the hundred and thirty Fossataro had brought to Nice would fit the lock above the combinations. In order to find it, Max had to discover which set it belonged to and try out all the keys in that set one by one. This could take anywhere from a minute to a whole hour. Max looked again at his watch. If nothing went wrong, he should have enough time. And so he proceeded to try every key.

Almost half an hour later, the 107th key opened the lock with a soft click and Max pulled the heavy steel door toward him with noiseless ease. The beam from the flashlight lit up shelves piled with sturdy cardboard boxes and files. There were a few items of jewelry and some money in the boxes, and documents in the files, which was where he turned his attention first. Barbaresco and Tignanello had shown him letters similar to the ones he was looking for, bearing the official Italian foreign office stamp, so that he would recognize them. He found them in one of the files: three typewritten letters each in a paper folder, numbered and dated. Bringing the light very close, he checked the letterheads, the content, and the signatures, as well as the name *G. Ciano* typed below. These were undoubtedly the letters. Addressed to Tomás Ferriol and dated the twentieth of July, and the first and fourteenth of August 1936, respectively.

He pocketed the letters and replaced the file exactly where it had been. Barbaresco and Tignanello had insisted on this, so that the Ferriols wouldn't notice immediately. In fact, before Max even began cracking the safe, he had noted the original positions of the combinations, in case he decided he needed to leave them as they were (some people were in the habit of checking the combination each time they opened their safe). But now, as he swept the flashlight beam over the study, with the forced window and muddy wet footprints everywhere, he realized it would be impossible to disguise the break-in. It would take him hours to clean up that mess, and he didn't have the proper equipment. Besides, time was running out. Susana Ferriol might be about to take leave of her hosts in Cimiez.

The cardboard boxes didn't contain anything of interest. In one of them he found thirty thousand francs and a thick bundle of notes from the Spanish Republican treasury, which, unlike the currency in the nationalist zone, were quickly decreasing in value. As for jewelry, Max figured that Susana Ferriol must have another safe in her bedroom, for there was very little in the Schützling: a gold locket, a Losada hunter case pocket watch, and a pearl tie pin. There was also a money pouch containing fifty-odd gold sovereigns and an antique brooch in the shape of a dragonfly studded with emeralds, rubies, and sapphires. With a pensive expression, Max flashed the light over the tracks he had left in the study. At this stage of the game, and with a trail like that, he thought, it made little difference. The brooch and the coins were risky items, easy to identify if the police found them on him. But money was money. Untraceable almost the moment it changed hands, money had no identifying marks and no other owner besides the person carrying it. And so, before closing the safe, rubbing his fingerprints off with a handkerchief, and putting away his tools, he seized the thirty thousand francs.

—ɯ—

The sky is sprinkled with stars. The nocturnal view of Sorrento and the bay from the rooftop is spectacular, but Max is in no state to appreciate the scenery. Exhausted from his exertions, hampered by the rucksack on his back, he is lying next to the cornice, trying to catch his breath. Beyond the hotel buildings of the Vittoria with their bright windows lies the dark expanse of the sea, bordered with tiny lights extending along the coastline toward the distant glow of Naples.

Somewhat recovered, the blood pulsing through his heart having calmed a little (that night he is happier than ever he gave up smoking eleven years ago), Max presses on. Slipping the rucksack off his back, he takes out the rope, knotted at fifteen-inch intervals, and looks around for something solid to secure it to. The faint lights nearby coming from the hotel allow him to see where he is going while he explores the edge of the roof, taking care not to trip. Finally, he fastens the rope with a double sheepshank around the concrete base of the lightning rod, and to be extra safe, coils it around the metal chimney flue. Then he slips the rucksack back on, counts six paces back toward the left and, stretching out along it, the rope fastened around one of his wrists, he looks down. The Russian chess player's suite is fifteen or twenty feet directly beneath him. He can see no light inside. Contemplating the dark abyss beneath the balcony, Max remains motionless, trembling with dread as his pulse starts to race afresh. I'm too old for this kind of caper, he thinks. The last time he found himself in a similar situation, he was fifteen years younger. Finally, he takes a deep breath and seizes hold of the rope. Grazing his knees and elbows as he clambers over the cornice and the guttering, he descends knot by knot.

Apart from his misgivings (Max is terrified his grip will weaken or that he will suffer a dizzy spell), the descent is easier than he had expected. Five minutes later, he is standing on the balcony, on solid ground. He feels for the glass door to the unlit room. How lucky if it has been left unlocked, he thinks, donning a pair of fine rubber gloves. But it isn't. And so he resorts to the diamond-tipped glass cutter he has used in the past. Positioning a rubber suction cup to hold in place the piece he is removing, he traces a circle six inches around the handle inside. Then he taps it gently, removes the cut out section, places it carefully on the ground, slides his hand through the hole taking care not to cut himself, and pushes down the handle. The door opens easily, and he steps across the threshold into the dark empty room.

Max acts quickly now, following the old method. He is surprised to discover that his heart is beating calmly and regularly, as though at this stage of the game age no longer mattered, and rediscovering the old ways had given him back an energy and a professional calm that a moment ago he thought impossible. Moving with extreme caution so as not to trip over anything, he draws the curtains and takes a flashlight out of his rucksack. The apartment is spacious, but smells musty, of stale tobacco. Indeed, there is a large ashtray full of cigarette ends on a low table, next to some empty coffee cups and a chessboard with the pieces jumbled. As he walks around, the flashlight illuminates armchairs, rugs, pictures, and a door into the bedroom and bathroom. Also, the surface of a mirror, in which, as he draws closer, Max can make out his own figure dressed in black, furtive and still. Alarmed, almost, by the sudden appearance of a stranger.

Moving the beam away, as though having given up trying to recognize himself in the mirror, Max lets his reflection slip back into the darkness. The light is now pointing at a desk covered in books and papers. He goes over to it and begins searching.

—m—

It was still dark and raining in Nice when Max stopped the Peugeot next to Gesù church and crossed the square in his raincoat and hat, walking carelessly through the rain-splashed puddles. There was no one about. The rain seemed to appear in misty, yellow swirls around the street lamp on the corner of Rue Droite next to the closed bar. Max reached the second doorway, which was open, and walked across the interior patio, leaving behind the patter of rain outside.

In the hallway, a dusty, bare bulb provided just enough light for him to see where he was putting his feet. On the upper landing, another light was switched on. As he mounted the stairs, the steps creaked beneath his sodden shoes, which still bore traces of mud from his recent sortie. He felt dirty, drenched, and exhausted, and wanted this to be over so that he could lie down and sleep for a while, before packing his suitcase and leaving. So that he could reflect calmly about his future. When he reached the landing, he unbuttoned his raincoat and shook the water from his hat. Then he pulled the brass doorbell and waited, with no result. This made him a little uneasy. He pulled the bell again and heard it chime inside. Nothing. The Italians should have been waiting on tenterhooks for him. Yet no one came.

"I'm glad to see you," said a voice behind him. Max started, dropping his hat on the ground. Fito Mostaza was sitting on the stairs leading to the next floor, looking relaxed. He was dressed in a dark, pin-striped suit with padded shoulders, and his customary bow tie. He wore neither a raincoat nor a hat.

"It turns out you're a responsible fellow," he added. "Reliable."

He spoke with a pensive, distracted air, as though concerned about something else. Oblivious to Max's unease.

"Did you find what you were looking for?"

Max stood gazing at him for a while, without replying. He was trying to figure out Mostaza's part in all this, and where he himself stood.

"Where are they?" he said at last.

"Who?"

"The Italians. Barbaresco and Tignanello?"

"Oh, them."

Mostaza rubbed his chin with one hand, smiling almost imperceptibly.

"There's been a change of plan," he said.

"I know nothing about that. I'm supposed to see them. That's what we agreed."

The lenses in Mostaza's spectacles glinted as he bobbed his head with a pensive gesture then raised it again.

"Of course . . . plans and agreements. Naturally."

He rose to his feet almost reluctantly, brushing off the seat of his trousers. Then he straightened his tie and walked down to where Max was standing. In his right hand was a shiny key.

"Naturally," he repeated, unlocking the door.

Mostaza stood aside, politely, letting Max through. He entered, and the first thing he saw was blood.

—⁂—

He has them. It was so easy finding Mikhail Sokolov's chess notebooks, that for a moment Max wasn't sure if they were what he'd been looking for. But now he is. A careful examination by flashlight with his reading glasses on has dispelled any doubt. Everything fits with the description Mecha gave him: four thick volumes bound in cardboard and cloth, resembling big, tattered accounts books, filled with handwritten annotations in small, compact Cyrillic script, diagrams of games, notes, references. The professional secrets of a world chess champion. The four notebooks were in full view, piled one on top of the other, among the papers and books on the desk. Max doesn't read Russian, but he easily identified the last entry in the fourth volume: half a dozen lines in obscure figures (Q4R, P3RQ, B4R, KxPQ) jotted down next to a recent clipping from *Pravda* about one of the Sokolov-Keller games in Sorrento.

With the notebooks (the book, as Mecha called them) in his rucksack, which is once more on his back, Max goes out onto the balcony and looks up. The rope is still safely in place. He gives it a tug to make sure it's secure, before preparing his ascent. But no sooner has he made a first attempt, than he realizes he isn't going to make it. He might have enough energy to reach the roof, but he will have difficulty climbing over the gutter and the cornice where, on his way down, he grazed his knees and elbows. He overestimated his capability. Or his strength. If he faltered, he would plunge to his death. Not to mention the effort of going back the way he came, descending the iron ladder set in the wall, fumbling in the dark, unable to see where he was putting his feet. And only his hands to cling on with.

The realization hits him with a jolt of panic that leaves his mouth dry. He stays like that for a moment, motionless, clutching the rope. Unable to decide. Then he releases his grip, defeated. Accepting that he has fallen into his own trap. Overconfident, refusing to accept the reality of old age and exhaustion. He will never reach the roof that way, and he knows it.

Think, he tells himself anxiously. Think carefully and quickly, or you won't get out of here. He leaves the rope dangling (it's not possible to pull it down from below) and goes back into the room. There is only one way out, and knowing that helps him focus on what steps to take next. Everything, he concludes, will depend on stealth. And on luck: how many people are in the building and where. Whether the guard the Russians usually leave on the ground floor also does the rounds between Sokolov's room and the door to the garden. And so, careful not to make any noise, treading heel first in his rubber-soled shoes, Max walks across the room, steps out in to the corridor, and closes the door quietly behind him. There is a light outside, and a carpet extending to the elevator and the stairs, which helps him advance noiselessly. When he reaches the stair landing, he stops to listen, leaning over the stairwell. Everything is calm. He descends taking the same precautions, peering over the banister to make sure his way is still clear. He can no longer hear properly, because his heart is racing again, and the throbbing in his ears is deafening. It's been a long time since he broke out in a sweat, he thinks. His skin was never prone to perspiring, but beneath his black trousers and sweater, he feels his undergarments soaking wet.

He pauses before the last stretch, making a renewed effort to calm himself.

Above the pounding in his head, he thinks he can hear a distant, muffled sound. Perhaps a radio or television is on. He peers down the stairwell again, descends the remaining steps, and creeps toward the corner of the lobby. There is a door on the far side, undoubtedly the one leading to the garden. On the left is a long, gloomy corridor and on the right, a set of frosted-glass doors, through which a light glimmers. That is where the sound of the radio or television is coming from, louder now. Max takes off the scarf still tied around his head, uses it to wipe the sweat from his face, then stuffs it into his pocket. His mouth is so dry that his tongue is almost stuck to the roof of his mouth. He closes his eyes for a few seconds, takes three deep breaths, crosses the foyer, opens the door silently, and goes outside. The cool night air, the scent of lushness beneath the trees in the garden, embraces him like a wave of optimism and vitality. Holding on to the rucksack, he begins to sprint between the shadows.

—◊◊◊—

"Sorry about the mess," Fito Mostaza said as he closed the door.

Max didn't reply. He was gazing with horror at Mauro Barbaresco's body. The Italian was lying sprawled on his back, in his shirtsleeves, in a pool of semicongealed blood. His face was the color of wax, his eyes two glassy slits, his lips parted, his throat slit from ear to ear.

"Go on through," Mostaza prompted. "And careful where you put your feet. It's rather slippery."

They advanced down the corridor, toward the end room where

Tignanello's body was blocking the doorway to the kitchen, one arm stretched out at a right angle, the other beneath his body. He was lying facedown in a pool of brownish-red blood that had trickled in a long stream under the table and chairs. There was an almost metallic odor in the room, subtle yet pervasive.

"Approximately five liters per body," Mostaza remarked with distaste, as if he found this truly regrettable. "That makes ten in total. Quite a spillage."

Max slumped onto the nearest chair. Mostaza stood watching him intently. Then he picked up a bottle of wine from the table, half filled a glass, and offered it to Max, who shook his head. The idea of drinking with all that just under his nose made him retch.

"At least take a sip," Mostaza insisted. "It'll do you good."

Eventually, Max obeyed, barely taking a sip before leaving the glass on the table. Mostaza, who was in the doorway (Tignanello's blood inches from his shoes) had taken his pipe out of one of his pockets and was calmly filling it with tobacco.

"What happened here?" Max stammered.

The other man shrugged.

"Occupational hazards," he replied, pointing at the body with the stem of his pipe. "Theirs, in this instance."

"Who did this?"

Mostaza looked at him with faint surprise.

"Why, I did, naturally."

Max leapt to his feet, knocking over the chair, but froze instantly at the sight of the object Mostaza had just taken out of his jacket pocket. With his unlit pipe still in his left hand, his right held a small, shiny nickel-plated pistol. And yet the gesture wasn't threatening. He was simply showing the gun in the palm of his hand, almost apologetically. He wasn't pointing it at Max: his finger wasn't even on the trigger.

"Pick up the chair and sit down again, will you? . . . Let's not be melodramatic."

Max did as Mostaza said. By the time he was seated once more, the pistol had disappeared into Mostaza's right pocket.

"Did you find what you went looking for?" he asked.

Max was gazing at Tignanello's body, facedown in a pool of semicongealed blood. One of his feet had lost a shoe, which lay on the floor, farther away. The exposed sock had a hole in the heel.

"You didn't shoot them," Max said.

Mostaza, who was lighting his pipe, contemplated him through a puff of smoke, shaking the match until the flame went out.

"Of course not," he said. "A pistol, even a small-caliber one like this, is noisy. No need to alert the neighbors." He opened one flap of his jacket to reveal the handle of a knife tucked inside, next to his suspenders. "This is messier, of course. But more discreet."

He glanced thoughtfully at the pool of blood at his feet. Apparently contemplating the appropriateness of the word *messier*.

"It wasn't pleasant, I assure you," he added after a moment.

"Why?" Max insisted.

"We can discuss all that later, if you wish. Now tell me whether you managed to get hold of the letters. Have you got them with you?"

"No."

Mostaza straightened his glasses with one finger and gave Max an appraising look.

"I see," he said at last. "Foresight or failure?"

Max remained silent. At that moment he was busy calculating how much his life would be worth once he handed over the letters. Doubtless about as much as those poor wretches who had bled to death on the floor.

"Stand up and turn around," Mostaza ordered.

His tone betrayed a hint of irritation, although he still didn't sound threatening. He was merely carrying out a tedious but necessary formality. Max obeyed, and Mostaza enveloped him in a puff of smoke when he approached from behind to frisk him, without result, while Max secretly congratulated himself for having the precaution to leave the letters under one of the car seats.

"You can turn around now. . . . Where are they?" Mostaza's pipe was clenched between his teeth, distorting his voice, as he wiped his hands, moist from Max's raincoat, on his jacket. "At least tell me you have them in your possession."

"I do."

"Splendid. I'm glad to hear it. Now tell me where, and we can get this over with."

"Get what over with?"

"Don't be so suspicious, it's a figure of speech. There's nothing to prevent us from parting on civilized terms."

Max looked again at Tignanello's corpse. He remembered the man's sad, silent expression. A melancholy type. He was almost sorry to see him like that, facedown in his own blood. So still and defenseless.

"Why did you kill them?"

Mostaza frowned uneasily, and the scar beneath his jaw seemed to deepen. He opened his mouth to say something unpleasant, but apparently thought better of it. He glanced at the bowl of his pipe, to make sure it was burning evenly, then looked at Tignanello's body on the floor.

"This isn't a novel." His tone was almost patient. "And so I have no intention of explaining everything in the final chapter. You don't need to know what happened, and I don't have time to stand around telling spy stories. Tell me where the letters are and we can wash our hands of this."

Max pointed at the dead body.

"Is that how you plan to wash your hands of me once you have them?"

Mostaza appeared to give the question some serious thought.

"You're right," he agreed. "No one has given you any guarantees, of course. And I presume my word isn't good enough, is it?"

"You presume correctly."

"Aha."

Mostaza sucked thoughtfully on his pipe.

"I should set you straight on a few details regarding my résumé," he said at last. "In fact, I don't work for the Spanish Republic, but for the government in Burgos. For the other side."

He winked, roguishly, behind his spectacles. It was clear he was enjoying Max's discomfort.

"You could say," he added, "it was a family affair."

Max was still gazing at him, horrified.

"But they're Italians. Fascist agents. Your allies."

"Look. It seems you're a little naïve. When you work at this level there are no alliances. Their bosses wanted the letters and so did mine. Jesus said we should be brothers, but he never said anything about cousins. I imagine my bosses consider these letters demanding a commission for selling aircraft a powerful ace up their sleeve. A way of having the Italians, or their foreign minister, by the balls."

"Why didn't you simply ask Ferriol for them—he's their banker, isn't he?"

"I've no idea. They give me orders, not explanations. I expect Ferriol has his own plans. Maybe he was going to demand some other form of payment. From the Spanish and the Italians. He's a businessman, after all."

"And what was that strange story about the boat?"

"The *Luciano Canfora*? . . . Unfinished business, which you helped resolve. It's true the captain and his chief engineer wanted to deliver the consignment to a Republican port. I persuaded them myself, posing as an agent of the Republic. We'd had our suspicions about them, and we were right. Afterward I used you to pass the information on to the Italians, who acted swiftly. The traitors were arrested, and the ship is now on its original course."

Max pointed at Tignanello's body.

"And these two . . . was it necessary to kill them?"

"Technically, yes. I couldn't control this situation with three people involved, two of whom were professionals. I had no choice but to take some of you out."

He took the pipe from his mouth. It seemed to have gone out. He turned it upside down and tapped the bowl gently against the table, emptying it. Then he took a last puff before putting it in the pocket not containing the pistol.

"Let's get this over with," he said. "Give me the letters."

"You've seen they aren't here."

"And you've heard my side of the story."

"So, where are they?"

It was absurd to go on refusing, Max realized. And dangerous. All he could do was try to gain more time.

"In a safe place."

"Well, take me there."

"And after that? . . . What will happen to me?"

"Nothing in particular." Mostaza looked at him, as though offended by his misgivings. "Like I said, you go your way, I go mine. Game over."

Max shuddered, vulnerable to the point of self-pity. For a moment his knees felt like jelly. He had deceived too many men and women in his life not to recognize the warning signals. He could see in Mostaza's eyes how precarious his future was.

"I don't trust your promises," he protested feebly.

"It makes no difference, because you have no choice." Mostaza patted the bulge in his jacket pocket, to remind Max of the pistol. "Even if you're convinced I'm going to kill you, it's up to you to decide whether I do it now or later . . . although I insist that isn't my intention. With the letters in my possession, there'd be no point. It would be an unnecessary act. Superfluous."

"What about my money?"

Max was making a last desperate attempt to gain time. To draw things out. But as far as Mostaza was concerned, the discussion was over.

"That's none of my business." He picked up his hat and raincoat from a chair. "Let's go."

Mostaza gave his pocket another pat as he motioned toward the door with his other hand. All of a sudden, he appeared tenser, more serious. Max went first, stepping over Tignanello and his pooled blood, and made his way along the corridor until he was standing next to Barbaresco's corpse. While he was reaching for the handle to open the door, Mostaza at the rear, Max took a last look at the glassy eyes and half-open mouth of the Italian, and was seized once more by that strange feeling of pity, of sympathy, which he had felt before. He'd grown fond of those two, he realized. Dripping wet dogs in the rain.

The door was stuck fast. Max gave it a tug, and the sudden movement, as it opened abruptly, caused him to stagger backward. Mostaza, who was behind him putting on his raincoat, also took a precautionary step back, one arm in his coat sleeve, his free hand half inside the pocket containing the pistol. As he did so, he trod in the semicongealed blood on the floor and lost his balance. Not completely: only a slight wobble as he tried to regain his footing. In that instant, Max realized with gloomy certainty that this was his only chance. In an act of blind desperation, he threw himself at Mostaza.

The two men slipped on the blood and fell to the floor. Max's first thought as he grappled Mostaza was to prevent him from taking out his pistol, but he quickly realized that his adversary was trying to reach for his knife. Fortunately, Mostaza's other arm was tangled up in the sleeve of his raincoat. Max made the most of this to gain a slight advantage by punching Mostaza repeatedly in the face, on his spectacles. They shattered with a crunch, eliciting a groan from Mostaza, who was clasping hold of Max as tightly as he could, trying to roll him over on his back. His skinny, wiry body, only deceptively fragile, was in fact dangerously strong. That knife in his hands would be the equivalent of a death sentence. Max's punches were relatively well placed and he managed to fend off the attack. They continued to wrestle, Max attempting to hold his opponent down and punch him, while Mostaza fought to free his trapped arm, as the two of them slid around in Barbaresco's blood. Frantic, his strength beginning to ebb, aware that if and when Mostaza succeeded in freeing his other hand he could consider himself a dead man, Max's long-forgotten reflexes came to his aid: the street kid from Calle Vieytes and the soldier who had defended himself with a knife in the Foreign Legion's brothels. Things he had done or seen others do. And so, with all the strength he could muster, he jabbed his thumb in one of his enemy's eyes. As it plunged deep into the socket there was a soft squelch and a savage howl from Mostaza, who slackened his grip. Max attempted to sit up, but slipped over again in the blood. He kept on until he managed to sit astride Mostaza, who was squealing like an enraged animal. Then, using his right elbow as a weapon, Max began hitting his adversary in the head as hard as he could, until the pain in his elbow became unbearable, Mostaza stopped resisting, and his battered, broken face lolled to one side.

Finally, Max slumped, exhausted, to the floor. He lay still for a long while, trying to regain his strength, until in the end he felt himself slipping out of consciousness and everything around him went black. He passed out slowly, as if he were falling down a bottomless well. And when he came to, a square of dirty, gray light was seeping in through the tiny window in the hallway, announcing the dawn. He moved away from the lifeless body, and dragged himself out onto the landing. Behind him was a trail of his own blood, for he had (he realized, painfully groping his leg) a gash on one thigh, a hair's breadth from his femoral artery. Somehow, in the last instant, Fito Mostaza had managed to pull out his knife.

12

The Blue Train

I T IS SIX in the morning and the telephone in Max's room at the Hotel Vittoria rings for the second time in fifteen minutes. This makes him uneasy. The first time he picked up the receiver, there was no voice at the other end, only a silence followed by the click of the connection being broken. This time he lets the telephone ring until it goes quiet. He knows it isn't Mecha Inzunza, because they have agreed to keep their distance. They decided that last night, on the terrace of Il Fauno. The chess game had ended at ten-thirty. Soon after that, the Russians must have discovered the break-in, the hole cut in the glass door, and the rope dangling from the roof. And yet, sometime after eleven o'clock, when, having showered and changed his clothes, a nervous Max had walked through the garden toward Piazza Tasso, he saw no sign of any commotion in the building occupied by the Soviet delegation. Apart from a few lighted windows, all was seemingly calm. Possibly Sokolov hadn't yet returned to his suite, he concluded, as he approached the main gate. Or (and this could prove more worrying than police cars parked outside) the Russians had decided to deal with the incident discreetly. In their own way.

Mecha was sitting at one of the far tables, her suede jacket draped over the back of her chair. Max went over and sat down next to her without saying a word. He ordered a Negroni and glanced about with an air of quiet satisfaction, avoiding Mecha's inquisitive gaze. His hair, still damp, was carefully combed, and a silk scarf showed beneath his open shirt collar, under his navy-blue blazer.

"Jorge won this afternoon," she said after a few moments.

Max admired her composure.

"That's good news," he said.

He turned to look at her, smiling as he did so, and Mecha guessed what that smile meant.

"You have it?" she said.

The question was rhetorical. He beamed. His lips hadn't displayed that look of triumph for years.

"Oh, darling," she said.

The waiter arrived with his cocktail. Max took a sip, savoring it at length. A little heavy on the gin, he noticed contentedly. Just what he needed.

"How was it?" Mecha asked.

"Difficult." He put his drink down on the table. "I told you. I'm too old for this kind of escapade."

"But you did it all the same. You got the book."

"Yes."

She leaned over the table, eagerly.

"Where is it?"

"In a safe place, as we agreed."

"Won't you tell me where?"

"Not yet. Just for a few hours, to be on the safe side."

She looked at him intently, studying his response, and Max

knew what was going through her mind. He recognized the old, almost familiar look of distrust in her eyes. But it only lasted an instant. Then Mecha lowered her head, as though ashamed.

"You're right," she admitted. "You shouldn't give it to me straightaway."

"No. We spoke about it before. That's what we agreed."

"Let's see how they respond."

"I just walked past the apartment block. Everything seems quiet."

"Perhaps they haven't found out yet."

"I'm sure they have. I left enough evidence."

She stirred uneasily.

"Did something go wrong?"

"I overestimated my strength," he said simply. "Which forced me to improvise."

He looked toward the main gates of the hotel, beyond the car and scooter headlights on Piazza Tasso. He imagined the Russians discovering what had happened, shocked at first, then angry. He took a few more sips of his drink to calm his nerves. It felt almost strange not to hear any police sirens.

"I almost got trapped in the room," he admitted after a few moments. "Like a fool. Imagine if the Russians had come back to find me sitting there, waiting."

"Can they identify you? You said you left evidence."

"I didn't mean fingerprints or anything like that, only signs of a break-in: a broken window, a rope. . . . Even a blind man would know the moment he walked in. That's why I say they must have found out by now."

He glanced about, uneasily. People had begun to leave, although a few of the tables were still occupied.

"It worries me that there's no movement," he added. "No response, I mean. They could be watching you right now. And me."

She looked around, frowning.

"There's no reason why they should connect us to the theft," she concluded after a moment's reflection.

"You know they'll quickly put two and two together. And if they have found out about me, I'm in trouble."

He was resting one hand on the table: bony, spotted with age. There were traces of mercurochrome on his knuckles and fingers, on the scratches from when he climbed up to the roof and shinnied down the rope to Sokolov's balcony. They still stung.

"Perhaps I should leave the hotel," he said after a moment. "Make myself scarce for a while."

"Do you know what, Max?" She ran her fingers gently over the red marks on his hands. "All this gives me a feeling of déjà vu. Of history repeating itself. Doesn't it you?"

Her tone was soft, infinitely tender. The lanterns on the terrace made her eyes shimmer. Max frowned, wistful.

"It's true," he said. "At least in part."

"If we could travel back in time, perhaps things would have been . . . I don't know. Different."

"Things are never different. They're fated. The way they have to be."

He called over the waiter and paid the bill. Then he stood up, to pull Mecha's chair out for her.

"That time in Nice . . ." she had started to say.

Max draped her jacket around her shoulders. As he withdrew his hands, he ran them over her arms for an instant, like a fleeting caress.

"Please don't talk about Nice," he murmured to her in a way he hadn't spoken to a woman for a long time. "Not tonight. Not now."

He was smiling as he spoke. And she smiled, too, as she turned to look at him.

—⟁—

"This is going to hurt," Mecha said.

She poured a few drops of iodine tincture on the cut, and Max felt as if she had placed a red-hot iron on his thigh. It stung like hell.

"That hurts," he said.

"I warned you."

She was sitting next to him, on the edge of a canvas-and-steel sofa in the villa at Antibes. She was barefoot and had on a long elegant robe, tied at the waist. A silk nightgown was visible where the robe fell open, revealing part of her naked legs. Her body gave off a pleasant odor, of recent slumber. She had been fast asleep when Max banged on the door, waking first the maid and then her. The maid was back in her room now, and he was lying on his back in a rather unbecoming position; trousers and underpants pulled down around his knees, exposing his manhood, and, at the top of his right thigh, the shallow gash a couple of inches long left by Mostaza's knife.

"Whoever did this, almost got you . . . Any deeper and you'd have bled to death."

"I know."

"Did he do that to your face, too?"

"He did."

Max had studied himself in the mirror in his room at the Negresco (a black eye, a bloodied nose, and a broken lip) two hours earlier, when he stopped off there to clean up his wounds as best he could, take a couple Veramons, and pack in a hurry, before checking out and leaving a handsome tip. Then he had paused for a moment in the entrance, beneath the glass awning onto which the rain was still beating down, surveying the street apprehensively, on the lookout for any unusual movement beneath the street lamps illuminating the Promenade and the façades of the nearby hotels. Finally, calming himself, he put his luggage in the Peugeot, started the engine, and drove off into the night, the car's headlights lighting up the white-painted pines along the road to La Garoupe and Cap d'Antibes.

"Why did you come here?"

"I don't know. Or rather, I do . . . I needed time to rest. To think."

Yes, that was the idea. There was a lot for him to think about. Whether or not Mostaza was dead, for example. Also, had he been acting alone, or did he have people out searching for Max at that very moment? And that went for the Italians, too. Immediate and future consequences, none of which, however hard he looked, offered any pleasant prospects. Added to that, the natural curiosity of the authorities when two (possibly three) bodies were found in the apartment on Rue Droite: two foreign secret services and the French police wondering who else was mixed up in all that. And, as if that weren't enough, how Tomás Ferriol would react when he discovered that Count Ciano's letters had been stolen.

"Why me?" asked Mecha. "Why come to my house?"

"You're the only person in Nice I can trust."

"Are you wanted by the police?"

"No. Not for the moment, anyway. But the last thing on my mind tonight is the police."

She was looking at him intently. Suspicious.

"What are they going to do to you? . . . And why?"

"It's not about that, it's about what I've done, and what they might think I've done. . . . I need to rest for a few hours. Treat this wound. Then I'll go. I don't want to cause you any trouble."

She points coldly at his wound, at the iodine and bloodstains on the towel she spread out on the sofa before making Max lie down.

"You don't call it trouble to show up at my house in the middle of the night with a knife wound in your leg, scaring my maid half to death?"

"I've said I'll leave. As soon as I am able to think straight and decide where I'm going."

"You haven't changed, have you? And I'm still a fool. The moment I saw you at Suzi Ferriol's house, I knew you were the same

Max as in Buenos Aires. Whose pearl necklace have you stolen this time?"

He put his hand on her arm. His facial expression, somewhere between sincere and helpless, was one of the most effective in his repertoire. Years of practice. Of success. With it he could have persuaded a hungry dog to part with a bone.

"Sometimes we pay for things we haven't done," he said, holding her gaze.

"Damn you." She shook his hand off her arm in a flash of anger. "I'm sure you pay very little. And that you've done almost everything."

"One day I'll tell you about it. I promise."

"There won't be another day, if I can help it."

He held her wrist gently.

"Mecha . . ."

"Be quiet," she said, freeing herself once more. "Let me finish doing this before I throw you out."

She laid a piece of gauze over the wound, and as she did so her fingers brushed his thigh. He felt her warm touch on his skin, and despite the wound, his body reacted to her flesh with its odor of recent slumber and still-warm sheets. Motionless, perched on the sofa, her expression as calm as if she were studying something unrelated to either of them, Mecha raised her eyes until they met those of Max.

Then she untied her robe, lifted her silk nightgown, and sat astride him.

—⁓—

"Mr. Costa?"

A stranger is standing in the doorway to his room at the Hotel Vittoria. Another, out in the hall. The old alarm bells start ringing before he is able to assess the real danger. With the resignation of someone who has been in similar situations before, Max nods without uttering a word. He notices the man casually take a step forward to prevent him from closing the door again. And yet he has no intention of closing it. He knows that would be futile.

"Are you alone?"

A thick, foreign accent. He's not a policeman. Or at least (Max swiftly considers the pros and cons) not an Italian policeman. The man in the doorway is no longer in the doorway, he is inside the room. He enters with ease, glancing about while the man in the corridor stays where he is. The man who has entered is tall, with lank, brown hair. He has large hands, and his nails are chewed and dirty. On his little finger he wears a thick gold ring.

"What do you want?" asks Max at last.

"We want you to come with us."

He has a Slavic accent. Almost certainly Russian. What else would it be. Max walks backward, toward the telephone on the night table. The lank-haired man watches him, expressionless.

"It wouldn't be wise to make a scene, sir."

"Get out."

Max points to the door, which remains open with the other man out in the corridor. He is short, his shoulders ominously broad, like those of a wrestler, bulging beneath a tight, black leather jacket. His arms hang loosely by his sides, ready to tackle any unexpected event. The man raises the hand with the ring, as if it were holding up an irrefutable argument.

"If you'd prefer the Italian police, that's no problem. It's your choice. We just want to talk."

"What about?"

"You know perfectly well what about."

Max thinks for five seconds, trying not to yield to panic. His heart is racing and his legs feel like jelly. He would slump onto the bed, except that this would be seen as a sign of surrender or guilt. An implicit confession. He curses himself silently for a moment. Staying at the hotel was a foolish, unforgivable mistake, like a mouse enjoying the cheese while the trap is springing shut. He never imagined they'd identify him so quickly.

"Whatever this is about, we can discuss it here," he ventures at last.

"No. There are some gentlemen who'd like to speak to you at a different location."

"And where might that be?"

"Not far. About five minutes' drive."

As he says this, the man with lank hair taps with one finger the dial of his watch, as if it were proof of reliability and precision. Then he glances at the man in the corridor, who enters the room, closes the door quietly, and begins searching the room.

"I refuse to go anywhere," Max protests, with a determination he is far from feeling. "You have no right."

Unperturbed, as though his interest in Max were momentarily suspended, the man with lank hair allows his colleague to carry out his duty. The other one riffles through the chest of drawers and makes a thorough search of the wardrobe. Then he looks under the mattress and the bed. Finally, he shakes his head and says four words in a Slavic language, of which Max can only understand the Russian *nichivó*: nothing.

"That no longer matters," the man with lank hair says, resuming the interrupted conversation. "Rights or no rights . . . the choice is yours. Either you talk to the gentlemen I mentioned or to the police."

"I have nothing to hide from the police."

The two intruders are quiet and motionless now, staring at him coldly, and Max is more alarmed by their stillness than by their silence. After a moment, the man with lank hair scratches his nose. Thoughtful.

"I tell you what we'll do, Mr. Costa," he says at last. "I'm going to take one of your arms, and my friend here will take the other, and together we'll walk downstairs, through the foyer to the car we have waiting outside. You may or may not agree to come quietly. . . . If you don't, there'll be a scene, and the hotel will call the Sorrento police. In which case, you can acknowledge your responsibility and we'll acknowledge ours. But if you come with us, everything will take place discreetly and without any violence. . . . Which do you prefer?"

Max is trying to win time. To think. To list possible or impossible solutions, ways of escape.

"Who are you? Who sent you?"

The man with lank hair looks impatient.

"We've been sent by some peace-loving chess enthusiasts, who want to discuss a couple of suspect moves with you."

"I know nothing about that. I have no interest in chess."

"Really? . . . You don't give that impression. You've gone to a great deal of trouble for someone your age."

While he is speaking, the man with lank hair picks up Max's jacket, which was on the chair, and hands it to him with an impatient, almost brusque gesture. As if his last reserves of courtesy are almost exhausted.

—⁓—

The suitcase lay open on the bed, ready to be closed: shoes in flannel bags, undergarments, folded shirts, three suits doubled over in the lid. A fine leather travel bag, matching the suitcase. Max was getting ready to leave Mecha Inzunza's house in Antibes for the railway station in Nice, where he had a seat reserved on the Blue Train. Count Ciano's three letters were hidden in his suitcase, the lining of which he had unglued and carefully reglued back together. He hadn't decided what to do with them, although keeping them in his possession was a risky business. He needed time to assess the significance of what had occurred the previous night at Susana Ferriol's villa, and in the apartment on Rue Droite. And to weigh the possible consequences.

He had just knotted his tie and was in his shirtsleeves, the buttons of his vest still undone, and was looking at himself in the bedroom mirror: his hair slick with pomade parted off center, his freshly shaven face smelling of Floïd cologne. Fortunately, he bore few marks of his struggle with Fito Mostaza: the swelling on his lip had gone down, and a little makeup (Max had used some of Mecha's face powder) had covered the bruising under his eye.

When he turned around, doing up all but the bottom button on his vest, she was standing in the doorway, dressed, holding a cup of coffee. He hadn't heard her come in, and had no idea how long she'd been watching him.

"What time does your train leave?" asked Mecha.

"Seven-thirty."

"Are you sure you want to leave?"

"Yes."

She took a sip, gazing pensively at the cup.

"I still don't know what happened last night. . . . Why did you come here?"

Max spread his hands. Nothing to hide, his gesture said.

"I already told you."

"You told me nothing. Only that you'd had a serious problem and couldn't stay at the Negresco."

He nodded. He had been preparing for this conversation for a while. He knew she wouldn't let him leave without asking questions, and it was true she deserved some answers. The memory of her flesh and her mouth, her naked body entwined with his, agitated him once more, throwing him for a moment. Mecha Inzunza was so beautiful that leaving her felt almost like an act of violence. For an instant, he reflected about the limitations of the words *love* and *desire* amid all this uncertainty, the doubts and the urgency of fear, with no guarantees about the future or the present. That dismal flight, to where and with what consequences he did not know, eclipsed everything else. Only after he had escaped could he ponder the effect Mecha had on his body and mind. It could have been love, of course. Max had never loved before, and so he didn't know. Possibly love was that unbearable wrench, the emptiness at his looming departure, the overwhelming sadness that almost supplanted his instinct to flee and survive. Perhaps she loved him as well, he thought suddenly. In her own way. Perhaps, he thought, too, they would never see each other again.

"Yes," he said, at last, "a serious problem. Or rather, a lethal one. Which ended in a rather nasty fight. Hence the need for me to disappear for a while."

She looked at him almost without blinking.

"What about me?"

"You'll stay here, I imagine." Max made a gesture with his hand that could have embraced that room or the whole of Nice. "I'll know where to find you when things have calmed down."

Still fixed on him, Mecha's eyes radiated a deadly seriousness.

"Is that all?"

"Listen," Max said, slipping on his jacket. "Without wanting to be dramatic, my life could be at stake here. In fact, there's no could about it. It is."

"Is someone looking for you? Who?"

"It'd take too long to explain."

"I have time. I can listen to however much you care to tell me."

On the pretext of making sure his luggage was in order, Max avoided her eyes. He closed his suitcase and pulled the straps tight.

"Then you're lucky. I have neither the time nor the energy. I'm still confused. There are things I wasn't expecting . . . matters I don't know how to handle."

The distant sound of a telephone reached them from somewhere in the house. It rang four times and stopped suddenly, without Mecha taking any notice.

"Are the police looking for you?"

"Not that I know of." Max held her gaze with sufficient composure. "I wouldn't risk taking the train if they were. But things can change, and I don't want to be around when that happens."

"You still haven't answered my question. What about me?"

The maid appeared. Madam was wanted on the telephone. Mecha handed her the coffee cup and they disappeared down the corridor. Max put his suitcase on the floor, closed his travel bag, and placed it next to the suitcase. Then he went over to the dressing table to pick up the things he had left there: wristwatch, fountain pen, wallet, lighter, and cigarette case. He was fastening the Patek Philippe around his left wrist when Mecha came back. He glanced up and saw her leaning against the door frame, exactly as she had been before she went off, and he knew straightaway something was wrong. She had news, and it wasn't good.

"That was Ernesto Keller, my friend from the Chilean consulate," she said with total calm. "He tells me someone broke in to Suzi Ferriol's villa last night."

Max remained stock-still, his fingers busy fastening the clip on his watch.

"How terrible . . ." he managed to say. "And how is she?"

"She's fine." Her voice was icy. "She was out when it happened, at a dinner party in Cimiez."

Max looked away, reached out a hand, and picked up his Parker pen, with as much calm as he could muster. Or conjure.

"Did they take anything of value?"

"That's for you to tell me."

"Me? . . ." He made sure the cap was on properly before slipping the pen into his inside jacket pocket. "How should I know?"

He looked straight at her, fully composed now. Without moving from the doorway, she folded her arms.

"Spare me the customary excuses, pretense, and lies," she commanded. "I'm in no mood for this nonsense."

"I assure you I haven't—"

"Damn you. The moment I saw you at Suzi's place I knew you were up to something. Only I never thought it would be there."

She strode over to Max. For the first time since he'd met her, he saw her face contorted with rage. An acute exasperation that tensed her features, clouding her expression.

"She's my friend. . . . What have you stolen from her?"

"You're making a mistake."

Motionless before Max, almost enraged, she glowered at him. It was all he could do not to recoil.

"The same mistake I made in Buenos Aires, you mean?"

"It isn't what you think."

"Tell me what it is, then. And what this robbery has to do with the state you were in last night. With your wound and the bruises on your face. . . . Ernesto said that when Suzi got home, the thieves had already fled."

He didn't reply. He was trying to hide his unease while apparently verifying the contents of his wallet.

"What happened afterward, Max? If there was no violence there, where did it take place? And with whom?"

He still said nothing. He had no more excuses not to look her in the eye, because Mecha had picked up his cigarette case and lighter and was lighting a cigarette. Then she hurled both objects onto the table. The lighter bounced off and landed on the floor.

"I'm going to report you to the police."

She exhaled into his face, from close up, as though spitting the smoke at him.

"And don't look at me like that, because I'm not afraid . . . not of you or your accomplices."

Max stooped to pick up his lighter. The knock had dented the top, he noticed.

"I don't have any accomplices." He slipped the lighter into his vest pocket and the cigarette case into his jacket. "And it wasn't a robbery. I got mixed up in something I didn't go looking for."

"You've spent your whole life looking, Max."

"Not this time. I assure you."

Mecha remained very close, staring at him sternly. And Max knew that he couldn't evade her questioning. On the one hand, she had a right to know some of what had happened. On the other, leaving her behind angry and bewildered in Nice was to add unnecessary risks to his already precarious situation. He needed a few days' peace. A few hours, at least. And then possibly he could manage her. After all, like the rest of womankind, she only needed persuading.

"It's a complicated matter," he confessed, exaggerating the difficulty of his admission. "I was used. I had no choice."

He paused for a moment, timing it to perfection. Mecha listened, waiting attentively, as if her life and not Max's hung in the balance. And then, after hesitating a little longer, before relating the rest, he told her the truth. Perhaps it was a mistake to go this far, he told himself. But he had no time to reflect about it and could not imagine another way out.

"Two men are dead . . . possibly three."

Mecha remained unruffled. Only her lips slackened around the smoldering cigarette, as if she needed more air in order to breathe.

"Is this related to what happened at Suzi's?"

"Partly. Or I should say, yes. Completely."

"Do the police know?"

"I don't think so, not yet. Or perhaps they do by now. There's no way I can find out."

Mecha's fingers trembled slightly as she withdrew the cigarette slowly from her mouth.

"Did you kill them?"

"No." He looked straight at her without blinking, wagering everything he had on that look. "Not one of them."

The place is bleak. A tumbledown villa, the garden overgrown with shrubs and weeds, on the outskirts of Sorrento, between Annunziata and Marciano, boxed in by two hills that block the view of the sea. They drove there in a Fiat 1300 along a winding road full of potholes, the man with lank hair at the wheel and the one in the black jacket on the backseat next to Max. And now they are in a room with peeling walls, where antique paintings languish amid crumbling plaster and patches of damp. The only pieces of furniture are two chairs, and Max is sitting on one of them, between his two chaperones, who are still standing. There is a fourth man in the other chair, placed opposite that of Max. He has pale skin, a bushy, ginger mustache, and unnerving, steely eyes with dark shadows under them. From the sleeves of his unfashionable jacket, two long, thin, pale hands emerge, which bring to mind the tentacles of a squid.

"And now," the man concludes, "tell me where grand master Sokolov's book is."

"I don't know what book you're talking about," Max replies calmly. "I only agreed to come here to clear up this stupid mistake."

The man sitting opposite contemplates him, impassively. Propped up against one of the chair legs at his feet is a worn-looking black leather briefcase. Finally, he leans over, almost lethargically, to pick it up, and rests it on his knees.

"A stupid mistake . . . Is that what you call it?"

"Exactly."

"You have a lot of nerve. I mean that sincerely. But I'd expect that from a man like you."

"You know nothing about me."

One of the squid tentacles traces a sinuous shape in the air, resembling a question mark.

"Know? . . . You're seriously mistaken, Mr. Costa. We know a great deal. For instance, you aren't the wealthy individual you appear to be, but instead the chauffeur of a Swiss citizen living in

Sorrento. Likewise, we know that the automobile you keep at the Hotel Vittoria doesn't belong to you . . . And that's not all. We know you have a police record, for burglary, fraud, and other petty crimes."

"This is outrageous. You've got the wrong man."

Perhaps this is the right moment to feign indignation, Max decides. He makes as if to rise from his chair, but instantly feels the man in the black leather jacket's hand firmly on his shoulder. The gesture isn't hostile, he notices. But persuasive, as though recommending patience. In the meantime, the man with the ginger mustache has opened the briefcase and is taking out a thermos flask.

"On the contrary," he says, unscrewing the top of the thermos. "You are who you are. And please don't try to deceive me. I've been up all night investigating this muddle. And that includes you, your past history, your presence at the Campanella contest, and your relationship to the young pretender, Keller. Everything."

"Assuming it's true, what have I to do with this book you're asking about?"

The other man pours some hot milk into the thermos cup, plucks a pink tablet from a pillbox, and takes it with a swig of milk. He looks genuinely tired. Then he shakes his head slightly, encouraging Max to desist with his denial.

"You did it. You climbed onto the roof in the dark and stole it."

"The book?"

"Precisely."

Max smiles, unflustered. Disdainful.

"Just like that."

"Not quite. You put a great deal of effort into it. An admirable amount, I must say. A superbly professional job."

"Listen. Don't be absurd. I'm sixty-four years old."

"That's what I thought this morning when I got hold of your file. But you look in good shape"—he glances at the scratches on Max's hands—"although I see you hurt yourself a little."

The Russian finishes the remains of his milk, shakes the cup out, and screws it back on.

"You took a huge risk," he goes on as he puts away the flask. "And I don't mean being caught by our men in the building, but rather when you lowered yourself onto the balcony, and everything else. . . . Do you still refuse to own up?"

"How could I possibly own up to such ridiculous nonsense?"

"Listen." The man's tone remains persuasive. "This conversation is off the record. The Italian police haven't been informed of the theft. We have our own security methods. . . . Everything could be straightforward if you return the book, assuming you still have it. Or tell us who you gave it to, who you're working for."

Max tries to think quickly. Returning the book is a possible solution, but that would be giving the Soviets solid proof that their suspicions are founded. Considering the way Moscow uses propaganda, he wonders how long it would be before they made their version of events public in order to reveal his links to Jorge Keller and discredit the challenger. A scandal like that would end the young man's career, destroying his chances of playing for the world title.

"They are all the grand master Sokolov's notes taken over a lifetime," the man with the ginger mustache goes on. "Important things depend on them. Future games . . . We must get them back, do you understand, for the sake of the champion's reputation, and the good name of our country. This is an affair of state. Your stealing the book is an act of aggression against the Soviet Union."

"But I don't have this book, I never had it. And I certainly didn't climb onto any roof, or enter any room other than my own."

The weary eyes contemplate Max with a baleful intensity.

"Is that your final word, for now?"

That *for now* is even more sinister than the steely gray eyes, despite being accompanied by an almost amiable smile. Max feels his resolve weaken. The situation is beginning to get out of control.

"I don't see what else I can say. . . . Besides, you have no right to keep me here. This isn't the Iron Curtain."

Scarcely has he uttered those words than he knows he has made a mistake. The last trace of a smile vanishes from the other man's lips.

"Allow me to tell you something about myself, Mr. Costa. . . . My knowledge of chess is, shall we say, limited. My true expertise is dealing with complicated matters in order to simplify them. . . . My job is to make sure that the grand master Sokolov's games proceed without a hitch. To safeguard his environment. Until now, I have carried out my duties impeccably in that respect. But you have upset all that. You have called my professional reputation into question, do you understand? . . . In the eyes of the world champion, my superiors, not to mention my own."

Max struggles to hide his growing panic. At last he manages to open his mouth, and without stammering, utters five words:

"Take me to the police."

"All in good time. For now, we are the police."

The Russian glances at the man with lank hair, and Max feels a violent, unexpected blow to the left side of his head, which makes his eardrum reverberate as if it has just burst. All at once he finds himself sprawled out, the chair overturned, face flat against the tiled floor. Dazed, head buzzing like a disturbed beehive.

"So, shall we make ourselves comfortable, Mr. Costa?" he hears a voice say, seeming to come from very far off. "While we continue our conversation."

—⚇—

When Mecha Inzunza switched off the ignition, the windshield wipers stopped and the glass glimmered with raindrops, distorting the view of taxis and horse-drawn carriages parked outside the triple-arched entrance to the railway station. It wasn't quite dark yet, but the street lamps in the square were already illuminated, their electric lights reflected on the wet tarmac, amid the grayish glow of dusk hovering over Nice.

"This is where we say good-bye," Mecha said.

Her words sounded sharp. Matter of fact. Max had turned to look at her in profile, motionless, her head bent slightly over the wheel. Her eyes gazing outside the car.

"Give me a cigarette."

He reached into his raincoat pocket for his cigarette case, lit an Abdul Pasha, and placed it between Mecha's lips. She smoked for a moment in silence.

"I don't suppose we'll see each other for a while," she said at last.

It wasn't a question. Max frowned.

"I don't know."

"What will you do when you get to Paris?"

"Keep moving." His frown deepened. "A sitting target isn't the same as a moving one. So the more difficult I make it for them, the better."

"Is it possible they might harm you?"

"Perhaps . . . yes. That is a possibility."

She had turned to look at him, her hand holding the smoldering cigarette resting on the wheel. The lights outside cast streaks from the wet windshield onto her face.

"I don't want them to hurt you, Max."

"I don't intend to make it easy for them."

"You still haven't told me what you took from Suzi Ferriol's house. How was it different from an ordinary robbery? . . . Ernesto Keller mentioned cash and documents."

"That's all you need to know. Why get involved?"

"I'm already involved." She made a gesture, embracing the two of them, the car, the railway station. "As you can see."

"The less you know, the less you'll be affected. They were papers. Letters."

"Private letters?"

Max preempted the unspoken disapproval in her question. "Nothing like that," he said. "I'm no blackmailer."

"What about money? . . . Is it true you stole some money?"

"Yes."

Mecha bobbed her head slowly, a couple of times. Apparently confirming her own suspicions. And she'd had a long time in which to reflect about them, Max feared.

"What possible interest could you have in Suzi's letters?"

"They belong to her brother."

"Ah. In that case, be careful." Her tone was sharp now. "Tomás Ferriol isn't the sort of man to turn the other cheek. And he has too much at stake to allow a . . ."

"A nobody?"

Mecha took a last draw on her cigarette, ignoring the smirk on Max's face. Then she wound the window down and dropped the butt outside.

"To allow someone like you to stand in his way."

"I seem to be getting in rather a lot of people's way recently. They must be lining up for my scalp."

She said nothing. Max glanced at his wristwatch: ten to seven. His train, which was arriving from Monaco, left in forty minutes, and he preferred not to wait around on the platform, exposed to prying eyes. He had reserved a seat over the telephone in a first-class sleeping compartment for one. All being well, he would be in Paris by morning: rested, shaved, and fresh. Once again ready to face life.

"Once everything calms down, I'll try to negotiate," he added. "To make something out of what fell into my lap."

She laughed softly.

"You say that as if it came out of the blue."

"I didn't go looking for this, Mecha."

"Do you have the letters with you?"

He hesitated for a moment. Why involve her further?

"That doesn't matter," he replied. "There's no need for you to know."

"Have you thought of giving them back to Ferriol? . . . Of coming to some kind of arrangement?"

"Of course I've thought about it. But approaching him has its risks. Besides, there are other possible customers."

"Customers?"

"There are two individuals. Or there were. Two Italians. They're dead now . . . It's absurd, but sometimes I feel like I owe them something."

"You can't owe them anything if they're dead."

"No, of course not. Not directly. And yet . . ."

He screwed up his eyes, remembering those poor wretches. The rain falling outside, the drops of water trickling down the glass made the scene all the more melancholy. He glanced at his watch again.

"And what about us, Max? Do you owe me anything?"

"I'll see you again once things have calmed down."

"I may not be here by then. They might exchange my husband for other prisoners. And there's more and more talk of another war in Europe . . . Everything could change soon. Disappear."

"I have to go now," he said.

"I don't know where I'll be when, as you say, things calm down. Or go wrong."

Max had reached for the door handle. Suddenly he paused, as though leaving the car meant stepping into the void. He gave a shudder, feeling vulnerable. Exposed to loneliness and to the rain.

"I don't read much," he said. "I prefer the cinema. I occasionally skim cheap novels when traveling or at hotels, the kind magazines publish. . . . But there's something I always remember. An adventurer whose motto was: 'I live by my sword and my steed.'"

Max tried to order his thoughts, searching for the right words to finish what he wanted to say. Mecha sat still, listening quietly.

Between the silences, only the patter of raindrops could be heard falling on the car. Gently, now. As though God were weeping.

"I feel a bit like that. I live by what I carry with me. By what I find along the way."

"Everything has an ending," she said softly.

"I don't know what that ending will be, but I know the beginning . . . I had few toys as a child, almost all of them made out of painted tin and empty matchboxes. Occasionally on a Sunday, my father would take me to a matinee at the Libertad cinema. Admission was thirty cents and they gave away sweets, and tickets for a raffle I never won. On the screen, with the piano accompaniment playing in the background, I saw starched, white-bib fronts, well-dressed men and beautiful women, automobiles, parties, and champagne glasses. . . ."

Max took his tortoiseshell cigarette case out of his pocket again, but didn't open it. He was content to play with the lid, running his fingers over the initials *MC* at the bottom, monogrammed in gold.

"I used to stand outside a cake shop in Calle California," he went on, "looking through the window at the pastries, cakes, and tarts. . . . Or I'd play along the banks of the Riachuelo on my way to La Boca, watching the sailors disembark: men with tattooed arms, who had come from places I imagined were fascinating."

He broke off almost abruptly, feeling awkward. It had just occurred to him that he could have gone on endlessly stringing together memories like this. He was aware, too, that he had never talked about himself so much to anyone. Not truthfully, not with genuine memories.

"Some men dream of leaving, and they do it. I was one of them."

Mecha remained silent, listening as though fearful of cutting the slender thread of his confessions. Max gave a deep, almost pained sigh, and put away the cigarette case.

"Of course there's an ending, like you say. Only I don't know where mine is."

He stopped looking at the lights and the blurred shapes outside, and, turning toward her, he kissed her spontaneously. Gently. On the lips. Mecha let him, without resisting the contact. A delicate, moist warmth that made the rainy landscape outside seem even bleaker to him. Afterward, when she moved her face away slightly, they remained close, gazing into each other's eyes.

"You don't have to leave," she whispered. "There are a hundred places here . . . near me."

He was the one who pulled away this time. Without taking his eyes off her.

"In my world," he said, "everything is wonderfully simple: I am what the tips I hand out say I am. And if one identity turns bad or his luck runs out, the next day I take on another. I live off other people's credit, without any bitterness or any grand illusions."

"Has it never occurred to you that I could change that?"

"Listen. A while ago, I was at a party, in a villa on the outskirts of Verona. Wealthy people. After dinner, at the behest of the owners, amid laughter, the guests began scratching the plaster off the walls with their coffee spoons to reveal the painted frescoes beneath. And as I watched, I thought how absurd everything was. How I could never feel like they did. With their silver coffee spoons and their paintings hidden beneath the plaster. And their laughter."

He paused for a moment to wind down the window and inhale the moist air from outside. Among the billboards on the station walls, political posters from Action Française and Front Populaire had been pasted: ideological slogans vying with advertisements for lingerie, mouthwash, or the latest movie, *Abus de Confiance*.

"When I see all those black, brown, red, or blue shirts, demanding affiliation to this or that group, I think that before the world belonged to the rich and now it will belong to the embittered. . . . I fall into neither category. Try as I might, I can't even feel bitter. And I certainly try."

He looked at her once more. She was still listening to him, motionless. Solemn.

"I think that in today's world indifference is the only possible form of freedom," Max concluded. "That's why I'll go on living by my sword and my steed."

"Get out of the car."

"Mecha . . ."

She looked away.

"You'll miss your train."

"I love you. I think. And yet love has nothing to do with all this."

Mecha beat the steering wheel with both hands.

"Just go. Damn you."

Max put on his hat and got out of the car, buttoning up his raincoat. He took his suitcase and travel bag out of the back and walked away without uttering a word or looking back, through the falling rain. He felt a piercing, grief-like sadness. A sort of premature nostalgia for everything he would long for later on. As he entered the station, he handed his luggage to a porter who led him through the crowd, toward the ticket office. Then he followed him until they reached the vaulted roof of iron and glass that covered the platforms. Just then, a locomotive came chugging into the station amid clouds of steam, dragging behind it a dozen dark blue carriages with a gold stripe beneath the windows bearing the words *Compagnie Internationale des Wagons-Lits*. A metal plate on either side showed the route: Monaco-Marseille-Lyon-Paris. Max glanced around, on the lookout for any disquieting signs. Two gendarmes in dark uniforms were chatting outside the door to the waiting room. Everything looked calm, he thought, and no one seemed particularly interested in him. Although that was no guarantee.

"Which car, sir?" the porter with his luggage asked.

"Number two."

He climbed aboard the train, handed his ticket to the conductor together with a one-hundred-franc note (a surefire way of winning the man over for the entire journey), and while the conductor was doffing his cap and bowing from the waist, he gave another twenty to the luggage porter.

"Thank you, sir."

"No, my friend. Thank you."

As he entered the compartment, he closed the door and pulled the curtain back, just far enough to be able to take another look at the platform. The two gendarmes hadn't moved and were still chatting, and he saw nothing to alarm him. People were saying their farewells and climbing aboard the train. There was a group of nuns fluttering their handkerchiefs, and an attractive woman embracing a man outside a carriage door. Max lit a cigarette and leaned back in his seat. When the train started to move, he looked up at the suitcase on the luggage rail. He thought about the letters hidden inside the lining. And about how he would stay alive and a free man until he disposed of them. Mecha Inzunza had already vanished from his memory.

—⁓—

Pain, Max realizes, sooner or later reaches a saturation point where intensity is no longer important. Where being hit twenty times is the same as being hit forty times. From that point on, what hurts are the breaks between blows, not each fresh blow, but the moments when your tormentor stops what he is doing to take a breather. When the numbed flesh relaxes and feels the pain inflicted upon it. The sum of all the previous blows.

"The book, Max . . . Where's the book?"

The man with the ginger mustache and the hands that resemble tentacles is talking, but his voice sounds distorted and muffled to Max, because his head is wrapped in a wet towel, making it difficult for him to breathe, even as it muffles his cries, absorbs some of the impact of the blows, and leaves no visible marks or bruising on his body, which is now tied to the chair. The rest of the blows are directed at his stomach and abdomen, exposed by the posture the ligatures have forced him to adopt. They are meted out both by the man with lank hair and the one in the black leather jacket. He knows it's them, because from time to time they remove the towel, and through the mist of his throbbing eyes filled with tears he sees them next to him, rubbing their knuckles, while the other man watches seated.

"The book. Where is it?"

They have just taken the towel off his head. Max gulps air into his bruised lungs, despite each breath stinging as if his skin were flayed. His blurry eyes finally manage to focus on the man with the ginger mustache.

"The book," the man says again. "Tell us where it is, and let's be done with this."

"I know . . . nothing . . . about any . . . book."

On his own initiative, under no orders from anyone and as a personal contribution to the procedure, the man in the black leather jacket suddenly punches Max in the groin. Max writhes beneath the ropes as this new pain radiates out into his thighs and chest. He wants to curl up, but that's impossible because his legs, chest, and arms are tied to the chair. A cold sweat breaks out over his whole body, and a few seconds later, for the third time since this started, he vomits bile, which dribbles down his chin onto his shirt. The man who hit him looks at him in disgust and turns toward the man with the ginger mustache, awaiting further instructions.

"The book, Max."

Still gasping for breath, Max shakes his head.

"Well, well." There is a hint of mocking admiration in the Russian's voice. "The old man is playing tough guy . . . at his age."

Another blow in the same place. A fresh spasm causes Max to writhe once more, as though something sharp were piercing his innards. And then, after a few seconds of intense pain, he loses control and cries out: a short, savage cry that brings him some relief. This time he retches without producing any vomit. Max sits with his head lolling on his chest, breathing unevenly and painfully. Shivering because of the sweat that seems to be freezing beneath his damp clothing, in every pore of his body.

"The book . . . Where is it?"

Max lifts his head, slightly. His heartbeat is erratic, with long pauses, followed by violent palpitations. He is convinced he is going to die in the next few minutes, and is surprised at his own indifference. His numb resignation. He never imagined it like this, he reflects in a moment of clarity. Letting himself go, punch-drunk, like allowing the current to drag you away into the night. But this is how it will be. Or so it seems. With all that pain and weariness wracking his body, it feels more like a promise of relief than any-thing else. Rest, at last. A long, final sleep.

"Where's the book, Max?"

Another blow, to the chest this time, followed by a explosion of pain that seems to crush his spine. Once more he is seized by violent retching, but there is nothing left to come out of his mouth. He urinates freely, wetting his trousers, with an intense stinging sensation that makes him howl. His head feels like it's splitting, and there is scarcely space for any coherent images among his jumbled thoughts. All he can make out with his blurred vision are white deserts, blinding flashes of light, vast surfaces undulating like heavy mercury. The void, perhaps. Or nothingness. Sometimes, into this nothingness old images of Mecha Inzunza appear, random frag-ments from his past, strange sounds. The one he hears the most is that of the three ivory balls clicking against each other on a billiard table: a soft, monotonous, almost pleasant sound that brings Max a strange kind of peace. Which inspires him with the necessary strength to raise his chin and look straight into the steely eyes of the man sitting opposite him.

"I hid it . . . up your mother's . . . cunt."

With that last word, he spits at the man with the ginger mustache. A pathetic string of bloody sputum that misses its target and dribbles to the floor between his own knees. The man with the ginger mustache contemplates the spittle on the floor with a look of displeasure.

"I have to admit it, granddad. You've got guts."

Then he signals to the others, who cover Max's head again with the wet towel.

—⁓—

The Blue Train was speeding northward through the night, leaving Nice and its perils behind. After draining the last sip of a forty-eight-year-old Armagnac and dabbing his mouth with a napkin, Max left a tip on the tablecloth and walked out of the restaurant car. Five minutes before, the woman he had shared the table with had stood up and made her way toward the same carriage as Max: number two. Fate had brought them together at the first sitting for dinner, after Max had seen her embracing a man moments before the train pulled out of the station. She was French, around forty years old, and wore with an easy elegance what Max's trained eye thought was a Maggy Rouff suit. He also noticed the gold wedding band on her left hand, next to a sapphire ring. They didn't engage in conversation when he took a seat opposite her, apart from the obligatory *bonsoir*. They ate in silence, exchanging an occasional polite smile when they caught each other's eye or the waiter topped up their wineglasses. She was attractive, he decided, as he took his napkin off his plate: big eyes, finely penciled eyebrows, and just the right amount of red lipstick. After finishing her *filet de boeuf-forestière* she said no to dessert and reached for a packet of Gitanes. Max leaned over the table to light her cigarette. It took him a while to open the dented lighter, and their first exchange on that pretext gave rise to a superficial, pleasant conversation: Nice, the rain, the winter season, the advent of paid holidays, the World Exhibition that was coming to a close in Paris. Having broken the ice, they went on to discuss other topics. The man she had bade farewell to on the platform was indeed her husband. They lived in Cap Ferrat for most of the year, but she spent a week in Paris each month for her work: she was fashion editor at *Marie Claire*. Five minutes later, the woman was chuckling at Max's jokes and watching his mouth as he spoke. Had he never thought of being a male model? she asked after a while. Finally she glanced at her tiny wristwatch, remarked on how late it was, took her leave of Max with a broad smile, and left the restaurant car. By a pleasant quirk of fate their compartments were adjacent: numbers four and five. The vagaries of trains and life.

Max walked through the lounge bar (which at that time of night was as busy as the Ritz), stepping over the gangway connection between the cars, where the rattle of the train and the drone of the wheels was loudest. He stopped at the end of the carriage, where the conductor was checking the list of the ten compartments in his charge by the light of a small lamp that made the gold-colored lions on his pocket flaps gleam. The conductor was a small, friendly looking fellow, bald with a mustache, and a scar on his head—from a piece of shrapnel on the Somme, Max discovered when he asked about it. They chatted for a while about battle scars, and then about sleeping cars, Pullmans, and international railway lines and trains. Max produced his cigarette case at the right moment, accepted a light from the conductor's book of matches bearing the company's insignia, and when they had finished smoking their cigarettes and exchanging confidences, any passing passenger would have taken them for old friends. Five minutes later, Max glanced at his watch, and in the tone of someone who, had the roles been reversed, would have done the same for him, asked the conductor to avail himself of his key to open the door between compartments four and five.

"I can't do that," the employee protested feebly. "It's against the rules."

"I know it is, my friend . . . But I also know that you'll make an exception because it's me."

As he spoke, he slipped into the conductor's hand, with a discreet, almost indifferent gesture, a couple of one-hundred-franc notes identical to the one he had tipped him with when boarding the train at Nice. The conductor wavered for a moment, although this was clearly more to do with upholding the reputation of the Compagnie Internationale des Wagons-Lits than anything else. At last, he pocketed the money and put on his cap with the knowing expression of a man of the world.

"Breakfast at seven, sir?" he asked, completely naturally, as they walked down the corridor.

"Yes. Seven will be perfect."

There was an almost imperceptible pause.

"For one, or for two?"

"For one, if you'd be so kind."

On hearing this, the conductor, who had reached Max's door, gave him a smile of appreciation. It was a pleasure (Max could read his thoughts) to work with gentlemen who still knew how to conduct themselves.

"Naturally, sir."

That night and the ones that followed, Max had little sleep. The woman's name was Marie-Chantal Héliard; she was athletic, passionate, and droll, and he continued to see her during his four-day stay in Paris. It provided him with the ideal cover, and moreover she gave him ten thousand francs to add to the thirty thousand from Tomás Ferriol's safe. On the fifth day, after much reflecting about his own immediate future, Max transferred all the money he had at Barclays Bank in Monte Carlo and drew it out in cash. Then he went to Thomas Cook on Rue de Rivoli, where he bought a train ticket to Le Havre and a first-class passage to New York on the transatlantic liner *Normandie*. As he was settling his bill at Hôtel Meurice, he placed Count Ciano's letters in a manila envelope and sent them via messenger to the Italian embassy without any card or explanation. However, before handing the envelope to the concierge together with a tip, he paused for a moment and smiled wistfully to himself. Then he plucked his fountain pen from his pocket and scrawled on the back in capital letters, by way of a return address, the names Mauro Barbaresco and Domenico Tignanello.

—⁓—

Max has lost all sense of time. After the darkness and the pain, the interrogation and the incessant blows, he is surprised that it's still light outside the room when they remove the wet towel again. His head is aching so much that his eyeballs feel as if they are about to pop out of their sockets with each erratic beat of his heart and rush of blood through his temples. And yet it's been a while since they stopped hitting him. Now he can hear voices speaking in Russian and make out vague shapes as his eyes become accustomed to the light. When at last he manages to focus clearly, he discovers a fifth man in the room: blond, burly, with watery, blue eyes that are gazing at him inquisitively. He looks familiar, although in his present state, Max is unable to order his memories or thoughts. After a moment, the blond man makes an incredulous, disapproving face. Then he shakes his head and exchanges a few words with the man with the ginger mustache, who has stood up and is also looking at Max. The man with the ginger mustache appears not to like what he is hearing, for he responds with irritation and a gesture of impatience. The other man answers back and their discussion grows more heated. Finally, the blond man utters what appears to be an abrupt command and storms out of the room at the very moment Max recognizes him as the grand master Mikhail Sokolov.

The man with the ginger mustache has gone over to Max. He studies him, as though appraising the damage. Apparently he doesn't find it excessive, because he shrugs and says a few gruff words to his companions. Max tenses again, anticipating the wet towel and more blows, but that isn't what happens. What the man with lank hair does is fetch a glass of water and place it, brusquely, to Max's lips.

"You're very fortunate," the man with the ginger mustache says.

Max drinks greedily, spilling the water. Then, with the liquid running over his chin onto his chest, he looks up at his interlocutor, who is observing him with a serious expression.

"You're a thief, a charlatan, and an undesirable with a criminal record," the Russian says, moving his face closer to Max until he is almost touching him. "Your employer, Dr. Hugentobler, will be informed of this today, at his clinic in Lake Garda. He will also discover that you have been parading around Sorrento in his clothes, with his money and his Rolls-Royce. And more importantly: the Soviet Union won't forget your actions. Wherever you go, we'll do our best to make your life difficult. Until one day someone knocks on your door to finish what we started. . . . We want you to think about that every night when you go to sleep and every morning when you open your eyes."

With this, he gestures to the man in the black leather jacket, and there is the sound of a knife blade opening in his hands. Still dazed, as if he were floating in a cloud of mist, Max feels the ropes slacken. A tingling sensation, which makes him gasp with surprise, flows through his swollen arms and legs.

"Now get out of here, and bury yourself in the deepest hole you can find, granddad. . . . Wherever you go, whatever you do, from now on you're finished. A dead man."

13

The Glove and the Necklace

H E HAS HAD a hard time getting there. Before straightening his clothes with an instinctive gesture and knocking on the door, Max looks at himself in a mirror in the corridor to check the visible ravages. To see how far pain, old age, and death have progressed since the last time. But there is nothing extraordinary about his appearance. For the most part, anyway. The wet towel did its job, he observes with a mixture of resentment and relief. The only marks on his pallid face are the dark rings of fatigue around his puffy eyelids. His eyes also look feverish, the whites bloodshot as though hundreds of tiny blood vessels had broken inside them. But the worst damage is what can't be seen, he concludes, as he takes the last few steps toward Mecha Inzunza's door, pausing to lean against the wall and catch his breath: the bruising on his chest and stomach; his slow, irregular pulse, which exhausts him, requiring a supreme effort with every movement and covers him in a cold sweat beneath the clothes that chafe against his raw skin. Only through sheer willpower has he managed to disguise his acute discomfort, forcing himself to walk upright as he crossed the hotel lobby. He has an intense, overwhelming urge to lie down somewhere, anywhere, to close his eyes and drift into a prolonged sleep. To sink into the oblivion of a void as peaceful as death itself.

"My God . . . Max."

She is standing in the doorway to her room, looking at him in astonishment. The smile he is forcing himself to maintain doesn't seem to reassure her in the slightest, because she hurriedly takes Max's arm, propping him up despite his feeble protests as he tries to take the last few paces on his own.

"What's wrong? Are you ill? . . . What's the matter with you?"

He doesn't reply. The distance over to the bed seems interminable as his knees begin to give way. Finally, he slips out of his jacket and sits on the edge of the bed with an immense feeling of relief, his arms clutching his stomach, stifling a howl of pain as he doubles over.

"What have they done to you?" she asks, understanding at last.

He doesn't remember lying down, but he is in that position now, on his back. It is Mecha who is perched on the edge of the bed, one hand on his forehead and the other taking his pulse as she looks at him with alarm.

"A conversation," Max finally manages to say in a choked voice. "It was just . . . a conversation."

"With whom?"

He shrugs. But the smile that accompanies his gesture dissolves into a painful grimace.

"It doesn't matter who."

Mecha reaches for the telephone beside the bed.

"I'm calling a doctor."

"Forget about doctors." He restrains her arm weakly. "I'm very tired, that's all . . . I'll be fine in a while."

"Was it the police?" she asks, her concern apparently extending beyond Max's health. "Sokolov's people?"

"Not the police. It's all in the family, for now."

"Devils! Swine!"

He tries to adjust his lips into a stoical grin, but only manages a lopsided pout.

"Put yourself in their place," he says, objectively. "Talk about a dirty trick."

"Will they report the theft?"

"I didn't get that impression." He feels his stomach, gingerly. "In fact, I got a very different impression."

Mecha looks at him as if she hasn't followed him. Finally she nods as she strokes his disheveled gray locks.

"Did my package arrive?" he asks.

"Of course it did. It's in a safe place."

Easy as pie, Max tells himself. An innocent package for Mercedes Inzunza left with Tiziano Spadaro, and delivered to her room by a bellboy. The old way of doing things. The art of simplicity.

"Does your son know about it? . . . About what I did?"

"I prefer to wait until the contest is over. He has enough on his plate already with Irina."

"What's happening with her? Does she know you're onto her?"

"Not yet. And I'm hoping she won't find out for a while."

A sudden spasm makes Max cry out. Mecha attempts to undo his shirt, wet with perspiration.

"Let me see what's wrong."

"It's nothing," he protests, pushing her hands away.

"Tell me what they did to you."

"Nothing serious. I told you, we just had a conversation."

The two honey-colored eyes are staring so fixedly at him that Max can almost see himself reflected in them. I like it when she looks at me like that, he says to himself. I like it a lot. Especially today. Now.

"Not one word, Mecha. . . . I didn't say a word. I admitted nothing. Not even about myself."

"I know, Max. I know you . . ."

"You may not believe this, but I didn't find it so hard. I didn't care, do you understand? . . . What they did to me."

"You were very courageous."

"It wasn't courage. It was just what I said. Indifference."

He inhales deeply, trying to get his energy back, although with each breath he is racked with pain. He is so exhausted he could sleep for days. His pulse is still erratic, as if his heart were emptying out at times. She seems to realize this. Concerned, she stands up and brings him a glass of water from which he takes small, cautious sips. The liquid soothes his burning mouth, but hurts when it reaches his stomach.

"Let me call a doctor."

"No doctors . . . I just need to rest. To sleep for a while."

"Of course." Mecha strokes his face. "Get some sleep."

"I can't stay here at the hotel. I don't know what will happen. . . . Even if they don't accuse me openly, I'm in trouble. I have to go to Villa Oriana and return the clothes, the car . . . everything."

He makes as if to get up, but she gently restrains him.

"Don't worry. Rest. That can wait a few hours. I'll go to your room and pack your bags. . . . Do you have the key?"

"It's in my jacket."

She holds the glass up to his mouth again and Max takes several more sips, until the pain in his stomach becomes unbearable. Then he lies back, exhausted.

"I did it, Mecha."

There is a hint of pride in his voice. She notices it and smiles with wistful appreciation.

"Yes, you did it. My God, you did. Incredibly well."

"When the time is right, tell your son it was me."

"I will. . . . You can count on it."

"Tell him I climbed up there and took that damned book from them. Now the girl and the book make it a tie, don't they? . . . Like you say in chess, a draw."

"Of course."

He grins with a sudden hope.

"Perhaps your son will become world champion. . . . Then he might like me more."

"I'm sure he will."

Max sits up a little, and clasps her wrist with sudden urgency.

"You can tell me now. He's not my son, is he? . . . At least, you aren't sure. Of anything."

"Come on, go to sleep now. . . ." She makes him lie back. "You old rogue. You wonderful fool."

—⁂—

Max is resting. At times he sleeps deeply; at others he drifts in and out of consciousness. Occasionally, he gives a start and moans as he emerges, confused, from rambling, meaningless nightmares. He feels a physical pain and a dream pain that become superimposed and mixed up, vying in intensity so that he finds it hard to distinguish between real and imaginary sensations. Each time he opens his eyes it takes him a while to figure out where he is: the light outside has gradually seeped away until the objects in the room have become indistinct, and now there are only shadows. She remains next to him, leaning against the headboard of the still-made bed, a slightly clearer shadow among the others surrounding Max, the warmth of her body and the glowing tip of her cigarette close by.

"How are you?" she asks, noticing that he has moved and is awake.

"Tired. But I don't feel too bad. . . . Staying still helps. I needed sleep."

"You still do. Sleep some more. I'll watch over you."

Max, still dazed, wants to look around. Intent on remembering how he got there.

"What about my things? My suitcase?"

"I've packed everything. I brought your suitcase in here. It's by the door."

He closes his eyes with relief: the contentment of someone who, for the moment, doesn't need to take charge of the situation. And finally it all comes back to him.

"As many years as the squares on a chessboard, you said."

"That's right."

"It wasn't for your son . . . I didn't do this for him."

Mecha stubs out her cigarette.

"You mean, not entirely."

"Yes. Maybe that's what I mean."

She has moved away from the headboard slightly to nestle alongside him.

"I still don't know why you started all this," she says in a hushed voice.

The darkness makes the situation seem very strange, he thinks. Unreal. As if in a different time. Another world. Other bodies.

"Why I came to the hotel, and all the rest of it?"

"Yes."

Max smiles, knowing she can't see his face.

"I wanted to be what I once was," he says simply. "To feel the way I did then . . . One of my most absurd plans was the possibility of stealing from you again."

She seems astonished. And skeptical.

"You don't expect me to believe that."

"*Steal* probably isn't the right word. Definitely not. But that was my intention. Not because of the money, of course. Not because . . ."

"Yes," she cuts across him, convinced at last. "I understand."

"That first day, I searched this room. I could smell traces of you.

Imagine. Twenty-nine years later, recognizing you in every object. And I found the necklace."

Max inhales her closeness, alert to each sensation. She smells of tobacco mixed with the subtle aroma of perfume. For a moment he wonders whether her naked skin, wrinkled, blemished with age, also smells the way it did when they embraced in Nice or in Buenos Aires. Probably not, he concludes. Or surely not. No more than his own does.

"I intended to steal your necklace," he says after a pause. "Nothing else. To seduce you for the third time, I suppose. To make off with it the way I did that night when we got back from La Boca."

Mecha remains silent for a moment.

"That necklace isn't worth as much as when we first met," she says at last. "I doubt you'd get half the price for it now."

"That's not the point. It isn't about whether it's worth more or less. It was a way of . . . well. I don't know. A way."

"Of feeling young and triumphant?"

He nods in the darkness.

"Of telling you I haven't forgotten. I didn't forget."

Another silence. And another question.

"Why did you never stay?"

"You were a dream come to life." He reflects before continuing, making every effort to be precise. "A mystery from another world. I never imagined I had the right."

"You did. It was there in front of your stupid eyes."

"I couldn't see it. It was impossible . . . It didn't correspond with the way I saw things."

"Your sword and your steed, right?"

Max makes a sincere effort to cast his mind back.

"I don't remember that," Max says at last.

"Of course not. But I do. I remember every word you said."

"In any case, I always felt you were a bird of passage in my life."

"It's strange you should say that. That was how you felt to me."

Mecha has risen to her feet and is walking toward the window. She draws the curtain back a little, and the electric lights from the terrace below outline her dark, motionless figure against the glow.

"But those moments kept me going all my life, Max. Our silent tango in the Palm Room on the *Cap Polonio* . . . the glove I put in your pocket that night at La Ferroviaria, the same one I went to pick up the next day from your room in the boardinghouse in Buenos Aires."

He nods, even though she can't see him.

"The glove and the necklace . . . Yes. I remember the light from that window on the tiled floor and the bed. Your naked body and my astonishment at how beautiful you were."

"My God," she whispers, as if to herself. "You were so handsome, Max. Suave and handsome. A perfect gentleman."

He laughs, obliquely. Between gritted teeth.

"I was never that," he replies.

"You were more so than the majority of men I knew. . . . A true gentleman is someone to whom being or not being a gentleman is all the same."

She walks back over to the bed. She has left the curtain open a crack behind her, and the faint glow from outside reveals the shapes of things in the darkness of the room.

"What intrigued me from the start was that your ambition had neither passion nor greed in it. That calm absence of expectation."

She is standing next to the bed and lights another cigarette. The flame from the match illuminates her bony fingers and manicured nails, her eyes that are fixed on Max, the lines on her forehead beneath her cropped gray hair.

"My God. You only had to touch me and I'd tremble."

She extinguishes the flame so that only the glowing tip of the cigarette remains. And, like a twin spark, a soft, coppery glint in her honey-colored eyes.

"I was just a young man," he replies. "A hunter intent on survival. You were what I said before: as beautiful as a dream . . . one of those marvels which we men only have a right to when we're young and daring."

She is still standing next to the bed, silhouetted in the semi-darkness, facing Max.

"It was astonishing . . . and you're still doing it." The red end of the cigarette glows twice. "How do you manage it, after all this time? . . . You knew how to cast a spell with your words and gestures, as if you were wearing a mask of intelligence. You'd make some remark that was doubtless not your own, something you'd read in a magazine or overheard someone else say, but which gave me goose bumps all the same. And although twenty seconds later I'd forgotten it, the goose bumps remained . . . And nothing's changed. Here, feel my arm. You're a weak, battered old man, and yet you still have that effect on me. I swear."

She has stretched out her arm and is feeling for Max's hand. Her skin, he confirms, it is still warm and soft. In that half-light, her tall, willowy figure looks the same as it did when he first knew her all those years ago.

"That smile of yours, tranquil and treacherous . . . and daring, yes. You've held on to that, despite everything. The old smile of the professional dancer."

She lies down beside him. Once again the proximity of her smell, her warmth. The red tip illumines her face, so close Max feels the heat from the cigarette on his own face.

"Every time I caressed my son, when he was little, I imagined I was caressing you. And that still happens when I look at him. I see you in him."

A silence. Then he hears her laugh quietly, almost blissfully.

"His smile, Max . . . Can you honestly say you don't recognize that smile?"

With this, she sits up slightly, and, feeling for the night table, stubs out her cigarette.

"Rest, take it easy," she adds. "For once in your life. I've told you, I'm watching over you."

She has curled up very close, nestling beside him. Max screws up his eyes, contented. At ease. For some strange reason, which he doesn't try to analyze, he feels compelled to tell her an old story.

"I was sixteen the first time I went with a woman," he recalls slowly, in a hushed voice. "I was working as a bellhop at the Ritz in Barcelona at the time. . . . I was tall for my age, and she was one of the guests, a refined older woman. In the end, she contrived to get me into her room. . . . When I realized what she was after, I did the best I could. And when we'd finished, while I was getting dressed, she gave me a one-hundred-peseta note. Before leaving, I went over to her, naively, to give her a kiss, but she recoiled, irritated. . . . And later, when I bumped into her in the hotel, she didn't even condescend to look at me."

He falls silent for a moment, searching for a nuance or detail that will enable him to place what he has just told her in a precise context.

"In the space of five seconds," Max says at last, "while that woman recoiled, I learned lessons I've never forgotten."

A long silence ensues. Mecha has been listening very quietly, her head on his shoulder. Finally, she stirs, coming closer still. On her skinny, almost frail body, her breasts feel small and skimpy through her blouse, not at all as he remembers them. For some strange reason, this affects him. It moves him.

"I love you, Max."

"Still?"

"Still."

Gently, instinctively they seek out each other's mouths, almost wearily. A melancholy kiss. Tranquil. Afterward they remain motionless, in each other's arms.

"Have the last years really been that difficult?" she asks after a while.

"They could've been better."

A succinct way of putting it, he thinks, having scarcely finished the sentence. Then, in a quiet, dispassionate voice, he launches into a sorrowful litany: physical decline, the competition from young blood adapted to the new world. And finally, to top it all, a spell in an Athens jail—the result of a series of mistakes and disasters. Not a lengthy one, but by the time he got out he was finished. His experience only enabled him to live off petty crimes and poorly paid work, or to hang around places where he could make a living out of swindling people. For a while Italy was a good place for that, but in the end even his looks went. The job with Dr. Hugentobler, comfortable and secure, had been a real stroke of good fortune. Now that was ruined forever.

"What will become of you?" Mecha asks after a brief silence.

"I don't know. I guess I'll find a way. I always have."

She stirs in his arms, as though about to protest.

"I could . . ."

"No." He restrains her, clinging to her more tightly.

She stops moving. Max's eyes are open in the half-light and she is breathing slowly, quietly. For a while she seems to be asleep. Finally, she stirs again, just a little, and brushes his face with her lips.

"Anyway, remember," she whispers, "I owe you a coffee if you ever pass through Lausanne. To see me."

"Good. Perhaps I will pass through one day."

"Please remember."

"Yes . . . I will."

For a moment, Max—astonished by the coincidence—thinks he can hear the familiar strains of a tango. Possibly a radio in an adjacent room, he thinks. Or music coming from the terrace below. It takes a while for him to realize that he is humming it in his own head.

"It hasn't been a bad life," he confesses in a hushed tone. "Most of the time I lived off other people's money, without ever having to despise or fear them."

"That seems like quite a good outcome."

"And I met you."

She lifts her head off Max's shoulder.

"Oh, come on, you old fraud. You met a lot of women."

Her tone is good-humored. Knowing. He kisses her hair softly.

"I don't remember those women. Not one. But I remember you. Do you believe me?"

"Yes." She rests her head on his shoulder once more. "Tonight I believe you. Perhaps you have loved me, too, all your life."

"Yes. And perhaps I love you now. . . . How can I tell?"

"Of course . . . How are you to tell?"

—⟋⟍—

A ray of sunshine wakes up Max, and he opens his eyes to the light warming his face. A bright, narrow beam of sunlight is streaming through the curtains drawn across the windows. Max moves slowly, laboriously at first, lifting his head from the pillow with a painful effort, and he realizes he is alone. On the bedside table, a travel clock tells him it is ten-thirty in the morning. The room smells of tobacco. Next to the clock is a glass of water and an ashtray containing a dozen or so cigarette ends. She must have spent the rest of the night with him. Watching over him as she promised. Perhaps she had sat there, quietly smoking as she gazed at him asleep in the early dawn light.

He gets up, dizzily, running his hands over his creased clothes. Unbuttoning his shirt he sees that his bruises have acquired an ugly, dark hue, as if half his blood had seeped between his flesh and his skin. He aches from his groin up to his neck, and each step he takes toward the bathroom, until his stiff limbs begin to warm up, is almost agonizingly painful. The image he discovers in the mirror doesn't exactly correspond to that of his good days: an old man with bleary, bloodshot eyes stares back at him from the far side of the glass. Turning on the tap, Max puts his head under the stream of cold water. He leaves it running for a long while to wake up properly. Finally he lifts his head, and, before drying himself with a towel, he once again studies his aging features, the water trickling into the deep furrows that line his face. He walks slowly across the bedroom to the window, and when he draws back the curtains, the light outside bursts over the crumpled coverlet, the navy-blue blazer draped on the back of a chair, the suitcase by the door, Mecha's belongings strewn about the room: clothes, a bag, books, a leather belt, a purse, magazines. Dazzled at first, Max's eyes slowly become accustomed to the brightness, and he focuses now on the azure sky and sea fused together, the coastline and the dark cone of Vesuvius in misty blues and grays. A ferry, setting out with hesitant slowness toward Naples, sketches the brief white line of its wake across the cobalt blue of the bay. And three floors below on the terrace, at a table (the one next to the kneeling marble woman looking out to sea), Jorge Keller and his mentor Karapetian are playing a game of chess, while Irina watches them, sitting slightly apart from the table, bare feet on the edge of her chair, arms hugging her knees. On the margins, now, of the game and their lives.

Mecha Inzunza sits alone, farther away, next to a bougainvillea, near the balustrade surrounding the terrace. She is wearing her dark skirt, and her beige cardigan is draped over her shoulders. There is a coffee set and some newspapers open on the table, but she isn't looking at them. As motionless as the stone woman behind her, she appears to be contemplating the view of the bay. As Max watches, forehead pressed against the cold windowpane, Max sees her move only once, lifting her hand to touch her hair, and tilting her head to the side with a pensive air before sitting upright once more and continuing to gaze out to sea.

Max turns his back to the window and walks over to the chair to pick up his jacket. While he is putting it on, his gaze lingers upon the objects on the chest of drawers. And there, where he couldn't help but see it, placed deliberately on top of a long, white woman's glove, he discovers the pearl necklace, glowing softly in the intense brightness filling the room.

Standing there facing the glove and the necklace, the old man, who moments ago was contemplating his reflection in the bathroom mirror, feels memories, images, and previous lives float to the surface, his mind ordering them with astonishing clarity. His own and others' lives suddenly join together in a smile that is at once a painful grimace. Although perhaps it is the pain of lost or impossible things that is behind this sad smile. And so, once more, a small boy with grubby knees walks, arms outstretched, along the rotten boards of a boat abandoned in the mud of La Boca; a young soldier climbs a hill strewn with corpses; a door closes on the image of a sleeping woman, enveloped in moonlight as hazy as regret. Then, in the weary smile of the man looking back over his life, there appears a whole succession of trains, hotels, casinos, starched bib fronts, naked backs, and jewelry glinting beneath crystal chandeliers, while a handsome young couple, impelled by passions as urgent as life itself, gaze into one another's eyes while they dance an unwritten tango, in a silent, empty room on an ocean liner steaming through the dark night. Unknowingly, as they circle in their embrace, the pattern of an unreal world whose weary lights are about to be snuffed out forever.

But that isn't all. As the old man stares at the glove and the necklace, in his mind's eye he sees palm trees, their fronds bowed beneath the rain, and a wet dog on a misty, gray beach, opposite a hotel room where the most beautiful woman in the world is waiting, on disheveled sheets that smell of moist intimacy and a serenity that is oblivious to time and to life, for the man at the window to turn toward her to plunge once more into her warm, perfect flesh, the only place in the universe where its strange rules can be forgotten. After that, on the green baize, three ivory balls click gently while Max stares intently at a young man in whom, astonishingly, he recognizes his own smile. He also sees up close two dazzling eyes, like liquid honey, looking at him as no woman has ever looked at him before. And he feels a moist, warm breath tickle his lips, while a voice whispers old words that sound like new and pour a soothing balm on his old wounds, absolving all the lies, the doubts and disasters, rooms in boardinghouses and squalid dwellings, fake passports, police stations, prison cells, the humiliation of recent years, loneliness and failure, the dim light of endless bleak dawns that erased the shadow that the boy on the banks of the Riachuelo, the soldier climbing the hill beneath the sun, the handsome youth who danced with beautiful women on luxury liners and in grand hotels, had firmly attached to his feet.

—◌—

And so, the vestiges of a smile still playing on his lips, lulled by the distant echo of all those lives that have been his, Max moves the pearl necklace to one side and picks up the woman's glove beneath it. Deftly, with a touch of elegant whimsy, he arranges it in his top jacket pocket, the fingers protruding like the ends of a handkerchief or the petals of a flower in a buttonhole. Glancing around the room to make sure everything is in order, he gazes one last time at the necklace lying on the chest of drawers and nods briefly toward the window, as though taking leave of an invisible audience clapping their hands in imaginary applause. Such an occasion, he thinks while buttoning his jacket and smoothing it down, might call for the accompaniment of the Old School Tango as he bows out with appropriate nonchalance. But that would be too obvious, he decides. Too predictable. And so he opens the door, picks up his suitcase, and strides down the corridor, into the void, whistling "The Man Who Broke the Bank at Monte Carlo."

Madrid, January 1990
Sorrento, June 2012